NOT NORMAL, ILLINOIS

Peculiar Fictions from the Flyover

NOT NORMAL, ILLINOIS

Peculiar Fictions from the Flyover

EDITED BY

Michael Martone

AN IMPRINT OF
Indiana University Press
Bloomington · Indianapolis

This book is a publication of
Quarry Books
an imprint of
Indiana University Press
601 North Morton Street
Bloomington, IN 47404-3797 USA

www.iupress.indiana.edu
Telephone orders   800-842-6796
Fax orders   812-855-7931
Orders by e-mail   iuporder@indiana.edu

♾ The paper used in this publication meets the
minimum requirements of the American National
Standard for Information Sciences—Permanence
of Paper for Printed Library Materials,
ANSI Z39.48-1992.

Manufactured in the United States of America

Library of Congress Cataloging-in-Publication Data

Not Normal, Illinois : peculiar fictions from the Flyover /
edited by Michael Martone.
p.   cm.
ISBN 978-0-253-21022-7 (pbk. : alk. paper) 1. Short
stories, American—Middle West. 2. Middle West—Social
life and customs—Fiction. I. Martone, Michael.
PS563.N68 2009
813'.0108977—dc22
2009009978

1   2   3   4   5   14   13   12   11   10   09

In Memory of
David Foster Wallace

Contents

NOT NORMAL, ILLINOIS

Peculiar Fictions from the Flyover

Introduction
In the Middle of the Middle of Middletown

ᔆ

MICHAEL MARTONE

IN 1980, I RETURNED TO INDIANA to introduce Theresa, who was from
Baltimore, to my home state and the Midwest in general. The region was
a mystery to her as it is to many people not from it. We had started in Fort
Wayne, my hometown, Gas City with its history of methane boom and bust
and glass, and Wabash with its electric lights. Indianapolis's near south-side
Chinatown. Bloomington's limestone quarries made famous in the recently
released movie *Breaking Away*. Further south, we spent a day with the few
remaining religious at the convent in Ferdinand. A nun our age took care of a
cadre of octogenarian sisters still in habit spending their last days embroider-
ing cardinals—the state bird—on flour sack tea towels. When we admired
their work they excitedly revealed to us a linen closet filled with such towels,

handkerchiefs, and napkins for us to buy. Business had been slow, to say the least, and the sisters grumbled about the more successful brother Benedictine monks, down the road at St. Meinrad, with their cheeses and bread. We visited the then decaying grand resort hotels of West Baden and French Lick still with railroad sidings we were told again and again that allowed the gangsters from Chicago to pull their private cars right up to the front door. In Santa Claus, we saw Santa Claus in Bermuda shorts leave the amusement park at the end of the day, and we weathered a tornado in an ancient motor court decorated with a painted plywood façade of never melting snow. Later, heading back north to Fort Wayne, we decided to spend a night or two in the old Hotel Roberts in downtown Muncie.

I have a long history with Muncie. My father had gone to school at Ball State, mainly to play football, but discovered there, while trying to enroll in ROTC, that he never had been born. The sergeant told him the Army had no record of his birth. It didn't matter. After the season, my father ran out of money and walked back home to Fort Wayne. My mom's brother, Wayne Payne, was a student there later, and I remember moving him into a second floor apartment with a rickety outdoor stairway. He took me to the college's homecoming parade where fraternity pledges dressed as Egyptian slaves hauled hawsers connected to overbuilt floats from which their active brothers whipped them to pull harder. As I watched, one slave escaped and ran straight toward the crowd on the curb. "Help me!" he yelled, grabbing my shoulders before he was dragged back to the float. Much later my uncle became a professor of health science and lived on Shady Lane with two cats that might have been the model for his neighbor Jim Davis's comic cat Garfield. My uncle's dissertation had been on the effect of education on weight loss. He discovered that those who received information on the deleterious effects of obesity tended to eat more, having been made anxious by the knowledge. Ball State was the normal school for Indiana. My brother, who is an elementary school teacher, studied there, as did my mother, who lived in Lafollette dorm as a 51-year-old doctoral student. David Letterman was a student there too, and the scholarship in his name is still awarded to the student who maintains a C or lower average. At Butler University, I once watched Letterman in the TV lounge of the men's dorm do the nightly weather for an Indianapolis television station. "Pig-sized hail is falling on Ohio." It seemed possible.

But in 1980 Theresa and I arrived at the Hotel Roberts, in Muncie. Checking in, we discovered the third Middletown study was in progress. And we learned it from the old men sitting in the lobby who mistook us for members of the team of new sociologists. They were quite ready to respond to the surveys they imagined we would soon be administering. They had been teens and young men during the first two studies in '29 and '34 and had spent the rest of their lives self-consciously reading the reports and surveys and papers the study generated about their lives. It must have been strange being a student of yourself as a subject. Their normal lives published as the norm. Even their eccentricities interpreted as typical now because they took place here in a typical city. And it wasn't just the old men in the hotel lobby who anxiously awaited the beginning of the third study. Every native we met was ready once again to reset that sociological baseline he or she was born into. Waitresses in the café, postal clerks, delivery boys wearing Ball U T-shirts, gas station attendants, clerks, baggers at the Marsh's, disc jockeys, priests and pastors—everybody didn't want to disappoint, to skew the curves and standard deviations they knew by heart. They aspired to act normal, a normal they had learned by reading about themselves. They hoped they were still adept in their practiced averageness.

During our visit we did see a few of the actual sociologists, on the sidewalks with cameras and clipboards, documenting the vacant storefronts, counting traffic in and out of parking lots, administrating instruments on street corners. Theresa could see the same Muncie the sociologists saw, strange in its normality. As a midwesterner I had felt natural being normal. No, not quite natural. It was more like feeling the artificial nature of being "normal." Growing up in Indiana, one had to work at it, work at being normal. There were standards of the standard standard to uphold. I didn't need her eyes, her outsider eyes, to see the now naturalized nature in which we natives were immersed. I had been told all my life that this was the place to be—in the middle of the middle. People like to say "act normal." And I did. Without thinking. It came easy to me. And, if I had a question about what that normal was, well, I had the manual I could refer to, a book of mirrors, us being us, documented in the Middletown studies. You see, anything we do here is normal. That is, because we do it here, it's normal. Says so, right here in this book.

That being said, what gives with an anthology called *Not Normal*? Collected here are fictions that do seem peculiar, deviations from the norm of the "traditional" story that is realistic in style and narrative in form. You will find the irreal here and the lyrical devoid of any story. I would like to think that, with this book, the Not Normal is the new Normal, that what we have here is a kind of postmodern regionalism of a region that has been hiding, for years, in plain sight. The midwesterners have been normal for so long that it seems normal that they are that way, and the details of normalcy, the construction of what is normal, becomes so, well, normal as to be a cunning transparent disguise. We forget that the normal is made up. The stories published here attempt, in a variety of ways, to make us see the normal once again, exposing the received and accepted notions of what is real or right or beautiful for what they are: received and accepted notions. These stories are designed, then, to defamiliarize us to us. By design, they are made to make you see, really see, the things you take for granted all the time for the very first time once again.

In stories, and in life, we are, famously, always in the middle of things. You have just completed reading an introduction to a book that is about turning all those middles inside out.

Patty-Cake, Patty-Cake . . . A Memoir

MAX APPLE

1

WHEN HE TOOK WALKS, G.R. HUMMED "Cruising down the River." Now and then he munched on red pistachio nuts and spit the shells over the curb. I had to trot to keep up with his long steps. Once we got to the bakery, he'd go donut wild. Cream puffs, eclairs, even the cherryfilled Danish were nothing to him. He headed for the plain brown donuts, what my father called fry cakes. He ate each one in two bites, coming down exactly in the middle of the hole everytime. Daddy would give him a couple dozen like nothing. Everybody on Franklin Street gave things to G.R. There wasn't a housewife who didn't feel proud to fry him a few donuts herself. And why the hell not? He raked their leaves, carried groceries, opened doors, and smiled at the old folks. He was an Eagle Scout. I was just his nigger sidekick but people liked me for being that. Much later I got good jobs, loans, even my own business because of being his sidekick. But when we started, it was G.R. that needed me. He used to think my old man gave him the donuts because he was my buddy. He didn't know for a long time how much people liked him.

"Christ," I used to tell him, "Daddy would give you fry cakes even if you stomped me once a week. He likes you, G.R. You're his neighbor."

In fact we were sort of double neighbors. Our houses were on the same block, and his father's paint store was just down the street from the American Bakery, where my dad was the donut and cake man.

G.R. and I hung around the Bridge Street branch of the public library. He read the sports books and I did the science fiction. Then we'd go to the bakery and he'd start to wolf down the fry cakes. He ate all he could, then stuffed his pockets. My old man just used to laugh and throw in a few more. A dozen was a light snack to him. After football games, he always had his twelve fresh ones waiting in the locker room. He never shared, although he was generous with everything else. He ate them with his cleats and helmet still on and sometimes mud all over his face.

When my father died, G.R. and I were in college. He came over to the Alpha Kappa Psi house, hugged me, and said, "Sonny, you know how he did it, you've got to take over." And like a dumb ass, I did. I made them at night in the big Alpha Kappa Psi deep fryer. But G.R. always paid for the ingredients.

You've got to remember that this was 1937, and he was the social chairman of the DU's, the best of the white houses, and a big football player, and I was still his nigger sidekick from home to everyone except the brothers of Alpha Kappa Psi, where I was the house treasurer.

It only took about an hour once a week or so, and he liked them so much that I just couldn't stop. It would have been like weaning a baby. I didn't want to put up with all his moping. G.R. wasn't unhappy much, but when he was, the whole DU house could burn up and he wouldn't leave his room. I was the only one he let in. He'd sit and stare at a 12 × 5 of his father and mother in front of the paint store. He'd say things like, "Sonny, they did a lot for me and no goddamn girl is going to ruin it." Or if it wasn't a girl, it was a goddamn professor or sometimes a goddamn coach.

After a mope he'd be good for two dozen and a half gallon of milk. The brothers used to call me his mammy. "The big old ballplayer needs mammy's short'nin' bread," they used to say when they'd see me starting up the deep fryer after an emergency call from someone at DU. That's why half the house called me mammy, even though my actual nickname was Sonny. In the Michigan *Ensign* for 1938, there I am in the group picture of the only black frat house in Ann Arbor. "Sonny 'Mammy' Williams," it says, "Treasurer." G.R. is all over the book with the DU's, the football team, the Audubon Society, the Student Union, the Intrafraternity Honor Council. I counted him eight times and who knows how many I missed.

I think the only reason I ever went to Ann Arbor instead of JC like my sisters was that he was going and he got me a piece of his scholarship somehow. But when he went to law school, I said, "No dice, ace, I'm not hauling my ass up to Harvard." And I got a job back in Grand Rapids working for Rasberry Heating. Law School was the first time he got by without the fry cakes and he said he was a grump all three years.

"I lost seventeen pounds and almost married a girl I didn't love," he told me when he came back. "I lost a lot of my judgment and some of my quickness. Harvard and Yale may have class, Sonny, but when you come down to it, there's no place like home." He came back from Harvard as patriotic as the soldiers shipping back from Guam a few years later. I met him at the Market Street station with a sign that said, "Welcome back, Counselor," and a dozen hot fry cakes. His Ma and Dad were there too and his brother Phil. He hugged us all, ate the donuts, and said, "If you seek a beautiful peninsula, look around you." Then he said it in Latin and we thought it was lawyer's talk and we looked the train station over real good. Then he told us it was the motto of the state of Michigan, which was founded in 1837 and was the first state west of Pennsylvania to have its own printing press. He said he wasn't leaving Michigan for a good long time, and if it wasn't for the war a few months later, I don't believe he would have.

The war started in December and he came back from Harvard in the June before that. The first thing he did was make me take my two weeks from Rasberry and head up to the Upper Peninsula with him. "To the thumb, Sonny, to the tip of Michigan where three great lakes sparkle and iron and copper dot the landscape."

I still couldn't say no to the guy so I went along even though I knew the Upper Peninsula was for Indians and not for Negroes.

We drove two days in my '35 Chevy, up through Cadillac, Reed City, Petoskey, Cheboygan. The roads were bad. When we had a flat near the Iron River, it took an hour for another car to come by so we could borrow a

jack. I wished all the time that we were on our way to Chicago or Cleveland
or Indianapolis or someplace where you could do something when you got
there. But old G.R. was on a nature kick then. I believe Harvard and no fry
cakes had about driven him nuts. While I flagged down the jack, he stood
beside the car and did deep knee bends and Marine push-ups. He took off
his shirt and beat his chest. "Smell the air, Sonny, that's Michigan for you,"
he said. People were suspicious enough about stopping for a nigger trying to
flag them down without this bouncing Tarzan to scare 'em worse.

When we finally got the ferryboat to take us to Mackinac Island, I knew it
was a mistake. The only negroes besides me were the shoeshine boys on the
boat, and here I was in a linen suit and big straw hat alongside Mr. Michigan,
who was taking in the Lake Superior spray and still beating his chest now
and then and telling everyone what a treat it was to live in the Thumb state.
Everybody thought I was his valet, so when I caught some real bad staring
I just went over and brushed his jacket or something and the folks smiled at
me very nicely. I didn't want trouble then and I don't now. I've been a negro
all my life and no matter how hard I try I can't call myself a black.

Another thing I tell people and they can hardly believe is that I don't think
G.R. ever once said anything about my color. I don't believe he ever noticed
it or thought about it or considered that it made a bit of difference. I guess
that's another reason why I didn't mind baking his donuts.

But Mackinac Island was a mistake for both of us. I was bored stiff by
talking about how good the food was in the hotel and taking little rides in
horse-drawn carriages. G.R. seemed to like it, so I didn't say much.

One morning he says, "Sonny, let's get clipped," and I go with him to
the hotel barbershop without giving it a thought. After being there a week,
I must have lost my sense, too, to just go along like that. He sits down in one
vacant chair and motions me to the other. There are a couple of thin barbers
who look like their scissors. I'm just getting my socks adjusted and looking
down at "Theo A. Kochs" written on the bottom of the barber chair when
my thin man says almost in a whisper, "I'm sorry, sir, but we don't do negro
hair." G.R. hasn't heard this because his barber has snapped the striped sheet
loudly around him and is already combing those straight blond strands.

I step out of the chair. "No hard feelings," he says.

"None," I say, "I didn't need a haircut anyway. I'll just wait for my friend
here."

"Fine," he says, and sits down in his chair to have a smoke while he waits
for another customer.

When G.R. gets turned around and sees this little barber lighting up, he says, "Sonny, c'mon, I thought we're both getting clipped this morning."

"I'll wait, G.R.," I say, hoping he'll let it go.

"No waiting," he says. "It's sharp country up here, we've got to look sharp for it, right, boys?" He looks at my little barber who blows some smoke and says, "I'm sorry, but we don't cut colored hair here. In fact, I don't think there's a spot on the island that does. We just don't get that much in colored trade."

"What do you mean you don't cut colored hair?" G.R. says.

"Just what I said." The barber is a little nervous. He stands up and starts to wash some combs, but G.R. is out of his chair now and facing him against a row of mirrors.

"What do you mean by colored?" he asks the barber.

My barber looks at his partner. I am getting pissed at G.R. for making something out of this. I should have known better. At home I wouldn't just walk into the Pantlind or the Rowe Hotel and expect to get a haircut.

"It's okay, G.R.," I say. "Sit down and let's get going. We've got lots to see yet, Indian villages and copper mines and remnants of old beaver trappers' lodges."

"I want to know what this man means by colored," he says, crowding the little barber against a display of Wildroot Cream Oil. The other barber, G.R.'s, says, "Look, mister, why don't the both of you just take your business someplace else." G.R. is a very big man and both barbers together don't weigh two fifty. He says it again. "I want to know what this man means by colored." He is trailing them in the white cover sheet with black stripes and a little paper dickey around his neck. He looks like Lou Gehrig in a Yankee nightshirt. My barber is afraid to say anything but the other one says, "Well, look at your friend's teeth real white, see, and the palms of his hands are brownish pink, and his hair is real woolly. I couldn't pull that comb I just used on you through that woolly hair now, could I?" G.R. looks surprised.

"And when you've got white teeth and pinky brown palms and woolly hair and your skin is either black or brown, then most people call you colored. You understand now?"

"But what's that got to do with haircuts?" G.R. asks. Nobody knows what to say now. The barbers don't understand him, so I step up and say, "They need special instruments to cut my hair, G.R. It's like he says, those puny little combs don't go through this, see. I got to go to my own kind of barber so he'll know how to handle me."

G.R. was edgy all through his haircut and he didn't leave a tip, but once we left the barbershop I believe he forgot the whole thing.

But the way he was with those barbers, that's how he operated with girls too. What I mean is, he didn't understand what they were getting at. And this was a shame because he really attracted the ladies. They didn't all come at him like ducks to popcorn, but if he stayed at a school dance for an hour or so, the prettiest girl there would be over talking to him and joking and maybe even dancing with him. He never did anything but talk and joke them. He'd walk home with me. I'd say, "G.R., that Peggy Blanton was giving you the eye. Why'd you pass up something like that?"

"Training," he'd say, or "Hell, Sonny, I came to the dance with you and I'm leaving with you." If there'd ever been a good-looking colored girl there I sure wouldn't have left with him. Don't get me wrong, G.R. was a regular man, nothing the matter with his glands; he just wasn't as interested in girls as most of us were. One weekend in college he drove to Chicago with me and some of the brothers of Alpha Kappa Psi. The brothers wanted some of that good jazz from down around Jackson Avenue and G.R. wanted to see the White Sox play baseball. He took a bus to Comiskey Park for a doubleheader and met us about eight at the Blue Box, where those great colored jazz groups used to be in those days. G.R. stood out like a light bulb. We'd been there all afternoon just mellow and strung out on the music. G.R. came in and wanted to talk baseball. Don't forget that in those days the White Sox really were white and the brothers could have cared less what a group of whites were doing that afternoon up on Lake Shore Drive.

"You should have seen Luke Appling," he was saying; "there's not a man in either league who can play that kind of shortstop." Nobody paid any attention to G.R. He didn't drink and the music was just noise to him. He had taken a book along and was trying to read in the candlelight at the Blue Box. You had to feel sorry for him. It was so dark in there you couldn't see your fingers at arm's length. The atmosphere was heavy with music, liquor, women. I mean the place was cool, relaxed, nobody doing more than tapping a glass, and he sits there squinting over a big blue book, underlining things and scratching his head like he's in the library. He was alone at a table so he could concentrate, but I kept my eye on him just in case anything came up. Pretty soon two really smooth numbers come over to his table. Now you'd call them "Foxes." They were in evening gowns and very loose, maybe even drunk. He was the only white man in the place and they kind of giggled at him and sat down. I couldn't hear a word they said but I watched every move. I could see because they'd started using a spotlight for the small stage and G.R. was a little to one side of it.

One of the girls starts rubbing the spine of the blue book. The other one takes his finger and puts it on the page. She uses his hand like a big pointer. Maybe she's asking him what some of those big words mean. They're both real close. I start to get a little jealous. I've been there all day with nothing like that kind of action. But, it's like I said, he had a way with the girls. They seem to be talking a lot. The girls are real dreamy on him, one under each arm. It looks like he's reading out loud to them because one of them is holding the book up for him to read from. Whatever he's reading is really breaking the girls up. One of them is kind of tickling his belly with a fingernail between the buttons of his shirt. Sam Conquest and his combo were doing a set then that really had us going. I mean, as much as I was keeping an eye out for G.R., I was into the music too and couldn't really be sure about what my buddy was getting himself into. All I know is that I slipped into the music for just a couple of minutes and when I looked back he was gone. So were the girls and his book. What the hell, I thought, anyone else would, why not G.R. too?

It wasn't until we got back to Ann Arbor and were alone together in his room that G.R. told me what really happened with those two girls.

"I was robbed," he said. "They got about four dollars, but it was all I had. I think Shirlene did it." He showed me his finger with a Band-Aid on it. "I cut myself on the sequins of her dress. She was giving me kind of a chest rub and my arm was around her. I thought she really liked me, Sonny. I cut my finger real deep on one of those sequins. Doris went to the drugstore for a Band-Aid. While she was gone, I think Shirlene got her hand into my trousers and took the four bucks. I was telling them about World War I. They were interested in Woodrow Wilson and the League of Nations. I don't know why they robbed me. If she would have asked me, I'd have given her the four dollars, you know I would have, don't you, Sonny?"

"G.R.," I said, smiling but real sad about him, "you good-looking DU social chairman, you football captain and White Sox fan, what the hell is ever going to happen to you in the real world? You can't tell robbery from love, you don't have the ear for music or the eye for color. You can eat donuts and tackle people, you're a good citizen. Get tough, get mean, drink whiskey, swear, slap some chicks around, fuck a few, stop saying yes ma'am, turn in your homework late, cut football practice, cheat on exams, wear dirty socks . . . I mean, Jesus Christ, be like everybody else." I broke down then. I liked him so much the way he was that it killed me to say these things, but I did it for his sake. Somebody had to warn him.

He put his arm around me while I sobbed. "Sonny," he said, "I'll try."

2
___

When he ran for Congress he laid off the fry cakes. By then, with his help in getting me a loan, guess who owned the American Bakery? He was making good money as a lawyer. I thought he was crazy to run for the Congress. When I heard it on the radio, I brought a dozen fry cakes fresh from the oven right up to his office in the Federal Square Building. He had a little refrigerator where he kept his milk and his lunch. I hadn't even taken off my white baker's outfit. Some court photographer happened to be in the building and snapped a picture of me in whites carrying the donuts and looking mad as hell. Right after he became the President, *The New York Times* printed that picture and I started getting flooded with requests from TV. That's when the President's baker thing got started. I sold the American Bakery in '58 and have hardly dipped a fry cake since then, but once a story gets on TV you're stuck with it. Never mind that I'm in auto leasing and sporting goods now; the "President's baker" is what I'm destined to remain.

But the day of that picture was an important one: it was the last day of our real friendship. I slipped past a secretary and gave him the dozen. His desk was full of papers. "Later," he said. "Right now," I told him, and I stood there waiting. He was always more sensible after donuts and milk. I went right to his refrigerator and brought out the bottle of Sealtest. I stood there until he was done. "G.R.," I said, "why the hell are you doing this? Aren't you the man who told me you'd never leave Michigan? You've got your friends here and your family, what's all this about going to Washington, D.C.? If you want politics, what about being mayor?"

"Sonny, there's a big country out there and most of it is full of Democrats. And there's untold Communists around the world just waiting to get their fingers on your bakery and my law office and everything else we've been working for."

"G.R.," I said, "if you leave this town you're making the mistake of your life."

He looked up at me from his desk. "Sonny, if you're not for me you're against me."

"Get your fry cakes in D.C.," I told him, "and your friends too." I walked out. I voted against him that time and in every other election, and as far as I know he never again tasted one of my donuts. He moved to D.C. that January. Every year I get a Christmas card and a district newsletter, but until he became President that was it. Not even a phone call when he was in town. What the hell, I thought to myself, he turned his back on his old friends but I guess it's what he really wanted. He spent twenty-five years in D.C. without me and without those donuts and he didn't seem to miss Michigan all that much either. I, who was his nigger sidekick and his college "mammy," never saw his wife or his kids. When his dad died I went to the funeral, but the crowd was so big I didn't even get into the chapel. At the cemetery it was private. I thought I saw G.R. in one of the limousines while they were loading the casket in, but you can't run up and talk to a man at a time like that. Yessir, G.R. and I were through, cold turkey, until that night last August when Nixon resigned.

To tell you the truth, until the minute it happened none of us believed Nixon would ever be out of there until '76. When they interrupted the Tigers game with the news, you could have knocked me over with a feather. People all over town started walking around the streets like they were drunk. The JCCs painted a big Home of the President poster and had it up at the northern city limits within an hour. My mother, who's in a home now, called up to remind me that she taught the President how to tie his shoes. He was fast, Mama remembered, and double knotted every time. And the truth is, although I had resented him being a Congressman all those years, I spent a few minutes just saying out loud, "G.R., Mr. President." I said it over and over. I was still saying it when I got a phoned-in telegram from his press secretary. "Sonny—Emergency. Air Force One will pick you up midnight Grand Rapids airport." It was signed G.R. A White House operator read it to me at ten o'clock while I was watching the newsmen do a wrap-up on Nixon. He wasn't officially President until the next day but already he could send Air Force One out to do his errands.

I knew what this meant. I packed a blue suit and my own deep fryer, and it's a good thing I did. With all the stuff in that White House kitchen, there isn't a single deep fryer. I heard one of the cooks grumbling that Jackie Kennedy had it thrown away and Johnson used to eat all his fries on the ranch. Nixon only cared for pan-fried. The cooks were mighty suspicious. Here was the new President who they didn't even know sending over his own old boy with a personal deep fryer.

I was met at the airport by a nice young fellow. He took my grocery order. The Presidential limousine waited outside the all-night Safeway while we shopped. I overbought, made twelve dozen because for all I knew he wanted to treat the whole cabinet. By seven on the morning of the day he was to become the President, G.R. had his fry cakes, crisp on the outside, soft on the inside. I was a little nervous in case I'd lost my touch but this was one sweet batch. An FBI man delivered all twelve dozen. The White House cooks treated me very uppity. They were all tears about Nixon, wondering whether he could stomach bacon and eggs for his last breakfast, and here I was whipping out twelve dozen donuts for the new boy. They didn't know if they could keep up with an appetite like that.

I hung around the kitchen because I didn't know where else to go. You wouldn't believe the chaos. Nixon sent back the coffee, bacon, and eggs. He was going to be on TV at ten. They sent up cream of wheat, rye toast, coffee, and vegetable juice. It came back too. The juice glass was empty but there were lipstick stains on it.

"The poor man hasn't moved his bowels yet," the cook said when he saw Nixon giving his last speech. "Without morning coffee, he is cement. He hasn't slept either. Oh God, what's going to happen to all of us?" He looked at me and then spit into the sink. We were crowded together watching a twelve-inch Sony color set.

I had a late breakfast with the kitchen staff and hung around the TV for G.R.'s swearing-in and his speech. I played some gin rummy with a few maids. Limousines kept pulling up outside but the whole place was quiet as a white funeral parlor. Just before noon that same young man who met my plane came into the kitchen and gave me an envelope. There was a regular Central Air Lines ticket in it, but for first class, a hundred dollar bill, and a note. The note said, "Just like old times. Thanks, G.R."

I watched him on TV with Nixon's kitchen help. They were all zombies by noon. One of them said he dreamed that Nixon changed his mind in the air and was going to phone in at eleven fifty-nine to say hold off that swearing-in. I was the only one blindly excited and proud. And I don't have to tell you that my man was cool as a cucumber and straight as an arrow. There were some snickers in the kitchen when the camera showed General Haig brushing some crumbs off the new President's lapel. I saw them in color, the yellow crumbs I knew. "Here fellas," I said, tossing the hundred in the air, "have a drink on your new boss."

I was home by nightfall and haven't heard from him since. I guess that he's trying to make a go of it with that bunch of cooks he inherited. Still, who knows G.R. like I do? When it gets really tough in that oval office he'll start to smell the fry cakes. When that happens, watch out Kissinger and the Joint Chiefs. Mr. Donut and Dixie Cream won't be enough. His lips will start to twitch and his teeth will bite the air. He'll remember the glorious peninsula and the three Great Lakes of the Thumb. His mouth will water for the real thing. And when that happens, in the pinch, The President knows old Sonny won't let him down.

Childhood · Detroit · Michigan

JOEL BROUWER

Childhood

SURROUNDED BY RAGWEED AND BURDOCK. The silo, crumbling then, invisible now. A nimbus of squirrel skulls glowing yellow in the dirt. My memory as empty. Did I climb to the barn's lightning rod, or just threaten? We weren't farmers. In summer, the dead man's fields, ours via probate caprice, sprouted gladiolus, blueberries, rhubarb. We watched bewildered, filled vases and bowls, but most of it rotted where it stood. The daffodils still come up without me to cut, rubber-band, and sell them by the roadside. Four cars a day came by. Here's the rusty coffee can I dreamed full of dimes.

Detroit

Snow plunges down the night, scatters in gritty bursts above the vacant lots
like salt into the fields of Carthage. I'm sixteen stories above, watching the
bedlam rush up and down the window like a biology-class film of blood cells
lunging at the gates of the heart and falling back repulsed, like your breath
through the telephone rising with *Florida* and falling with *Never.* Through
the cracks in the sidewalk below, spidery arms of chickweed clutch at women
torn from magazines, spin them in a frozen cotillion. If every streetlight on
the block's shot out, where's that glow coming from?

Michigan

Smoke a pack of Kools in the dunes. Then he'll push your hand down his
swimsuit. Hold the damp cold there. Smell alewives. Then he'll do you, and
that's it. Back to the campground. No talking. Coppertone, hamburgers,
Frisbee. Suggest a walk on the pier to see if the fish are biting, though you
couldn't care less. *Too small, son. We're throwing them back.* Good soldier-talk
to remember for later, when someone's older brother wants payback for the
rum and the storm's chasing boats to harbor like a dog after rabbits. *Fish biting, kid?* Too small. They're throwing them back.

Beginnings

ROBERT COOVER

IN ORDER TO GET STARTED, HE WENT TO LIVE alone on an island and shot himself. His blood, unable to resist a final joke, splattered the cabin wall in a pattern that read: It is important to begin when everything is already over.

This maxim, published on the cabin wall between an outdated calendar and a freshwater fish chart, would have pleased him. He had once begun a story about the raising of Lazarus, in which Jesus, having had the dead man dragged from the tomb and unwrapped, couldn't seem to get the hang of bringing him around. There was an awful stink, the Jews crowding around were getting sick, and Jesus, sweating, was saying: Heh heh, bear with me, folks! Won't be a minute! If I can just get it started, the rest'll come easy!

This, then, was his problem: beginning. And having begun: avoiding resolutions. Thus, there were worse jokes his blood might have played on him. Its message might have read: All beginnings imply an apocalypse. Perhaps, in fact, that's what it did say, how was he to know? Pulling the trigger, he thought: This is working! I'm getting on!

It was comfortable, that cabin, roomy and clean-smelling, with walls of unvarnished Norway pine, Coleman lanterns for light, a wood cookstove, and a long pine table with a yellow checkered oilcloth he'd bought for it, big enough to eat on and write on at the same time. There was a bay out front with a small pier for the boat. He was alone on the island, except for a few squirrels, frogs, muskrats, the odd weasel, birds, porcupines. The nearest people were about a mile's boatride away.

He rarely needed these people, though sometimes he visited them when his imagination failed him or he ran out of peanut butter. On these occasions, they often told him stories, astounding him with their fearless capacity for denouement, and he'd return to his island shaken, thinking: I'm the last man alive on earth! Once they told him about a man who had come to one of the islands to write, but on arriving had shot himself. Yes, he told them, that was me, and they noticed then that his head was coming apart, and on the wall was a message: You ain't seen nothin' yet, friends!

He once wrote a story about a man who was born at the age of thirty-two with a self-destruct mechanism in his gonads, such that he could be sure of only one orgasm before he died. This man traveled all over the world, seeking out the perfect mate for this ultimate experience, but blew it one night in a wet dream on a jet flight over Bangkok. What was fascinating about this story was neither his travels nor his dream, but rather the peculiar physical appearance of a man kept so long in the womb. He had rather liked this story and stayed with it longer than most, but had had to abandon it finally when he'd heard about the new cults forming aboard jetliners.

Well, we've made a start, his blood said on the wall. Nothing else matters. The people who had come to identify the body crowded around, staring in disbelief. This is impossible, they cried. That story wasn't true, it was only a legend! They noticed that he'd left the coffeepot on the stove and it had boiled over. They pointed to it and said: Aha!, satisfying thereby their lust for motive, but they couldn't conceal a certain disappointment. They scratched about, however, and finally found enough peanut butter for two sandwiches, though there wasn't any bread. Well, at least we haven't come for nothing, they said.

There was nothing primitive about this island. He had a shallow bay to bathe in, a cabin to eat and sleep in and an outhouse to shit in, a chair to read in, wild blueberries for breakfast, saws and axes for cutting wood, a boat to go to town in, and he could write anywhere. If he subsisted largely on peanut butter, that was his own fault, because he even had a gas refrigerator and stove. These he used as little as possible, though, because his principal hardship was exchanging used butane tanks for new in town, then single-handedly dragging the loaded one back to the boat, later heaving it out of the boat and up the steep hill to the cabin, and finally setting it up in place and lighting it without blowing himself up.

As for the old wood cook stove, he loved it. When the lake was darkened by a storm, or at night, he could sit for hours in front of it, watching the flames, warming himself, brewing coffee, frying up feasts of fish and potatoes when he had them, imagining a life free of settings forth, and so immortal. What limited his use and diminished his enjoyment of the stove was the need to chop wood for it. He found it took about as long to burn the wood as it took to cut it. There seemed to lurk some kind of unpleasant moral here, and it was this more than the hard work, which in his womb-wrinkled condition he should have welcomed, that made him use the cook stove less and less. He would have abandoned it altogether, but for his insomnia. On bad nights, he could stare at the flames, each one new, violent, unique, and sooner or later all this variety would put him to sleep.

An ordinary island then, with ordinary trees and bushes, ordinary bugs, birds, and reptiles, ordinary lake water lapping it about, yet even before pulling the trigger, he recognized that there was something suspicious about it, as though it might have been, like the air he breathed, just another metaphor. So many otherwise solid and habitable islands had gone that way in the past, it was a kind of pollution. Perhaps he should have shot himself in the boat on the way to the island, spared the world another bloody epigram and the island this transgression, this erosion. It was Adam did the naming, why did Eve get all the blame?

Because she was near at hand. This was her offense: affectionate trespass. She wanted company. She couldn't leave well enough alone, she had to turn up and tax his vocabulary. She must have come there sometime between the pulling of the trigger and the loosing of his blood and brains against the cabin wall. He named her many times over, but never Eve, having after all a certain integrity. What could he say in her behalf? That she helped him drag the butane tanks up the hill. But she helped him use them up faster, too, contaminating his days with history.

Yet he was grateful, because he was able to throw away everything he had written before she had come there, and this altered the fuel balance, permitting more fires in the cookstove. Also she was good at finding blueberries and cleaning fish, chopping off their heads like false starts. But she confused him by insisting she had been there first, he was the newcomer to the island, and she lifted her skirts to show him the missing rib. It was at this time that he began to suspect that he, not the island, was the metaphor. He began a story in which the first-person narrator was the story itself, he merely one of the characters, dead before the first paragraph was over.

He returned the rib to her and discovered it was more blessed to give than to receive, though this was not accomplished without some bloodletting. They found much peace and pleasure in this sharing of the rib, and called it fucking. Thus, he was still naming things. Perhaps because it rhymed with luck: fucking, they thought, was good for it, good for the raw nerve ends of his navel, too. I think this is the beginning of something, he said, as his hips bucked. Though they never let it get in the way of their struggles with one another, it always proved useful whenever they began to repeat themselves. It was almost like a place, somewhere to go when the island and his work became hostile and wounded him, an island within an island.

Small wonder, then, that he took to inventing stories in which time had a geography, like an island, place moved like the hands of a clock, and point of view was a kind of punctuation. He assigned numbers and symbols to death, love, characters, unexpected developments, transitions, then submitted them to the rhythms of numerologies. He invented a story with several narrators, each quoting the next, the last quoting the first and telling the story being told. He began another, added footnotes, subfootnotes to the footnotes, further footnotes to the subfootnotes, and so on to exhaustion, which came early: he still had something to learn about pacing himself.

The woman, like all women no doubt, was always the same woman and never the same woman twice. Sometimes she was pregnant, sometimes she was not. Sometimes she soaped him up when they bathed in the bay, and then they fucked in the water, or else on shore, under the trees, in the cabin, out in the woodpile, less often when she was pregnant. She did her best to hide the children from him for fear he'd eat them. Sometimes she was distracted and then he did eat them. He was always sorry about it afterwards, because he missed them and they gave him constipation for a week. In which case, she cared for him, scratched his head, gave him enemas, strewed the path to the outhouse with rose petals.

The outhouse was a short walk away from the cabin by the thick forest of pines, poplars, birch, and dogwood. It was strictly for the relief of mind or bowels, since it was their habit to pee wherever they were when the need hit them, except inside the cabin. Sometimes, at night, simply out the front door into the moonlight, hoping not to get bit by mosquitoes. Hoping did little good, they got bit anyway. This added a certain purpose and energy to their fucking, true, but did little to improve their technique. It was like the sting of conscience, teaching them to murder or be damned.

The children were less scrupulous about their toilet, with the result that the cabin often smelled worse than the outhouse. On such days, he would take the boat out on the lake and fish for walleyes and bass, pretending to be the Good Provider. He was not lucky at it, though, and hated taking the hook out, so sooner or later he'd go on into town and buy fish at the store. The woman was always amazed at his luck in catching fileted fish. It's a parable, he explained, and put the gun to his head. Soon I'll be able to dispense with this gun altogether, he thought with his scattering brain. It's like taking a cathartic.

Sometimes he thought that might be the way to get started at last: with a cathartic. But what if the trouble was heartburn? For it was true, his writing was a vice and tended to alienate them. He found he did no writing at all while fucking, and vice versa. It could be even worse in between times, when he wasn't sure which he was doing, or should be doing. He ate better than when he lived alone, slept better, she even took to chopping the wood and dragging the butane tanks up by herself, he had all the time in the world, and yet if anything he was writing less. He used to spill beer, ashes, peanut butter, kerosene into his typewriter, and hardly noticed; now she kept it clean for him, and it kept breaking down. Whenever an idea really gripped him, she would cry and accuse him of leaving the island; he'd apologize and take her for a ride in the boat, wondering where it was he'd been. She diapered the children in the climaxes of his stories, doing him a service, but she also borrowed his typing ribbon for a clothesline and mistook his story notes for a grocery list, nearly poisoning them all.

And yet, she was indispensable. When he complained about the suffering of the artist, she added more fruit to his diet, and in truth he suffered less. Alone, he used to sit in front of the cookstove and listen to the stillness beyond the flames; now there was her breathing. And who else was there to read to? He realized he had been writing so as to be able to sleep at night, but she could purge his guilt with a simple backrub, confirming his suspicion that it was nothing more than a cramp in the lumbar region. When he reasoned that perhaps he needed the writing, after all, to stay awake in the daytime, she sent the children in to play with him. He began a parody on Plato's cave parable, in which he celebrated, not the shadows, but the generosity of the wall.

Also, it became important to delay the climax. Thus, he got involved with spirals, revolutions, verb tenses, and game theory. There were puns that could make endings almost impossible, like certain very thick prophylactic devices. He started a story about a man who was granted a wish by a good fairy and who promptly blew the circuits by packing the universe out with good fairies. He applied Zeno's paradox to a suicide bullet, and kept it up all night. He invented a story about Noah in which the old man starts by making the door and the window, then can't figure out how to build the ark around them. God, too, is confused by this approach, but is too proud of his storied omniscience to admit it, and so provides dogmatic solutions which turn out to be self-contradictory. Many volumes of profound arguments ensue, explicating God's wit. Noah meanwhile builds himself a captain's cabin, complete with yellow oilcloth and Coleman lanterns, but God, annoyed by its pretensions, turns Noah into a pillar of peanut butter and then invites the animals in, inventing the Eucharist. Enough of these false starts, these dead fish heads, he reasoned, taking his children down to the bay for an afternoon swim, and the flood will never come.

It was beautiful, that little bay, clean and quiet, cool, with only the occasional leech like a cautionary tale. Sometimes a turtle would swim in, looking for the old days. The woman would kneel on a flat rock at the lip of the bay like Psyche, washing out diapers, as though to impress upon him the inadequacy of his revisions. On sunny days, schools of tiny fish would arrive like visitors from the city, white and nervous, and birds would come down, looking for action. His children splashed at the edges, played in the sand, scrambled about in the boat, chased toads, cried when they got ants on them, peed on the bluebells and each other, ate mud. Now and then, one would drown or get carried off by the crabs, and he'd wonder: why do we go on making them if they're just going to quit on us? Oddly, neither the woman nor his balls ever seemed to ask that question, and he felt alienated. He contemplated a detective story, in which all the victims and suspects are murdered, as well as the detective and all those who come to investigate the murders of the detectives who came before. But he was an intransigent realist, and he knew, as he climbed up on the small pier, that he'd probably bog down in the research. He dove off, projecting out a multivolume work on the blessings of mortality to be entitled, *Adventures of a Mongoloid Idiot*, and struck his head on the bottom, thinking: all this from the pulling of one trigger!

The message on the blood spattered wall was a learned discourse on the forty-seventh chromosome of mongoloid idiots, and its influence on the prime number theorem of imminent apocalypse. Was it enough to say that he'd shot himself because he'd let the coffee boil? Probably it was enough. He'd apparently run out of bread and had been eating his peanut butter between manuscript pages. His typing ribbon was missing. First lines lay scattered like crumbs and ants were carrying them off. One of them read: In eternity, beginning is consummation.

Much of the island was unvisited, being too thickly overgrown with trees and brambles. You could sink up to your knees in pulp from the last era's forest. His children occasionally wandered off and never returned. Perhaps there were ogres. Probably not, for they'd have heard them snorting and farting on still nights. Sometimes they took the boat around the shore of the island, gathering bleached driftwood. One of these twisted shapes led him to a story about a monster that was devouring the earth in bits and drabs as though to simplify its categories, but he threw it away, recognizing it as genteel autobiography. On one corner of the island, amid tall reeds, herons nested. Their long graceful necks seemed to give them an overview that spared them the embarrassment of opening sallies. If my head was on a neck like that, he thought, I might not have to shoot it off.

The cabin itself sat in a small sunny clearing above the little bay, with a view out over the lake and other islands. Now and then, a boat passed distantly, put-putting along. He wondered about the people who used to tell him stories. They probably died when the bombs fell. Yes, some politician did it one morning in a fit of pique or boredom, blew the whole thing up. The earth was never revisited. In time, the sun burned out. The cooling planet shuddered out of orbit and became a meteor, disintegrating gradually in its fierce passage through eons. Nothing was ever known of man. He may as well have never existed. He liked to sit in a chair in front of the cabin in the warm sunshine, gazing out over the blue lake, contemplating the final devastation, and thinking: all right, what next? He could just imagine that politician, the last giant of his race, pushing the button and thinking: This is one day they won't soon forget!

He sat in the chair less often when the woman was on the island, for he seemed then to attract chores and children like flies. At such times, he would go up and sit among the spiders in the outhouse, contemplating his aesthetic, which seemed to have something to do with molten flats, hyperbole, and scarecrows. He wanted to write about Job's last years, after he'd got his wealth back, but lost his memory. He thought: the central theme should be stated in the title and then abandoned altogether. He had a story about a soldier who'd been in a foxhole for fifty years and who, having forgotten entirely who the enemy was or what his rifle was for, crawled out one day and got shot. He could call it: *Beginnings*. He planned to write about Columbus voyaging to the end of the world and, more or less abruptly, finding it. He imagined an Eden in which nothing grew, but always seemed about to. To keep Adam from starving, Eve turned herself into an apple, which quite willingly he ate, forgetting that without her he could never find his way out of the place. He shat and called the turd Unable, because this was his prerogative. He wiped his ass and, glancing at the paper before dropping it down the hole, saw that it read: Once upon a time they lived happily ever after. Maybe I've got cancer, he thought.

Though on still days the outhouse could be a little suffocating, the smell was not really unpleasant. It was said that people who grew up in the days of outhouses often longed for that smell for the rest of their lives. The same could be said for piles of dead bodies, the important thing being the chlorinated lime. And to keep the door open.

Of course, that was an open invitation to bees and wasps. One thing leads to another, he thought, and that's how we keep moving along. The blast of the gun, the crash in his skull, were already fading, shrinking into history, wouldn't hear them at all soon, feel them at all. Once, frantically shooing a yellow jacket out the door with a rolled-up manuscript, he hadn't noticed the wasp that had gone down the hole, while he'd bobbed up off it. He sat down and then he noticed it. He yipped all the way down the path, through the cabin, and on down the hill to the bay, and what the woman, ever his best critic, said was: Hush, you'll wake the baby. After that, he always took a can of bugspray with him on trips to the outhouse, learning something as he squirted about the essential anality of the apocalyptic aesthetic.

At this time, he was also a great killer of flies. He carried a flyswatter around with him, indoors and out, and when he couldn't think how to start a story, he killed flies instead. There were a lot of first lines lying about, including a new one about an apostate priest in a sacred-fly cult who'd begun to question his faith during the ritual of Gathering at the Pig's Ass, but there were a lot more dead flies. It's too bad they're not edible, said the woman. She prepared him a fresh pot of coffee, then took the boat to town to have another baby and get some food.

He knew that what he was doing was good, because the flies were holding the earth together. He swatted them badminton-style, caught them on the hairline edge of sills and chair arms, laid jelly-blob traps for them and outscored that holy fiend the tailor, and always with a smiling self-righteous zeal: cleanliness is next to—WHAP!—godliness! He felt like Luther, his finger on the trigger, splattering dark ages against the cabin wall like brains. It's the beginning of something, he thought, wielding the flyswatter like a pastoral staff. A disease perhaps. The coffee was boiling over on the stove when the woman returned. I think I missed my calling, he said. It's a boy, she replied, and opened her blouse to give it suck.

He understood there was nothing banal about giving birth, even to mongoloid idiots, and through the first half dozen or so, he suffered nearly as much as she did, or so he told himself, writing odes to navel strings and the beauty of ripe watermelons to keep his mind off the unpleasant tearing sensation in his testicles. He began a story about a man who brings his wife to the hospital to have a child. They're both excited and very happy. The wife is led away by the doctor and the man enjoys a sympathetic and good-natured exchange with the staff. The delivery seems to take longer than it ought, however, and he begins to worry. When he asks the staff about it, he gets odd evasive answers. Finally, in a panic, he goes in search of the doctor, finds him at a party, roaring drunk and smeared to the ears in blood. He realizes that in fact he's in some kind of nightclub, not a hospital at all. The doctor is a stand-up comedian, delivering a dirtymouth routine on the facts of life and using his wife's corpse as a prop. The worst part is that he can't help laughing. Ah, what shall we do with all these dead? He wondered. The island was becoming a goddamn necropolis.

He'd even managed to kill the snake and the frog, though the woman had spared them. It was as though they couldn't escape their natural instincts toward snakes, his panic, her affection. The frog was just one of those innocent bystanders who come along to thicken the plot, like himself or Jesus Christ. The woman was bathing in the bay, standing in the shallow water, haloed about with suds, just kissing the surface with her vulva, and he was on his way down the path with shampoo and towel to join her. There was a snake across the path and he stopped short, his heart racing. Its mouth was stretched around the bottom half of a frog. He could see the frog's heart pounding, in fact he could hardly see the frog for its thumping panic. He ran to the woodpile and grabbed up an axe. The woman, who had seen his heart pounding in his ears and eyes, came up to see what had frightened him. Her bottom half was dripping wet, and there was soap scum in her pubes. He was trembling as he crept up on the snake with the axe: he thought that the frog might be a decoy, a secret ally, that *he* was the one the snake was after. It's some kind of identity crisis, he realized. The frog's eyes blinked in the snake's maw. The woman kicked the snake gently. It disgorged the frog, feinted as though to strike, then suddenly was gone. Stupefied still, he hopped a few feet into the underbrush and began a story about the old serpent, left behind in Eden after the action had moved elsewhere, who comes on a frog, green as the New Testament, first one he's seen in years, swallows it, and dies of indigestion. She nudged him in the ass with her toe, but he only cowered there, his heart thumping in his ears. She saw that he was in trouble and went down to secure the boat against the coming storm.

It's always like this, he thought. You just get started and then the storm comes. He knew that if he wrote a story about the heath, after Lear, the Fool, Poor Tom and all the rest were dead and gone, just the heath, the storm raging on, phrases lying about like stones, metaphors growing like stunted bushes, it would be the most important story of his age, but he also knew the age would be over before he could ever begin. He no longer believed there would be any message on the cabin wall: let's have no illusions, he thought, about blood and brains. Outside, the wind was howling, the boat was bumping against the pier, and pine branches swept the cabin roof restlessly. They

sat inside and played strip poker, starting naked so as not to delude themselves. He drew a pair of Queens and a King, but the woman beat him with
a heart flush. Off with his head! she screamed. What have I got to lose? he
said. The wind blew in and swept the cards away. In bed, their sheets flapped
like sails.

He awoke the next morning, tangled in first lines like wrinkled sheets.
The windows were smashed and birds lay about with broken necks. The
woman was down at the bay, rinsing diapers, the children huddled about her
like the sting of conscience. He went out to pee and saw that the boat had
sunk. First lines lay all about like fallen trees, shattered and twisted. Columbus, his hips bucking, was voyaging to the end of the world, crying: This is
working! I'm getting on! Jesus was raising mongoloid idiots from the grave
like fileted fish, pretending to be the Good Provider. He half hoped that, as
he peed, the boat would bob to the surface, but it just lay there on the bottom
in a gray sullen stupor, only its gunwales showing like a line drawing for a
suppository or a cathedral window. He felt as if he'd opened one too many
holes in his body, and the wind had blown in and filled him with dead bees.
It's time to leave the island, he told the woman. I've already packed, she said.
We'll make a fresh start, he shouted, but she couldn't hear him because the
children were crying. She was bailing the boat out with the diaper bucket.
A fresh start!

But back in the cabin, the coffee was boiling over on the stove and he saw
there was no bread for the peanut butter. Everything seemed to be receding.
They were back in the boat, and as they pulled away, the island suddenly
sank into the lake and disappeared. Hey, look! he cried. You did that on
purpose, the woman said. You always have to try to end it all! He had his
reasons, but they didn't justify such devastation. Who was he to be the last
giant of his race? Who was he to christen turds? So much for fresh starts. He
might as well not have pulled the trigger in the first place. But it was done
and that was an end to it. Or so it said on the cabin wall.

Some Notes on the Cold War in Kansas

⚜

ROBERT DAY

THERE WERE THREE OF US WHO WERE friends in those days when I was a young boy and lived in a small town in Kansas: Me, Benny and Than (short, I suppose, for Nathan). We were all members—the only members—of The Society of the Secret Shed.

It was the 1950s, and one winter, Grandmother White caught me putting snowballs in the basement freezer to use the following year for a summer snowball war. I say Grandmother White "caught me" because she was sure that the snows in Kansas—and all across America—were laced with "Russian radiation." Grandmother White was my father's mother.

"We'll have to throw it all out," said Grandmother White. She meant the food in the freezer: half a steer bought from—and butchered by—a local rancher. Some sausage from a farm pig. Bacon as well. Two catfish from

Wagnall's pond I had caught that fall and was proud to have done so. Vegetables and strawberries from our garden that we had picked and frozen the previous summer. Whole chickens we bought live from the Simms' down the road. It was Grandmother White who had slaughtered the chickens, chopping their heads off with my father's hatchet and then hanging them by one foot from the clothesline, using her collection of string. It was my job to catch the chickens as they flopped and ran—however briefly—headless around our back yard.

"I don't know," my mother said, looking into the freezer. "It seems such a waste." When my father got home from work, he made the decision: the food stayed.

"Your son will glow in the dark and parts of him will not be useful," said Grandmother White. "The rest of us will get tumors before our time. And warts too thick for a found penny to rub away. I know about the Russians." Grandmother White's real name, I later learned, was Grandmother Wakowski.

The snowballs could go, said my father. But the food stayed. He winked at me to say we'll find someplace else for the snowballs. Which we did.

"Parts of him will not be useful," said Grandmother White, glancing at me. I thought she meant my throwing arm and that I would lose at summer snowball war—or worse, that I would be unable to play baseball in the local Three-Two League. I held my right arm with my left hand. My father patted me on the back. We stored the snowballs in Uncle Bert's freezer. Don't tell your grandmother, my father had said.

The Girl Next Door

Sharon Fulton (for some reason I always thought of her by her full name, never just Sharon, or even Sherry—which is what her mother, and mine, called her), Sharon Fulton went to the Catholic school (Bishop Something or Other), while I attended Hickory Grove, the public school. I did this over the protests of Grandmother White, who might have changed her name but not her religion. Hickory Grove was a brief bike ride away from where we lived; Sharon Fulton's school was on the far north side of town.

Sharon Fulton's bus picked her up fifteen minutes before I had to leave for Hickory Grove, so as I got ready in the mornings, I could see her standing at the end of her driveway. Yellow became my favorite color because it seemed to be her favorite color: yellow blouses when school started and then again in late spring; yellow sweaters in fall; a yellow and black winter coat; yellow dresses that blossomed with the fifties foliage of petticoats and in which Sharon Fulton would, while waiting for her bus, twist her hips this way and that, as if to get them to settle. It was because of Sharon Fulton that I was always on time for school. It is also true that until the day I dug the atomic bomb fallout shelter, Sharon Fulton and I never spoke. And after that we never spoke.

Binoculars

Than's father had a pair of binoculars. "Navy beer bottles," he called them. From Than's house I could read our name on our mail box. I could see to the bottom of the lot and the line of small trees that hid the Secret Shed. If you stood on a chair, you could spot the flagpole on our school, even if the flag wasn't up.

"Let me see. My turn," is what the three of us would say as we passed around the binoculars. Once, I saw Sharon Fulton standing in her front yard. "That's enough," Than's father said just at that moment. He had been in the war (as had my father), and I suppose he wanted to be careful about his souvenirs from those days. "That's enough," and Sharon Fulton vanished from sight.

Civil Defense

Than and Benny and I were Boy Scouts. For a merit badge, we needed to perform some kind of "public" service.

"I think we should clean up Turkey Creek," said Than one day at the shed. "It's full of bottles, and cans, and trash. We could use my uncle's pickup." Than was always trying to figure out how to make use of, or ride in, (front or back—but the back was preferred) his uncle's pickup. "It's got a winch on it," said Than, as if that were the clincher. He cranked an imaginary handle.

For Benny's part, he was always plotting ways to use his .22—a bolt-action single-shot rifle that had been provisionally given to him the previous Christmas and which could only be used with his grandfather present, and then only for target practice on tin cans. Benny's father had been killed in Germany.

"I think we should shoot the pigeons at the Co-Op," said Benny. "My mother says they're a menace." Benny aimed a long stick and fired off a few shots at some starlings on the power line that ran above the shed. "Dead menace. Bang. Dead menace. Bang." "Menace" was a new word for Benny.

"I think we should join the Civil Defense," I said. "That way we could get binoculars to look for Russian bombers." I held up two rounded fists to my eyes and turned my head this way and that, scanning the Kansas sky for enemy planes. The dream of binoculars to look for Russian atomic bombers beat out the pickup truck and the pigeon menace.

The Secret Shed

It was an old chicken house located on a bank above a small nameless (and mostly dry) creek that ran into Wagnall's pond. Overgrown with morning glory vines and ringed with a barricade of sunflowers and thistle, it was hidden (so we thought) from everyone but the three of us. The shed had board floors, under which the three of us stashed various odds and ends ("totems" Than called them) that we would get out when we gathered for the meetings of "The Society of the Secret Shed."

It was at these meetings that we decided what we would do for the rest of the day: snake hunting was always on the list; tree climbing usually; skating if Wagnall's pond was frozen, stone skipping if it was not; snowball war, winter or summer. Just as important, we planned what we would do the following week, month, and year.

This list included floating down the Smoky Hill River to the Kansas River on a raft, and then to New Orleans by way of Chicago. As the only fisherman among us, I would be responsible for catching fish. Benny would shoot squirrels and rabbits and birds with his .22; and because he liked to build fires—he built the one that finally burnt down the secret shed—Than said he would cook.

Our plans also included taking turns walking and riding double on Dan (an appaloosa that Benny's grandfather owned) to Montana to see Niagara Falls, then taking the A Train to New York City. However, our best trip was hitchhiking to Kansas City and 12th and Vine to see a "burr-lee-q" show (This latter adventure was something Benny's brother, Leroy, had already done—hitchhiking and all). But, whatever our agenda, we never began a meeting of The Society of the Secret Shed without putting our totems on the two-by-fours that ran along the walls of the shed, each of us claiming a wall that was not used by the door.

Than had a bird's head skeleton, a horseshoe (that I coveted), plus a pretty nasty-looking rabbit skin that had been pried off the asphalt road that we took to Hickory Grove. He also had a collection of various animal bones—part of a jaw, some vertebrate, what might have been a leg bone, ribs—that he was trying to assemble into a composite animal on the floor of The Shed, and over which we would have to step as we moved around.

As for Benny, he had a flattened quarter that had been crushed by the local grain train after we put it on the tracks; a spent CO_2 cartridge he said we could use to make a bomb by filling it with gun powder and attaching a firecracker fuse; and two live 50-caliber machine gun rounds that his uncle had brought back from the war. Benny also claimed he was going to bring down some "Mexican" playing cards of his brother's with pictures of naked women on them—but he never did.

My totems were a greenish stone I found in a large catfish I had caught and cleaned. I would also put out a Lazy Ike lure, whose treble hooks I had straightened with a pair of pliers so I could claim—which I did—that a huge bass named Godzilla had struck the bait with such force he flattened the hooks.

But my prize totem—prized by all of us—was a page I had ripped out of a paperback book that had been in the rack of the local drug store. The page (page 126) had the words "brassiere" and "breasts" toward the bottom. The complete sentence ran: "When Lola turned around, George saw that she had unbuttoned her blouse so that he could see her black brassiere and the tops of her white breasts." The following sentence was the fragment: "Then Lola took off her blouse and reached behind her and un-" which broke off at the gully between page 126 and 127 (a page none of us had the nerve to return to the drugstore to steal).

At more than one meeting of The Society of the Secret Shed, we decided to find Lola—or a Lola—and invite her to join us on our trip to New Orleans. We were also inspired to name the raft for her: *The Lola*. Our hope was that a real Lola could go from page 126 to page 127 as we drifted toward Chicago by way of 12th and Vine streets in Kansas City. In the meantime, we had memorized her sentence and a half with the same fidelity we had memorized the Pledge of Allegiance we recited each morning at Hickory Grove Grade School.

Beyond our totems, it was required by The Order of the Secret Shed that each of us have a secret, secret, secret (being three, we thought of three as a sacred number) totem that was stored somewhere deep in The Shed. Both the location of this Triple Secret Totem, and the object, itself, were not to be revealed to anyone, thus Benny had something somewhere, and so did Than—and I did not know what or where.

For my part (and I have kept my secret all these years), I had hidden in a crevice in a beam above the door a letter I was in the process of writing to Sharon Fulton, it's opening sentence being: "I like yellow to" [*sic*]. Even then I needed an editor.

Physicals

"Yes," I am saying over the phone. "There are three of us, and we all want to join the Civil Defense. For our Boy Scout merit badge."

"Good for you," says the man at the other end. I cannot now recall by what means I tracked down whomever I am talking to, but somehow I had found my way to a pleasant and, as it will soon turn out, patient man. "What would you and your friends like to do for the Civil Defense?"

"We want to be spotters," I say.

"Spotters?" he says.

"Yes," I say. "We want to look for Russian atomic bombers."

There are moments in everybody's youth when they know they are being fools. You don't know exactly why—or even for sure what it means to be a fool—but by some means you leap into your future, and you know that when you look back you will see yourself as very silly. In spite of this awareness, I go on.

"We want to look for Russian atomic bombers with binoculars. We would take turns during the school week. But in summer and on weekends we would all look. We each want our own pair."

"With binoculars?" says the man.

"Yes," I say.

"I see," he says.

"We can climb trees," I say. "And we have a tree that gets us up to the roof of the shed, so we have a good view from there." There is a pause.

"Do you know about physicals?" he says.

In point of fact, he had asked me if I knew about "physics"—not "physicals." Probably he was about to explain that whatever Russian atomic bomb was going to be dropped on The Shed (not to mention the Hickory Grove Grade School) would have been cut loose from the Russian atomic bomber somewhere around Denver, so that no matter how high a tree we climbed, no matter how powerful were our binoculars, or how diligent our looking through them from the roof of The Shed, we would not be able to see the Russian atomic bomb until it became its mushroom cloud.

However, for me, in hot pursuit of three pairs of binoculars and all the fame that would come with them, it made perfect sense that you would need physicals in order to be in the Civil Defense and issued Civil Defense binoculars. You had to have a physical to play in the Three-Two League, didn't you? There might even be a training program to get into the Civil Defense. If we had to take Civil Defense physicals, that might mean a day off from school, complete with the kind of excuse young boys dream of: *I won't be in class on Friday Miss Anderson because I have to take a Civil Defense Physical.*

I saw myself returning to school with my binoculars hanging around my neck. *"Navy beer bottles we call them,"* I would say to anyone who asked. I might even be required to stand at the classroom window—instead of taking my regular seat—all the better to scan the sky. At recess, the three of us would be "posted" around the playground looking Westward (we always assumed the Russians would come from Colorado or California). And finally in this movie I am making in my mind, I am sure no one at Hickory Grove Grade School (not even Miss Anderson) would be allowed to talk to us when we were on duty.

Then there was Sharon Fulton. Of course, someone would be assigned to look out for the Catholic girls at Bishop Whatever It Was. Someone would have to patrol the outer fence of the playground with binoculars scanning the sky. Someone would have to yell: Russian atomic bombers! Take cover! Under your desks! Russian atomic bombers! Sharon Fulton would faint. Someone would have to carry Sharon Fulton off the playground in her yellow dress. That someone would be me.

"We'll take physicals," I say. There is silence at the end of the line.

Pubic Hair

It was Leroy, Benny's older brother, who first grew pubic hair. We even knew to call it "pubic hair" because you learned about it in Boy's Health, taught by the high school basketball coach, a Mr. Allen, who Leroy said was "doing the do" with Miss Anderson. Leroy was a hood.

Not that Leroy showed us his pubic hair; it was just that Benny reported on it from time to time. Benny's brother also shaved, had a switchblade knife, and kept a rubber in his wallet (he did show us the rubber one day when Than and I stopped by). Later Leroy would get Roberta Taylor "hot"—whatever that meant. (What it finally meant was that Roberta Taylor got pregnant and was shipped off to Sharon Springs to her grandmother's farm.)

Leroy's pubic hair made us wonder about girls, and what, in Than's terminology, was "down there?" We couldn't really imagine what was "down there," this being well before *Playboy* showed us anything but breasts and buttocks—and in those days young boys in rural Kansas did not often get a hold of *Playboy*, so even breasts and buttocks were scarce items.

"I wonder if girls have pubic hair," Benny said one day at The Shed. Nobody said anything for a moment. For my part, I was hoping our meeting would be short, as in my mind I had composed two more sentences of my serial letter to Sharon Fulton, a letter I would only take out when Than and Benny had left.

"Girls do not have pubic hair," I pronounced.

"How do you know?" said both Than and Benny.

"Because only boys have pubic hair," I said. "That is why it's in Boy's Health."

"Stern says his sister will take down her pants for a dollar," said Than. Stern was Leroy's age. He, too, was a hood, and Stern was his last name, not his first, which made him even more of a hood than Leroy. Stern's sister was our age. We had heard this before about her. But a dollar was a lot of money for us, as we got a quarter a week allowance (Benny probably got less) and could only put together another dollar or so by doing extra chores. Then there was the question of who would ask Stern's sister.

"I think girls do have pubic hair," said Benny.

"They can't have pubic hair," I said, "because they don't have beards."

"Why wouldn't they have pubic hair in Girl's Health just like we have pubic hair in Boy's Health?" said Benny.

"They have breasts instead," I said. "We don't have breasts in Boy's Health. We have pubic hair. So it's even-steven." To this day I love reasoning from limited available evidence.

"Do you think girls have pubic hair?" Benny asked Than. Than thought a moment. It seemed a long time. I was beginning to lose track of the two sentences I was going to write to Sharon Fulton.

"I think," said Than finally, "that girls have pubic hair, but that they shed it in the summer." It seemed right.

"I agree with Than," said Benny.

"So do I," I said. Meeting over. After we left, I doubled back and got out my letter to Sharon Fulton and wrote my two sentences and then went home, happy in the knowledge that someday, somehow, she would find it—maybe in the rubble of nuclear destruction.

It would be later that summer that the three of us would get a dollar together and draw straws to see who would ask Stern's sister to take down her pants (Benny lost). When she finally did it, standing in a small clearing up hill from the shed while the three of us sat on the peak of the roof, we were not really able to see what we saw—or tell anyone what we had seen. However, we all agreed she did not have pubic hair.

"I told you," I said.

"It's still summer," said Than. "They don't grow it back until Thanksgiving."

Grandmother White, Television, Warts, and the Reading of Codes

We didn't have a television and neither did Benny or Than. Than's uncle in Kansas City had a television, and he told Than that you could see *The Lone Ranger* on it. This did not seem possible to us.

"He comes right into the living room. Tonto, too," said Than.

"What about Silver?" asked Benny.

"Silver, too," said Than. "You just turn on the television and the Lone Ranger and Tonto and Silver all ride around. And talk. Just like on radio only they're in your living room."

"I don't believe it," I said. But I did. I imagined Silver and Tonto and the Lone Ranger all projected into our house, riding along while canyons and rivers and bandits and hostile Indians appeared in front of the divan or by the kitchen door or in the hallway that led to my bedroom— all as the plot required. How this happened, I wasn't sure, but I was sure I wanted it to happen in our house.

"Who's going to clean up the mess?" said Grandmother White. We were at supper, and I had asked if I might have a television for my "big" Christmas present, even though Christmas was months away.

"I don't think we can get television out here," my father said. "You have to be near a city."

"What mess?" said my mother. She was as alert to household untidiness as was Grandmother White.

"From all those cowboys and Indians traipsing through the house," said Grandmother White. "You heard the boy. That whole Ranger gang he listens to on the radio comes out of the television and into the living room. We don't need that."

"I don't think that's the way it works," said my father. "I think they are all on a screen like at a movie theater."

I was greatly disappointed to hear this, as my father was usually right about such things. But maybe not always.

"I'll clean up the mess," I said. "It can be one of my chores."

"We can talk about it later," said my mother. That meant that we would not talk about it later. If she had said, "I'll talk to your father," that meant, "I'll fix it with your father," just as my father's wink meant he'd fix it with my mother by hiding my snowballs in Uncle Bert's freezer. In such ways do children learn to read codes.

All of this talk in code may have diverted my grandmother's attention from *The Lone Ranger,* but it did not divert her attention from a wart that had recently come up on my index finger, and which she saw as irrefutable evidence of the spread of Russian radiation.

"I have a found penny," she said, "and we have a dishrag."

"Mother," said my father. That meant stop with this superstitious nonsense.

"Not that it will do much good," said my grandmother.

"Parts of him may already not be useful."

"Grandmother White!" said my mother in some alarm.

Grandmother White was quiet for a moment, and then under the table I could feel her foot tap mine. That meant if I'd let her rub my wart with her found penny so she could wrap the penny in the dish rag and bury it, she'd give me a quarter; it would turn out to be the quarter I'd contribute to have Stern's sister take down her pants.

Benny

Sometime during high school, Benny went to the Army. He was sent there by the local judge who said it was either the Army or jail. Or reform school. Benny had begun blowing up mailboxes with cherry bombs; then he blew up a toilet in high school with a CO_2 cartridge filled with gun powder; then he stuffed a potato into the exhaust pipe of the local patrol car; then he ripped a rubber machine off the men's room of the Texaco station; finally, he started shoplifting (he was caught stealing boxes of Russell Stover candy from the drugstore where I had stolen Lola's page 126). In the Army, he was first stationed in Korea; then he went to Vietnam. While I was taking graduate courses at the university, and Than was finishing his degree to be the veterinarian he is today, Benny was fighting in the Tet Offensive. Where he was killed. A fact I have only recently learned.

The Bomb Shelter and Sharon Fulton

Not long after Stern's sister had taken down her pants, I was digging a hole near The Shed to bury a bird I killed with my slingshot, and Sharon Fulton came up. I am to become a man who will never know what to do or say when first in the presence of women I find attractive. I once told a woman who had put on a stylish pea coat over her rather ample upper body, "My, what big buttons you have." What I said to Sharon Fulton was: "I'm digging a fallout shelter." It seemed like the thing to say to a girl whom I had saved a number of times by spotting Russian atomic bombers with my binoculars—not to mention carrying her to safety from the playground after she had fainted.

I suppose Sharon Fulton stood there for a moment and watched me digging my hole. I hoped she hadn't noticed the nearby dead bird. I did not look up.

"Why?" she said. It would turn out to be the only word Sharon Fulton would ever say to me. I looked up. She was wearing yellow. I went back to digging.

"Because there are Russian atomic bombers coming," I said.

"Why?" she said. I stopped digging. I stood by the pile of dirt I had made. I put my foot on the dead bird. I remember thinking I had not imagined Sharon Fulton's voice.

"They are slow bombers," I said. I struck a pose by leaning on my shovel. Again, she asked why.

"Because they are very heavy," I said. "They have all this steel plate, and our fighters can't shoot them down because the bullets bounce off. We've been shooting at them for a week now, and nothing happens. They are over Hawaii and pretty soon they'll be over Guam." I made the rat-tat-tat sound of the 50-caliber machine-gun fire I supposed would come from the front end of an F-86 fighter. I did this with a series of finger jabs meant to convey the bullets themselves, but which caused me to drop my shovel and shift my foot off the dead bird.

Sharon Fulton looked at the sky. She looked east, toward her school and mine. There was nothing there. Nothing but clear Kansas sky all the way to Kansas City.

"They are coming from the west," I said, and, after picking up my shovel, pointed toward our houses up the hill. "When they get here, they will black out the entire horizon. That's why you need an atomic bomb shelter. Otherwise when the radiation spreads, parts of us will become useless."

Sharon Fulton was crying. I am about to become a man who does not know what to do when women cry.

"You can't come into my atomic bomb shelter if you cry," I said. Sharon Fulton turned her back on me and walked away.

"Stern's sister took her pants down," I said. "For a dollar."

Sharon Fulton began running up the hill toward home, all yellow and lovely in my mind to this day.

At supper, my mother wanted to know if something was the matter. Grandmother White said she hoped I hadn't tried to dig up the washcloth with the found penny in it, because I'd get covered with warts just from touching it.

"Mother?" said my father. Here, he winked at me. As I didn't wink back, he said, "What's the matter, son?" I didn't know what to say.

And still don't.

Unless it is something to Sharon Fulton after all these years, and across what miles that separate us I do not know: Yellow is still my favorite color. Even today, I don't know what to say to women who are to me now what you were to me then. I hear the sound of your voice. And the sound of your crying. If only you had fainted, I would have known what to do. My mother could never understand why I started being late for school. When Than burned down The Shed that winter, my letter to you went up in flames, but I remember every word of it—including the final sentence I added after you left me alone with my bomb shelter. It is code for all that I have written above, which I am now tapping out to you. Wherever you are. Whoever we have become.

The One Marvelous Thing

﹋

RIKKI DUCORNET

THE NIGHT BEFORE ELLEN WENT SHOPPING with Pat, she dreamed she was gazing at a painting that created the illusion of a portal opening upon a grove of citrus trees. Within it a naked goddess tossed grain to a large rose-colored bird. Awakening alone in a room so banal it made her weep, she dressed for the day without enthusiasm.

Ellen has never liked Pat. A child of inherited wealth, Pat is addicted to the buying and selling of properties. The neighborhood is rife with seedy real estate made over into Tuscan villas. Everywhere you look, unedifying brass kokopellis tirelessly tootle on a glut of green. Weird Vietnam vets and old folks too stunned to answer a doorbell have been swapped for earnest acrobats of both sexes. They canter past at all hours accompanied by dogs the size of Hondas sporting alpaca leg warmers. Sundays their gimlet-eyed brats shriek from atop toy castles constructed of Indonesian teak.

Because she dislikes Pat, it makes little or no sense that Ellen accepts to join her shopping. Against her better instincts and before she can change her mind, she is belted into Pat's SUV and already alienated. Today Pat's glazed lips are unfamiliarly swollen, her hair thrashing with extensions, and her contacts tiger agate.

"Enhancement," Pat confides huskily in response to Ellen's eyeballing, "is the name of the game."

Ellen, who thinks she is referring to a T.V. program, wonders: "What's it like?"

"Great!" says Pat. "Why settle for less than better?"

"I'm so out of it!" Ellen acknowledges with a small, self-deprecating laugh. "I thought best was good enough."

"Don't be a fool!" Pat scolds her. "Best can *always* be bested! Lamb chops, pesto, Super Tuscans, sex—" She laughs with all her teeth. "Yes, sex *can* be better! Look in the box. In the back seat."

With difficulty, Ellen twists around, and reaching, feels something notched and carved. A bone whistle? A slip of oiled wood? Claws are they? Teeth! She recoils with horror.

"Uzbekie sex toys!" Pat carols, careening into Wormwood's vast parking lot.

There is a line, maybe three hundred people, waiting for Wormwood to open. Her bosom enhanced with Ralph Lauren counterfeit squash blossoms, Pat marches past them, Ellen in tow and already breathless. Knocking on the great glass doors, Pat manages to get someone's attention.

"We're here!" she shouts gaily, "with All International. You must let us in!" Scowling, a salesclerk shakes his head *no*, but Pat, her steel tempered with honey, insists. "We have an appointment with the manager," she gyrates, "and we're already a little late! Please?" she wheedles, "please? Please?" When the door opens, she gives his hand a squeeze. A moment later they are wading in a sea of leather sofas, all indigo blue.

"Truth *is* the consequences," Pat dogmatizes, "especially of lies. We are *here*," she insists, impatient with Ellen's troubled look, "right where we should be. On top of the food chain."

"Here with All International," Ellen snorts as Pat surges on.

"Stop it, Ellen," Pat says. "Stop being a nincompoop. In a minute the doors will open and those bitches out there will tear the place apart. If we're not on our toes, El, we'll miss out on the one marvelous thing." They are surrounded by recliners, and because Ellen continues to look unconvinced, Pat assures her: "There is *always* one marvelous thing."

A low roar swells and overtakes them. All at once Wormwood is thick and fast with women, some piloting anxious looking infants on wheels.

"Shit." Pat snarls. They are making their way around archipelagos of Welsh coffee tables. "Fuck them," she says. "Fuck THAT!" And she bolts.

"What *is* it?" Ellen calls after her. "What's wrong?" Pat has taken off in a dead heat towards a faux antique Roman birdcage over six feet high. Butter yellow and well greased with gold leaf, it glitters. Beside it, a clerk with a nervous disorder fumbles with a credit card.

"You can't have that!" Pat shouts at a startled brunette, handsome and dappled with freckles; "Sorry! But the cage is ours. Take a look," she tells the clerk, "it has a 'hold' ticket on it." Swimming in his red jacket, the geriatric clerk appears dazed.

"There was," the brunette speaks evenly, "no hold on this." Ellen thinks she is lovely, with an open, ironical face.

"Yes there was," Pat lies breezily. "I put a hold on it last night. For All International."

"You can take your All International," the woman says kindly, "and shove it. You and your wimpy sidekick."

Mortified, Ellen cringes. She likes the other woman. Likes her bangs, her hazel eyes, her freckles and her spunk. *I am a wimp*, she thinks. *Or I wouldn't be here. Tagging along with Pat!* She looks into the woman's face and smiles.

"What's All International anyway?" the woman asks her, almost tenderly. "I doubt it's real!" Leaning close to Ellen she whispers: "I don't think your friend is, either."

"She isn't," Ellen returns her whisper.

"Give her back her credit card," Pat directs the old codger. "Do it."

"I'm Magda," the woman tells Ellen, and thrillingly touches her wrist there where the pulse quickens.

"I'm waiting!" Pat says, beginning to look scary, "For you to give her back her card! Stop clutching it! For god's sake!"

"You are being abused," Magda tells the clerk, "by a mythomaniac. Don't let yourself be pushed around like that. A man your age!"

Ellen thinks the clerk must be eighty, at least. Like so many elderly Americans forced into servitude, he is held together with denture glue and surgical bolts. He has recently recovered from a hip replacement he could not afford. He cannot recall who saw the cage first; he can barely remember his own name.

"Hugo," Pat says reading his breast pocket, "you remember me. I came in last night before closing and told you to put a hold on the birdcage. You remember me. Hugo."

Hugo considers this. Hugo is, after all, his name. Yet he is frightened. His hands are shaking.

"Don't let her persecute you," Ellen says.

"Fuck you!" Pat shouts. "Fuck you, Ellen! Fucking traitor!"

"I have *birds*, Hugo," Magda tells him. "Thirty Australian Zebra finches. Each one has a name. And when one begins to sing, all the others join in. Zebra finches sing in syncopation. They've been doing so for tens of thousands of years. My birds will find their happiness in this cage—but only if you say so, Hugo. It's up to you." The clerk studies the birdcage with real intensity. "This woman—she'll make a phone booth out of it, a urinal—who knows what? Please, Hugo. Be kind. Process my card."

"Screw her, Hugo!" Pat explodes, "the sentimental twat! Screw her, goddamnit!"

"Hey!" says Hugo.

Pat presses her card upon him, but he pulls himself together, straightening his jacket and balancing on his elevator shoes.

"Now, now . . ." he offers. An ancient fire is stirring in Hugo's hollow chest. In his distant youth he was a missionary, and once convinced a headhunter to embrace the greater Power. He begins to process Magda's card.

"Hugo," says Pat. "What the fuck?"

"I'm a Mormon." Hugo says this with dignity.

"What?" Pat barks, now totally out of control, "what the fuck does that have to do with this transaction? I'll tell you what it has to do with this transaction! Not a fucking thing!"

"I'm a Mormon," Hugo repeats, his teeth all arattle, "and I am offended by your manner, Ma'am. My name is Hugo," he tells Magda who nods and signs the receipt.

"Shit," says Pat. "Fuck this." Stomping off she leaves a stench of sulphur and white diamonds in her wake. "Fuck you, Ellen!" she shouts as she eclipses. "I'll *never* take you shopping again."

Later that evening as they lie together sweetly entwined, Ellen asks Magda where her birds are.

"What birds, Pussycat?" Magda yawns, and languorous, stretches.

"The finches," Ellen says. "The thirty synchronized finches."

"I have no finches," Magda tells her.

"What's the cage for, then?" Ellen laughs, heartily amused.

"For you, little one," Magda says, taking Ellen's lower lip between her teeth gently. "To curl up in at your leisure like a cat. Like a cat that has eaten up all the little birds one by one. Their feathers, their feet, their tiny skulls."

"Yes!" Ellen purrs her approval. "And each and every one of those birds is named Pat."

Visions of Budhardin

❦

STUART DYBEK

THE ELEPHANT WAS THERE, WAITING in the overgrown lot where once long ago there had been a Victory garden, and after that a billboard, but now nothing but the rusting hulks of abandoned cars. The children grew silent as they gathered to inspect it: the crude overlapping parts, the bulky sides and lopsided rump, the thick squat legs that looked like five-gallon ice-cream drums, huge cardboard ears, everything painted a different shade of gray, and the trunk the accordion-ribbed hose from a vacuum cleaner. They stared back at Budhardin's eyes looking at them through the black sockets above the trunk. The holes were set too close together for a real elephant and made it look cross-eyed and slightly evil.

They couldn't see inside where Budhardin sat on a stool looking out at the world, his feet on pedals, hands manipulating levers, body connected to a network of lines and pulleys, a collar gripping his forehead for swinging the limp trunk, a clothesline tied around his waist running out the tail hole.

The children walked around, examining it from every angle.

"What in the fuck!" Billy Crystal said. He took his knife out and carved the date into the plaster rump and after it his initials, B.C.

Most of the kids chuckled even though they were familiar with the initials joke. A few threw stones, watching them bounce off, leaving dents in the paint job. Others had run across the lot to the alley, rummaged through the garbage cans, and began their bombardment of rotten tomatoes, banana peels, apple cores. Pedro "Chinga" Sanchez raced in balancing a glob of dogshit on a popsicle stick, arcing it as if it were a hand grenade. It splattered high off the humped back and was followed by a rain of beer cans and Petri wine bottles. Buddy Holly Shwartz sneaked up behind, grabbed the tail, and gave it a yank.

"Hey, it's just a goddamn clothesline!" he announced. They tried to light it up but nobody had any lighter fluid on him, so all they were able to do was get it smoking like a slow wick.

The elephant had closed its eyelids and stopped swinging its trunk from side to side. It stood perfectly still while they discussed pulling its trunk out by the roots or coming back with some gasoline to roast it.

"Ah, fuck it," Billy Crystal finally said, and they wandered off in little groups.

After they'd gone Mr. Ghazili, who owned the little combination grocery–candy store on the corner, shuffled over. As always, even in winter, he wore his house slippers, still speckled with pink paint from some job long ago. He stood looking up at the elephant, chewing his cigar. Little by little the elephant raised its lids.

"That's you in there, isn't it, Budhardin?" Ghazili said. The elephant nodded its trunk.

"You might look a little different, but I'd recognize those eyes anywhere . . . same as used to stare up at me through the candy counter. Yeah, you liked them licorice whips. I remember the time you bought out my whole supply and went outside giving 'em away to all the kids telling 'em you were Jesus Christ. So they tied you to a phone pole and started beatin' you with them licorice whips. I had to run out there and untie you."

Two tears rolled down the elephant's face.

"Yeah, I remember . . . always alone . . . except for that friend—what was his name?—kid who got tanned over . . . And now, a big tycoon! Yeah, I been readin' about you in the papers. Used to try and show people, but nobody around here's too interested in that kinda stuff, you know. Wouldn't of believed it was the same little fat kid anyway."

Budhardin didn't answer. He had failed to provide the elephant with a mouth.

"Your tail's smoking pretty bad back there," Mr. Ghazili said. He went around and rubbed the sparks out of the fibers. They stood looking at each other. Fistfuls of silver dollars, wristwatches, rings, suddenly issued from the trunk, spilling at Ghazili's feet.

"No, no," he said, "I don't want nothing. Just came by to say hello." He shuffled closer, his slippers crunching over the pile of coins, and patted the bump right above the elephant's trunk, then shuffled away.

Budhardin stood alone watching the day get older inside the sweltering body, wishing he could have told Ghazili the story. It was a story about two peasant boys on their own—their families dead, perhaps from plague. They find a huge plaster elephant standing in a field, left behind by a circus, and take to living in it. But the elephant is in poor repair and at night swarms of rats try to get in through the holes. During the day they wander about the deserted countryside scrounging for food. Once, they come upon a village, completely lifeless, with everything locked, and stare in through the bakery window at a fabulous display of cookies and frosted pastries.

He couldn't remember how it ended. It had been two years since the story had begun recurring in a series of haunting flashes and he still was unable to get beyond the two boys standing before the bakery window, their faces pressing against the glass. Sometimes people would say it sounded vaguely familiar, but, like him, they found it impossible to recall the ending.

He let his mind drift and found himself counting cars that passed. It was rush hour. He remembered how he and Eugene used to stand on the corner making endless surveys of cars. Long lists of dates and check marks under columns headed CHEVYS, MERCS, HUDSONS. What made it exciting was when something unusual came by, like a Packard, Eugene's favorite, a model called the Clipper. It had a silver captain's-wheel emblem on the hood. Eugene was always planning how someday he'd pry one off and mount it in his room. Instead he was killed by a maroon '52 Studebaker. The kind in which the front and rear look almost identical, both shaped like a chrome artillery shell—a model Eugene hated passionately.

They'd planned their Dreammobile together—the car they'd drive across-country to the Pan American Highway down to the Amazon—fins like an El Dorado's, long low hood like a Kaiser's, curves like a Jaguar's. They disagreed on whether it would have chrome spoked wheels or spinners with small blue lights.

They'd plan and wrestle on the "Boulevard," a four-foot median strip of grass separating double-lane traffic. Flat on their backs, rolling over each other between the roar of engines, the rush of tires only inches away on each side from where they struggled, gulping exhaust fumes. Of course Eugene was no match for Budhardin's greater bulk, but Budhardin would usually let him win. Eugene would wind up, flushed and panting, kneeling on Budhardin's shoulders to keep him pinned, and Budhardin would relax under the light body, turning his head in the crushed grass to watch the hubcaps spin endlessly by.

Once, when they were lying like that in the middle of five-o'clock traffic, a motorcycle jumped the median strip. The biker flew over the handlebars and before he hit they both distinctly heard him yelling, "You motherfucker!" at whoever had forced him out of his lane. Somehow he got back up, but when he took off his helmet blood was trickling out of his ears, and when he tried to talk all that came out was a reddish-pink froth. He sat down hard and slumped over, choking, and the next thing Budhardin knew, Eugene had run over and was cradling the biker's head in his lap so he could breathe. Later, walking home, Eugene started to cry because he had blood all over his jeans and he figured his old man was going to beat the shit out of him for ruining a pair of trousers.

After Eugene died somebody had drawn a circle with pink-colored chalk on the street and an arrow pointing to it with the words EUGENE'S BRAINS. Even after a season of fall rain and traffic, on his way to school he'd still been able to see the faded chalk letters on the asphalt before they finally vanished under snow.

It was getting dark now. He began to pedal. The elephant lumbered across the lot, crunching over tin cans, crashing through blowing newspaper. He turned up the alley, his shadow blotting out the shadows of the power lines against the backyard fences. He kept moving till the moon slid unbearably across his eyes in silver spots and blood rushed in waves through his head, making him too dizzy to take another step. He'd known that he was going to pass by the spot, but he hadn't expected his reaction to be this strong. It was the smell—the same smell after all these years—of rain-rotted wood, decaying leaves, catpiss fungi, of some wonderful weed the name of which he still didn't know, and behind it all the hint of damp flower beds. He stuck his trunk into the narrow Secret Gangway and inhaled.

He butted his head against the dark opening between two garages, but it was impossible for him to get any closer to the backyard on the other side. Even back then, as a child, he'd been barely able to squeeze through.

Eugene had discovered the place. He had been going there with Jennifer R., who was a grade ahead of them. Through the passage there was a yard with grass sprouting up like a wheat field around their knees. A broken birdbath stood in the middle, lopsided and dripping moss. Off to one corner, under a huge oak, was an old arbor so completely entwined with vines that the light inside was green. An old invalid lady owned the house, but her back-porch shades were always drawn and once inside the arbor, no one could see in.

They used to take turns going under Jennifer's dress. The elephant began to shudder, standing there with his trunk still in the gangway, remembering it. First the green sunlight inside the arbor and then kneeling down and entering the world of Jennifer, her legs and the way the light came through the flowered dress she wore, palms sweating, taking down her panties and *looking.*

He'd kneel there for a while and then it would be Eugene's turn and then his turn again. Once, on the way there, Eugene said, "I'm going to kiss it today." And so when it was Budhardin's turn he kissed it too. And Jennifer said, "Oh! He kissed me there!" to Eugene and Budhardin pulled his head up, feeling himself blushing, and said to Eugene, "Didn't you?" And Eugene was rolling around laughing.

Another time Eugene brought a little rubber hammer from a play-tool kit and they took turns tapping Jennifer. She seemed to like it.

The time after that Eugene asked her if she wanted to see them. At first she didn't want to but finally she did.

"We'll both show her," Eugene said. "One, two, three, pull it out!" Budhardin tried but he couldn't. He stood there frozen with guilt and embarrassment, his fly open, on the brink of damnation.

"C'mon," Eugene said, and then he reached into Budhardin's unzipped trousers and pulled out his penis. They both had boners. Jennifer started giggling. Eugene was playing with himself. He tried to get Jennifer to but she wouldn't. She was afraid of germs.

"Look, no germs," Eugene said, grabbing Budhardin's and jerking it gently.

The elephant was moaning and ramming his huge gray head into the telephone pole that stood in front of the gangway, concealing the entrance from view of the alley. Now that the dizziness had passed he was all twisted up inside and realized he couldn't just stand there anymore, he had to keep moving.

He could move off, but he couldn't stop thinking. He remembered the time they went to Ghazili's and bought balloons, then walked down the alley toward the gangway.

"What are these for?" Budhardin asked.

"You put them on your prick," Eugene said.

They practiced with a few. Budhardin struggled with a red one, stretching it over the head of his penis.

"It looks like Santa Claus," Eugene said, laughing. He had worked a yellow one partially on. "You know what I'd like to try? Sticking one of these up Jennifer and then blowing it up inside her. I wonder if she'd like that."

They were jerking each other off while talking.

"How could they have made this a mortal sin?" Budhardin said.

"A mortal sin!" Eugene looked at him, shocked. "Whataya mean a mortal sin?"

"It's against the Sixth Commandment," he said. He'd thought Eugene had realized that, that they had been sharing in a pact of mutual damnation. The closeness of damning themselves together had actually been more important than the physical pleasure.

"I wouldn't have done it if I'd of known it was a mortal sin." Eugene was looking at him as if he were weird. "You mean you knew it and still did it?"

"It's okay," Budhardin said quietly. "If you didn't know it was a mortal sin then it wasn't one."

"You sonofabitch," Eugene said—he was almost crying—"I coulda kept doing it then if you hadn't of told me!"

After Eugene went to confession he told Budhardin he'd never go to the arbor again. The priest had made him tell the whole story and for penance told him to wait until no one was looking, then to put his finger in the flame of one of the vigil candles and hold it there a moment, only a moment. And then to meditate on how eternity was a never-ending series of such moments, except the fires of hell were not one tiny flame but an inferno roaring like the bowels of a furnace.

Without Eugene, Jennifer wouldn't return either. Budhardin felt more alone than he ever had before. He could still remember in third grade, before he'd made Holy Communion, asking the priest, "If God is good how could he create something as terrible as hell?" The priest had explained that maybe hell really wasn't full of fire, that the real torture was the terrible loneliness of God withholding his love. Now he knew what that meant. Before he met Eugene he'd accepted himself as damned. From as far back as he could remember he was secretly aware of possessing a genius for understanding catechism, and it became clear to him early that he could never accept what was necessary for him to be saved. Like Lucifer, he was too proud to bow and scrape for God's love. But he hadn't grasped the extent of the pain—not until he was cut off from Eugene, could see the look of repugnance that came into his face, realized he had been cast aside as an "evil companion." He couldn't endure it, and so he decided that to win back Eugene's friendship he'd have to win his soul.

He went to Frenchie—an older, crazy guy in his twenties, who'd been in the Navy, knew every dirty joke in the world, had naked women tattooed on his ass, wore sandals, a little mustache, and a knot of beard growing out from under his lip instead of his chin. Everybody knew Frenchie was weird and avoided him. He'd come up to kids on the street, grinning as if he were their best friend, and mutter through yellow teeth, "How 'bout a little, my man?"

Frenchie traded him a pack of dirty playing cards. On one side were regular suits and numbers and on the other were photographs of people doing

things together he'd never even imagined. He showed Eugene the deuce of
hearts, on the other side of which was a woman smoking a cigarette with her
snatch. They went together to the arbor to look at the rest.

"Look at the size of their pricks!" Eugene said. "I can hardly wait till I
get older."

"Let's see if you got any bigger," Budhardin said.

That set the pattern. Without Jennifer it became more intense between
the two of them. And afterward Eugene going to confession and promising Christ he wouldn't do it anymore. Father Wally warned him he was
turning into a homo and urged him to pray for strength to withstand these
terrible temptations. Sometimes after they did it Eugene would get sullen.
Once he started to cry. But there were other times when he said he didn't
care anymore, would suggest that they try something new off the cards,
and Budhardin would feel a flush of joy, knowing that he had gained in his
contest with Christ.

One of the times that touched him most came when Eugene was serving mass. It was the feast of St. Lawrence, a martyr who had been grilled
alive rather than deny his faith, and Eugene was wearing a white-lace sur-
plice over a cassock, scarlet for blood. The bell rang for Communion. Father
Wally turned, holding the chalice full of hosts, and stopped, as always, to
give Communion to the altar boys first. They knelt before him on the plush
carpeted steps leading to the altar, their eyes closed and mouths gaping in
readiness (the way Eugene had knelt before Budhardin the day before). He
could see Eugene's face blushing in the candlelight and the look twisting the
priest's features when Eugene bowed his head, refusing to receive the host,
Father Wally suddenly realizing that someone with mortal sin on his soul
was helping to serve mass.

They never openly kicked Eugene out of the altar boys. He was just never
asked to serve mass again. Eugene never complained, but Budhardin could
see something changing within him—as if he were living in a trance, the
way he slept through class with his head buried in his arms or how he walked
into streets without checking traffic. That's when Budhardin conceived his
plan of collecting the souls of the other boys, till there would be no one left
in innocence to swing the censer or carry the heavy missal from the right
side of the altar to the left during the Offertory or to mumble the Latin re-
sponses. He'd show them the cards; he'd tell them the names of the others
who'd already seen them. Frenchie let him use his basement to show stag

films. Budhardin took them there one by one, running the film in the dark, the light passing through cobwebs, focused on the cinder-block walls, and just at the right moment he'd stop the machine and ask them, "Would you trade your soul to see what comes next?" He already had the deeds made out, ready to sign. They always laughed when they scrawled their names in the light of a flickering candle.

The elephant gazed up. He had been traipsing down the alleys for blocks, crossing the empty streets in between, and continuing on. Now he could see the spire of the church rising over the two- and three-story roofs against a moon as pale as a pane of smoked glass. He remembered walking down the same alley in a cold drizzle and seeing the spire shrouded in fog the day of Eugene's requiem mass.

Inside the church everyone was weeping and he was never more struck by the brutality of the service, with its incredibly gruesome *Dies Irae:*

> O day of wrath! O dreadful day!
> When heaven and earth in ashes lay,
> As David and the Sibyl say.

He knew that inside the catafalque Eugene's soul was black as the black-silk vestments of the priest, black as the woolen habits of the murmuring nuns.

> What terror shall invade the mind
> When the Judge's searching eyes shall find
> And sift the deeds of all mankind!

Eugene had died in mortal sin and now while they were chanting he was burning in the fires of eternity. He wouldn't have been surprised to see the flames begin to eat through the coffin from the inside out.

> Before Thee, humbled, Lord, I lie,
> My heart like ashes, crushed and dry,
> Do Thou assist me when I die.

And finally he knew none of it was true, not hell nor heaven, nor good, nor evil, nor God, nor any trace of Eugene called a soul. Only eternity was real. And him standing in the alley in the rain. He had turned then and walked to the arbor. Jennifer was there, dressed in black and crying. He was crying too. Rain was running in rivulets through the lattice and he got down on his knees in the mud and buried his face against her, trying to burrow up her skirt. She struggled away from him, slapping his face, slipping backward. He fell on top of her and tried to open his trousers.

"It's true what they say about you," she hissed. "I hope they get you like they said."

"What?" he said. She'd stopped struggling.

"After the funeral, they're going to get you . . . all the boys. For stealing Eugene's soul."

And that evening he was awakened by a soft howling outside his window. In the yard he seemed to see figures moving. He got back in bed. He heard stones tapping against the pane. He looked out the window. In the yard he saw the figures beckoning to him, chanting, "Give us our souls."

Sometimes he'd wake and there would be a garbage-can fire just beyond the backyard fence and it would seem to him someone was in it softly screaming. No one spoke to him at school—students or nuns—it was as if he were invisible and he stopped going. One night he heard the pebbles again. He looked out the window. The yard was covered with snow. There were children below, digging a hole, a grave in his backyard, and lowering a dirt-smeared coffin into it. "Here he is," a voice said, "close to you. Give us our souls in return." The next morning he burned the deeds in an empty coffee can, scattered the ashes along dawn-empty streets, and left for what he thought would be forever.

The elephant stood before the massive church doors curling his trunk around their wrought-iron handles, but the doors were locked. He looked at the sky. It was growing lighter—not the sky itself but the expanding halos of the streetlights.

There was a side door he had used when it had been his job to ring the bells. They had given him the job because he wasn't able to be an altar boy—they couldn't find a cassock to fit him in third grade, when they picked the torchbearers, and without first being a torchbearer one could never be an altar boy. The bells were operated electrically. It was simply a matter of inserting a key at precisely the right second and switching on the bells for the correct number of rings. He'd listen to the bongs spreading out across the neighborhood and picture himself swinging from the rope, scattering pigeons, up in the steeple.

As always, the door was open. Inside, it was dim; none of the electric ceiling lights were on. Only the glow from the racks of multicolored vigil lamps and the red sanctuary light suspended above the altar. The statues stood in the niches, colored reflections flickering off their martyrs' wounds, their stigmata, their muscles knotted in spiritual exertions, their eyes stony with visions.

He dipped his trunk in the holy-water font and sucked, then quickly swooshed the water out. It was salty and stale from a thousand fingertips, with some kind of fungus floating at the bottom as in a dirty fishbowl. The tottering font crashed to the floor, shattering marble.

He shambled up the aisle toward the altar. The communion rail was closed and he tried to climb over it. The rail swayed beneath his massive weight, then collapsed in a succession of snaps like a chain of firecrackers

The altar was carefully set: vases of lilies, candles in their golden candelabra, the enormous red missal Eugene used to struggle to carry. Budhardin swept them off with one flick of his trunk, trampling them all into the carpet, then, rearing, seized hold of the base of the enormous wooden crucifix that hung over the altar, dominating the front of the church. His trunk coiled around Christ's nailed plaster feet, the blood streaming down like nail polish from hundreds of wounds above. He could feel something give and thrashed harder. High above, Christ's head shook loose, bouncing down off Budhardin's back and rolling down the altar stairs before finally coming to rest, blue eyes staring out at him from thorn-studded brows. He turned back, letting the cross take the entire weight of his body, wrenching his torso wildly back and forth till it all suddenly gave, toppling slowly like a tree, dragging the entire wall above the altar down with it.

When he came to, he was halfway down the stairs, luckily still resting on his stomach. A cloud of plaster dust hung thick like incense in the red light of the sanctuary lamp. He was surrounded by rubble, and parts of plaster and marble bodies lay strewn about him, hands still folded in prayer, broken wings, pieces of halos. Where the ornate reredos had risen above the altar was now a gaping hole, BX cables dangling through shredded lathes. The tabernacle still remained, cast iron and indestructible as a safe.

He slowly forced himself up, the broken timbers sliding off his back, and remounted the stairs to finish the job. Before the tabernacle stood the monstrance, like a gold Inca sun flaring out dagger rays, and at its center a huge empty eye, where an enormous white consecrated host—Christ's body and blood—would be inserted during Benediction. He slid the monstrance aside and parted the silken curtains that concealed the tabernacle doors.

"Dear God! What are you doing?" a voice screamed from the back of the church. An old nun came doddering up the aisle from out of the dark shadows, holding a tray of colored votive candles, probably here early to arrange the church for another day.

"What are you doing?" she shrieked.

In the gleam of candles he recognized her—Sister Eulalia, more bent and wrinkled than ever. He stood staring as if he expected her to realize who he was and start to scold. Instead the candles were clattering to the floor from her tray.

"Dear God," she kept repeating, "oh, my Christ!" Her eyeballs looked swollen behind rimless spectacles; he could see her toothless mouth gasping for breath as she began to choke, leaning against a pew and clutching at her heart. He didn't want to see her fall.

He turned back to the tabernacle, ripped the curtains away, and swung open the golden doors. The light inside seemed blinding, like radium cased in lead. He heard a cry slice through the hollows of the church, more like a war whoop than a scream, and felt a sudden weight on his back. Sister Eulalia was atop him, kicking chunks out of his hide with her sturdy nun's shoes. He tried to reach back for her with his trunk, but she gave it a twist that almost tore it off, then started lashing him across the eyeholes with the floor-length walnut-bead rosary she wore coiled around her midsection. Half blinded, he trumpeted in pain, staggering down the stairs, stumbling over the altar rail, while she lashed on, drumming with her heels and shouting curses.

He swung his body around and around in circles, trying to pitch her off, reared and bucked, but she hung with him. His body careened off the front pews and into the rack of vigil lights in front of the grotto of Our Lady. Her body was sandwiched between him and the rack. He heard her gasp and slammed her against the rack again and again until she crumpled to the floor.

He looked at her lying there among the shattered overturned candles spreading out their puddles of tallow, her black veil covering her face like a Muslim woman's, her shredded habit up around her hips, exposing her black underwear. The church was reeling. He fingered her with his trunk, pulling away what was left of the habit. She opened her eyes and looked up at him in terror.

"No, no," she screamed, "I'm a bride of Christ! I'm God's wife!"

What am I doing, he thought, has it come to this? He plodded away, wanting only escape, down the center aisle to the front doors, but they were still locked. His head was clearing, but his ears had started to ring. To ring wildly! Then he realized it was the bells.

He hurried down the side aisle toward the doorway he'd come in. Just as he feared, Sister Eulalia had dragged her battered body to the bells and was sounding the alarm. Before he could make it to the door the rest of the nuns had swarmed into the church.

He turned from them and lumbered back down the aisle, his rump skidding as he tried to cut the corner, knocking over another rack of vigil lights. The nuns rushed after him, some of them clumping through the pews to cut him off. He galloped past the main aisle, remembering there was one more door he still might escape through—the sacristy entrance. He hurdled the broken communion rail, two nuns hanging on to his tail.

The altar boys, led by Billy Crystal, came storming out of the sacristy holding their long-pole candle extinguishers like lances. He braked and wheeled, scattering nuns, and reversed field. The church was a screaming echo chamber. The rear was in flames where he'd smashed into the virgil lights. He tried to fishtail a corner but his momentum was too much and he crashed headfirst through a confessional. His body was wedged so tight he couldn't move.

They hauled him out through the sacristy exit, still stuck in the confessional box, and set him on his side, where he lay futilely kicking his legs. He was in a little garden the nuns tended in back of the church, a rock grotto with a goldfish pond, a garden hose trickling water over the rocks. In front he could hear the sirens of fire trucks and smell the billowing smoke. All around him people were pacing and whispering, and someone was winding chains around his legs.

"The firemen want to come around back this way," a voice warned.

"No, not till we get rid of *him*."

He could hear the forklift's metal wheels grinding toward him down the flagstone path. The forks lowered and the chains were slipped over them, then the forks hoisted Budhardin, and they all began their silent procession out of the grotto and down the alley. It was just past dawn—gray light streamed through his sockets.

They marched slowly behind the jerky pace of the forklift: altar boys in one column, still holding their extinguishers, and nuns in the other, telling their beads in unison.

The alley wound behind the water-filtration plant and they left it for a huge storm drain, the forklift traveling so smoothly down the concave passageway that the procession had to jog to keep up. When they finally re-emerged, the sunlight was blinding.

They stood where the drain ended in a broad lip that angled into a steep concrete runoff above the drainage canal. He could smell the acrid industrial stench of the sludge-thick water below mixed with the gentle scent of the milkweeds that sprouted in long shoots like a curtain along the bank. They were murmuring the Sign of the Cross over him and when they got to "and of the Holy Spirit" he felt them all shove together. He began to roll slowly at first, picking up velocity till he was traveling trunk over rump, the wooden confessional splintering around him and gray chunks of his body flying off, faster and faster till he bounced through the high weeds, somersaulting over the bank and landing with a resounding *bonk* in the metal bottom of a garbage scow.

He lay there stunned, as much from the fact he wasn't drowning in the quicksand like water of the canal as from the concussion. He heard the bees he'd disturbed buzzing above him angrily in the crushed milkweed. He heard shouts and realized they had seen what had happened and were coming to finish him off. A huge hole had broken open in the elephant's side and the sky he looked out at was so blue he wanted to live just to see it. Why did they have to shout so? Lukewarm rust-stained rainwater that had gathered in the bottom of the scow was soaking through the cracks in his hide. He could see bits of mosquito larvae, suspended flecks of rust, swirls of grease. He licked it off his dry, cracked lips. The water sloshed back and forth across the bottom of the boat. A shadow passed overhead, blotting out the sun. Suddenly it struck him he was moving! He looked up into the girders and saw wheeling pigeons beneath the underside of a bridge. He could see the traffic passing overhead. The scow floated out from under, back into the sunlight. It was in the middle of the river. On each side huge glittering walls of skyscrapers loomed like canyons of glass.

He shifted so he could peer out of the eyeholes. The drop gate was partially lowered and he could see out of the front. The scow was entering the mouth of the river, passing the light tower on the delta. The water was dark brown but beyond that he could see the green horizon of the sea.

"Hey"—someone was knocking on his head—"hey, Elephant." He turned back toward the gaping hole and found himself staring into the angelic face of Billy Crystal. "Hey," Billy said, "I told them I was gonna see if you was dead, but instead I untied us and pushed off. You shoulda heard the assholes yelling. Fuck them!"

Budhardin smiled.

"Where you think we're heading," Billy Crystal said, "Europe?"

"Maybe," Budhardin said, "or maybe the Yucatan. Depends on the current."

"Well, we got rainwater to drink and garbage for bait and your tail for a line, and I can use this as a fishing pole," Billy said, shaking his extinguisher. "The only trouble is there's rats sittin' up on the bow."

"Don't worry," Budhardin said, "there's room enough for both of us in the elephant."

"South of the border!" Billy Crystal said, his choirboy mouth breaking into a grin. "Fucking A!"

River Dead of Minneapolis
Scavenged by Teenagers

❧

MARK EHLING

UNTIL YOU SWIM THE RIVER, AND SPEND TIME watching what floats downstream, you're kind of surprised at first there are so many dead people. I swim under the trestle—Third Bridge, Hennepin Avenue, then back the whole length again—and I see the bodies. They float past at one and a half miles per hour. You can swim out and touch them. And you can check their pockets for money.

One thing I've noticed is that the meat on a drowned man—the flesh, not skin—is white, very bright white meat, and it looks exactly like sturgeon.

The other thing is that heads don't look like heads. They look like shrunken, very old potatoes. A guy might hook into, and then lift up, a drowned man with a gaff and then set that body dripping onto the bow of a tug boat or a timber barge in broad daylight and think to himself: *Now all I gotta do is find the eyes and I'll know I'm lookin' at a head.* But sometimes you can't find the eyes. You can't find ears. Noses, maybe.

There is no sound under water—no sound except the sound of water itself. There's no light. One thing that happens under the river in darkness is that a fish as long as a tall man will bump into my leg or my face. For a moment, there is a hairy, air-breathing descendant of apes suspended in water, which is me, listening to the sound of water, and he is suddenly hit in the face by a fish. And for a moment the ape-thing and the fish-thing are down there thinking of each other. Some other guys I know have felt this and screamed. But under water it doesn't sound like a scream. It's just bubbles.

I don't know where drowned men come from. They just come from upstream. There is a bum's camp on Nicollet Island—at night you can hear the fights. Or maybe the drowned men come from the Yacht Club, which is not a club, but a bar on Marshall Avenue with the words YACHT CLUB written on it. It is many blocks from the river. Maybe guys get drunk there, walk ten blocks west, and trip.

It's nothing to touch a body. You swim out there and just take the arm and guide him into shore. You can't squeeze too hard, because drowned flesh is fibrous and weak and your fingers can push through it as if it were cake. Then a smell comes out of the skin-holes. So you learn to gently lead and hold, like walking grandma to Mass. One thing I always say to myself is, *Dead guys don't need money in Iowa.* So I take their coins and the crucifixes from around their necks, and I gently send them back out, in a manner of speaking, to sea. It's either the sea or the power plant.

A drowned body—if it floats well and does not hold fast to a root or a sunken log—will drift under the train trestle, flow past the hobo camp, float under the Third Avenue bridge, and then reach a junction with two forks: starboard, and it tumbles over the falls and continues south. Maybe Muscatine. Maybe the Gulf of Mexico. If it veers to port, that man's journey is done: stuck in a grate at the intake of the St. Anthony Falls power plant, damming the water and stopping up little scraps of paper and twigs.

I have seen how the men from the plant pull up a body with gaff hooks and poles. I see how they sit at the intake rail and wait for cops and light cigarettes and smoke. I can't touch the body anymore. It's theirs.

When I sit under the bridge and watch the plant workers pull up the bodies, I know that I am committing the sin of envy. I want their job, instead of the one I soon will have: serving concessions at the Jednota Hall to the

Slovaks. To pass the time, I dive for scrap metal. Sometimes there is none. I put my clothes back on and get ready to go home. In about three weeks I start my summer job for real. I pick up a rock and throw it at the power plant. It doesn't even come close. It hits the water. It does exactly what you'd expect a rock to do. It sinks.

Fuck with Kayla and You Die

LOUISE ERDRICH

ROMAN BAKER STOOD IN THE BRIGHT and crackling current of light that
zipped around in patterned waves underneath the oval canopy entrance to
the casino. He wasn't a gambler. The skittering brilliance didn't draw him
in and he was already irritated with the piped-out carol music. A twenty,
smoothly folded in his pocket, didn't itch him or burn his ass one bit. He had
come to the casino because it was just a few days before Christmas and he
didn't know how to celebrate. Maybe the electronic bell strum of slot machines would soothe him, or watching the cards spreading from the dealer's
hands in arcs and waves. He took a step to the left, toward the cliffs of glass
doors.

As he opened his hand to push at the door's brass plate and enter, a white
man of medium height and wearing a green leather coat pressed his car keys

into Roman's palm. Without waiting for a claim ticket, without even looking at Roman beyond the moment it took to ascertain that he was brown
and stood before the doors of an Indian casino, the man walked off and was
swallowed into the jingling gloom.

Roman waited before the doors, holding the keys. All of the valets were
occupied. He held up the keys. A few seconds later, he put down his hand and
clutched the keys in his fist. No one had seen this happen. Roman turned away
from the doors, opened his hand, and saw that one shining key among the
other keys belonged to a Jeep Cherokee. Immediately, he spotted the white
Cherokee parked idling just beyond the lights of the canopy. An amused little
voice in his head said go for it. He didn't think it out, just walked over to the
car, got in, and drove away.

You couldn't call this stealing, since the guy gave me the keys, Roman
told himself, but we are on a slippery slope. He checked at the lighted gauge
of the Cherokee, and saw that the tank was nearly empty. There was a Super-
stop, handy, just down the road. Roman drove up to the bank of pumps and
inserted the Cherokee's hose into the gas tank. Eight dollars worth should do
it, he thought, and then he wondered. Do what? In the store, he decided he
should be methodical, buy something to eat or drink. Afterwards, he would
know what to do. The complicated bar of coffee machines drew him, and he
stepped up to the grooved aluminum counter, chose a tall white insulated
cup, and placed it under a machine's hose labeled French Vanilla. He held the
button until the cup was three quarters full, and let the nozzle keep drizzling
sweet foam on top. Then he figured out which plastic travel lid matched his
cup and pressed it on, over the froth. So as not to burn his hand, he fitted the
cup into a little cardboard sleeve. He paid for everything out of his twenty,
and walked outside. It was a warm winter night in the middle of a thaw. Bits
of moisture hung glittering in the gas-smelling air. There was a very light
dust of sparkling fresh snow sinking into the day's brown slush.

"A white Christmas, huh?" said a woman's voice, just to the left.

"Yes, it will be enchanting," Roman answered.

He was the kind of person people spoke to in situations that could easily
stay completely impersonal. His face was round, his nose pleasantly blunt,
his eyes wide and friendly. His smile was genuine, he had been told. Yet
women never stayed with him. Perhaps he was too comfortable, too nurtur-
ing, and reminded them of their mothers. Desperate mothers who wanted
their children home before dark or wouldn't let them out of sight. Now, in

addition to being motherly, plus the kind of person people spoke to on the streets or while pumping their gas, he was the type into whose comfortable palm strange white men trustingly pressed their car keys.

And house keys, too, and other keys. Roman jingled the set before his eyes and then fit the correct car key into the lock. He got into the car and carefully set the cappuccino into the cup holder before he drove to the edge of the parking lot. There, he turned on the dome light and opened the glove compartment. He found the car's registration, folded in a clear plastic sleeve, and the proof of insurance, too, with numbers to call. The owner's name was Torvil J. Morson and his address was 2272 West 195th Street, in the closest suburb. Roman took another drink of the milky, sweet, deadly tasting cappuccino. Then he put the cup back into the holder and drove carefully out of the lot.

The casino was prosperous because it was just far enough from the city to be considered a Destination Resort, and yet close enough so only an hour's quickly diminishing farmland, pine woods, and snowy fields stood between the reservation boundaries and the long stretch of little towns that had blended via strip malls and housing developments into the biggest population center in that part of the Midwest. Roman knew approximately how far he was from 195th street, and it took him exactly the 45 minutes he'd imagined to get there, find the house, and pull into the driveway, which he wouldn't have done unless he'd seen already that the windows were dark. The house was a small one story ranch style painted the same drab green as the jacket of the man who gave Roman the car keys.

Roman got out of the car, walked up to the front door, used the key. Just like that, he entered. Once in, he shut the door behind him and wiped his feet on a rough little welcome mat. The house had its own friendly smell— slightly stale smoke, cinnamon buns, wet dried sour wool. A powerful street-light cast a silvery glow through the front picture window. As his eyes adjusted, Roman stepped onto grayish, wall-to-wall carpet, and padded silently across the living room. His heart slowed. The carpeting soothed him. He went straight across the room to the kitchen, divided off by only a counter, and opened the freezer section of the refrigerator. He'd heard that people often kept their jewelry and cash there in case of a burglary or fire. There was a coffee can in the freezer, but it only held ground coffee. A few other promising Tupperware containers held nothing but old stew, alas. Roman shut the insulated door and rubbed his hands together to strike the chill from his

fingers. Then he walked down the hall. He stepped into a bedroom, turned
on the light. Posters of pop stars, stuffed animals, pencil drawings and dried
flowers were taped to the walls. A teenage girl's room. Nothing. He turned
out the light and found the master bedroom, the one closest to the bathroom.
He was just about to turn on the light when the sound of breathing, or the
sense of it, anyway, in the room, stopped his hand.

Then it didn't sound like breathing, but something else, sighing and watery. A fish tank, Roman thought. He listened a bit longer, then switched on
the light and saw, on a table next to a window, a small plug-in fountain. The
water coursed endlessly over an arrangement of smooth, black stones. Roman thought this must belong to the man's wife. He frowned at himself in the
dressing room mirror, and adjusted the lapel of his jacket. The wife, or the
teen, or another member of the family might return while he was standing
in the lighted bedroom. Yet Roman had no prickles up his back, no darts of
fear, no sense of apprehension. In fact, he felt as much at home as if he lived in
this house himself. He was even tempted to lie down on the big queen-sized
bed neatly made up with a purple quilt and pillows arranged upon pillows.
Where had he read about this? Goldilocks! This bed looked comfortable.
He thought of the three bears. There was a Mrs. Morson for sure, thought
Roman. He pictured a bear meditating by the fountain. A meditator probably
wasn't the type who would own gold and diamond jewelry, but he still had
to check. There was not a safe on the closet floor, or even a velvety box on
the top of the dresser or in the drawer that held underwear. No, there was
only underwear, and it was decent, fresh cotton. What am I doing, thought
Roman, with my hands in Mrs. Morson's underwear?

He shut the drawer firmly and sat on the edge of the bed.

I'm not going to find any cash, he decided. Mr. Morson has taken it to
the casino. Treading down the hall and back across the soft carpet, he felt
cheated. What had happened with the car keys was a once-in-a-lifetime
thing. Roman had never before done anything that was strictly criminal.
But this break-in, where he hadn't had to actually break in, this was given
to him. It was as though Mr. Morson had invited him to travel to his house
and look for valuables. And nothing there! The house was very still now, the
street outside utterly deserted, the neighboring houses dim and shut. Roman
sat down on the couch, wishing that he had the rest of his cappuccino, but
he'd left the cup in the car. There was a tremendous energy to the quiet, it
seemed to him, a seething quality. He felt that he should do something bold,

or important, with this piece of fate that he'd been handed. As he was thinking of what he might do, someone knocked on the door. Roman's first instinct
was not to answer. But the expectant quality of the silence was too much for
him. He went to the door and opened it. There stood a woman and a man,
both in coats but wearing no scarves or hats. The woman held a wrapped gift.
The man carried a crock-pot out of which there issued a faint and delicious,
smoky, bean-soup scent.

"Oh, thank god!"

The woman stepped into the entryway, the man also, both exuding an air
of conspiratorial excitement.

"Very clever, keeping the lights off," said the man.

"But isn't that his car?"

"He gave me the keys and I just drove it here," Roman told him. The man
gave a scratchy laugh that turned into a cough.

"Where should I put this?" He lifted the Crock-Pot slightly.

"In the kitchen?" said Roman.

"Let's put his presents in there, too," said the woman. "You must work
with T.J. Have we met?"

"I'm Roman Baker."

"You look like an Indian," said the woman.

"People tell me that!" said Roman.

"Okay, and I'm Willa and that's Buzz with the seven bean soup. It's his
specialty. Just the countertop lights! No overhead!"

"Right!" Buzz sounded gleeful. "Is Zola back yet? Did she get the
cake?"

"I think so," said Roman. His skull suddenly felt tight, his eyes scratchy
and shifty in their sockets. "I feel bad," he mumbled. "I don't have a gift.
Maybe I should go out for sodas or beer."

"Oh, T.J. won't notice. T.J. will have a shit fit. I think we should all hide
behind the counters and the couch. Will you get the door, Roman?"

"Come on in," said Roman, as he opened the door. "Wipe your feet." Two
young men and an older woman stood on the steps. One man carried a neatly
foil covered bowl. The other held a large, pale, tissue-wrapped gift.

"We brought Mom," one of the young men squealed, "she's drunk. She's
such a hoot!"

"I drank a strawberry wine cooler. I'm loaded," said the elderly lady in
a prim and sober voice. "Let me in so I can ditch these two idiots. Does he

suspect?" She eyed Roman with a flare of exasperation, her scarlet mouth down-twisted.

"Not in the slightest," Roman told her. He helped her out of her coat while the two young men settled their things in the kitchen.

"Very clever, all the lights out," the lady muttered, "Zola says he'll pee his pants."

"That's pretty much what Willa says, too," Roman told the lady. Steering her toward the couch, he startled himself. A picture formed in his mind. It was himself. Crouched on the carpet. Out of control. Pissing his own pants and howling with surprised mirth.

"They're sending me out for more strawberry wine coolers," he said. He patted the woman's hand.

"You're an Indian," she said, severely and as if imparting information to him.

"A big one," said Roman.

The others in the kitchen were whooping with secretive anticipation. Roman touched the keys in his pocket, walked out the door. As he neared the white Cherokee two more people stepped into the driveway, asked him in low and enthralled voices if anybody else was there.

"Go on in," Roman told them. "Willa and Buzz are organizing everybody."

"Oh God!" said the woman. "I saw his car! I thought he'd got home already. Zola's following us. She'll be here any minute with the cake."

Roman jumped into the car, backed down the driveway, and drove the opposite way down the street from the way he guessed Zola would arrive.

Back on the turnoff to the highway, he thought, right or left? But it was inevitable. He headed toward the casino. The cappuccino was still warm and on the way there he finished it. He started to feel good. Yes, he had been given the Morson's keys, the keys to their life, and he'd visited that life. Enough. Nothing had happened after all. He hadn't taken anything except this car—for a drive. As he neared the vast casino parking lot he slowed and carefully reconnoitered, watching for extra security or flashing lights in case the Cherokee had been reported stolen. But all was bright and calm. Gamblers were walking to and fro, those who had self-parked. Others were waiting with their claim tickets on the swirl patterned carpet in the lobby underneath the lighted canopy. Roman eased the car into a marked space cautiously, far from the activity, and took his empty cappuccino cup with him before he locked the car's door.

That was your little adventure, he told himself. Now what? But he knew what. He walked back to the casino entrance and walked through, into the icy bells and plucking, continual ring that did predictable and pleasurable things to his central nervous system. He breathed faster in excitement. Possibly, the sound depressed left brain action. He felt connected to an irrational and urgent universe of lucky chance. His fingers twitched. First things first. He scanned the seated players looking for the green leather jacket, which was all he remembered about Morson. He decided to make a sweep, starting at the far end of the casino, checking the men's room first. He went up each row and down each row, passed behind each glazed, ghostly player. It took so long that he thought of giving up and simply turning the keys in at the lost and found. But then, there was T.J. Morson, green jacket slung behind him, staring into the lighted tumble of little pirate cove symbols on his machine's curved torso.

Roman tapped his shoulder and Morson waved him off, not to be bothered. Roman watched the man shove in three more quarters and hold his breath. Then sit back, dazed, rub his hand over his face.

Roman touched his shoulder again. "Happy Birthday."

"What?"

Morson turned and focused on him. His face was clean-cut and perfectly square, a solid Norwegian jawline, pale eyes, hair already white and thin, a little tousled. He was falling into heaviness around the neck and then below, like Roman, it was pretty close to a lost cause. Roman dangled the keys. "You dropped these, I think?"

Morson slapped the pockets of his pants.

"For God sakes, thought I had it parked!"

Roman gave him the keys and turned to go, but he couldn't, not quite. He took a last look at Mr. Morson and saw that something was very wrong with him. T.J. Morson was sitting there with his mouth open, staring at the car keys. Not moving.

"Hey," Roman bent toward him, then waved his hand before the man's eyes, "you okay?"

"No," said Mr. Morson. He shut his mouth and then slowly, like a very old man, stood and shrugged on his jacket. He dropped the keys, picked them up. Sat back down and stared once more at the machine. Slowly, from his pants pocket, he drew a bit of change. Held it out questioningly to Roman, who rummaged in his own pocket and exchanged what Mr. Morson offered for a quarter. Morson held it a moment, then played it. Nothing.

"You okay?" Roman asked again.

But Morson was staring vacantly before him. His mouth was open and his hands were shaking.

"Not all right, not all right," he muttered.

"Hey," said Roman, "come on. Get up. Let's go sit in the cafe. I'll buy you a coffee."

"What I need is a drink."

"Yeah, well, maybe." Roman helped steady Mr. Morson. They walked down the aisle of light and sound, along a short hallway, and into a small interior restaurant where the waitress gave them a booth for two and poured their coffee.

"Cream. Lots of it. Thanks," Roman told her. She left the pot and a bowl of tiny plastic servings of flavored half-and-half.

"Thank you," said T.J. Morson, staring at the brown pottery cup. "And thank you for returning my car keys." His voice was heavy as a pour of concrete. The syllables seemed to harden as they fell from his mouth. "Well," he looked up, scanned the country-themed room, "this is it."

"What are you talking about?" asked Roman.

Morson put his face in his hands and then slowly pushed his hands up his face and over his hair. "That was it," he said again.

"Listen." Roman was beginning to feel alarmed. "It's your birthday. You should be heading home." He thought of all the excited people waiting in the living room of the Morson house, crouched behind the sofa and chairs and kitchen counters, the lights off.

"Weren't you supposed to be home a while ago?"

Mr. Morson looked at Roman, frowning now, momentarily distracted. "Who are you?"

"I'm a friend of Buzz and Willa," Roman told him. "Look, I'm going to let you in on something that's going to cheer you up. You've got to go home now. I'm not supposed to say a thing about it, but they're planning a surprise party in your honor. Zola's got the cake. Even as we speak, they are in your house, waiting for you. They have presents."

Telling this to Morson was surprisingly difficult. Roman felt the bleeding sensation of envy when he imagined stepping onto the warm, thick carpet. The blast of noise from friends. The bean soup. Beer. Cake.

Mr. Morson said nothing.

"You can't just leave them waiting there." Roman heard a note of accusing desperation in his voice.

Morson shook his head, now, as though his misery was a fall of water washing over him. His brilliant white hair lifted in the staticky air. Roman felt like reaching over and patting it down, but he kept his hand curled around his coffee cup.

"Fuck's sake, I can't go back there," said Morson wearily. "They don't know. Zola has no idea about this . . ." he waved his hand toward the casino through the glass doors of the restaurant. "I play when she's at work, when I'm supposed to be at work, except I don't have a job, see. That's over. She doesn't know I put a second mortgage on our house, a line of credit, then topped it. Cleaned out every one of our accounts." He stared fiercely, disconnectedly, at Roman. "There's nothing," he said. His mouth was suddenly and frighteningly sharklike, an impersonal black hungry v. A bubble of spit formed at either corner. "They'll take the house and then my car. They'll take her car. And Kayla . . . Oh god."

Morson dropped his face into the bowl of his hands. Roman thought he might either break down and sob or leap up and rake his fingers down the wallpaper. Which would it be? He was feeling oddly disconnected. Maybe this was the way a shrink felt, listening to the woes of a client from behind a clear shield of therapeutic immunity.

With a thick, jerky movement, T.J. Morson struck his hands together.

"I don't even smoke," he said as though appealing to Roman, "I don't drink. But this . . ." again he waved at the lights and bells outside the door. "I think, I know, I had the vision or whatever, that because it was my birthday I could turn it all around if I had just, say, a couple hundred. And I knew where to get it. So today after Zola went to work and Kayla was at school, I sneaked back to the house and I searched Kayla's room. She has this little passbook savings account with me as her co-signer. But where does she keep the passbook? So I dug through the stuff in her drawers, her closets. Can you imagine this?"

Roman's mouth opened. Better than you know, he thought. But Morson went on quickly, "I found her secret things. They were under the bed, in this cigar box she had covered on top with a piece of paper. You wouldn't believe this knowing how sweet Kayla is, what a good girl. The box was labeled with a purple marker FUCK WITH KAYLA AND YOU DIE. Here she's a good little student, all As or Bs, never given anybody whatsoever any trouble in her life before. So this tough little message . . . I mean . . ."

Morson stopped and drank some coffee.

"It got to you," said Roman.

"Yeah," said Morson. "Anyway, I took the passbook. Withdrew two hundred and eighteen dollars worth of baby-sitting money."

Roman nodded, poured another coffee for himself and stirred in three creamers. And yet, he thought. Here is a man for whom people will give a surprise party. Roman tapped the sugar packets, drank the rest of the coffee, put the money down on top of the check.

"I have to get out of here," he said to Morson, who stared at him for a moment, then widened his eyes and broke the look off with a cunning little grin.

T.J. Morson followed Roman out the door of the cafe. On the way past the banks of moving lights and bells and trilling knockers, he said, "C'mon. I hit, we'll split."

Roman kept walking. Morson grabbed the sleeve of his jacket. "Please," he said. Roman started at the sight of him. Morson's eyes were rolled back so the whites showed. His lips were drawn away from his gums in a guilty snarl. Roman felt in his pocket, flipped out a quarter. Morson opened the hand that held the car keys. Roman took the keys and gave the quarter to Morson, who played it. The two men watched the rolling tabs of symbols spin over and over, whirling, clicking into place in a disparate row.

"Okay, you satisfied?" said Roman.

Morson wiped his hands slowly on his hips and then followed Roman out the doors, across the gleaming, wet parking lot, over to the Cherokee. Roman still had the keys. He opened the doors and got into the driver's side. Passive, concentrating on something invisible just before him, Morson got into the passenger's seat and shut his eyes. But suddenly, as Roman pulled out of the parking space onto the highway, Morson mumbled "thanks anyway," and opened his door to jump out. Roman managed to hook his hand in the

remembered. Maybe Buzz simmered his beans with garlic, or wine, or some kind of herb. Maybe it was the sorrow, or the strangeness. Perhaps Buzz had added a few drops from a vial of Liquid Smoke. Then again a ham bone. Or the fact that these beans were all different types. Roman finished the bowl and put it down.

"You want another?" said Willa.

"It's good," Roman nodded.

She got up to refill the bowl and Roman took over patting Buzz on the back, slow and regular, two or three pats to each of his sighing breaths. He kept feeling the wrench when he'd pulled Morson toward him, in the car, the way Morson had twisted, striking the bridge of his nose. There was the weight of Morson off balance, in his arms, the smell of his hair tonic, after-shave, and the smoke of the casino and the coffee on his breath.

Now here he was eating Morson's bean soup with Morson's friends and no doubt in two or three days he would be tasting Morson's cake. Roman shut his eyes. His thoughts flickered.

"I'll be right back."

He set the beer down, got up, walked down the hall just like an old friend who knew the place. He opened the door to Kayla's room, walked in, shut the door behind him and knelt on the floor beside her bed. Reaching underneath, he groped for and found the box that he could see, once he turned on her little homework lamp, was indeed labeled FUCK WITH KAYLA AND YOU DIE. He handled it carefully. You shouldn't have fucked with Kayla. Psychic time bomb for the girl, though, wasn't it? Morson had replaced her little passbook. Roman flipped to the last page, then tore out a deposit slip. Same bank as his. Anyone could make a transfer, he supposed. He put the passbook back, lay the cigar box on the floor and snapped the sides flat. Then he slipped the box back underneath the bed. He walked back to the living room, passed behind an intense discussion of who should go now to the hospital, who was needed, what arrangements. In the kitchen, he paused at the sink for a drink of warmish, chemical-tasting suburb water. He set the keys to the Cherokee on the counter. Then he slipped out the back door.

All You Can Eat

ROBIN HEMLEY

SARAH, JAMIE, AND I ARE at this pancake social given by a local church. Not that we're churchgoers, it's just that we like pancakes. We never use syrup though, only butter. Bad for our teeth, you know. I remember when sweet meant good and wholesome, but now you can't trust anything that doesn't say "sugarless" or "all-natural" on the bottle.

I didn't want to come here in the first place. In fact when Sarah suggested it, I blew up. My weekends are the only times I have to relax, and crowds of churchgoers aggravate me. I work hard at the office all week. I'm up for promotion. Our marriage is going to hell. Our son loves his toys more than us. And what does Sarah want to do? She wants to go to a pancake social just because Aunt Jemima is supposed to attend. The Real Aunt Jemima.

So what? I say. There's no such thing as the Real Aunt Jemima anyway. There's probably a whole horde of these Aunt Jemimas traveling around the country, appearing at pancake socials. But my arguments have no effect on Sarah. We never want to do the same things. My idea of an enjoyable Sunday is staying home and reading the newspaper, watching *Meet the Press* and then *60 Minutes* later on. I'm the type of guy who can't go a day without knowing what's going on in the world. If you wanted, you could quiz me and I'd know everything. Yesterday there was an earthquake in Peru, and it killed three hundred people.

Sarah, on the other hand, couldn't care less about news. All she's interested in is fixing up our house and taking Jamie to places like this. Last week it was the circus. The week before that she took the kid to one of those tacky little sidewalk sales called Art Daze. When we're alone together, we have nothing to say. I want to talk about Iran, and all she can think about is wood paneling in the den.

The meal is one of those all-you-can-eat deals. I've only had about four pancakes and I'm ready to go home, but I can't even suggest it because Aunt Jemima hasn't shown yet. All I can do is stare across the table at this fat man who's too busy pigging out to notice me. He's got his head bent so low to the table that his tie is soaking up the syrup on his plate. That's gluttony for you. As far as I'm concerned, gluttony is the worst sin by a long shot. And he's not the only one pigging out here. It seems like my family is the only one that knows how to eat decently.

The fat man sees me staring and lifts the corner of his mouth in a half smile. "You don't like pancakes?" he says, and adds, "This here's sure a bargain."

I don't have time to answer because the minister gets up on stage and announces that Aunt Jemima is here.

Out she comes, fat and dressed just like you see her on the syrup bottles: red polka-dotted kerchief, frowsy old dress, and a pair of tits that belong in a 4–H fair. The kids don't know who the hell she is, so they keep eating their pancakes like nothing's happening while the old woman thanks everyone, especially the children, God's children, and tells us all how much she loves us.

Sarah leans over to my side and whispers, "I didn't realize she'd be such a racial stereotype."

"What do you expect of someone named Aunt Jemima?" I say.

The minister sits down at the piano, and Aunt Jemima turns around to tell him something, I suppose what key she's in. At that moment, all the parents grab the bottles of syrup on the table and show the kids just who Aunt

Jemima is. When she turns around again, they go wild, now that they've seen her face on a mass-produced product. My Jamie starts to clap and yell along with all the others. Over the general roar in the church basement you hear a few parents telling their kids to eat their pancakes before they get cold.

"Before I start my song," says Aunt Jemima in a deep melodious voice, "I want to say a few words to y'all. Now I travel around the country singing to good folk like y'all, but I don't only sing, I have a message to bring. When you see me on a bottle of syrup, what do you really see? You don't just see old Aunt Jemima. You see all the things in life that's sweet and good, all them simple things in life, like maple syrup."

"Simple things in life," I tell Sarah. "Who's she fooling?"

"Relax, Jack," says Sarah. "If you'd stop acting like a skeptic for a minute, you might enjoy yourself. Just remember your blood pressure, okay?"

"I remember," I say. "I don't need you to remind me. But if I have a heart attack and drop dead, I want you to move my body. I don't want to be found dead among a bunch of churchgoers. Next she's going to start talking about family values."

But she doesn't. She goes right into her song, "He's Got the Whole World in His Hands." She's got a deep gospel voice and sways to the music while the minister accompanies her on that old piano with half the keys chipped away. While she sings, she makes motions with her hands. When she gets to the word "world," she makes a circle. When she says "hands," she cups her own together and looks piously up at the ceiling. After two verses, she stops and says, "Now I want all you children, God's children, to sing along with me and do all the things I do with my hands. Now when I say children, I don't just mean the young ones," and she gives us her famous syrupy smile. Everyone laughs, even me. I don't know, maybe there's not all that much difference between me and these churchgoers, and anyway, what's the use of arguing with such a sweet old woman? So I grab Sarah's hand, even though we just had an argument before breakfast, and she smiles at me like people do only in movies or rest homes, sort of vacant.

Sarah and I have had a lot of arguments recently. She's always reading these dumb women's magazines and trying out the things that they tell her to do. "101 Ways to Fix Chicken Pot Pie for the Man You Love," and stuff like that. Poor Sarah. She's been trying for the last fifteen years to make me happy, but the more she tries, the more bored I get with her. There are some people who aren't meant to be happy, and I'm one of them. I don't like happy people. Sarah is completely the opposite. Her favorite word is "tickle." She likes to go to movies that tickle her, and if she ever reads a newspaper, it's only to scan the columnists who tickle her.

A couple of weekends ago, Sarah spent hours shellacking the covers of women's magazines onto the walls of our bathroom. Of course when I saw what she was doing, I was furious. "Sarah," I said. "This is the tackiest thing I've ever seen. I mean, you might as well turn the whole house into a 7-Eleven."

"I just thought it would brighten up the place," she said. "Don't you think it looks cheery?"

"It looks cheery as hell," I said. "I don't need cheeriness when I'm on the john."

Sarah sat down on the edge of the tub. Then she grabbed a pile of magazine covers, threw them over the drain, and turned on the water full blast. A model's face was on top, and the face just bounced up and down under the water pressure like it was doing some kind of strange facial swimming stroke.

For the first time in a while, I was scared for Sarah. I had an aunt who killed herself with sleeping pills, and this seemed to be just the kind of thing someone would do before they offed themselves. So I gave in. I let her shellac the bathroom so that now it looks like a newsstand. Then I took her out to dinner, and I didn't even mention the fact that the Soviet Union had rejected our latest arms proposal, though it was on my mind.

Now Sarah's acting like we've never argued in our lives. She's just giving me that silly smile of hers.

"I'm glad we came," I say to make her happy. "Pass the syrup."

"But you don't like syrup."

"That's true," I say. "I don't know what's come over me. It just looks so sweet, so wholesome."

"Daddy, can I have some syrup?" says Jamie.

"No. You remember your last checkup, don't you?"

"Oh, let him have some," says Sarah. "A little couldn't hurt," and she smiles at me. But she doesn't need to smile. Her hair smiles for her, flipping up on either side of her face, a phony style that went out fifteen years ago.

"Well, it *does* look good," I say. I pour some onto my pancakes and take a bite.

Yum.

Aunt Jemima's well into her song again, and everyone is singing along, following her motions with their hands. When she gets to the part about the "itty bitty baby in His hands," they all rock their arms back and forth. Some of the younger children don't know how to rock a baby and look more like they're sawing some object in half.

Babies. Sarah's wanted to have another child for a while, but I don't. She's so old-fashioned about that sort of thing. If I tried to tell her about exponential population growth and about starvation, she wouldn't understand me at all. She'd probably just smile and say, "But we're not some starving tribe in Africa, honey. We can afford another child." I've known Sarah long enough to know this is exactly what she'd say.

But it's all right. This anger towards Sarah will pass. Right now, I feel happy and know that the whole audience is thinking the same thought: Everything is fine. We're all safe together in the hands of this fat old woman. She looks like she could shelter us from anything.

The shy-looking minister at the piano feels it too. He's pounding his fingers up and down on the keyboard, his skinny churchgoing rump half off the bench just like Jerry Lee Lewis. And the whole plaster ceiling is shaking, bits of it raining down on us like God's white teeth. Then the song ends, and everyone is tired and sweating. My brain is sweating from all this thinking. Maybe I should stop thinking and relax, like Sarah says.

I smell my armpits. That roll-on antiperspirant I use really *does* last a long time. As the commercial says, men sweat more than women, but you couldn't tell it by old Aunt Jemima. She's got two wide circles around her armpits, and she says, "It's a mite hot in here."

Everyone agrees. All this combined body heat makes the place hotter than an oven. I look over at Jamie. In between songs, he's wolfing down pancakes like he's never tasted food before. And the syrup. His pancakes are swimming in it. Empty bottles line our long table like dominoes, and our waiter is working his butt off bringing stacks of steaming hot pancakes and bottles of maple syrup to everyone. I've never seen Jamie eat like this. Sarah and I have to feed him protein pills just to keep him from going anemic on us.

And that fat man. He's sure getting his money's worth. I've never seen anyone put away this much food.

I don't know what it is with him and me. We've been having this silent fight ever since we sat down, with him just smiling that weird half smile at me. I don't know why I feel so hostile toward this particular fat man. Maybe it's really guilt. Maybe I'm hostile because I have a lot of fat inside *me*, not the kind you can weigh. I'm really a skinny guy. Invisible fat.

"I sure wish Jamie would eat like this all the time," I tell Sarah.

"Me too," she says. "Maybe we should feed him pancakes morning, noon, and night." She sends me another vacant smile that doesn't mean anything. It's just polite. I look around the room and half the people in here have that same polite smile on their faces.

Anyway, what's she saying? Morning, noon, and night. I don't know about that.

I pour milk into my coffee with a moo-cow creamer, which is sort of disgusting if you think about it. I mean, the people who invented these things must have known that it looks like the cow is puking into your coffee.

I take a few bites of my pancakes, swishing them around in the syrup with my fork. Yum, yum. They're such simple things really, brown on the outside, fluffy white inside. But they're so good. I never realized before that covering them with syrup makes all the difference in the world.

Aunt Jemima is singing another song now, called "Pancake Lady." None of us know the words, so we just let her sing while we laugh along in between bites.

> Pancake Lady makes pancakes for me
> Pancake Lady makes pancakes for free
> Eat 'em up, eat 'em up, one, two, three
> Pancake Lady's got a hold on me

Suddenly Jamie gags and yells with his mouth full, "Look, there's a fly in my pancake. Yuck, there's a fly in my pancake."

Sure enough, Jamie's fork has uncovered a little fly, snugly wedged in a piece of white fluff, its itty feet and its bitty head sticking out.

"Jamie," says Sarah. "Don't make such a fuss over a little fly. You're going to spoil everyone's breakfast."

"Your mother's right," I say. "Have some more syrup and eat your pancakes."

"But I'm not hungry anymore. It's gross. A gross, dead fly in my pancake."

As soon as Jamie says gross, the fat man looks over at him with a pained expression. I put my arm around Jamie's shoulder and hug him to me so that his mouth is squeezed into my armpit. I smile at the fat man and whisper to

Jamie, "You're embarrassing me, you little twit. Finish your pancakes or you won't eat for a month."

Jamie's mouth is so firmly planted in my armpit he can barely move his lips. "Daddy, you're hurting me," says a voice like the dummy of an amateur ventriloquist.

The fat man leans across the table and pokes his fork at my son. "Nice little boy you got there," he says. And then he does something disgusting. He sticks out his fat cow tongue, covered with big chunks of chewed-up pancakes. If he wasn't an adult, I'd think he had shown me his slimy food on purpose.

"Oh yes," I say, a little flabbergasted. "He is kind of nice. Jamie, thank the nice fat man."

Oh shit, I didn't mean to say that. I look at the fat man, but he's just smiling at me, taking big bites from his stack of pancakes.

"Daddy," says Jamie, his voice like the sound of a TV in another room. "Please let me go. I'll eat anything."

I free Jamie and tell him, "Now be a good boy and eat your pancakes and syrup."

Jamie looks all right, just a little red in the face. He picks up his fork, pours syrup on his pancakes, and then makes a big ceremony of cutting away the piece with the fly. He slides it with his fork to the side of his plate.

"His mother spoils him," I tell the fat man, and Sarah gives me a "wait until we get home" look.

I glance at Sarah and wonder why she still wears her hair in that phony flip that went out of style fifteen years ago. I just wish we had something like syrup to pour on our marriage.

Yesterday we were talking for the millionth time about having a kid, and I said, "Look, I bet you don't even know who the prime minister of Japan is."

"Maybe I don't," she said. "But that's because I don't bury myself in things that don't matter."

"The world doesn't matter?" I said.

When Sarah argues, she gets irrational. All she did to answer me was to recite this kids' rhyme, "Here's the church, here's the steeple. Open the doors and see all the people." She also made the corresponding motions with her hands, first interlocking her fists, then pointing her index fingers into a spire, and then opening up her hands and wiggling her fingers at me. After that she stuck out her tongue and locked herself in the bathroom. A woman like that certainly can't handle another child. Still, there was something sort of endearing about her at that moment.

Aunt Jemima finishes the song and we all clap for her. I wonder where she's been for the last fifteen years. Things sure do seem a lot simpler when she's around.

I look over at the fat man for a second. This time he looks me directly in the eye, and with a wink, opens his mouth as wide as it will go, showing me a mouthful of stuff that looks like foam rubber.

"Listen, mattress-face," I say. "I've had just about enough of you," and I get ready to send him a punch, though I'm sure he's got enough flesh in that shock-absorbing face to suck up half my arm. I'm halfway off the bench and across the table when Aunt Jemima starts into her next song, "Camptown Races." As soon as I hear that soothing voice, I just can't get up enough energy to be angry anymore. I float back nice and easy to my bench, like a paper cut-out doll.

I lean over to Sarah and whisper, "Speaking of racial stereotypes, what do you think of this one?"

"It's lovely," she says, smiling at me and blinking like she's in some 1960s beach party movie.

Aunt Jemima tells everyone to sing with her, and so we sing.

The kids love this song. Most of them don't know the words, but they sing along anyway. They especially love the line "Doo dah, doo dah" and won't sing anything but these words. The song soon turns into a shouting match among the children, most of them substituting "Doo dah," and then "Doo doo," for all the words in between. I sort of resent this alteration of the original, but no one else seems to mind. Aunt Jemima looks like she's having a blast, dancing around the stage like a voodoo queen, her enormous hands waving in front of her.

The fat man is yelling "Doo doo" in my face.

Plaster chips fall from the ceiling as the song ends, and with hardly a break, Aunt Jemima leads us in "The Hokey Pokey." The minister's hands flop up and down on the keyboard like a marionette's. Everyone rises from the benches and crowds in between the tables to do the Hokey Pokey dance. There's not enough room for a circle, so we make two lines facing each other. Like two Zulu armies dancing before a battle, we shake our feet, then our hands, and then we turn ourselves around.

Aunt Jemima's voice rises above us, singing, "That's what it's all about."

I am suddenly disturbed by the fact that I am shaking my hands and feet at the command of an old woman. If someone from the office were to come in now I would certainly be passed over for promotion. They'd make life unbearable. "Glad you're working for us," they'd say. "We need a man around the firm who knows his Hokey Pokey."

But I can't stop doing the dance. This is ten times better than watching "Meet the Press." It's hard to worry about work, divorce, or even the world when you're doing the Hokey Pokey.

When the song finally ends, everyone in the church basement groans. We want more, but Aunt Jemima says she's tired. In fact she looks completely drained. Her kerchief has fallen off, and she doesn't even have enough strength to pick it up. But we want an encore. The crowd's past control, with everyone shouting and hooting for more.

"I'm about ready for some more pancakes and syrup," I tell Sarah over the noise.

"Daddy?" says Jamie. "I'm tired. Can we go home?"

"We'll go home when I say so," I tell him. "We can't leave in the middle of Miss Jemima's last song. She'd be offended."

"You're good people," Aunt Jemima tells us. "Real fine people. Now before I sing my last song, I want to ask you, what's the best food in the whole wide world?"

"Pancakes!" we yell.

"And what tastes better on pancakes than anything else?"

"Syrup!"

Why, there's nothing we wouldn't eat for this fine woman.

With tears in her eyes, she leads us once again in "He's Got the Whole World in His Hands." We're still standing from the Hokey Pokey, and so we sway along.

When she says "world," we all make a globe. When she says "hands," we cup our hands like we're holding robins' eggs.

Then she sings, "He's got you and me brother in His hands," and clutches her chest. We all clutch our chests. She collapses on the floor, and everyone except for the minister at the piano collapses with her.

Lying on the floor like that, we sing until all the verses are done.

After the song ends, the basement is quiet except for our breathing. Slowly, we rise to our feet, all except Aunt Jemima, who remains on the floor, her arms folded on her chest, her eyes closed. She's quite a gal, joking around like that.

The minister gets up from his piano bench, steps over Aunt Jemima, and yells, "Three cheers for Aunt Jemima."

We all cheer, but she's so modest, she doesn't even respond. She just stays on the floor, that syrupy smile fixed on the ceiling.

I sit down with the rest of the crowd.

Then the waiters spring out of the kitchen, carrying trays of steaming hot pancakes and new bottles of syrup, and we begin to eat again. I have a voracious appetite. So does Jamie. He's shoveling pancakes into his mouth. The piece with the fly is gone. He must have eaten it. In fact, everyone is eating with so much gusto that no one has time to talk. All you can hear is the *squish squish* of people chewing pancakes, like the sound of an army walking in wet shoes.

People are smiling and laughing. I smile at Sarah. That hairstyle of hers is the most attractive thing in the world right now, except of course, for pancakes with lots of syrup.

I lean her way and say, "I've been thinking, Sarah. I've changed my mind. Let's have a baby."

"Let's have lots and lots of babies," she says.

"Gobs and gobs of babies."

"Daddy?" says Jamie with a cute expression of concern on his face. "If you have lots and lots of babies, will you still love me?"

"Why certainly, young man. That's what it's all about."

"Ooh Daddy," he says. "I love you as much as pancakes."

"With lots of syrup," I reply. "That reminds me. I could use some more."

I ask the nice man across the table to pass the syrup, and he kindly obliges. Then I see that a couple of paramedics have come to take Aunt Jemima away. No one else seems to notice. Maybe I'll find out what happened to her on the news, but then again, maybe I won't. I'm sure she'll be all right. I don't know, it's just a feeling I have, that all of us are safe together.

13 Remotely Related to South Bend, Indiana

LILY HOANG

1. Coming from Texas, I was sure that Indiana was somewhere between Connecticut and Maine. The first time I visited, I saw the large mass of water to the west of the city. Confused, I thought, maybe Indiana is just north of California.

2. For my first few months here, I lived in grad housing. I came to understand that things are flatter in the Midwest. And whiter.

3. If the Midwest were crammed into a pie chart, divided by race, Asians would occupy a thin, single line. When my brother came to visit, school was not in session. He asked where the diversity was, only he said it in a much more blunt manner. Not that

he cares about things like that. He just wanted to know where the football players were hidden.

4.   I used to live in a house. It was huge and old. I lived next to a witch, who called herself a gray witch. She charged people fifty bucks an hour to tell their fortune, or whatever else could fit into that time frame. I also lived next door to a crack-head, who on one particularly intoxicating night, burned down the majority of the house. Luckily, he had passed out on the ground or else he would have died from asphyxiation.

5.   From above, the city seems to be a pristine garden, a sprawling metropolis, the perfect place to live. From below, this place must look like all other places. From eye level, you can see so far that the landscape itself seems to always be shifting.

6.   People seem to both scream and speak more slowly to me here. It must be because I don't speak English.

7.   To the west of the city, there's another smaller, richer city. People, once they reach a certain pay rate, move to the smaller city with iron gates keeping them safe.

8.   The witch's husband is legally blind. Every day, he drives to the courthouse, where he runs a small café. People see him drive—cops, judges, attorneys—and no one stops to think that maybe it's not a good idea.

9.   Indiana is nowhere even remotely close to Connecticut, Maine, or California, as a point of clarification, lest you become confused.

10.   I used to live next door to a retired priest. Count it now. That makes a witch, her blind husband, a retired priest, and a crack-head who burned down his house. The retired priest was a strong proponent for *The Vagina Monologues*. Even being a feminist, there's something that makes a woman blush when she hears an 83-year-old retired priest say the word "vagina."

11.   Before the whole burning a huge hole in the house incident, the crack-head—while clearly not sober—stood in my front yard, looking past me. When I screamed, he ran towards the backyard and repeatedly slammed his body against the gate. When I screamed again, he stumbled onto my front porch and walked into my door

more times than I could count. Then, he fell asleep on the doormat. It was made of twill and could not have been very comfortable.

12.   There's one hill in South Bend. It varies in size depending on which side you take.

13.   One day, the witch stopped me before leaving to tell me that if I ever saw that good-for-nothing husband of hers, to call the police immediately. Turns out that he had an affair with another woman he'd met on the internet. The witch told me, as I was rushing off to some appointment, that he'd flown her into South Bend and brought her home. Can I believe that he'd brought that slut into her home? The witch told me that her husband drugged her so that she fell into a coma-deep sleep for the weekend. Then, she told me he fucked this internet girlfriend in the backyard, which I can see from my backyard.

It'd be going on for years, she told me.

Years, I thought. Funny what crystal balls don't tell you.

14.   Because even towns in the Midwest need something to grow on.

Happy Film

LAIRD HUNT

THIS MORNING, AWARE THAT, AS USUAL, they had all taken up their positions around me, leaning onto the edge of the bed, video camera switched on, I kept my eyes firmly shut, stuck my fingers in my ears, held myself very still, and began silently counting. This mechanism, however—which throughout what has been a challenging winter has allowed me, with surprising efficacy, to recuse myself, even as I continue to fulfill my contractual obligations—has begun to deteriorate, and it is all I can do at times to keep murmuring my lines. These lines—drafted by the film crew's second oldest member, whose highly determined flair for the absolutely ordinary has had undeniable influence on the project—are handed to me at the end of each day's filming, are read over and over again by me each night, and must be uttered by me, my contract states, at the appropriate moment "even when counting." Of late, as I say, my ability to regulate a steady and appropriately incremental stream of numbers while at the same time murmuring, "where are my shoes," "the dog is not happy," "be still, I am having a good dream," etc., has occasionally broken down, so that I have either lost count, or, which is worse, forgotten my lines. These audible lapses are dealt with swiftly. My contract states that in such cases I am to "receive buffets and hard poking." This morning, for example, my mind hiccuped, my hold on the triple-digit numbers I was running through weakened, and I said, "Oh yes, sure, I would like some binoculars," instead of, "Oh yes, sure, I would like some binoculars too." Given that at least three of them immediately launched themselves onto me, it is probably not difficult to imagine that despite my best efforts, I had not even reached 175 before I gave up and, making some vain attempt to dislodge them by flailing my legs and arms around a bit, emitted a scripted groan, then hauled myself out of bed.

Once I had brushed my teeth and shaved and taken care of other tedious necessities, which at any rate I was able to see to in privacy, even if I could hear them all milling around outside the bathroom door, arguing about how best to frame this morning's bathroom exit shot, I went down in a sea of jostling arms and legs to the kitchen, which was indeed "a lower-case holocaust" of overturned boxes, puddles of milk and patches of sodden multicolored balls and wedges of factory standard early morning product. Having launched the one or two "rather stale and half-hearted reprimands" required of me, I secured a clean bowl and spoon, cleared a space at the table, and, selecting the nearest box, apportioned myself a small quantity of what turned out to be an actually fairly pleasant mixture of wheat squares and marshmallows that I covered with milk and, suffering two of the smaller members of the crew to crawl up onto my lap, tucked into.

Those of you familiar with my Rabelaisian gustatory predilections described in earlier Happy Film press materials will no doubt be wondering what has become of my appetite—indeed, it has been some time since I last breakfasted on that wondrously copious ensemble of eggs and breads and meats and pastries described by the Happy Film publicity team therein. Suffice it to say that an addendum to my contract states that "Father/Subject must lose weight" and I have been obliged to cut back. So much so, in fact, that at times during the shooting of scenes in which "Father/Subject regards himself in the mirror or considers the fit of his shorts," I have had a difficult time manifesting the enthusiasm I am meant to exude when I utter, "Oh, yes, definitely, wow!" At any rate, breakfast, meager as it was, passed pleasantly enough, and by the time I was finished I realized that they had all left me and I was somewhat alone. I put it that way, because it is 1) always possible that even during these ostensible off-screen interludes, when I am supposed to relax and recruit myself, one or more of them is hiding somewhere with the camera and 2) never very long before one or more of them have returned—i.e., it is never possible, successful moments of counting excluded, to settle into the feeling of being off-screen. This is troubling. Often during these so-called off-screen moments I allow myself to say this aloud. I said it aloud this morning, just after I had finished clearing the table and making a stab at cleaning the floor. I had just finished shaping the "g" at the end of troubling when, more fuel for the curious admixture of pleasure and malaise that has characterized my entire day, my Wife/the Producer walked in.

"Have you eaten?" she said.

"Yes, I have eaten," I said.

She appeared to have just returned from the grocery store and perhaps one or two of the other errands of which she likes to give me detailed accounts. This morning, however, rather than launching into a description of her travails at the large slice of meat establishment or at the moist and dry cheeses shop, she simply looked at me, set her bag of groceries on the counter, sat down at the table and sighed. This sighing of hers was, all things considered, quite a quick and pretty sound, not one of those awful, elongated, saliva modulated exhalations she is capable of, more like a little triangle of colored plastic being flipped by the wind. Of course, in former days, and as recently as last fall, I would have been only too eager to share this rather choice, I think, verbalization with her, and perhaps even to have expanded and refined it—the piece of plastic might better have been pictured as ovoid in shape, and rather than being flipped by the wind, it might better have been described as being quickly rolled. All I found myself in a position to do this morning, however, was give her a quick glance, say "ahem," and ask her, as my contract states I must ask at least once each day, including off screen, "When will this charade end?"

"Never," she said.

"Well, all right then."

The rest of the morning passed uneventfully enough. The day's script had me pottering around the shed, banging at things with my tools, sketching a little in one of the children's abandoned notebooks, periodically looking at the remote camera and nodding in a "friendly and knowing way." After a not unreasonable amount of this and that then, my Wife/the Producer called me in to lunch. I went in. I sat down. I let the youngest crew member pull at some of the hairs on the back of my hand. I felt pretty good. I turned to the camera and said, "Circle, Leo, My Macintosh, Miss Darling!" It was at this juncture that bits of a rather unpleasant scene, the one that I think of every day, began to float before my eyes.

Since I have been asked in this brief on "Father/Subject's State of Mind" to shed as much light as possible on "Father/Subject's motivation," it strikes me that it might be useful to pause here a moment and explore these bits, which not only speak to the question of motivation, but also to the aforementioned notion of charade. For the purposes of this exploration I submit, first, the following teaser, which is taken from the soon-to-be-released Happy Film posters:

HAPPY FILM

His family had been gone!
He had not expected them to return!
They returned!

Second, the following related, slightly dramatized, no doubt partially symbolic, narrative account excerpted, for convenience sake and with Happy Film crew permission, from Father/Subject's character file:

So disoriented was he during the first few minutes of their return that he simultaneously allowed himself to be ridden around the room by as many as three little revenants at once and to be scolded by their mother for having let both the house and himself go in their absence. It wasn't until he had given each of the smaller ones a swing around the room and had assisted in a failed cat's cradle that the full implications of the situation sunk in and he collapsed onto the couch.

What's wrong with Dad? one of them asked "his wife."

Why don't you ask him, "his wife," or whatever it was, said.

This suggestion brought the questioner within arm's reach of his position, and he held out a hand to see if he could touch her.

Mom, Dad's acting weird! she said.

One of her brothers seconded this assessment, apparently obliging "his wife" to come out of the kitchen, where she had been furiously cleaning.

What's wrong with you, are you sick?

He didn't answer. She came over and stood in front of him with her fists bunched on her hips. This brought his hand out slowly again.

Yes, that's my stomach—my God, what's gotten into you?

I am going to count to 100 and then you will all be gone again, he said.

Are you kidding, buddy? the female entity standing in front of him said.

He shut his eyes. He counted. He said, "Away with ye, foul demons!" When he opened his eyes again most of them were gone. The only one left was a fabulously clever simulacrum of what had been his smallest boy. When it saw that he had stopped counting it went over and sat beside him, affecting more or less the same slouched position he had adopted, its little legs barely breaching the couch's edge. They sat there together for a while, then he began, ever so slightly, to hyperventilate. Apparently not much impressed by his condition, the simulacrum proceeded to roll over, drape itself across his legs and punch him in the stomach.

Will you play cars with me, Daddy? it said.

And it was at precisely this moment that he perceived, in the far corner of the room, the remainder of "his children" somehow collectively holding the video camera (purchased by him) pointed in his direction.

Turn that thing off, he said.

Vroom, vroom, said the little thing on his lap.

We're making a movie, do something weird, Dad, one of the others said.

Don't, he said, shutting his eyes, call me that.

Even if I admit that some of the bits and pieces I contemplated as I sat there, fork in hand, mouth slightly open, diverged (though not regarding the implicit question of charade) from this account in what might fairly be characterized as key particulars, I suspect it will come as no surprise to learn that when the bits and pieces did not speedily dissipate, I tried counting. The counting did not work. I opened my eyes. Of course the camera was on. Of course all 7 or 8 of them were looking at me. Attempting, as it were, to put the best face possible on my face I smiled, said, "the shopping cart is full of boxes," and set to eating the carrot and orange gelatin salad that I found in one of the little bowls in front of me. It wasn't very long before the requisite clinking and slurping, interspersed with the occasional injunction from my Wife/the Producer's end of the table to "slow down," could be heard. When the first course had been completed, two or three crew members cleared the table, and my Wife/the Producer busied herself about the stove. A moment later, she set an attractive loaf of meat on the table near me and, producing a knife and a stack of plates, asked me to serve. I accepted the knife and began to dole out appropriate portions—half slices to the smallest, large and very large slices to the others, a medium-sized slice for myself. A bowl of boiled carrots and potatoes was then sent around and we all began eating again.

After one or two minutes, my Wife/the Producer gave me a prompt, which was "Well?" and I set to "spontaneously extolling" the loaf's fine qualities and admirable textures. It was, I have now decided, because I went on at some length, perhaps longer than my prompt would have indicated, that one of the younger crew members said, "it's your favorite, right, Dad?" which remark was immediately followed by instructions, from one of the older crew members, for the speaker to shut up, an injunction that was accompanied from beneath the table by a dull thud.

"Mom!" the offended party howled, before launching her own booted foot in the direction of her attacker, and a moment later a regular kick-fest had begun.

Again, while it is quite fair to say that the narrative account I include above has a measure of the fictional about it (especially when it treats the business of "my" hand coming out and groping and so forth) it would not be true to say that the teaser does. It is true that my family left me, so to speak, late last Autumn, and it is true that I did not expect them—indeed would not have thought it quite possible for them—to return. And it is true that they nevertheless did do so. When this state of affairs is compounded by the ever-expanding exigencies of Happy Film, whose generally preemptive scripts and situations have very nearly succeeded in blotting out the personal nature of the fatherly and conjugal contribution I have been pleased for so many years to make to our little household, I expect it will seem nothing but reasonable that I have become increasingly withdrawn. Not least from my Wife/the Producer, who, after all, has enthusiastically underwritten the entire Happy Film exercise and was of course chiefly responsible for engineering the near-miraculous return, not to mention other troubling events last fall. All I have had to do is think of this and any little inklings I might have had of, say, accompanying her on one or two of her errands around town or slipping, late at night, out of the guest room and into what was once our bed are squelched. I should note, however, that I am not at all times entirely happy about this state of affairs and there are moments when quite the contrary is the case. Indeed, there are instances when, tempted by the chance image of walking side by side with my Wife/the Producer down the local supermarket aisle or, even, of lifting, so to speak, the goose-down quilt off her bed, I have engaged in counting or even saying "La, La, La" and the like in hopes of holding off the memory of her previous offenses. This strategy has, alas, yet to work; it has been quite some time now since I let the goose-down quilt, etc., settle over me. At any rate, I mention all this simply to provide context for the surprise everyone (myself included) felt when after not too terribly much jostling and kicking I brought my hand down on the table and said, "Enough!"

"You heard your father," my Wife/the Producer said, and in short order all the kicking and wriggling had stopped.

"But she wasn't supposed to say anything like that," the aforementioned older crew member said, glaring at his sister.

"That's all right," my Wife/the Producer said looking at me. "Isn't it?"

"I'm not sure," I said.

"Well, I think it is."

"Then it must be."

The rest of the main course passed without incident. I ingested small but generously seasoned mouthfuls of meat and vegetables and thought about my day and my curious state of mind and, aware that I was up against a deadline, began mentally shaping the opening sentences of this brief. Several of the convives made the remarks and witticisms one is accustomed to enduring at the domestic table, and my Wife/the Producer contented herself with offering me the occasional prompt. According to my script, at a given moment during the meal I was obliged to sing something, and I did so. I have a nice singing voice and this went off very well. In fact the truth is, much about the day seemed at that moment to be going very well, or at least somewhat better than the average. So much so that for a few minutes I entertained the notion of beginning this brief with some sort of positive or at least neutral formula—perhaps, it struck me, a light-hearted remark about the weather, which hasn't been all that bad lately, and certainly agreeable enough for me to enjoy pottering about the shed and so forth. It also occurred to me that I might just as well make mention, in the opening lines, of the strong stand I had taken during the meal and about how well it had been received and about how happy this had made me. Or rather, it struck me as I thought more carefully about it, how confused this had made me, since my strong stand hadn't been scripted and no one had objected. The singing, of course, had made me happy, not the strong stand. The singing and the vegetables and the loaf of meat.

"Would anyone like to hear me sing something else?" I said, looking directly at the camera.

No one answered.

I returned to thinking. And it wasn't any time at all before I found myself back at the bits and pieces of involuntary memory that had opened the meal, which led me to think of my recent failures in counting, and, in turn, to the previously mentioned series of events last fall involving my Wife/the Producer and, to a lesser extent, the rest of the crew.

At that time, I was in the grips of one of my little enthusiasms. This particular enthusiasm regarded a certain work of undeniable literary merit and, by extension, the creator of that work of undeniable literary merit. I engaged in some dress-up activities and in some minor fantasizing. I wrote a few fan letters. I made the occasional attempt at proselytizing family and community members. I purchased a video camera—which, yes, has now become *the* video camera—in hopes that we might, all 7 or 8 of us, put on reflective sunglasses and act out some of the scenes from the work in question, then watch the results together at our leisure. My family took this all poorly. They decided this quite circumscribed range of activities said incontrovertible things about my thought process and inner being. Once, for example, I overheard one of them talking on the phone about her "crazy dad," and my Wife/the Producer's sighs were frequently interspersed with expletive-surrounded calls for me to come to my senses, etc. I might add that this latter, in the course of what I feel obliged to describe here as her machinations, was not above, discreetly I suppose she imagined, inviting certain third parties over to further strengthen her hand. One was an extremely large young official whose job it is to counsel children at the local school. She sat with us for quite some time and asked me questions, including about the reflective sunglasses I was wearing and about the plot and structure of the work of undeniable literary merit, all the while stuffing brand-name cookies into her mouth. "I will not answer any of your questions," I told her. Another, I found one afternoon sitting in the living room with my Wife/the Producer, and when I came in they stopped talking and looked at me. He had creepy investigative authority written so clearly all over him that I walked right over and bonked him on the head.

Fortunately, this line of remembrance and concomitant low spirits were soon countered by the remaining bites of meat and sauce on my plate and by the rather charming spectacle of the smallest of the crew members, who, as overcome in his own way as I was, had fallen into a doze, his little head threatening at any moment to droop onto his plate. This diversion—which was interrupted only by a momentary squabble at the far end of the table to do with camera angle for the upcoming shot—was followed by one or two other fairly pleasant moments, and I soon found myself in an almost acceptable pleasant frame of mind. "Well, that was fundamentally delicious!" I said, which is a line my contract allows me to emphatically pronounce during any meal at any time. It was just as I was letting my own head droop towards my plate that they turned out the lights and, with a great deal of yowling, brought in the cake.

"My God," I said.

"Happy birthday, honey," my Wife/the Producer said.

"But . . ." I said.

"Look at the camera," my Wife/the Producer said.

They all began singing.

I have been told I have ten minutes to hand over this brief so that it can be reviewed by the relevant Happy Film crew members before they head up to bed. This is a shame, because I could go on. I could relate in detail how, while they sang "For He's a Jolly Good Fellow" over and over again, I ran to my room, retrieved my script, returned to the table waving it around, said, "Can I ask a question?" was ignored, turned to the camera and repeated this, was told to blow out the candles and cut the cake, blew out the candles and cut the cake, doled out substantial portions, had a few bites, looked into the presents they produced, put on a slightly torn paper crown and cut a few capers next to the table, then ran out of the room again. I could relate how I spent the remainder of the day in the shed and how I felt in the aftermath of an event that I took to signal (though I register it will take some time to confirm this) the household's entry into a new phase of Happy Film, a phase, if I understand it correctly, in which substantive parts of each day's script would go *unscripted* and must somehow be inferred. I could, in this connection, analyze at practical length the curious inversion carried out by my Wife/the Producer late this afternoon when she stood in the doorway of the shed and asked *me* when this charade would end. How she stood there, hands on hips, eyebrow raised, looking over my shoulder at the remote camera. How I finally realized that of course I should make some answer.

Long Walk

SANDY HUSS

SOME OF US ARE DRAWN TO IT. Reiteration. Like Richard Long, who blazed a path in a meadow by insisting, by walking, whose only marks were ephemeral: let's call it Art. What is temporal is also enduring: each footfall a special instance of what the body is always anyhow doing. All walking amounts to this walking, to the weight of a body on the planet, to the bending of the grasses, the piling of stones into cairns, the inevitability of the trace.

By now it seems that Long has walked
nearly everywhere: in the Himalayas
and the Andes, on Dartmoor and in
Africa. Sometimes he simply walks and
records his journeys on a map. At other
times, he has continued to make his
unobtrusive marks in the landscape: not
just with stones, but with driftwood and
seaweed and bits of shrubbery as well.
His preference is for the more remote
and uninhabited, even exotic landscapes; there is a melancholy absence
of any human trace except his own
photographs. The configuration of his
walks and the form of his marks have
remained unwaveringly simple: circles
and squares, spirals and straight lines.
—*John Beardsley,* Earthworks
and Beyond: Contemporary
Art in the Landscape

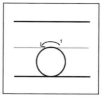

Forensics makes hay with this, the spreadsheet of
one's leavings: there's no such thing as a clean crime
scene, the body is an outmoded factory with no emis-
sion controls. It walks the earth like Pigpen in a cloud
of its own exhaust. Clothes shed their fibers, carpeting gloms to the soles of shoes, the shoes themselves
with their particular tread and patterns of wear leave
imprints as idiosyncratic as the crooked keys of type-
writers back in the day. Stuff splatters and splinters and
shatters and shreds. There is no fresh air: we swim a
soup that's far from primordial, ride a prevailing wind
of bad behavior, screams of terror, clenched fists and
spastic bowels. We enter it naively at our peril. We
admit it to ourselves.

You're walking with Blackie, in winter (else you would be biking), beneath a grim, gray, lake effect sky. You've come to think of this as the pinnacle of Walking, self-locomotion par excellence. Not in any Wordsworthian sense: there is nothing Picturesque about it, nothing either Thoreauvian, nothing meditative or explicitly self-improving—instead, a principle of physics as it might be demoed in the lab. Bodies in motion tending to stay in motion. Blackie's motion, her inclination, hands clasped behind the back support her Army Surplus knapsack, head bulleted by a skullcap pulls you both along. Shorter than you by enough to matter, she sets the pace and keeps it up, fueled by a fury or a longing that you don't understand. Both of you in second hand coats, hers army green with epaulets & brass buttons, yours not as hip, nor your backpack either, but beneath you too are uniformed in threadbare jeans and a flannel shirt. There is a revolution afoot.

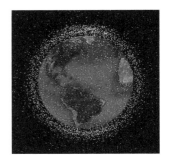

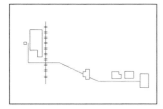

A thing is a hole in
a thing it is not.

—*Carl Andre, Symposium at
Bradford Junior College, 1968*

Out the door to the stench of cat food from the factory opposite, the greasy afterburn of animal rendering, speed *is* of the essence here: you both smoke: there is only so long you can hold your breath. The lurch down the block and around the corner: if you can just cross the train tracks the miasma will sail downwind. Past undistinguished houses leased for chickenfeed to other students, in a neighborhood long since given over to the factory, resigned to its marginal status, a built environment barely knocked together, now coming apart. Still, in the spring, when the cat food operation is over and the ketchup making has yet to begin, a mock orange will bloom.

A contour line between two interlocking figures has a double function, and the act of tracing such a line therefore presents a special difficulty. On either side of it, a figure takes shape simultaneously. But, as the human mind can't be busy with two things at the same moment, there must be a quick and continuous jumping from one side to the other. The desire to overcome this fascinating difficulty is perhaps the very reason for my continuing activity in this field.
—*M. C. Escher, "The Regular Division of the Plane"*

It is a funny thing about addresses where you live. When you live there you know it so well that it is like identity a thing that is so much a thing that it could not ever be any other thing and then you live somewhere else and years later, the address that was so much an address that it was a name like your name and you said it as if it was not an address but something that was living and then years after you do not know what the address was and when you say it is not a name any more but something you cannot remember. That is what makes your identity not a thing that exists but something you do or do not remember.
—*Gertrude Stein,* Everybody's Autobiography

Walking's claim: intimacy with one's surroundings. Connected to the planet, sole to soil, one opens to knowledge that vehicular travel over the same route inevitably blurs. Changes in terrain reverberate in the body, which becomes tuned to all the currents as they flow. The body remembers what the brain is too dumb to even register: beyond one's willing and doing one comes to feel At Home. And so too perhaps with the perfect walking partner: one meshes with the other's pace, the other's warp through the woof. A sympathy springs up between the bodies: together the air is cleaved, shit sidestepped, single files wordlessly created so that others can pass.

Ceci n'est pas une sortie metaphysique. You are two girls walking to school, to the library on Saturday morning, where you'll study all day to earn your dissipation in the bars that night. You stop at the student union with its Morse-encoded tiles that somebody—nobody you know—has supposedly deciphered, where cafeteria workers cook your breakfast, hot and greasy, stoke you with coffee, and send you back out. This last stretch is the coldest, out into the deforested former cornfield that is the New Quad. Out from the sheltering huddle of the dark old buildings into a wind-filled aisle of nothing much Yet. If it were a weekday, the new science buildings to the north would be open, and Blackie would lead you through crowded corridors from building to building, emerging for mere seconds between buildings—not even long enough for your glasses to defog. But it's Saturday, so she bends with still more determination, you both bend, you both lean, you both bewail that the library is so far away. You think you know more than you do. You've proved to yourself that you're up for it, this driving stride. Nobody ever asked before: who knew you could deliver? You think it counts for everything, this shared insertion into the weather, the street map, the social grid. It makes you think you couldn't betray her, that Once There, you are always there, permanent, if not fixed.

Language is like a road; it cannot be perceived all at once because it unfolds in time, whether heard or read.

—*Rebecca Solnit,* Wanderlust: A History of Walking

Round

✣

LILY JAMES

1

TOLEDO WAS BUILT ON A BEAUTIFUL PLAN, all up and down interstate
75, and back and forth along the Maumee River, with the University in the
Southwest end, and the Lake up in the Northeast. Of course in a circle there
are no ends, nor are there ends in a line which continues, point to point, until
it reaches east and west together. When the tornadoes came to Toledo, they
were the worst tornadoes in the history of the world, and all through our
little lives they rampaged, smashing the city into a horror. Yet there we still
were, living. It hadn't been worthwhile to get out.

He and I were married and our baby had been born a sea turtle. I was prepared to be sharply disappointed, except that in the breadline we had seen a
large poster proclaiming the advantages of a sea turtle child, and I found that

the myth of mother love was true. We treated him as a normal baby, and we knew that he would live forever, or nearly, as sea turtles are known among mammals for longevity. So he could be taught and would learn many things and outlive us. Barring the chance that disease would befall him, he could depend on a happy future, and his father to his credit loved the baby dearly, although he had been married before, and with that woman he had fathered a normal baby, a boy, a wonder.

I had always lived in Toledo because of the beauty of it, and because people are supposed to live on land. But the tornadoes came and with the sound of trains they marched across me and my city. It was a day I faced like the catfish in a circular pond, when the bass finally says, "Hey, bottom feeder, isn't it time we emerged?" and he goes down in circles through the water right down to the muck, creating a whirlpool, counting off 12, 13, 14, 15 until the water begins to spin and rise, upending the pond and spilling up onto the grass. This was the effect of the tornado on Toledo and me.

2

We awoke in the refugee camp on Interstate 75. People were setting up tribes and keeping close in families or groups of single office employees who were born in other cities. We camped beside a creek in Rossford, having scavenged some pottery and candles from our building. Our group was made up of me and my husband, and I had my baby with him and he had his child with Shell, and Shell was there with us too, with her other child who was already born before they met. That girl was not connected to my husband or me, she was only connected to Shell, and Shell to my husband through the boy they had together, and he to me through the sea turtle. So there were five of us, counting the infant. If we had stood in a line, the parenthood would have been clear: first me, then the others, and then Shell's child standing last in line. What I felt, and what I had always said to him, was that Shell's old lover should be there, and that he and I should have a baby together, and then we would all be a big circle. It was a big joke that I had regularly said.

Of course the father of Shell's daughter was a psycho. He had left Shell high and dry. The daughter had always referred to my husband as Father, and I was the stepmother to all the children really. Even my own child, who was a sea turtle, and could not be expected to grow up thinking of me as his mother. How do the perfect families form? In circles. Families who form in a line can be destroyed as easily as blowing down paper skyscrapers.

3

Shell was wild. She was mother to no one. She spat at me, angry we were all forced together by the ruin of Toledo. We had never been comfortable with each other, and without my husband around to prevent it, we frequently fought. I would interpret her questions to mean that she thought I was stealing, and she would assume that my good intentions toward the children were greedy, meant to shut her out. I decided to walk around the perimeter of the city, mark out a path around the whole thing. I was tired of living in a city laid out on a beautiful plan. I want one of those cities with a bypass around it, like a rim, like a wall, a city that doesn't leak into a lake, a protected city, one with land all around it, like Fort Wayne, or Columbus.

I mostly just wanted to get lost for a while. Walking around put me in a kind of a trance, and by the time I had gotten around to Airport Highway, my fatigue led me to irresponsibly take a ride in a Volkswagen. We got on the freeway and fled South in the car. I said for the driver to make a left, and left, and left, and drive left around the whole thing without slackening pace, until we had worn a hole in the ground which could be filled with water, a breaker for wind, a protection against wild animals, a moat.

"What thing," he asked me, "What thing?"

He thought I was fucking crazy. And he left me in Maumee, wandering through a mini-mall, one of those long plazas with a parking lot, one that contains a dry cleaner and a bagel place, a sports equipment retailer and a copy shop. The river was there, bisecting everything. The river and then the lake.

I met up with someone I had known in high school. A man I had always identified by his habit of resting the sole of one foot against the arch of the other, a soft and tall freckled man with whom I felt really safe. He was wearing a white puffy jumpsuit over his clothes but he had taken the helmet part off.

"What's that," I said to him.

"CBR suit," he said.

We talked easily, walking back to his car, viewing the spreading waste-land of the suburbs. It was so easy to talk to him! He wanted to know what I had been doing since school, and I enjoyed telling him as he drove me back. We parked on a sidewalk, and then as we approached our camp I saw Shell's daughter come running up to us. With a happy smile I greeted her. I was surprised to see her welcome me. She ran however right into *his* arms and he called her by name and it was obvious they were blood related. This was then the psycho father, first lover of Shell, the missing link in our outer wall of family. Who had left Shell pregnant and lost, contributing to her downfall. This non-person from my old high school was that very same guy. Remarkable.

Back at the camp, his little girl clung tightly around his neck. With him and Shell locked in conversation, and my husband cooking up macaroni for the children, there was nothing for me to do but languish beside my infant's tank, and pretend to stroke him, though I was afraid of harming his baby shell. Then darkness came and we all felt it was important for him to stay with us. They had been affected by me and my desire to close the circle. Desire perhaps too strong a word. Paranoia about the circle so dangling. Frustration. Not desire. Don't fall into that trap.

It was night. Shell lay with my husband on her cot, their hands tangling and their voices low and parental. They lay on their backs, and their eyes didn't meet. They were languidly touching each other as parents will, and they were parents. They were discussing the futures of their children. The boy they had created was a kind and talented person, needed safekeeping, shepherding, thought. They were taken with it. They were all sewn up comfortably. I could hear them like I used to hear my parents when I half-slept in the back seat of our car. The voices, noise never reaching the distinction of words, but a sound that comforts. I lay down half on top of our new friend, Shell's ex-lover. His white suit crinkled so I started to peel it off him and he let me remove it. I leaned my back against his stomach and he supported me. I didn't know about it. We didn't talk about it. I think I fell asleep.

It should have become apparent to me that night as I lay drowsing that a city with a wall around it falls anyway. A city like Columbus is the same as a city like Chicago. There is no safety in a freeway that lets you circumnavigate. I had in my sadness forgotten the third dimension. A circle is still at the mercy of birds and those attackers which fly at you from the top. There is no such thing as strength. It is irrelevant. The world will never escape from weather.

4
—

It was a day for minor blemishes. I was moments away from menstruating, and I found in the morning a hard little pimple forming at the corner of my lip. I had heard someone telling someone at the spigot that all wounds were to be treated immediately at the field hospital. But what could I do? There weren't many clouds or many cars on the road, but there was always at least one cloud, and some traffic. That day I heard a lot of people saying that we should just move to a new city, get jobs, rebuild. But I didn't have a job, and it wasn't our responsibility to rebuild an entire apartment complex in which to rent rooms. There were already people in any other city we could choose. Why displace others so that we were no longer displaced? From the ruined Toledo we could move either East or West. But which way? Going out to the coast was like rolling down a hill. Would we stop? Would we be able to stop ourselves from rolling all the way out?

Still, minor prophets rose up from among scavengers, and urged us to start over. Did we listen? Would we be moved? Well, little boys are always throwing money into lakes. When they run out of coins, they pick up pebbles and then rocks. If they are determined enough they may cause the water level to shift and we will spill out to get away from them. For now they are lunatics at the dime store. No one listens. The ruins of Toledo are full. There is no rim around the top, just a jagged, broken edge. You can't go out too far or you will risk falling out. And once you fall out, you will never stop falling.

So go ahead. Stand in your room and say "This building will survive the greatest tornado, and the only thing that can knock it down is my own dynamite that I make myself!"

5
—

I lived in fear that I would be caught on the videotape of a tourist who had come to personally record the "unbelievably massive destruction." The tourists wore black boots and moved in groups of four. Of course when it happened it happened. I hoped I looked more feral than I was. I wished I had a hunk of cheese and a hunk of bread. I think it is more picturesque that my wrecked clothes were very expensive. We did not always live in rags. I felt very well except for the diarrhea. The tourist industry had become huge in the suburbs, people with gas masks, protective suits. Maybe someone would hire me as a tour guide—here the old glass tower, there the old stone cathedral. Everything is now "the old." They should burn it all, but who's going to pay money to see that? You don't improve a bad place by lighting it on fire. You don't let anything out that way, or keep anything away. Once, Toledo had sparkled in the dawn, alight with possibilities. Now something was sour down inside it. Me in my torn dress, linen, hem half melted, and the tourists stomping through the rubble, taking pictures, collecting artifacts.

Let x be the number of pigeons in a city; then x is the number of miserable disenchanted creatures, each one mangled, each one having suffered some agonizing wound to the foot or wing. Shell's daughter and I are miserable and disenchanted also. We have an adversarial relationship. She is a beautiful child, sort of Slavic, and her eyes represent a level of maturity which coupled with her age can only signify demon possession. She used to use her mother against me, and but now she uses her father against my husband. It is a ridiculous mockery of domestic life, when we huddle under trees in October, each adult eyeing his or her respective cot, the children playing with scavenged dolls and trucks, all sipping the tea, which someone has hoarded away.

"I think we should move to California," said Shell that night, ever one to be lead by new ideas. This is perhaps what makes her inspiring to men and scary to me. She has no doubt because she has no established beliefs. Anything could be next for her. "California has always been the place for us," she continued, the new fall wind blowing her hair around her lipless face, "It's just taken this change for us to establish ourselves as a group."

Her ex-lover's eyes sought the skies, but absently. Perhaps he wasn't listening, or perhaps he didn't want to be her traveling companion. Shell had no "current" lover. It seemed legally proper that these two should resume sexual intimacy, under the circumstances. Yet they regarded each other with coldness, and I couldn't decide which way I wanted it to go. If they produced another child together, then their bond would be twice as heavy as Shell's bond to us, and they would break away, leaving us with her son or else rending the son in two, taking half away and leaving us the rest. If he produced a child with me, then we would all be enclosed, complete, and many times defined by the laws of Euclidean geometry. We would have an area, a circumference, a radius, chords. It was a question of who to include. Did I want to be alone with my husband?

Shell lit a cigarette and prodded my husband's ankle with her foot.

"Come on, Tim," she said, "Pick up your pets and get out of here. I'll go too." I turned to him anxiously to see how he would answer. My husband is not a placid man. He has not accepted many things as stated. The times have been frequent when he has asked someone to please hold on a minute.

"No," he said, "The sea turtle couldn't make the trip. Not in a tank."

"Maybe we could go by boat," said Shell, "And drag him along behind."

"Don't go trying to establish direction," said my husband. "I know how a line moves. Single file or abreast. Can you think of a more absurd way to travel? And who's going to march first? Who's going to stand at the end of the line? Put away your boring idealism. I want no more discussion. Everyone! Go to bed!"

And so, our days were consumed with scavenging and the maintenance of our camps and ourselves. Our nights were colored by the posturing of adults and the whining of confused children. We were murderously tired all the time.

6

I had terrible trouble getting Shell's daughter to sit for hair brushing. She was squirming. She was slapping. With the arrival of her "real" father, I had been demoted from stepmother to disposable nanny. Pain made her cry and threats of pain made her stare resolutely into my face, those deep frightening eyes ready to claim deity. She never stopped crying voluntarily. My husband's shouting she respected, but my voice, even when reasonable, even when desperate would not sway her. She was a tiny child, and full of rage. She led her half brother into deceit, tantrums, and theft. The boy was simply good, pleasant to talk to, and easy to amuse. He was younger and a male, always less complicated. I think I sincerely loved him. But I couldn't stand the daughter. No, I couldn't stand her.

I went out scavenging with Shell's ex-lover. The city was still full of things we could use. His name was Fred. Our conversations about the old days in high school rang hollow among the debris and desperation for food.

We couldn't even be happy. Now it wasn't an interesting and surprising circumstance, us being together. Now it was the magnetism between two ends of a rope, which could be used to contain cattle, or pieces of lumber. There was much unspoken between us. The sky hung low over the empty streets and some buildings still stood high, with their peaks grazed off, leaving one floor exposed at the top. Looking up and around I felt tiny, because it was vast. Looking down at a piece of paper I felt ownership, because here the marketplace had forsaken its possessions, and they were free to anyone who would take abandoned wealth.

I don't know if he was feeling favored to be allowed out with me. In some ways, he should have been feeling very privileged. After all, in high school, he would never have had this hold on me. Now he was free to leave me buckled to my tribe, or he could impregnate me and thus staple himself in as well. He probably liked it. We left the whistling space of the street and all the irrelevant potholes and entered a building through a wall. The elevators were all unsafe, and the stairs perilous also. We climbed from floor to floor on collapsed ceilings, giving each other hands up, pushing through holes in plaster and wood. Inside a great hulking corpse like this, you conceive of burial as a sudden structural failure. You look for air pockets, and try to plan ahead. He was the protection and so I followed. And we encountered dead bodies. Which were rotted. And we found bags of beans and a comfortable chair, and I sat there. He hovered behind the chair and I sat staring at the colorful wall mural.

"Maybe we should build a roof of bricks over our heads," he suggested. "I could come here every day and bring back a load of these bricks over here, and we could plaster them together with concrete." I could tell he was thinking of floor plans. I said it was more important to have a wall. The wind and the draft were savage.

7

Arriving at the camp with our arms full of bricks, we found Shell sick with fever. She was as fragile as anybody else. She was lying on the ground with a sweater pulled over her, her feet kicking distractedly, wanting covers. Fred and I lifted her into a cot and covered her with a quilt, and I breathed onto her face to warm it. Her eyes opened right into mine, and they were as the eyes of her daughter, challenging.

"I'll never get any more sun," she said, "Never any more sun after this."

She was right. The sky had been overcast for weeks. I had considered it a blessing, given our exposure. The clouds were close and foggy.

"And then winter will come and I'll die," she went on into my face, "and you will be weighted down with all my children and all yours and you'll sink right down to the bottom, and you'll die too. A group of children. A gaggle of children. A dependency of children."

"You're not going to die, Shell," I said, brushing away her daughter, who had crept up to her mother's side.

"Is mom going to die?" she asked loudly, with a lot of manufactured sorrow. The tears had already sprouted out of nothing.

"And I'll come back from the dead," Shell said, her lips so thin and white and her eyes rolled back pathetically, "I won't leave you alone forever. I will come back from the dead and you'll see me. If it is at all possible I will come back from the dead and see you."

She was looking directly at my face and her words sounded ominous and threatening although they could have been lines for a dying lover to say to the bereaved. That woman hated me so much I believed she would actually die. I looked up at the tree over us as it edged out the gray sky in hard little malformed knobs. Around us the city was fractured, it straggled broken, from north to south bits were separated. Bits forgotten. I remembered the whirl and rush of the storms that broke it. When the electricity went out, we lost track of the rest of the world.

"Can we build that wall already?" I shouted at Fred, "Do you really intend to allow her this melodrama?"

When I said to Shell, "I WILL NOT LET YOU DIE" I meant that I would protect her from death, that I would save her from pain, that I would stand bravely between her and hell. I meant that I would deny her release from everything that is bleak, grim, gray, and knob-edged in this world, because I did not think her worthy of that liberty, and I did not think I could look at the bleak things alone forever, with two men, and three babies, and no home.

8

The children refused to eat beans, even when we referred to them as "summer blossoms," and even when they saw us eating them in great quantities. It was as if their young limits had been reached, and they would accept nothing but SpaghettiOs in a colorful can, preferably endorsed by a cartoon super hero. Shell was taking her beans in a watery paste, hand-fed by me, whimpering between bites that she would never leave me, threatening me with daily visitations from the grave. After a week of her illness, I was getting tired of her dark tone. My husband kissed me deeply, putting one strong hand behind my neck to support it against his kiss, and the other hand over his eyes, to hide his increasing preoccupation and remote ill humor. He announced that he was going into the suburbs to find some food that the kids would eat without a fight. "We could all cooperate a little more," he said to them. By this he meant that I should sleep with Fred and close our straggling line into a circle. He knew that Shell was fading fast, probably because of the magnetic pull which had concentrated itself not on their son but on her own body. Two ends will always polarize. In a circle a charge is distributed throughout the curve continuously, creating force fields outward and inward, which protect and defend and defend and protect. From me to the sea turtle and from him to the husband, to the boy, to Shell, to the girl, to Fred and through our congress back to me. Well, all right.

When he entered me I could feel three pairs of eyes on me and I knew that my sacrifice was appreciated. Like a welding tool, Fred forged a new link, a final link. With the sea turtle rampaging in his confinement, and Shell and her daughter serenely clasping hands at her cot, it was almost as if no plunging and thrusting were necessary. The force of a circle closing is inescapable. My pregnancy was certain, like a bear trap snapping shut. With this connection made, I felt myself rising fast, as if at last I had been dragged under a ship. Having spent my entire life hanging over one side, looking in this same portal, I had been pulled with a rope under the keel, and now I could feel just as near, just as part of the other side, as the motion I had started would pull me up and over and down, under and up again, ceaselessly connected.

9

For months we ran free like electrons in a wedding band, around our set course, contained, tight, no one as strong as myself, pushing toward birth. Shell developed the ability to give orders, and began expectorating constantly. Fred became regular in his construction of wall after wall, containing us in brick. My baby sea turtle learned to execute fantastic tricks. My husband acquired a car. Our situation seemed daily to improve. Many people, like us, found themselves stabilized in this new lifestyle. Their habitats became gradually permanent, and they developed sources of income based on marketing goods from the old city, or cooperating with the tourists, offering samples of blood or hair for them to take away. Or they engaged in specialized agriculture. We were interviewed by reporters. We were exposed on public television. A breed of celebrity rose from the rubble, people who sought the spotlight, considered themselves exemplary or representative, believed they could spawn fashion trends. This one missing half a head of hair, this one whose fingernails had fallen off. It was common to see refugees driving around quite freely in cars they had seized and repaired, running out to the suburbs for dinner and then back to their fortresses to sleep. I still believe that people from other cities actually moved into our camps, identifying the potential for establishing radical cults.

My husband had responded with optimistic indifference to my tryst with Fred. He hoped that everything would go well for me. He hoped that I would feel better and better. He hoped that my life would improve with the birth of the child. We had sex with increasing frequency as I became more visibly pregnant, by my choice. I liked sex all the more because it recalled for me that acute moment of junction that I had felt with Fred, possibly the most satisfying moment of my life since the tornado. My husband kept busy reviving his consultancy. While his office and his staff were gone, his brain was left by the tornado intact and therefore his business was sound. He rented himself out by the hour, sometimes spending long days in the suburbs working for the flourishing corporations that always situate themselves near disaster. I should have said to him, "One day is like any other day, and in the constancy of our love there is no" and then I should never have said, "Today I feel so strange" or "This time we will do something entirely different" or "Let us leave Toledo and discover the continent of Europe."

10

It was a day in which I craved cigarettes for the first time since I had become pregnant. I told him we would have to take the car to a convenience store so that I could buy just one pack of Camels, because it wouldn't hurt me to have just one pack, and anyway, it had been days since I'd been in the car. We left Shell asleep and Fred playing with the children and plastic figurines, my sea turtle baby circling his tank moodily, bored, unable to decide what to do with himself. The family's peaceful revolutions could be marked, quantified, dated, tracked, always on the same track, always on the same ring, bounded easily. As we drove away we talked about things the children had said, playthings we intended to make for them, and other trivialities. He wanted to drive. At the convenience store he decided to stay in the car, since he didn't want to be seen with a pregnant woman buying cigarettes. He laughed about it, because it was perfectly allowable and understandable. He said he didn't mean to make me feel guilty, and looked at me, and we both had the giggles. It was fun to be out with him in the car for a change.

I pranced into the store, having left the keys in the ignition and the car running with him in it, the driver's side door unlocked. When I came back out smiling, I saw that the car and my husband were gone and had been abducted. Then have I never felt so foolish. I had seen on a sign how these murderers would linger and wait until a car was idling unlocked with a careless passenger, and then jump in with a gun, push the passenger aside, throw the car in gear and be off. It was so sudden, so ridiculous, that I called out to him as if he were still speeding away, and then I stood there heaving. But, I thought, I have been an idiot, and I have been blind to the third dimension.

For every ring there is an outside that is up, and for every orb there is an outside that is time, and there will always be erosion, and there will always be intrusion, and there will always be reason for paranoid defenses. Me with my family gathered around in the safest orbit, like a group of fish which defend themselves so brilliantly against the predators of the sea, only to have the dearest of their number captured by a marauding bird of the air and spirited away screaming.

Anton's Album

JANET KAUFFMAN

1.   All right. In the grape arbor, and in the shadows, you can see me. He put me in there, just to look out. This is September, and he had forgot to prune in the spring. Look at the tangle.

2.   The embassy, the rear door; and those are two bluebirds, one caught in flight, landing on the gravel the way they often do, tilting their wings and flashing that bluey blue. He's caught the corner of Geoffrey's car, accidentally, the gray blur over there.

3.   That's not me, not on your life. That's Angelique. When he called the embassy and ordered up an angel, she's the one who showed.

4.   Me again; I think this was the birthday dinner for Geoffrey. Anton called this shot "Consideration." He asked me to bring in the

butter dish, and I only said, just like he would, "Give me a chance to consider."

My hair was longer then, what a shame.

5.   When Geoffrey moved out, Anton blamed the neighborhood. People with money were buying the houses, and there were two seasons: sandblasting season and winter. Anton hated it. "Literacy does this to a neighborhood," he said. "The bums move out."

He took a picture when the couple across the street came outside in coveralls to paint their wrought-iron fence.

6.   These two, I'm not sure I can remember their names. Anton ignored introductions; he had the idea that people would make themselves known. These two stopped in about once a year and brought tins of smoked salmon; and Anton took a day off and we got some Bibb lettuce and cheese from Gaccione, two blocks down. Gaccione'd say, "Tony, baby. Tony, you deserve the best!" Always the same lip-smacking.

After a while, the wine bottles arranged themselves on the table like bowling pins. These two guys, one was called Bob White, I believe that was it, a bird's name, told long stories involving motor troubles, leaking boats on the Yukon River, and Anton would sit there tearing a lettuce leaf down the middle and shaking his head side to side, "Oh, no, don't tell me."

I like the way they stood here, though, one behind the other, the same shoulders, like a two-headed man.

7.   It's hard to believe, but this is Anton's mother. She came by train before Christmas that year, and when I kissed her cheek, she said, "I take it this is the child." From then on, she was like anybody else.

When I did her hair, Ice White, Anton took a picture, and she touched one hand behind her head and tipped up her chin, like a star.

8.   Another picture of Anton's mother and me. Anton never made excuses—he wasn't a photographer. If somebody turned and the face washed out, that suited him. He said what he wanted was evidence.

"You two were here," he said about this one. "Here's the evidence."

9.   Angelique again, in her blue dress, all the sequins. I'll tell you what I know about her. Her mother was Serbo-Croatian, and her father a Marriott-Hilton. She told this story as a way of accounting for how easily she could "dance in rooms—or not!" Then she howled, with her very smart laugh.

Anton was taken, I won't say smitten. He was taken. We had special foods, artichokes, fresh shrimp, red lettuce, asparagus with lemon grass and butter. Geoffrey did his work in the living room, reports on his lap, some secret, some not, he was just there, comfortable, out of the way, while Angelique put on music. I didn't mind. Why should I? I learned how to lounge, how to sprawl on a chair with upholstered arms, how to listen to anything, you name it.

Anton said, "What a sad life," talking about her; but he never would say it about himself.

10.   And Geoffrey, in the arboretum. He came along as a favor, although he claimed no admiration for trees and no liking for gravel paths, which suggested corduroy to him, a texture he found unnatural. I gave him a walking stick—it was sassafras, and I peeled the bark off—and he sank his teeth into that, as I suggested, for a taste, before walking through the beech wood. By the time Anton took this picture, Geoffrey admitted there might be a pleasure or two, somewhere in the wild; and so he waved the walking stick, and he smiled. That's how simple he was.

11.   True Value Hardware, that's right. This was my birthday, and my present was, I could take a picture anywhere I chose. Anton said, "Anywhere. You choose."

I said, "The place on the calendar."

And, very quick, Anton said, "And I say which calendar!"

If I had said one word—Crete, Lapland, anywhere—I'd have been there, to this day. It could have happened. Anton was not much for premeditation. His idea was, you could only think something through after the fact.

Since it was his present to me, I accepted. I'd forgot we had more than one calendar.

After the cake, instead of boarding a plane and flying to the Arctic Circle to take a picture, or flying to England, we took Geoffrey's gray Olds over to Nebraska Avenue. The boxwood at the entrance to the store is sliced off the edge, just like the calendar picture, and the sun on the glass doors is about as bright.

12.   I suppose this is Anton's favorite photo of the embassy, an incomprehensible picture, the heads of everybody lost off the top. But Anton said it was all right, he liked the colors. At the swimming party, the men posed in the pool, and here they are, the big shots, naked chest after chest after chest. They're columns of pink, peach pink, and the water is plain blue.

13.   Geoffrey sent a picture of his room in Paris, the rue Victor-Cousin.

"Rue," Anton said. "Ruin." He gave me the photograph to throw in the wastebasket.

It was a dark room, if I remember correctly, with the camera aimed out the window toward the rooftops across the street, with some of the windows over there shuttered and some open.

Anton decided to take this picture, out the front window of our place, with the frame of the window the frame of the picture, and the roof of the house across the street cutting a low triangle, green-shingled, and the white sky above it, all around, very bright, your large city sky, no color, probably ozone.
You can see, though, he never sent the picture to Geoffrey. He kept it here.

14.   All right, look. Here he is. Nothing I can say will show you Anton better than this, enthroned, on the back porch in the ratty gold chair. That's not his Amish hat, that's mine, to match my hair, and Geoffrey took this picture.

These are all out of order.

This was the summer, and we were celebrating Independence Day, waiting for the fireworks, doing nothing the way we did it best.

Anton set up the tripod, the timer, and tried to take a picture of the three of us, arranged, he said, so that nobody outshone anybody else, but it didn't work. After a couple of foul-ups, Anton picked my hat off my head and said to Geoffrey, "There's one shot left. Take me."

He sat back in the chair, the wide-brimmed hat on his head. In the shade, he grinned with his eyes, but you can see the uneven tips of his front teeth, which hardly anybody ever saw.

It's a good picture. That's how he looked that afternoon. This was a lucky shot, and I'm lucky to have it because usually Anton wasn't very good at looking good.

15.   Here is the old woman who moved into Geoffrey's car in the alley for three nights. She didn't speak English. Anton finally gave up pointing at the door.

16.   There aren't any other pictures, those last months. Anton stopped taking pictures. I was ready for it when he told me to leave, I should be on my own. I kissed his fingers.

I said, "What's far away?"

"Calcutta," he said. "Anchorage. How about a ticket to Anchorage?" His mouth stayed open.

"One way to Anchorage, that's fine."

"It's not a pretty place," he said.

I let my mouth sag, too, and didn't say anything. I just looked back at him until he said, the way I always say it, "All right."

At the airport, I asked if I could take a picture, and Anton rolled down the car window and looked out. He didn't look pretty, not that day. I took this picture, though, and I'm glad he let me take it. I took his album, too, out of the living room rubble.

I wouldn't take anything else. I owe him too much. His idea was, it was the same with humans as with God: after you saw the ruin, that's all there was. The rest didn't matter. The idea pleased him, when it didn't make him ugly. And it pleases me, too.

A History of Indiana

❧

JESSE LEE KERCHEVAL

ALL HIS LIFE, LANCELOT WALKER would remember the plague of squirrels.

At that time New Hope had existed for just thirteen months. The whole first year no one knew anything, and that was painful. No one knew when to trust the thawed earth enough to plant. No one knew when the frost would come again. That year there were three families and Walker, their bachelor. Even so they couldn't agree on anything. Walker wanted to name the settlement Camelot. He didn't see any harm in it.

"Camelot, Mother of Harlots," declared Mrs. McLintock, the matriarch of the two Georgia families. Mr. Bingham, who was English, thought it smacked of monarchy. "Too much history," he said, "it doesn't seem American."

So New Hope it was, though Walker thought it a melancholy choice. It implied a trail of blasted hopes behind them, and even if that was true, he didn't see why they had to make it official.

That first spring they couldn't even agree what to plant. Walker and the two Georgia families were for corn, but Bingham wanted to plant wheat and hedge with potatoes. "Well, think of Rome," Walker said, trying to lend a little perspective to their troubles. "Do you think Romulus and Remus knew right off what to do?" It seemed to Walker they probably had less to go on, if they were raised by wolves.

"I suppose you think they planted corn," Mr. Bingham said.

"Well, I'm sure as hell they didn't plant potatoes," Walker said.

"Rome," Mrs. McLintock said, "is the Seven-Headed Beast that was and is not but will be."

They planted. The corn and wheat grew. The potatoes rotted.

Walker spent the first January snowed in his cabin, making up a list of names for plants people had spent the summer calling things like pricky bush and big bud. He went through Livy and Mallory—Brutus Blade, Cleopatra's Tears, Excaliber Leaf. He didn't mean to lose the next time.

By the second March things began to repeat themselves, and life seemed on the edge of predictability. The snow melted on time. The ground warmed up, and everyone planned on planting both corn and wheat. Three Welsh families came straggling over the creek and cleared land. That doubled the population, and the whole of New Hope had Mrs. Bingham's second annual piano concert to look forward to. None of the new families had been at the first concert, of course, but they realized what it meant on the frontier to take part in a second annual anything.

It was at the second annual concert that Lancelot Walker met Gwen Llewellyn for the first time.

"Guinevere," Walker said, taking her hand.

"She's just a plain Gwen, Mr. Walker," her father corrected as his daughter became the first person in New Hope to have her hand kissed in greeting. But Gwen had never heard of Arthur's queen and didn't know she was in danger of history. She paid more attention to the piano, which rose from clawed feet to a music stand carved into two griffins—rampant. She had never seen one before.

Walker was sorry she wasn't looking at him but respected her for her love of music. The first concert had been his doing. He was at the Binghams' one morning arguing corn versus wheat and staring at the only musical instrument in New Hope when something rose up in him. He pushed past Bingham and into the kitchen where Mrs. Bingham was boiling porridge.

"Spring awaits you, Persephone. Rise up and play for us!" he cried out to her.

Mrs. Bingham put her spoon down, wiped her hands on her apron. "All right, Mr. Walker," she said. "Since you put it that way."

Mr. Bingham had to put up with cold porridge while his wife rehearsed, but now, in the second year, he was inclined to see it as a sacrifice for the greater good.

"Karl Ditters Von Dittersdorf," Mrs. Bingham said and seated herself at the piano in a thunderstorm of purple silk.

"Alas, that once great city," Mrs. McLintock whispered to her daughter, "that was clothed in purple."

The music started.

Gwen's father always said of his daughter, "That one's closed tight as a fist." But at the instant Mrs. Bingham struck the first chord, Gwen looked at Walker and caught him looking at her. She took the music as a gift from him. He smiled, and she smiled back.

When Mrs. Bingham had played every note she knew, repeated exactly the previous year's performance, the concert was over. New Hope clapped and rose, stretching. It was then that Walker heard a sound like something hitting the roof.

"Is that hail?" someone asked. Mr. Bingham opened the door.

The fence, the yard, every tree and stump was covered with squirrels. Walker went out. Squirrels were running across the roof, and it did sound like hail. They chased each other in circles in the yard like leaves might in a storm. But mostly they looked and sounded like squirrels, hundreds and hundreds of squirrels. Squirrels chewing on the rails and shingles and the bark of the trees. Squirrels as far as anyone could see.

"The wheat!" Mr. Bingham ran by with an ax. When the first dead squirrel came flying out of his grain bin, they all broke and ran—"The corn cribs!" There was much nailing of boards across cracks before each family went to bed under its own roof of squirrels.

The squirrels were still there in the morning. Still there the next day. They ate the swelling buds off the trees. Walker couldn't get over how strange it was no one had seen the squirrels' arrival. "Where do you think they came from?" he asked Bingham.

"Better to ask where we should go," he said, and everyone shook their heads. There was no point in planting corn or wheat if the squirrels would eat it as soon as it came up, and, if they waited much longer, it would be too late to clear land and plant somewhere else—in New New Hope.

"The Lord Jehovah smote the Philistines," Mrs. McLintock said, "with a plague of hemorrhoids."

The next day it rained, but the wet squirrels still sat and chewed. Everyone's roof leaked.

"What we need is some information," Walker said as they all sat in front of the McLintock fireplace. "I mean how often do the squirrels come? Not every year—we know that. But every other year? Every hundred years?"

"How about how long do they stay?" Mr. Llewellyn put in.

"Or how to kill them?" said Mrs. McLintock.

"More like, should we head north or west?" said Bingham.

Walker stood up. "Indians," he said, "are the ones who'd know."

"There aren't any Indians here," Bingham said, and, for the first time, this seemed a bad omen not a good one. What if the Indians knew better? Or had all starved?

"In Lewis and Clark's journal," Walker said, "there's report of a tribe of Indians on the Ohio descended from a Welsh prince named Madoc. I met a trader on the way out here who'd heard about them and said damned if he didn't have half a mind to go see."

"White Indians?" Bingham said. "Welsh Indians?"

Llewellyn shrugged—he'd gotten here.

"I'm going east to find out about these squirrels," Walker said. Everyone looked east. "But I need someone who speaks Welsh." Llewellyn stopped looking east.

"I'll go," Gwen said.

"A woman might be less threatening," Bingham agreed.

Walker shook Llewellyn's hand. "Think of your daughter," he said, "as the Joan of Arc of New Hope."

They left the next morning. The first day every tree they passed was top to bottom with squirrels. The second day they could still hear squirrels moving from branch to branch. But the third day the forest was quiet and empty. The fourth day they came to the Ohio. They went upstream until they found a ford and waded across. On the other side, they sat and put their boots on.

The bank was steep and seemed to have been reinforced with cut logs. Smoke rose from a fire they couldn't see. After a while, a woman came to the top of the bank and threw off some trash.

"Hey!" Walker said. The woman shrugged. They sat a while longer, and four men appeared and began to pick their way down to the river. One sat on a boulder about twenty feet off, and three came on. Then another sat down, and another, until finally the oldest man sat down so close his knees touched Gwen's. The Chief had straight dark hair a little longer than Gwen's. Walker thought he saw a resemblance.

"Okay," Walker said, nodding to Gwen.

"'r wiwerod," Gwen said, wrinkling her face and bringing her hands up like paws. Walker heard one more distinct wiwerod and then the Welsh really started to fly. Gwen kept up the pantomime as well, adding a bushy tail to her squirrel. She held out an open hand, let one finger rise from it like growing corn—before her other-hand-as-squirrel nibbled the finger back down to the ground. Gwen's sentences started to go up at the end, and Walker guessed she'd gotten past facts into questions. She pointed east. She pointed west. She shrugged. The Chief started to talk. He pointed at them. He pointed at himself. He tapped his nose twice. The Chief's face was blank—but then he was an Indian. Gwen's face was too, but no more than usual.

"Well?" Walker said.

"I can't understand him," she said, "and I don't think he understands me either." They all looked at each other. Then the Chief turned around and yelled to the man behind him, who passed it on, and another man came down from the invisible village—the trader Walker had met.

"How the hell are you?" the trader asked, sitting down next to the Chief.

Walker told him about the squirrels.

"Well, damn," he said.

"He doesn't seem," Walker said, nodding toward the Chief, "to speak Welsh."

"Well, Goddamn."

"How do you talk to them?"

"I parlay French—all the Indians on the Ohio speak a little of that. You want I should talk to him?"

"Please."

"Les ecureuils," the trader started, wrinkling his face at the Chief in his own squirrel imitation. The trader turned back to Walker. "What do you want to ask?"

"Where the squirrels came from and how we can get them to go back there."

The trader asked.

The Chief answered.

"Well, damn," The trader said. "He says that you're asking the wrong questions."

"Damn yourself," Walker said.

"Ask him," Gwen said, "to tell us what he knows about the squirrels."

The Chief swam his hand through the air as he answered.

"He says," the trader translated, "that they're fish." The Chief drew a wavy line in the dirt with his finger. "And fish swim in a river."

"What's that supposed to mean?" said Walker.

"Well," said the trader, "sometimes I don't understand them myself. It could be I'm getting all the words but not what they mean—I mean, would the Chief here get what I meant if I told him I was washed in the blood of the Lamb? But then again," the trader shrugged, "he could be just jerking you around."

The Chief stood up. He took Gwen by the shoulders and kissed her firmly on each cheek—as if she were Joan of Arc. Then he left, his men following.

"Well, Hell," the trader said, leaving too. "Don't do anything I wouldn't do."

They recrossed the river. "Fish," Walker said.

"Fish," he said again when they stopped for the night, and put his head in his hands. "Fi . . ." he started, but Gwen stopped him. "Don't say it," she said and, taking off her dress, made a gift of herself.

"Can I talk to your father?" Walker said to her later. "You do know I want to marry you, don't you?"

Gwen rolled over. "You're asking the wrong questions again."

In the morning they began to see squirrels passing in groups overhead. The next day the trees were full of them. One squirrel to a square foot of bark, Walker figured.

"Swim," Gwen yelled at them, flapping her arms. Two panicked squirrels ran forward and fought for a places on the next tree, their place in the rear taken in an instant.

Walker kicked a tree "Swim." A half-dozen squirrels ran forward, and a half-dozen behind them moved up. "Sshh," he said, and they stood quiet. Even without prompting, every few minutes some squirrels changed trees—always moving forward—toward New Hope.

"Stay here," Walker said, and went off the path. After about fifty feet, the squirrels thinned out; after sixty, the trees were empty. He came back.

"They're going somewhere," he said.

"To New Hope."

"Maybe."

When they reached New Hope, there was no smoke coming from the Llewellyns'. Standing outside Walker could tell the place was empty, but Gwen went in anyway, closing the door behind her. The other chimneys were still smoking so Walker knew everyone hadn't cleared out yet. He went through New Hope to the woods on the other side. The trees were full of squirrels—still moving west.

When he got to his cabin, he saw Gwen out planting his corn. She straightened up and handed him the sack. By the time New Hope realized they were back, he had a half-sack of seed corn in the ground.

They all stood dumb watching him plant. The squirrels watching too. "What's this?" Bingham asked when Walker got to the end of the field.

Walker put down the sack of corn. "These squirrels are headed somewhere, and I intend to follow them until I find out. But first I'm going to get in my early corn."

"A time to plant," Mrs. McLintock said. She nodded at the squirrels, "and a time to pluck."

Walker put in another half-sack—as if an extra ten pounds would hold New Hope until he got back. It was almost dark when he left his cabin.

"Dad left the family Bible for me," Gwen said. She held a large book against her chest.

Walker took her arm, which was as thin and hard as a tree branch. "He knew you might need it," he said.

"Go on," she said, shaking her head, shaking her arm free. Walker started toward the woods. Looking back, he saw her standing with the book open in front of her, though it was too dark to read. "That which is far off," she called, "and exceedingly deep, who can find it out?"

They all sat watching Walker's field. They were in agreement now. If the first shoot came up and got eaten, they would leave. The day after Walker left, three trappers drifted in and started banging away at the squirrels.

"How much do you get for a squirrel fur?" Bingham asked them when they'd made a big pile in the middle of town.

"Nothing," one of them said, and spit. "We're gonna jerk 'em." Which Mrs. Bingham explained to her husband meant dry the meat for winter. But when the trappers slit the squirrels their knives hit bone right under the skin. There was no meat on them and their stomachs were full of splinters. The trappers shot a few more, out of habit, then gave it up and sat with everyone else watching Walker's invisible corn.

After six days, there was still no sign of Walker or his corn. The grass on the edge of the field was starting to sprout and each blade seemed to come up under a squirrel. Mrs. McLintock shook her head. "I have lived an alien in a strange land," she said.

"So we have," Bingham said.

"Me and mine will be leaving," Mrs. McLintock said, "at sunup." Then Bingham thought Walker had been right about the town's name—How sad to leave New Hope behind with old. The trappers spent the day digging lead shot out of the dead squirrels. Then two of them headed west. Maybe they'd run into Walker or find out what had become of him and maybe not. At any rate west was the direction they always went—west and further west.

"Head north," the trapper who stayed behind advised Mrs. McLintock, while whispering in her daughter's ear, "Come west." Everyone except Gwen spent the night packing. But the Llewellyn's hadn't left Gwen anything that needed packing, so no one could tell if she was going to leave or stay.

It was the quiet that woke everyone up. When Bingham opened his door and saw no squirrels, it was almost as much of a shock as seeing the squirrels the first time. The roof was empty, the fences, the trees. An hour later, Walker came home. He went right to his field, stood looking at it until everyone in New Hope was there. Then he told them what had happened. It was a story he only told once, but everyone remembered it. Years later a New Hoper working for the Indianapolis Free Democrat Locomotive would write his own version and put the story into history.

The reports coming to us recently from Chicago of the sightings of strange airships should not be taken by the public as a thing altogether without precedence. A certain respected citizen of New Hope—well known in the state as a honest, non-drinking man—thirty years ago saw such a sight right here in Indiana. "The vessel was thirty feet in length," he reported, "and shaped like a bread pan with a loaf risen in it—all the color of new tin. Near the vessel was the most beautiful being I ever beheld. She was rather over-size, but of the most exquisite form and with eyes of sapphire and features such as would put shame to the statues of the ancient Greeks. She was dressed in nature's garb and her golden hair, wavy and glossy, hung to her waist, unconfined excepting by a band of glistening jewels that bound it back from her forehead. The jewels threw out rays of light as she moved her head. She was plucking little flowers that were just blossoming from the sod with exclamations of delight in a language I could not understand. Her voice was like low, silvery bells, and her laughter rang out like chimes. In one hand she carried a fan of curious design that she fanned herself vigorously with, though to me the air was not warm, and I wore an overcoat. On the far side of the vessel stood a man of lesser proportions, though of majestic countenance. He also was fanning himself with a curious fan as if the heat oppressed him.

"Was this," I wondered, "Adam and Eve come to earth again?"

The newspaper reporter didn't mention the squirrels, years later maybe they didn't seem important. But squirrels there certainly were as Walker made his way west. He had to tie his hat on to protect himself from squirrels who, missing a particularly inspired forward leap, fell to the ground like two pound hail. On the second day he began to hear a sound, a single high note that seemed to shift from one ear to the other. He shook his head. The squirrels around him shook theirs. The third day he came out of the woods on the edge of large clearing. The squirrels were so thick on the ground that he couldn't move without stepping on them. Walker was afraid they might panic suddenly when he got into the clearing. A thousand squirrels would run up the tallest thing in sight—him. So he cut a branch and moved forward, sweeping a dozen squirrels aside for each step. In the middle of the clearing was the bread pan. And the naked woman. The high-pitched noise was coming from the ship. But the woman opened her mouth and made a sound that wasn't too different from the one the ship was making. It made his ears itch. Walker, thinking about the Welsh Indians, almost lost heart for the whole business. But he went forward, starting Gwen's squirrel imitation. It helped that there were a thousand thousand squirrels in a circle around him to point to by way of example. He pointed east. He did the finger-as-corn eaten by hand-as-squirrel. He rubbed his stomach, sucked in his cheeks—tried generally to look faced with starvation.

It was then he saw the man. The woman said something, and the man came around from the other side of the ship, making marks on a piece of flat tin. Nine hundred thousand and one, nine hundred thousand and two . . . He's counting the squirrels, Walker realized, watching each mark. The woman finished talking to the man and turned back to Walker. She pointed to her ship. She held up three fingers.

"Three what?" Walker asked.

She pointed at the sun, then moved her arm three times in an arc across the sky, her breasts making their own gentle revolutions.

"Three days," Walker said, holding up three of his own fingers in acknowledgment. The woman nodded. The man moved away, marking on his tin again. The woman watched him for a moment, then shook her head, and something in the way she did it made Walker think, "She's his mother."

The woman looked back at Walker and smiled. She took him by the wrist—her hand was hot. She pointed at him, touched her own chest, pointed at the ship, pointed up. Walker threw his head back and looked at the sky, blue and endless overhead. He felt he was at the bottom of a deep clear well. His lungs ached. He wanted to swim up, burst into what was beyond, into air he had been waiting all his life to breathe. The woman was looking up too. Her fingers burned on his wrist. Against the blue of the sky, her face was white as milk—inhuman. Walker wondered if he knew her name and spoke it, would she disappear with a puff of smoke and a scream like Morgan le Fay? She looked down, and her face was flushed. She looked lonely. Walker shook his head. He took her hand from his wrist and touched it to his lips. It was like kissing a stove. She blushed—red spreading from the roots of her hair to her breasts and maybe lower, though Walker didn't look.

He could feel her watching him as he swept his way out of the clearing. The squirrels stood on their hind legs, and it struck Walker that they looked like little humans wearing fur suits. When he looked back from the edge of the woods, the afternoon sun gave them fur halos. For three days the trees he passed were more full of squirrels than ever. The third night he slept as trees groaned with squirrels. He woke up to absolute quiet.

"They're really gone then," Bingham said.

Walker nodded.

"They was angels," Mrs. McLintock said. "Unfallen creations of God like Adam and Eve, walking naked and not ashamed."

"Well," Walker said, "maybe."

"And they're in Heaven now," she said. "Oh, behold! I heard the voice of many angels round about the throne and the beasts and the elders: and the number of them was ten thousand times ten thousand, and thousands of thousands."

"Angels," Bingham asked, "or squirrels?"

"But why," Mrs. Bingham asked, "didn't you go with her?"

"Because Gwen's agreed to marry me," Walker said. Gwen shook her head, but let Walker take her hand.

"Because you had corn in the ground, you mean," Bingham said.

Mrs. Bingham sighed, as if she saw years of cooked porridge and concerts clearly before her.

Then Walker heard a scratching sound. Everyone else heard it too. On a tree beside his cabin was a squirrel. There was no mistaking that. But it was completely white—an albino. The trapper drew a bead on it with his rifle, eased his finger onto the trigger.

"Don't," Walker said, and knocked the barrel up. The ball went whirring through the high branches. The squirrel didn't flinch. "It's deaf." He stood at the base of the tree. "Swim!" he yelled, "Get!" The squirrel looked like a white X painted on the tree. It hadn't heard its other-worldly summons.

"His head and his hairs were white like wool," Mrs. McLintock cried out, "as white as snow! And his feet like unto fine brass, as if they burned in a furnace! And out of his mouth went a sharp two-edged sword! And when I saw him—I FELL DOWN AT HIS FEET AS DEAD!" She went over like a tree. "Thank You, Jesus!" she said as her sons carried her inside.

Everyone went home to plant.

Gwen put her arm through Walker's. "You should have let him shoot that squirrel," she said. "It won't bring you luck." Walker shook his head.

The squirrel looked down at him with eyes as blue and empty as the sky.

Still Life with Insects

BRIAN KITELEY

Beetles dislodged by drilling into exposed
heartwood of a standing Maple. Part of the tree
had fallen, splitting a section of the trunk.
—*Northfield, Minnesota, May 4, 1952*

THE COOK WALKED A WIDE ARC around the empty dining room in the
La Crosse Hotel and finally stopped at my table as if by accident. From his
side appeared the bag lunch I'd ordered with my breakfast. This boy looked
intelligent and too young to be a fry cook. He asked me what I was reading.
"Just an entomology journal," I said, my gaze distracted by the dust motes
and sunlight. Shadows of people too brightly lit to make out passed by the
picture window on the street below. "Oh," he said, disappointed. "I want to
write a novel. My dad wants me to go to work in his brother's bank." This
comment hung in the air for a moment until I decided to clean my glasses
with the cloth napkin. A middle-aged man entered from Division Street,
bringing a gust of hot air. He carried a doctor's bag and frowned at me. "If
you don't mind, sir," he said. "I'd like to have a word alone with my son."
I never saw either of them again, but the way the father took his son by the

neck, as if the boy were still a child, and his tone of voice with me, as if I were giving his son bad advice, reminded me of someone I could not quite place. The sandwiches the cook prepared, however, were excellent—Wisconsin cheddar so sharp my lips burned, oily ham, and great watery slices of tomato someone must have been sorely tempted to pick weeks before they finally arrived in my sandwiches.

After my appointment in La Crosse, I drove seventy miles before I stopped for lunch and a bit of collecting in a handsome wooded valley that lay between rolls of black farmland. An undergraduate field biology class came upon me—the forest belonged to their nearby college—and the professor asked me to talk about the sort of insects I found in these parts. My little lecture and, later, the warm colors inside a stand of blooming Red Osier dogwoods convinced me there was no need to rush off to Le Sueur, which was next on my itinerary. I had parked my car beside a phone booth crowded by these dogwoods. Inhaling the steamy smell of honey and burnt rope, I began to search the flowers for sap-drinking beetles. The telephone rang. I reached through branches and brambles into the phone booth, as if this were a perfectly natural thing to do.

"Hello?" I said. "Dad," my son Henry said breathlessly. "I called Helen down at the central exchange and I asked if she could pretty please find the phone number of your field office—" "Field office," I repeated, laughing. I had called my wife from this phone half an hour before, to tell her I would not be home today after all.

Henry kept bantering along in a happy, excited voice I had not heard since he and Helen broke off their engagement. He was saying, "I told Helen it was a family emergency. I come home from a big Philo exam and find a mother and baby brother looking about as glum as a couple of Ukrainians. I figured it would be easy to trace the call, since you called collect. In case you're wondering, the cost of this conversation is on Minnesota Bell, the monopoly with a heart."

Most people enjoy my son's sense of humor and storytelling, but no one as much as he does. He took a breath, and laughter strangled his efforts to refill his lungs. "Dad," he said after a moment. "Are you there?" I nodded, watching a chipmunk on the bridle path through the phosphorescent green of early spring leaves. The path sank into interior forest and pleasant darkness, shielded from the hot afternoon sun by a canopy of oak and maple. I remembered to speak. "I think so," I said.

Then she spoke and her image disappeared. "Do you remember the trip to Vancouver we took after your last breakdown? You didn't say a word the entire trip, just let your head bounce against the train window. I could tell you were alive only by the breath that formed on the glass. But I didn't mind. In Vancouver at the Finnemores, you walked twenty miles a day so you would exhaust yourself to sleep at night. The first day you went back to work in Calgary was the hardest day of your life." "I remember," I said. But I have no memory of this period, so I rely on other people's versions of these dreamlike incidents. A janitor found me the morning after my collapse and said, "You were sprawled out there on the lab floor as if you'd passed out. But, get this, you had neatly folded your glasses beside you."

Ettie asked, "But do you remember how sweet it was to come home after that first day back at work? I've never seen anyone so happy." I'd forgotten. The smell of French toast and bacon. My younger son Greg flying about the living room with his arms as propellers, oblivious to my ridiculous, triumphant return. I asked how Greg's arm was. "Why on earth do you want to know that?" Ettie snapped. This happened three years ago, I realized with a shock. Greg used his left arm as a propeller walking to school one day and the arm simply snapped. He didn't hit anything. The bone was congenitally weak. He found his brother a few minutes later and said, "I think I hurt my arm." Henry, who is nearly a decade older, saw the bone jutting out of Greg's shirt and sent him home. "Why did you let him go alone?" I asked Henry, horrified, but vaguely aware I might have done the same thing myself. "He knew the way," Henry had sobbed.

"I've called the minister," Ettie was saying. "He'd be glad to come over any time tonight." The minister was twenty-seven years old and unmarried. He arranged debates between me and the fundamentalist crowd on evolution. "He's young enough to be our son." "Nonsense," Ettie said. "Both his parents died in that awful plane crash in La Crosse." There was no disputing this logic. "I've put fresh sheets on the guest bed if you—" "Ettie," I said. "I'm not trying to avoid you."

"Then what *are* you doing?" she said tartly. This made me pause. I could hear traces of other conversations over the line. Other husbands and wives trying vainly to stay in love.

"You missed dinner at the Akers," Ettie said. The accusing tone of the first half of this sentence softened to guilty pleasure at gossiping the last half. "I'm glad you went anyway," I said. "How did you know? Bob Aker picked me up, but then I recalled Helen's parents had promised to drive me. You remember Helen's parents, Jean and Jack?" "Of course," I said. "I saw someone who looked just like Jack this morning at breakfast in La Crosse. He made an unpleasant impression on me." It wasn't the face of the cook's father, as much as his manner, which reminded me of Jack.

"Did he now? Well, when Jean and Jack arrived, Jean suggested I drive with Jack, so she could go with Bob Aker. She wanted to see how a Cadillac felt. Of course, you know Jack, he was furious. He didn't say a word to me the entire trip to Golden Valley. I tried to keep a conversation going, but it was like talking to a pig in mud, all grunts and groans." "I like it when you talk dirty," I said. "I do not. Where was I? Oh, at dinner Jack continued sulking, except in a crowd it became both more embarrassing and less noticeable. But Jean recognized it the moment Jack and I walked in the door, and periodically she would take him aside and whisper fiercely in his ear. But he never changed. The poor woman. Before dinner, he just sat by the antique gun case, staring straight ahead. Then at the table it was as if he wasn't there. He chewed his food and Jean tried to keep conversations going, but we could all see his behavior just ate away at her. Bob Aker once tried to involve Jack in the general chatter and said, 'The lumber business sure seems to be booming.' Jack's retort stopped the dinner talk cold."

"What did he say?" I asked, curious, but also there, in the Akers' sumptuous dining room, feeling the chilly pleasure of their hospitality. "It wasn't what he said," Ettie replied in a quiet voice. "It was how he said it: 'We have nothing to complain about, but we're certainly not getting rich.'"

"He envies the Akers?" I said. "Well anyone would." "No," my wife said. "He's insanely jealous. It was Jean driving with Bob that set him off. But the most extraordinary part is that he apologized to all of us. Not that night, but by post the next day. Everyone got a humble letter. Mine said he was terribly embarrassed by his childish conduct. He was not sure his wife would ever forgive him. He said he was sorry he ruined an otherwise festive evening."

"Ettie," I said. "This man's daughter may marry our son." "Oh dear," she said. "And I heard from the Akers that Jean threatened to leave him once and for all. She's done it before." "We could celebrate a marriage and divorce before the same justice of the peace." "Do stop it," Ettie snapped. She paused. "I don't dislike Jack as much. It took courage to write those letters." "It took a wife standing in the driveway, suitcases in hand."

"Of course he was wrong. He hardly ruined a festive—just a moment there. What did you mean this man's daughter might marry our son?"

"You're the one at home," I said. "Don't you see how Henry maneuvered this phone call? He wasn't doing it to reconcile his dear old parents." "Oh lord," Ettie said. "This phone call. We've been on for hours. We'll go the poor house." I reminded my wife of Helen's arrangement. "The phone company is paying for the call." "Are you certain? I don't think it's right. Someone will find out." "Ettie," I said, wanting to change the subject. "I miss you. I think I will come home tonight."

"Who could that be?" she said. "Someone's at the door." "Fine," I said, angrily. "I'll hang up." The shadows on Route 19 had grown longer. The light of the interior forest had turned violet. I could do another tour of collecting on the bank of the river. A swallow zigzagged underneath the tent of leaves. But my wife had left the phone. "I'll get it," I heard Henry cry. I thought about hanging up, but curiosity and affection for this other interior kept me on the line. Our old house came alive again to my senses. The warm light in the kitchen that spilled into the foyer at a jagged angle. Ettie standing just beyond the light, like a superstitious cat, untying her apron strings. Henry bounding down the front stairs to intercept Greg at the door—an unknown head refracted by the stained glass of the door's porthole window. Somehow I knew who stood straightening her dress on the front porch. I heard Henry's high and cheerful voice; then it dropped an octave and I could feel my son blushing the way he always did when his emotions ran ahead of his ability to articulate them. Ettie spoke one or two indecipherable words, but she also fell silent. For a long moment there was no sound at all, except the tick of the Banff Hot Springs clock above the phone and the uphill chug of the refrigerator.

Ettie's whisper caught me off guard. "It's Helen. They've made up. You should see."

"I can," I said. "But I'm on my way home. I'll call Le Sueur from there."

"Well if you want to," Ettie said dreamily. "But don't come home on my account."

Mobile Axis: A Triptych

CLARENCE MAJOR

Liberties

LIGHT TOUCHED EVERYTHING and thereby shaped the direction of my gaze. I suddenly had a vision.

We enter the bedroom. Standing at the foot of the bed, we have a particular view of its objects: two chairs, five pictures, a mirror, a washtable, a towel on a nail, two doors, perhaps three. We take liberties with what we see.

I have stood in this corner, in this bedroom, many times, overwhelmed by the tricks it plays on me.

In the churchyard I feel nervous. I follow my eyes. They seek the red roof first. Move up the complex lines of the bell tower and down the line of the roof to the far left. Spot the red roof in the far background. It's the tip of a house on a low street that slopes down past the church. My eyes have their own intelligence yet they are pulled back by the footpath and come all the way down to the grass just in front of me. They repeat these motions.

I notice the brooding blue sky and the blue windows of the church. The angle of the light is brilliantly impossible, compositionally correct: the grass around this—the back side—is partly shaded by the presence of the awesome church. Light falls directly onto the church just above the shaded area. This gives my heart an ache it has never felt before.

Is this really the back side of the church? If not, why do I feel such extreme dislocation, even stress? This side of it seems to be engaged in a radical argument with convention. (At the same time, I happen to know that the other side is not as intricate and therefore not as interesting.)

Nothing was consciously planned.

There he is, and I still don't know what to make of him. I have a three-quarter view of the right side of his face. He has the distant look of a man who has pulled himself away from all human contact. He is not happy but feels safe, finally. Perhaps he has just been released from some hospital. It is winter. He wears a heavy overcoat and a wool cap. He is not in his own country and although he might feel homesick—along with his deeper sickness—he is not going to acknowledge it.

He looks suspicious or skeptical or maybe only critical. No, this is a look of scrutiny. Morbid depression and calm scrutiny. I've never seen him smile or even appear to be at peace with himself. Art never makes him happy.

He attempts to recreate himself. He makes the connecting parts work, in a way. In this recreation, the face seems most important to him. Yet he is not about to cry out for mercy or salvation. The face would make you think so. In his recreations of himself—his face mainly—I see what he sees: the limitations of the flesh. I see the uselessness of the material world. I see his point of view—the impasse he's reached. Yet I also see that his aspirations have not completely died.

Has he cut his hand in an accident? The right hand is bandaged. All lines move toward the bandage. The eye swings up away from the hand toward

the face, studying it, circles the cap, comes down the right side and takes in
the insecure mouth, the collar of the heavy green coat, continues up again,
down again, settles on the bandaged hand.

Every time I try not to look, my eyes are drawn back to it. As usual, it's
a three-quarter view. The longer I look the more likely I am to change my
mind. It might not be a bandage but some sort of mitten.

I've rarely seen him from any other angle. Today his eyes seem particularly close together. They are slightly below eye level, my eye level. This
arrangement makes the sharp line of the mountain range behind him very
severe in its bluntness.

He has a dazed look. The last thing the eye collects is the steam of his
breathing, lifting on the winter air. Despite the furious heat of the background—orange and red—the total effect is one of severe cold. He is obviously extremely cold—shivering, frostbitten.

Everything in and around him is airtight in its relationship to everything
else. Spiritual defeat broods in his face, in the seclusion of his mood. He in
himself is not a subject matter.

Is his theme suffering?

Are we to find no way to avoid biographical information in these recreations of this man?

Cause is no longer connected to effect.

The Industrial Revolution has yet to happen.

The revolution in interpretation itself? With nothing much to work with,
how do we know we're doing our best investigating the nature of human
activity or the stars and moon, God and the Devil, the eighteenth century,
or the man with the mitten?

We come back to him. He is standing at an oblong window looking out.
We're outside looking at him framed by the window. Through the glass we
see him all at once rather than in detail. At least at first. It's January or Febru-
ary, as usual. The country doesn't matter but it's not ours yet we live here.

We're looking up at him. Three-quarters to the left. He's stood here at
least forty different times. The composition is blunt and simple. A design of

squares, rectangles, and one circle, put together in a manner which keeps the eye returning to his miserable eyes. The lines of the blue coat and the arm and the hand—with nothing to do—suspended in the space just below his heart, are hard lines, stretched like a tight canvas. They direct the journey of our eye away from his face and back to it.

Does he possess a sense of himself? What does it mean, in the first place, to perceive one's self and the objects surrounding one's self?

Of course he's not asking such questions. He's into the pleasure principle, being far too smart to bother himself with the abstract side of the brain.

I'm thinking this. When the stimulation of the physical world surrounding him is withheld he becomes disoriented, as has been shown in sensory deprivation experiments I've subjected him to. He waits for his senses to feed him information. Should he eat the cheese? Can he take a shower now?

Nothing has changed. I am his mirror. Through me, he might recreate himself—yet again. The image of himself is no simple model but more primarily my stimulus. The human perception of him as object begs for variety—which is why I prefer to watch, say, a dog walking by beneath the window than to stand here motionless at the fence watching only his motionless, framed figure, in the window. It is a defense against boredom and the otherwise assurance of monotony.

Yet his mission to recreate himself persists. He too selects himself as stimulus and model. But with an important difference: he himself is his most familiar territory.

Knowing that it is not possible to duplicate anything seen, my sense of vision allows me to select from what I see of him in the window. Not all of him is seeable, recordable. To record his emotional substance—the misery in his eyes, for example—I have to arrange and rearrange him, stretch or shrink him, play with the distance between him and myself.

Each of the forty times he's come to this window he has appeared different. You would have thought him a different man each time. Photographs of him taken minute after minute also show a different person. At certain times he seems small for a grown man, at other times, he appears as a very large man, one with thick arms and a bull's neck. His eyes are sometimes slanted. His skin color varies from dark to pink. All the same, he never smiles.

It is several months later. He's at the same window but out here it's warm, so the season is different. He might be too hot in the house with the window closed, but there he is, standing there, as usual. Judging from his expression, he is undergoing some terrible crisis.

Again. This time he's very thin and in a blue suit. He looks like a skeleton. He's holding something—perhaps a palette or a platter. If it's a palette he's an artist, if it's a platter he's a waiter. He's looking out toward me—not *at* me—but beyond, to the left.

High above his head, hanging on one leg of what looks like an easel is a real skeleton. It looks like a mocking replica of his own body. The suspended skeleton seems to be gazing down at the man standing at the window. His gaze is one of astonishment and horror. I can see beyond his shoulder into the dimness of the room. There's a white door back there surrounded by a wall filled with framed paintings. Each face in each picture represents a version of the man at the window.

Women in Love

It's a clear night and the sky is full of stars. There's a barefoot pregnant woman standing in the yard. To her right is a two hundred year-old yardtree in which two nightbirds are communicating—

coo-claws coo-claws coo-claws
pee-cow pee-cow pee-cow

Inside the house, another woman is sitting submerged in warm water in an antique bathtub. She's watching her belly shimmer beneath the water.

Then she climbs to her knees, holding the edges of the tub, and she stands to her full height.

She now appears to be an unmovable mass: made of something other than flesh. There is no way she is ever going to move again.

She is one-sided, about to topple but she will never fall. She will continue to lean like this. Her arms are too short for her body. She could never reach her feet with those arms. Her head is also too small for her body.

Back to the pregnant woman. She has been joined by two other women. One is seated on the ground to her left and the other, also seated, is to her right. The one on the left is breastfeeding an infant. She's closer to me though she seems farther away and therefore smaller than the pregnant woman.

The seated woman would have had more foreground had she felt more important than the standing woman. Yet I do not sense that the woman in the background is actually in the background. Rather, what I sense is that in this yard these three women are serene mother-naked beings waiting for godknowswhat.

There is no background, no foreground. All aspects of the yard space are equal. In coming out here under the stars they have chosen also to ignore the rules of retreating-advancing colors. The pregnant woman now reaches down to the grass and takes up a blue shawl and throws it across her shoulder.

The right-side woman is now standing off several feet from the other two. She has her back to them. She seems to be angry, as she glances over her shoulder at them. Across her shoulder hangs a red shawl. She too is barefoot.

The moonlit yard is mostly in shades of blue.

From my point of view the scene might work better rendered in aerial perspective. That would be radical but much like a map showing the house, the yard, the women, trees and bushes. And I might even still be able to hear the birds.

Here are three or four other women in the market place.

In a window above the market is a woman with a mandolin.

The women pick through the green pears, searching for red ones. Meanwhile, the woman in the window leaves, leaving a square of black space.

One of them buys a rabbit and has the butcher chop off the legs and whack the body into four pieces. She watches him with great skill.

Another one is selecting olives from a barrel of brine. She is using a dipper.

This is the climate, as I see it:

Despair, serious illness, dread, anxiety, mortality, jealousy, perversion, dread again, the feeling of loss, the dance of death, loneliness.

At one point in his life an artist I know said that without illness and death he would have been like a ship without helm. A writer I read, once attempted to explain what he was after when he said, ". . . pain and perspiration."

So, the climate contains people.

Here they are:

A sick woman in bed.

A sick man on a road screaming.

A jealous man in the act of discovering his wife making love to her lover.

Men who are judges seated at a long table while a young woman parades before them.

Young lovers embracing in a dimly lighted room.

Broken workmen stumbling home from the mine rattling their lunch buckets.

A grief-stricken man opening the door for four visitors.

The sickbed where the dead body lies fully covered by a blunt white sheet. A young woman in the foreground looks toward a corner of the room. There are large black circles around her eyes. Her long black dress reaches her throat.

Is the screaming man, by any chance, also holding his ears? No. Is a town visible in the background? No.

The screaming man here on the long road does not represent Human Nature but is naturally human. He is running home. Sexless, nearly boneless, bodyless, miserable, he is running home. Everything swirls around him.

(There is the famous photograph of the Vietnamese girl running, naked, on a receding road, away from some disaster. Napalmed and in unbelievable agony, she runs toward the camera. General W. said the child had burned herself on a hibachi.)

So, there was no bridge. Only the road.

But *now* there is a bridge—and it's crowded.

Shocked into readiness, we watch the mob approach. Angst. The sense of desperation in the faces—as they come toward us—is chilling. They are moving in on us.

Our eye level shifts in a most disturbing manner. Nine faces are very, very visible. They are stark, yellow-white, bloodless, pious—and judging from the manner of dress—belong to beings severely distressed and repressed.

The mood of the people rushing us across the bridge is generated most dramatically by an external factor: the sky behind them. It is full of red urgency. They are fast-walking zombies. Grotesque and blunt, carved out of wood, their quest is to turn themselves into water.

When they hit us we are absorbed by their madness.

Again, the sick woman, in her sickbed, in her sick-chamber, is dying. I stand in the far corner watching the comings and goings. This is family grief—etched large. This family has known the sequence of death, from grandparents to infants. Now, the mother. The cause of death? In the old days it was tuberculosis, then it was cancer. Now it is AIDS.

My own mortality hangs on me like the rags on a scarecrow. I feel deeply the effects of the family's grief.

Mourning figures, usually in black, drift in and drift out. They are ghost-like, bloodless, seem barely to hang on. I have seen these same folk gathered and regathered in other groupings, sometimes around gravesites or coffins or other sickbeds, in fives, in tens, in threes. (Dying Mr. Chapman gave away everything he had in fours.)

Usually one female figure stares away from the rest of them, toward a wall, looking as though she can see into eternity. Her sense of loss is incalculable. Her arms are folded across her chest like a lithographic crucifixion. She seems almost ready to sink into the earth while the rest of the grief-stricken visitors move as though they recently broke loose from gravity and are now about to float softly up through the roof and beyond into the clouds.

What amazes me is the stillness, their finalized mood. The massive presence of the floor beneath my feet and the green wall behind the brooding figures suggests a closure which operates as a space sealed off from all signs of life. The light in which we stand or sit or lie is artificial. The room reeks of misery and the smell of decay. I have not adjusted to it nor to the smell of medicine.

Although I have stood here in this corner watching longer than I care to remember, I have yet to see the face of the dying woman. It's almost as though her individuality doesn't matter. She's Death with a capital D. I can see her hair but the covers of the bed are so heavy and pulled so far up around her face that it is impossible, from this angle, to determine anything about her. She might be my grandmother or my mother.

(It was the same a month ago—no, two months ago—when she used to sit up. She sat there in that armchair facing the window with the daylight pouring in on her and at times it made her look healthy. We thought she might recover. I saw only the back of her head in those days. When I entered the room there was always a nurse facing her—washing her face or dressing her—and therefore facing me as I entered to see how she was feeling. It was always the nurse who told me how the sick woman felt. She never seemed the center of her own composition. The nurse was more at center and I had the feeling she'd taken the old woman's suffering and dramatized it as her own.)

It is not I who suffers jealousy this time. It's the husband of my lover. Pity all three of us.

We have stage presence.

My lover is in a purple robe. It is opened down the front and she is mother-naked beneath. I love the swell of her belly though she is not pregnant.

We're in the garden under the latticed grapevines. (No apples, thank you. No scarlet red garments, thank you.)

We're not touching, not yet. Perhaps I am wooing her from this side of the wings. (Speculation has it that our affair is about to be discovered, that her husband, a friend of mine, is about to enter the house unexpectedly, walk through it and out into the garden and discover us together—by that time, embracing under the latticework.)

Call him Stanley.
Call her Dagmar.

Stanley now comes into the yard and Dagmar and I are embracing. Rather than flying into a rage on sight of us, Stanley backs away, stumbles, crosses the yard and stands with his head pressed against the fence. His body seems limp with the emotion that has suddenly hit it from within.

Like figures on a stage, Dagmar and I continue to embrace and to kiss and fondle each other. This is to increase the dramatic tension. The audience loves it and understands all the emotions going on.

Over where Stanley stands are large trees. They and he are in the fore-ground—at least from the audience's point of view. Therefore everybody thinks the story is primarily Stanley's. He's larger, better focused.
Dagmar and I are ironically insignificant, only villains, in the back-ground.

Although Stanley has no intention of creating a cartoon effect, he never-theless flirts with it. When he stops crying and lifts his head from the fence and looks toward the audience, his features are rather exaggerated. Rather than wanting to cry with him, the audience is tempted to laugh at his pain. A philosophical trick has been played on Stanley: he is not the serious center of his own universe.

Despite his foreground location, he begins to go out of focus and Dagmar and I come into focus. With the emphasis shifting to us, it is like a painting of a cornfield taking up ninety percent of the canvas with a ten-percent view of a strip of great historical ruins—squares, monuments, signs of Western civilization far off in the background. In this latter view, there is no doubt about the creator's intentions.

Dagmar and I kiss again. We are locked in a drypoint embrace. Our touch is aquatinted.

Later, we are in her bedroom with the heavy drapes drawn and we stand there against them embracing still. A tiny strip of female light steals through an opening in the closed drapes. I touch the lower part of her belly and she says, "Ethics takes place above the waist, morals below."

I, the larger figure, stoop a bit in order to fully embrace Dagmar. I feel her whole body lifting up into my strength with all her passion. The kiss continues, with her head thrown back, and mine bent over hers. There is a level of selflessness achieved in the moment. It is in stark contrast to the anxiety and despair we both feel when we are apart.

After we make love we go out for a walk, oblivious to Stanley, of course, although we know his anxiety and despair. On Main Street the color vibrations are soft, almost peaceful and the tonic moments of sound are muted and we can hear Abbe Costel matching the tonal effects of do, re, mi, fa, sol, la, ti, do, with colors—with emotions!—such as *do* with skyblue or *mi* with the yellow-gray of Main Street or *sol* with the quiet red of the firetruck screaming up out of Nature.

Our eye level, strangely, is above the horizon line. This is unusual for Dagmar and me because we are not especially tall. Perhaps our passion has disoriented us or things have been moved around out here. It's hard to say. We are literally looking down on the passing cars and the other evening-strollers filled with their own anxiety and despair. The faces of the people we pass are large and red.

There, also strangely, is not the slightest fear that Stanley will suddenly leap from an alley and drive a knife into my neck or into Dagmar's.

Another time. I'm watching dog-tired men leave work, headed home to wives who love them. Their lunch buckets slap against their thighs. They are filthy with coal dust. A powerful compositional line holds them together, keeps them moving miserably in the same direction—out this way, toward me.

I step to the side, fearful they may plunge forward, like slabs of a half-demolished building, and crush me.

They walk in the middle of the paved road. I move to the nearest of the two sidewalks, which is asquirm with monstrously lovely boys and girls with purple and green hair, all eager to be seen.

I lean against a barbershop wall and watch the workers go by. Their appearance suggests hotness and a muddiness that carries exhaustion, a lack of spirit. Packmules of chaos, despair, joyless reflections of each other, they bump along. Monotony is the name of the game. Redfaced, they are vehement and sensuous in an explosion of earth colors—browns, blues, juxtaposed with bloody reds and desperate orange.

The curved lines they follow are not those of Hogarth's curve of beauty—though beauty, certainly, may be found here, as in the call and response of two lovebirds first thing in the morning just outside the midsummer morning window when it is already muggy before six.

They zig-zag, they blunder along, brutal, aggressive, mean-spirited. There's violence in every step. They clash with each other, clash like moral positions at a drunken party.

They remind me of Death on the march. I remember the film of ditches full of victims of the gas chambers and other slaughters, real and filmed elsewhere, and there were curves to those ditches too, as there are curves to the lives of these men, to this street, to their bodies, as they move.

They will work till they die—if they're lucky. In the winter they will shovel snow. They, as charcoal studies, propose a skeptical future for humanity. This is not in any way a glorification or damnation of the working class.

I'm now turning, watching their backsides as they shuffle toward the vanishing point. Still in the framework, I feel the fierce effects. They are impetuous as they sneer back at the punks along the sidewalks and all the while gravity seems to be pulling their dead souls forward, out of the frame, perhaps into a pit (like the one they've just left), an abyss at their toetips.

There's a hazy moon, pyramid-gold in color.

I've climbed the fence of the racetrack. It's just after midnight. Place is totally silent except for a thump wop thump wop thump wop in the distance. It must be a horse. Somebody's out here this time of night riding?

I stay in shadows of the grandstand. The sound comes closer. Then I see the rider on a yellow nag. He's a ghost carrying a spear. He goes around and comes back. He's apparently tirelessly galloping around and around the track under the unfocused moon.

This scene, I know, says more about what remains *after* death than what is hoped to be understood before.

She wears a paint-stained white medical smock, having been unable to find a painter's. At her easel, she is surrounded by five erected card tables on which her brushes, thinner buckets and oils are scattered. The sky light falls across her left cheek and hits the tilted surface of the canvas at an angle she's worked out to reduce glare.

The painter in her studio is working carefully and slowly on a landscape view of an old rotten barn on Route 52 near Walker Valley, New York. Outside the studio window she can hear early morning birds—

dippty-sweet dippty-sweet dippty-sweet
swifty swifty swifty swifty
dippty-sweet dippty-sweet

Here, in the studio, the spirit of the birds get into her work as she paints the sense of the objects—rock, barn, sky distant farmhouse, hillside, tree—and what she achieves here (more than out on location) is a synthesis of the things. Being on the spot might limit her imagination.

(A man is walking across a field throwing seed from his apron pocket in a pattern like music. Behind him is the horizon and the cool presence of firstlight.)

I am reminded of a friend's struggles with *his* sower—a common motif—and his breakthrough with a seated Arab figure, which he considered a failure, but also which, because of its experiments with foreground perspective, opened the way for all decorative painters who came after him because of the way he *tilted* the foreground space.

The Ghetto, The Ocean, The Lynching, and The Funeral

This is a man-made world, one so closed off from Nature that the angular patterns seem to reinforce the sense of stone and flesh, hard and soft.

A black minister climbs the steps, possibly toward his own apartment.

Life on the stoop is lively: a girl sitting midway of the steps, a boy also beginning to climb up, holding to the railing. A baby in a carriage, on the

The Digitally Enhanced Image of Cary Grant[1]
Appears in a Cornfield in Indiana[2]

MICHAEL MARTONE

IN SEPTEMBER, BENJAMIN DAY, his wife Irene, and their two sons Norbert
and August witnessed the miraculous and seemingly spontaneous appearance of the actor Cary Grant (in his role as Roger Thornhill in Hitchcock's

1. Cary Grant was born Archibald Leach on 18 January 1904 in Bristol,
   England, to an overly possessive mother and distant father.
2. Admitted as the nineteenth state in 1816. The area was controlled, by
   France until 1763 and then by Great Britain until 1783. Population
   5,490, 260. Or a borough of west-central Pennsylvania, east-northeast
   of Pittsburgh.

North by Northwest)[3] in the opposite oncoming unpaved shoulder of U.S. Route 41 at Prairie, a rural Greyhound bus stop, near Ade, Indiana, halfway between Chicago and Indianapolis. The bewildered apparition responded (as the Days, on the way to Irene's sister's place in Kentland, pulled over to park) with a look of anxious anticipation as if he (Cary Grant)[4] had perhaps come to this spot to rendezvous with a person or persons unknown to him at this otherwise deserted location (the very situation portrayed in the movie). Cary Grant[5] (who the Days had recognized only from his performances in movies and mainly then when replayed on television) flickered on the side of the road, the pattern[6] of his tailored suit[7] strobing in the bright sunlight. Seemingly vexed and appearing to be searching for words, the actor (who the Days believed had been dead for years)[8] undid the button on his jacket and, squinting, looked both north and south, scanning for traffic before beginning to cross the empty highway approaching the Days' automobile in a rather sheepish manner. "Hi," it (or he) said. "Hot day." Mr. Day responded with, "Seen worse." There was a long uncomfortable silence during which the solid projected image of the screen actor wavered and seemed to dissipate. Through the translucent chest of the tongue-tied matinée idol, the Days now noted an emerging insect-like speck on the horizon of what would become

3. Originally known as *The Man in Lincoln's Nose*, *North by Northwest* came by its official title from *Hamlet*: "I am mad north-north-west."

4. For the rest of his life, he felt that his insecurity with women, his desire to control them, stemmed in large measure from being led to believe that his mother had abandoned him.

5. He had been offered many millions to write his autobiography. He refused, saying he didn't want to embarrass anyone, including himself.

6. Glen plaid checks, originally known as Glen Urquhart checks. Glen plaid, sometimes referred to as "Prince of Wales" checks, was initially woven of saxony wool and was later found in tweed, cheviot, plied, and worsted cloth.

7. Brooks Brothers introduced the No. 1 sack suit in 1895. Designed to fit all body types, the suit offered soft natural shoulders, a single-breasted jacket, and full plain-front trousers.

8. 11:22 PM, 29 November 1986. Massive stroke. While visiting Davenport, Iowa, with his *Conversation* show.

the menacing crop dusting biplane[9] growing larger as it a) approached or b) became visually enriched by continuing production of escaped free radical holographic microwave carrier pixel transmissions or c) grew in the mass pixilated mind of the hysterical family Day seriously effected by an hallucinogenic toxin produced by secretions from mold spores present on the rye bread of their recently consumed ham sandwiches or d) became another (along with the miraculous image of Cary Grant) actual blessed mystery of The Lord God Almighty. The ultimate of the above list of options chosen by the Days (devout Roman Catholics) themselves during their recovery and currently under investigation by the Diocese of Fort Wayne/South Bend as an actual miracle attributed to the intercession of the Beatified Wendell Willkie and commemorated by a small shrine on the spot and its inclusion in the officially sanctioned pilgrimage of St. James of the Starry Fields. "Are you supposed to be meeting someone here?" the resolidified image of Cary Grant asked the inanimate Days who then (as if on cue) shook their heads *no* in unison. "Oh, then a, then you're name isn't Kaplan?" At this point the details of the event in the Days' retelling become somewhat sketchy. But there is a transition of some kind as the distant airplane[10] on the horizon metastasizes above their heads, leading to the reenactment of the celebrated chase of Cary Grant by the aforementioned crop dusting biplane[11] through a cornfield[12] in Indiana. On the first pass, Grant falls down onto the dirt[13] covering

9. The single-engin Stearman biplane was originally designed as a simple, sturdy, military, two-seater trainer. The history of agricultural aviation dates back to 1917 when a cotton field in Louisiana was dusted.

10. The aircraft is flown with a constant throttle, the pilot regulating the altitude with the stick. If the airplane is equipped with an adjustable propeller, which is kept in course pitch. Longitudinal trim is mostly set in neutral. Some pilots prefer a slight nose-up setting, which gives additional safety in the event of striking birds or other incidents.

11. It is evident that prolonged low-altitude flying puts severe strain upon the pilot and calls for very special qualities.

12. A polystichous diploid with unisex inflorescences and rigid rachilla.

13. Alluvium: soil deposited by water such as a flowing river. Duff: soil found on the forest floor, leaf litter, and other organic debris in various stages of decay. Eluvium: soil and mineral particles blown and deposited by the wind. Gumbo: fine silty soil known for its sticky mud.

his head as the plane swoops low then running again only to collapse once more into a "shallow depression" as the overtaking plane unleashes a barrage of automated[14] weapons[15] fire (the end result of which is the eruption of soil all around the prostrate and vaporous Cary Grant spraying him with the resulting vaporized dirt). Scrambling up from the ground, Grant then runs back to the highway to flag down an approaching car that passes through him without slowing down. He turns and runs (and falls), pursued by the rapidly accelerating, diving biplane into a stand of dried corn[16] (brittle in the wind kicked up by strafing plane flying a few feet above the tasseled stalks). The plane circles for another pass, this time emitting contrails of aerially applied insecticide[17] on Cary Grant's suspected location in the rows of corn. The cloud of descending poison[18] blankets him (a ghost in a ghostly cloud). He reaches for a handkerchief and covers his mouth and nose. Flushed and flushed from hiding, Grant breaks back into the open, heading for the highway once again (where in the movie a fuel tanker truck will run him over and then said truck receives in a fiery crash the too closely pursuing menacing aircraft). But then Cary Grant just disappears in mid-stride as the Days

14. An automatic weapon is one in which the process of feeding, firing, extracting, and ejecting is carried out by the mechanism of the weapon after a primary manual, electric, or pneumatic cocking as long as the trigger is held and the supply of ammunition in the belt, feed strip, or magazine lasts.

15. These weapons embodied simple blowback actions and were chambered for cartridges from caliber .45 to 9mm with magazine capacities of 25–32 rounds and operated in cyclic rates of 500–600 rounds per minute at a maximum effective range of two hundred yards.

16. Corn demands a quantity of water because it sweats, or "transpires," heavily. A full-grown plant on a hot July day in an Iowa cornfield will transpire five to nineteen pounds of water, while an acre of plants will transpire seven hundred and twenty tons.

17. DDT is an abbreviation derived from the common name d(ichloro) d(iphenyl)t(richloroethane). The proper name for the insecticidal compound is 1,1,1, tricloro-2,2*bis*(parachlorophenyl)etane.

18. The storage of DDT on human fat is a consequence of its differential solubility. DDT is almost completely insoluble in water but much more soluble in non-polar solvents, including lipid tissue.

gape (their memories of the event expired or their memory of the movie incomplete). The airplane (too) vanishes. "But what has really happened?" the narrator intones. The Days of Ade, Indiana, have told their story to a variety of interested governmental, religious, academic, and media entities whose representatives descended upon this part of Indiana like flights of menacing crop dusting biplanes. The recounting of events has now been transcribed and archived (as well) assuring that the next appearance of Cary Grant in Indiana will be all the more complete (approaching perfection in its exactness, in its subsequent re-iterations), looped (as it were) back into this place (the focal point of a few feet of framed film) this place that (most will tell you) wasn't on the map (perhaps), never really existed before the movie (*North by Northwest*) was produced and shown and brought this tiny sacred (what?) precinct (stuttering) to a kind of life . . .

"Hangin' Hawkins"

Talking to My Old Science Teacher about Drawings in which I Killed Him

BRIAN McMULLEN

Half my life ago, as a fifth grader at Maumee Valley Country Day School in Toledo, Ohio, I began to draw a lot. I would go to my oversize Christmas-present sketchbook on weekday afternoons, when the Nintendo was off-limits, and fill it with made-up stuff: new comic book characters and sketches for video game sequels. One afternoon, though, I decided to draw a picture of my science teacher, Mr. Hawkins, hanged at the gallows. I liked drawing that picture. I liked adding the details: the drooling tongue, the unzipped fly, the "1-800-GALLOWS" service mark. In four more after-school drawings, I brought new kinds of secret justice to the mean Mr. Hawkins: a guillotine, a meat cleaver, and a peashooter.

For Cabinet *magazine's "Enemy" issue, I thought I'd try to find Mr. Hawkins, show him the secret drawings, and ask to have a telephone conversation. This actually worked. Mr. Hawkins, who is now retired, was kind enough to talk with me for three and a half hours. Here are some excerpts from the conversation.*

BRIAN McMULLEN: My first question is—you've seen the drawings now. Do you have any questions?

MR. HAWKINS: Oh, I don't think so. They're pretty straight-forward.

BM: Okay.

MH: Over the years, there were lots of talented artists who did this sort of thing. Was there a Franklin[1] contemporary with you?

BM: Yeah, Matt Franklin. Did you catch him with drawings of you?

MH: Well, no, but his younger brother did this sort of thing. I don't know if he drew me, but he drew these kinds of pictures. He was a really fabulous artist for that age. I mean, I would have to say better than you in his ability to depict reality.

BM: Okay.

MH: But he was into heavy metal and all kinds of stuff, so a lot of his drawings were pretty gory and pretty violent.

BM: Were they secret?

MH: Well, some were and some weren't. Every kid in the entire UI[2] knew he was an artist. He would illustrate his projects and also just draw pictures, for the fun of it, that were fairly dramatic. I never saw him do anything like this, but he and I had a very rocky relationship, so it wouldn't surprise me at all if somewhere in his stuff are pictures a lot like these.

BM: I see.

MH: But you know, I don't remember you and I having any particularly difficult times.

BM: Well, outside my mind I don't think we did. I liked approval, I hated to get caught, and I hated the thought of having my name written on the board.

MH: Uh-huh.

1. All names besides Mr. Hawkins and P. T. Barnum have been changed.
2. UI = Upper Intermediate, the title of the combined fifth and sixth grades at Maumee Valley Country Day School.

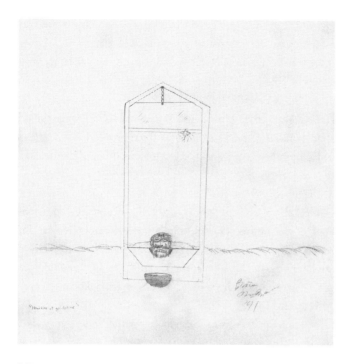

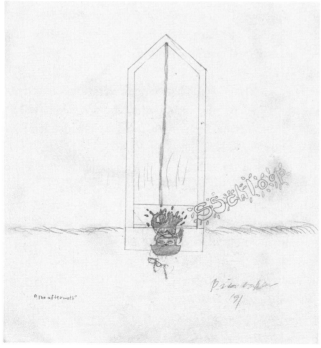

BM: In fifth grade I remember thinking—in a big vague way, you know—that you were mean. Before I decided to send you these drawings, I tried to come up with a list of reasons why I thought you were mean. First on the list is your gruff voice. And your directness. You're not a coddler, as I recall.

MH: Yes. Very true. The only kids I would coddle were the ones I'd identified as having some sort of emotional problem.

BM: I remember you were the first teacher I heard swear.

MH: Yeah, probably.

BM: I was around the corner, in Mrs. Burke's room, playing a word game. Suddenly, your chalk tray—the big, five-foot-long, magnetic one—fell off the board. The sound was unmistakable. In reaction, you said *damnit*. The word grumbled out of you like—and I had this analogy pre-prepared—like a warning groan from a dormant volcano. It was low and soft and everywhere. I was scared. You scared me.

MH: Hmmm.

BM: There was also this time when you gathered up everyone's Nintendo Game Boys into a black Hefty bag before we got off the bus for Camp Joy. You were the Grim Reaper.

MH: At the time, did you understand why we did that?

BM: Well, yeah. The integrity of the trip—it was the trip to the Joy Outdoor Education Center in Clarksville . . .

MH: Right.

BM: The Game Boys would have completely compromised the point of the trip. A bunch of kids staring into screens would have killed, or seriously hurt, the group bonding that was supposed to happen.

MH: And we didn't explain that to you?

BM: Well, I'm sure you did. But there's hearing the explanation and then there's giving up the fragile, favorite toy.

MH: The team of teachers, probably long before you guys, had made decisions about how to handle situations like this, the collection of distracting materials like Game Boys.

BM: But you were the guy holding the Hefty bag.

MH: Yeah, right. And there would have been somebody else on the other bus with another Hefty bag.

BM: I hid my Game Boy from you.

MH: [*laughs*] Really?

BM: I thought it would get scratched or broken. You plus garbage bag equaled problem. But I didn't use the Game Boy the whole trip. I was afraid you'd catch me. You seemed to have eyes everywhere. A dormant volcano, Grim Reaper with eyes everywhere.

MH: That was a myth we encouraged.

BM: Another and I think really important thing that helped me think you were mean was the beard. The neat, full, black-and-white beard. Do you still have the beard?

MH: Oh yeah.

BM: You were my only bearded teacher until high school. I have this theory that the beard was a key part of your authority.

MH: Really?

BM: Yeah. Remember the P. T. Barnum musical?

MH: Yeah.

BM: It was surprising enough to see you, the science teacher, on stage. Everyone else was a student. But the really shocking thing was that you had shaved your beard. You came out beardless and you danced all around, singing this song about feeling like a kid again. Suddenly you were this big lovable softie. When you took the beard off, a wall came down.

MH: I hadn't thought about it, but that makes perfect sense.

BM: Your smile beamed. For the first time, maybe, people could see what it looked like. The smile.

MH: All through the rehearsals, there was no discussion of the beard coming off. But my wife and I, weeks before the show, talked about how weird it was for me to be up there, singing like a kid and having this beard on. I said, "I think I'll shave it off." And she said, "Well, I guess so." She wanted to know if I'd ever shaved it off before.

BM: Had you?

MH: No, never since 1968 when I started growing it, in Japan, in my first year of teaching. Not for an illness or anything. So during the opening numbers of the show, I went back to the restroom and shaved it off. It was incredibly painful. The whole time I was doing it, I kept asking myself, "Why did I think to do this? But oh well, I can't stop now, with half the beard gone. I have to continue."

BM: Was it physically painful?

MH: Oh yeah. I had a styptic pencil with me to stop the bleeding, and I used bits of toilet paper. I didn't think the bleeding would stop before I had to head down the aisle, but it did. My own mother-in-law didn't recognize me. My wife had to tell her it was me. And the looks on the faces of the kids who were supposed to be responding to my cues, they were incredulous. Their jaws were down to their knees.

BM: It was shocking, you in the spotlight, beardless.

MH: And that was the desired reaction.

BM: Does the beard keep you warm?

MH: [*laughs*] Not particularly. It's good when you're skiing. In the summer, I keep it short. There were some times in the '70s when I wore it long, when it was momentarily fashionable, but since those days I haven't let it grow longer than an inch and a half or so.

BM: Are you the kind of guy who's sensitive to fashion trends? I wouldn't guess that you are.

MH: Not particularly. I buy clothes for their particular, you know, use-value rather than for how they look. I bought Carhartt working clothes long before they were fashionable. I buy them because they're the best.

BM: In this first drawing, "Hangin' Hawkins," with the "1-800-GALLOWS," I've put you in . . . Do you have the drawings with you?

MH: Yeah, they're right here.

BM: I've put you in a cable-knit turtleneck sweater and white loafers. If you were to go to the gallows, what kind of clothes would you wear? Were these a good guess?

MH: [*laughing*] I don't know. I always think of that situation. I mean, not for myself to be in it, but you wear whatever the person's given you to wear. You don't have a choice.

BM: If you had to make one last fashion statement on the gallows, though.

MH: I don't know. I guess it would depend on what I was being hanged for.

BM: For being a mean teacher.

MH: [*hint of annoyance*] Yeah, right. I wouldn't care what I was wearing at that point. The sweater in that drawing is something I would have worn a lot in the winter. But I don't understand the shoes.

BM: I think those were the shoes I felt comfortable trying to draw. My dad had some loafers with elaborate tasseley tongues. They weren't white.

MH: They wouldn't have been my shoes, that's for sure.

BM: Let's switch over to the meat cleaver drawing.

MH: Okay.

BM: That's Bobby Larkin holding the cleaver.

MH: What was the students' impression of Bobby Larkin?

BM: He was not a very smart kid, but he was a fun kid. He would do things that were, uh . . . He was my friend, but I didn't see him as an equal. I took advantage of the kid. There was this incident where I had this idea to send you magazine subscriptions using Business Reply Mail cards.

MH: Uh-huh.

BM: That was my idea.

MH: Uh-huh.

BM: I'd bring these subscription cards from my mom's magazines in to school, and my regular friends—my bring-home friends—thought the idea of sending you the magazines was kind of funny, but I didn't ask them to do it. I didn't think they would have actually done it. They liked the idea in theory.

MH: You didn't do it, did you?

BM: I did do it.

MH: Oh, it was you? It wasn't Bobby Larkin?

BM: It was Bobby and me, both.

MH: Oh, okay. Because we assumed right off the bat—I told my colleagues about it—we assumed it was Bobby Larkin because we couldn't think of anyone else who would do that. Although I do have to admit, we sort of wondered how he would have gotten the idea. [*laughs*] Luckily, it wasn't a big problem. All I had to do was call up the magazines and tell them I hadn't subscribed, and that usually took care of it.

BM: So they actually sent you copies of these magazines? *Better Homes and Gardens?*

MH: Yeah, whatever it was.

BM: Did you read any of them?

MH: Oh, I don't know. At first I assumed it was a computer error. My information accidentally got entered in the wrong place. But after several magazines came, one of my colleagues said, "Someone's doing it to jerk your chain." Our person of choice was Bobby Larkin because, I don't know if you knew this, but we were afraid of him.

BM: [*laughs*] I didn't know.

MH: Not terrifying afraid, but we were afraid in the sense of thinking he might do something. I mean, you know when Columbine happened? We all thought, "This is something that Bobby Larkin could have done if the situation were different."

BM: Man, I don't know. I guess I can see that perspective. But one thing I liked about Bobby was that what you saw was what you got. He wasn't a seether. Maybe he was scary because he was incapable of creating a façade, or seemed to be. Anyway, his recklessness was different and exciting. He was not afraid, so to speak, to get his name on the board.

MH: A lot of our fear was centered around the kinds of things that you might not have seen. Things he did to other kids. And the kinds of things he wrote about were worrisome. For a kid to be able to express those kinds of things, in writing, in school, as part of an assignment, made him a candidate for "let's watch him."

BM: So his writing was expressive. Was it good?

MH: It was really bad. Extremely violent. And, to be fair, all boys in fifth and sixth grade, or almost all, write that kind of stuff. I did too. One of my hobbies when I was that age was planning bank robberies.

BM: [*laughs*] Neat.

MH: [*laughing*] We even went as far as to go downtown and walk into a bank so we could see what it looked like inside. I mean, it didn't last long. It went on for about a month, and then we ran out of gas and went on to something else. But Bobby's stuff seemed strange to us.

BM: We talked about you shaving your beard for P. T. Barnum. There was this other weird, surprising fifth-grade theater moment. I don't remember the details, but it was at the spring talent show . . .

MH: The blackface thing?

BM: Yeah! On talent show night, I just remember these two girls coming out in front of the whole school—teachers, parents, everyone—with shoe polish on their faces. And they spoke with this thick embarrassing drawl. What happened?

MH: What happened was we had some kids who wanted to do this skit. So they went through all the rehearsals, and they never used blackface. They never suggested it or brought it up. While they were preparing, we were very careful to have discussions with them about one particular part of the skit . . .

BM: What was the skit about?

MH: Well, in this one part there were two mothers, one black and one white. Each one had a child. There were black and white characters, but the skit wasn't about being black and white. We had discussions with the kids, telling them to be sure they didn't camp it up.

BM: Were they using the thick drawl in rehearsals?

MH: They were trying all kinds of things. We asked them to be careful. But blackface never entered into it.

BM: Did the students write the script?

MH: No, it was a canned script. Anyway, two of the kids in this skit were really into acting. I remember—and forever this moment has hung with me—I remember I was backstage walking around in the area where they were preparing, and I leaned my head in the door and said, "You guys are on next." And I saw them putting on blackface. But it was just a fleeting instant, and I moved on to what I was doing, and they went onstage. It didn't register on me quick enough to stop them. I mean, I could just say I never saw them at all. But I did see them. It didn't dawn on me fast enough to say, "You can't do that." And so they went on, and oh man, all hell broke loose. We scheduled several meetings with parents. We explained that the kids didn't have any idea that this was wrong. It took about two weeks for everyone to come out mollified.

BM: I remember a big school meeting the day after the show. I was excited that something big was happening. People had messed up. We were missing class. During the big meeting, you stood up in front of everyone and you broke into tears. Before that, I don't think I'd ever seen a teacher cry.

MH: That's because you weren't in my literature class. Every time I would finish a sad book, I'd always cry.

BM: Really?

MH: Oh yeah. There's a book called *A Day No Pigs Would Die*. I read it aloud with the kids every other year I was at Maumee Valley, and I've never been able to get through the ending without crying. Kids would tell their younger siblings about it, to look forward to it.

BM: So your tears became an event to anticipate. Old Faithful.

MH: Yeah.

BM: What happens at the end of the book?

MH: The main character buries his father and takes over as a man in the family. And the way it's written is so touching. Even the hardest kid gets touched by the end of that book.

BM: I see.

MH: Even Bobby Larkin might have been touched.

BM: I'm happy we could talk. I'm going to send you a subscription to *Cabinet*. Don't cancel it.

MH: Oh, sure. If you need more, call back.

P.S. While preparing for this conversation, I called 1-800-GALLOWS, the phone number on the gallows in the "Hangin' Hawkins" drawing. The number, I learned, belongs to Ventura Metals, a manufacturing company in Ventura, CA. (Motto: "Meeting all metal needs.") At their website, *www .venturametals.com*, I discovered that 1-800-GALLOWS also spells 1-800-4-ALLOYS—the company's official phone-number spelling.

I called Ventura Metals back and asked if they could make me a makeshift gallows—a 15-foot steel pole, bent 90 degrees at the 10-foot mark, suitable for anchoring in the ground and suspending 500 pounds. It turns out that, yes, with two weeks of lead time, for approximately $700 postpaid, the people at 1-800-GALLOWS will make-to-order and ground-ship, to your United States residence, an actual gallows.

A Harvest

GLENN MEETER

"We shall come rejoicing, bringing in the sheaves."

Ah, Spring is in the air, and the blood leaps to the highway's call. Fields from Kansas to the Panhandle lie white unto the harvest, and north from Dakota to Athabaska's smoking muskeg the acres of green blades glitter, potentially gold. Each time the earth turns around the sun spreads eighteen hours of light at your feet like a rose and silver rug. In a dozen ports of entry comrades and customers wait, scanning the sky which bulges profitably blue, and pray your safe arrival. Grain prices climb with the arc of the sun, the great plain labors with bread for the world, and your harvesters wait for you, greased, gassed, insured. Come along!

If you hesitate I can understand. You, like myself, are no tiller of soil, no giant in the earth, no warrior, pioneer, entrepreneur, no Hemingway hero

either (bull fighter, expatriate soldier, wounded fisher for trout), but more of
an Updike sort of fellow, a dealer in certain abstractions, propositions, positions, promotions, situations . . .

An expert. Our offices maintain forever a temperate, shady, though well-
lighted climate. We do work that is also done by women. How to suspend
disbelief in a job that follows the seasons, rises with the dawn, engages heavy
machines against the earth? And how to imagine ourselves part of such a
thick-fingered family as this, where wives get up in darkness to bake bread
for their men, make their breakfasts, clean their boots, and then deferentially
wake them, obeisance in the touch of their hands?

"Hank—"

A genuflection in the dark doorway; on his bed the god stirs, phlegmatic.
"Coffee's ready—Hank?"

Imagine only a marriage. One female child in this tribe of farmers and
mowers, escaping the usual fate of exposure to the elements, was allowed to
grow up and go to the city: there you married her, partly from that romantic
streak that makes you sometimes mention that your grandfather lived "on
the land." And so here you are on the prairie, en route to metropolitan in-ser-
vice expense-paid and tax-deductible conference, convention, symposium,
or workshop, breathing the once-a-year air, getting your hair cut for a dollar
and a quarter, and storing the mind with second-hand rural delights.

You are no harvester. You feel that, though their smiles around the groaning board concede that freeways are as worthy an opponent as nature; you
feel it in the pallor of your fingers on rough-textured slices which they cut
from thick, legendary loaves and butter with the high-priced spread, loyal
to their guild. You are no harvester but you agree to a harvest of sorts: you
will drive with an older brother (he leaves his farm to a sixteen-year-old
son) seven hundred grassy miles south, so that he can replace the youngest
brother on a combine crew. This youngest brother, now swinging a John
Deere across Oklahoma like Alley Oop on a brontosaurus, must be brought
home and fitted with uniform and sleeping bag and kit, for he is going to war.
Not the real war—that would cast some melancholy over the trip. This is
only a summer practice for the National Guard, two weeks in the Black Hills
like a vacation (the mother laughs, fitting South Dakota's coyote emblem the
wrong way on his sleeve, and contentedly, as if sewing baby garments, does
her stitches again); and so you look forward whole-heartedly to your part in
this son-gathering expedition, your part which consists, as you admit with a
deprecating laugh, mostly of going along for the ride.

Secretly you feel otherwise. Your journey is only two days, but a day to fruit flies and to God is as a thousand years, and space too is experience, like time. From the beginning, swimming awake in the wake of dawn (your wife, resuming country courtesy, treads softly round your altar), splashing costly water on your eyelids (uncertain of bathroom manners where toilets, a recent innovation, flush reluctantly), breakfasting to the hushed flutes of wood doves, you sense in this journey a numinous significance, something to be memorialized beyond mere quantities of mileage. The stacks of homemade buns, the phallic Thermos, the wife's goodbye, the father's blessing ("Good luck," as he puts on his hat for the fields), the sunglasses, the shaving kit, the auto club's *Great Plains Guidebook* unfolding mighty alluvions of glacier and river and road, and the geography of the trip itself, south and north with nature against the course of westering civilization, down the continent's midriff with buffalo and red men and no others until the harvester crews—this gives an aureole of purpose even to keeping a drowsy driver awake or transporting a boy from work to rituals of war. Suffused with lightness and power, you make with the roughboned farmer beside you (Gerald, pronounced with a hard *r* like the clashing of gears) an emblem of spirit and flesh like the prairie-and-cloud horizon, on your right as you roll to the south.

"Farming seems . . . Impersonal, nowadays. Nobody builds barns anymore. Only sheds. Quonset huts. I bet the last real barns were built thirty, fifty years ago."

An easy opening but his nod is brief. Perhaps he senses what you now recognize, that in the in-law's extension of sibling rivalry you minimize his job by subsuming it under your own. But acres of morning silence marshal your argument: as the grass breathes quietly, wet with sleep, sunlight speeds infinitesimal packs of energy down conveyor-belts to each green plant. A lark spirals upward, following the phrases of its song, life imitating art. Trees in windbreaks angling stiffly north and west deny the non-Euclidean curves of earth. Thermos-shaped silos, bullets, aim at the sky. The Missouri River, mapped by Lewis and Clark, dammed by Army engineers, is an artificial lake; crossing it, and crossing a line purely intellectual, academic, you enter a new state where people owe allegiances in a different direction and even wildlife is preserved in different seasons, under different rules.

"The modem farmer is citified, really. Half engineer, half scientist. And market analyst. And politician. Lobbyist. Plants and animals don't have much to do with it." He smiles as at a falsely clever witticism. "How about Harlan?"

Harlan, the oldest brother, is known to love the creatures which he raises for slaughter. It is easy to show that Harlan's ability to call a hundred Herefords by name, making fine discriminations in spine-length, placement of eyes, and whorls of white hair, or, bending over a patch of native sod, to name the individual gramma and buffalo grasses and blue-grass and fescue, annuals and perennials, up to fifteen varieties symbiotically existing in one square foot of "grass"—that this is less instinct or love of earth than sheer intellectual power, categorizing and abstract.

Though eroded grease on his pin-striped bib overalls proclaims him a Quonset and machine, not a barn man, Gerald shrugs and steps on the gas, leaving in his dust a town named for the philosopher Spencer. "Well, Harlan always had a memory on him." His bulk on the front seat puts you in his field of gravity, so that you have to lean slightly toward the window. Your point is, the whole ecology of the plains is a web of civilization's weaving—cattle from Scotland and England and Holland, the horse from Spain, the Chinese elm, the Russian olive, the exotic pheasant, the wheat itself, all from Asia, hardly one thing unimported in all the rustic prairie . . . Asia evokes the Guardsman who is the goal of your journey, and with him the image of ships passing on the Pacific, one heavy with bayonets and the other with wheat and pheasants and silver-leaved trees. You swing to an explanation of the excesses done in the name of progress, the making of the Dust Bowl, the slaughter of buffalo, the ravishment of the Black Hills—these should not be charged to the rational or civilizing principle but to its opposite, a naked instinctive greed. These were mere practical men, their trouble was they didn't *think*.

Gerald keeps his eyes on the road, which glitters now in the sharper angle of the sun. His answer is to ask for lunch, an instinctive rhetoric that forces you to woman's subservience: you serve, he eats and drinks, driving easily with one hand through Greeley, Nebraska. Greeley, a town with shaggy elms and sewers that hump the road, was named for a journalist who was himself named Horace after the Roman poet; and as you consider this link between the cultures of Rome and Greeley, Gerald says, "Somebody had to kill them though. Else we couldn't raise any crops."

He means the buffalo. But in the wake of his seriousness poets, journalists, and all their progeny of wordsmen seem to expire feet up on the prairie, bull calf and cow, useful like the bison to exhibit in museums or for the delicacy of their tongue. Outside the narrow sundrenched streets of St. Paul Gerald jabs a finger: "There's wheat." It is his language, harsh vowels and burred

consonants, that has power. *Thairʒweet*. There's wheat, there's wheat; Garden
City has froze *out*, but here by God there's wheat!—Gerald giving *by God* its
full significance, *here, by divine pleasure, our daily bread*. Green waves break
past the window into individual spears, drilled in rows. There's wheat. In
Red Cloud, home of Willa Cather, where the sons of pioneers have built
a Willa Cather curio shop and museum in an abandoned dry-goods store
where a white-haired lady has lunch alone from wax paper and Dixie Cup,
Gerald stops for gas and lets you take the wheel.

Downs, Osborne, Luray, Russell, Great Bend, St. John, Pratt. Map-
knowledge is a poor substitute for Gerald's blood-memory, seasons of pushing the big rigs over weary hills. Kansas, announced by signs as the home
of sunflowers and Miss America, offers empty, rock-edged fields, farmed
by remote control from the irrigated towns. It is a mistake that no one lives
between Downs and Osborne or walks the twenty-two miles between Osborne and Luray or touches with his hand the stone fence-posts between
Luray and Russell. Dead houses, gray eyeless skulls where once Eisenhower
and Dorothy of Oz and Olympic distance-runners and Miss America lived;
thousands in your city hole like lab-mice while in all non-urban Kansas only
a lineman in a tin hat and an orange-vested road crew breathe the country air,
which they taint with fumes of tar. Man should live in harmony with nature:
Gerald agrees, speaks of shooting deer in Wyoming while his eyes are on
the wheat. Yellow already. Be cutting before Oklahoma. It is hot, your back
aches, your eyeballs burn, the white line like a carpenter's tape zips to your
forehead. There is fatigue in doing nothing but sitting in control of power.
In the cool sky a white hawk swims, sailing with dignity though pursued
by small frantic housekeeping birds down a secret river of air. A truck on
its back, wheels and dirty belly skyward amid alarmed red flags, floods you
with the sweetness of existence. Why not live like hawk or bird or Negro
boy on a bicycle (Kansas was a slave state once, but in this boy in Pratt or
the black nurse sashaying through the heat of Medicine Lodge appears no
sullenness like that on the faces of black strivers in your city, born bitter
and consciously oppressed)—why not this simple state of being? Ah, down
here the Mobil gas man speaks softly Southern and you bless the memory
of unpainted wooden signs of Pentecostals, Baptists, and Brethrens who replace the Midwest Gothic Lutherans and Catholics and tight-sphinctered
Reformed, whose metal advertisements back North always took the shape
of shields or arrows. The Methodists have been with you all the way, like
the poor, but down here they too build churches of wood not brick, speak

slow, live warm and easy like the soft-barked cottonwoods not ranked in rows but sauntering, graceful, following in lazy curves the flow of water and the land.

Wheat is being cut. Leathery men and kerchiefed peasant women, the flash of whose bare arms is more seductive than all Hollywood. Cramped in a crazy speeding furnace which perverts the sun's love, your right leg growing numb, you envy the laboring man his nightly sweet-breathed sleep, still more the exhausting no-nonsense heavy-limbed coupling which you imagine to take place when the sun goes down in Kansas.

> Oh the people never wed
> Or so I've heard it said
> They just tumble into bed
> In Kansas.

This tune together with Champlin, "Great Name in the Great Plains," drifts through the brain's dry channels into Oklahoma. Big-armed combines shoulder you to the ditch, and their drivers, kings of the road, hold left hands as blinders to the sun and happily chew one thought, the four-dollar acres of Kansas tomorrow. You envy them, yes, and heavy instinctive Gerald, since Nature is the name of all paradises—but how, without you, would they abstract an ideal from even the barns wombing their own childhoods, hay cattle and boy one warmth with mice and lantern and cat against the snow? Without you, without vision, they were blinded lemmings who trampled their way to disaster, Quonset huts, war . . .

Gerald takes the wheel. It is a relief to bathe the mind in longing for supper and bed. Fatigue swims out of Chester, Seiling, Taloga. Though your journey began in June it's August, Dakota's yellow dandelions gone to seed, the green wheat burned white, and below the Canadian River's trickle (Drink Canada *Dry*), hardly a stalk uncut. Cicadas sing in the evening heat. Dust blows from fall plowing, burros on the red rock chew brown grass. Hills, horses; tractors, plains. At Hobart conical mountains loom like promises unfulfilled from the horizon you will never reach, and glad of it—Abilene, Laredo, salt and oil, Mexico and the other Americas funneling poverty down to the Horn, the thought of those miles daring to exist to be traveled in other journeys burdens the mind like a concept of stars or religion.

"There they are."

Washed clean for Kansas, trucks bearing Gerald's name stand at roadside tailing docile green elephants. Gerald is renewed; while you stay in the car he braves a farmer's dog to find the trailer parked near a field of pinto beans. There the youngest brother and his crew stow beer-cans and pack guitar, records, dirty bedding, socks, hats, paper-backed history, and pornography, moving on. "A bitter run," says the crew, mocking careful epic Gerald. "Ah, 'twas a bitter run." One, who averages less than average at Chadron State, so says the youngest brother, is wearing a Harvard sweatshirt. Showered, sunburned, using life's first razor, they trust nightfall and a clean truck to bring them the girls of Oklahoma. As for you, after supper with the brothers-in-law (chicken in jackets of batter), after wandering Hobart's dark streets to pay hospitable but accurately profit-taking garagemen and restaurateurs, you lie dirty and relaxed on one of Hobart Hotel's three-dollar beds while Gerald on another sleeps vigorously, his breath threatening the springs. Floating free of him in the rattle of air-conditioning like a soul leaving a body, you have a thought he would never have, that life, like your journey, is half over; and you ask, sinking asleep, not disappointed but in a curiously self-congratulatory way, pleased with your discovery, what, oh what have I done, what have I left behind me but the miles?

Morning brings June again, dark-bellied clouds on a cool wind. A long-tailed swallow, trailing straw, hovers near the combine's cutter-bar arm, measuring against hereditary minuscule blueprints: before she darts away you see the tiny wing-pits working hard, red against the trim white chest as if she sweats blood. Everything, the sky, your body, is washed clean. You travel now with Brian, the youngest; leaving the others plodding behind, you speed to Chester, where you breakfast on doughnuts (only a nickel in the wheat flour Bible Belt, good measure, pressed down, running over), and Brian arranges jobs for his crew through the agency of the café waitress.

"He *was* waiting on some fellows from Minnesota. I *believe*."

Uh-huh. Well, whatever he wants to do. We'll be in today, is all.

"Well, he ain't but one big field, I know *that's* ready now . . ."

Uh-huh. Well, far as that goes, we could start within three, four hours. Maybe less. If he wants to have it done.

"Well, I could *call*, I s'pose . . ."

Well, uh, we've got two trucks. If he needs any hauling. And two rigs. If you think he wants it done right away.

"Well, why don't I just call him, then."

Well, I guess it wouldn't hurt. We did four hundred acres down to Hobart.

Tall, pale, thin-legged, narrow-faced, Brian is different from his brother. His speech is submissively persistent. At twenty-three the captain of delicate mortgaged equipment and a crew of eighteen-year-olds, he rouses your admiration. Unrolling morning miles of Oklahoma you consider his difference from Gerald: seventeen years younger, born into war and prosperity, depression dust forgotten, brought up on TV and flush toilet, his system tuned not to Yankton but Kansas City and Minneapolis for the Big Leagues there. He is further from Lewis and Clark by a long generation but dresses more like the West: black grainy high-heeled boots, tight-legged pants with peaked pockets, three-button-cuffed shirt, suede jacket with outlined shoulder-piece, and a felt Stetson, stylized version of his brother's beat-up straw. Whatever his role, Pecos or Wild Bill or one of the James Boys, he takes it seriously, the back seat is crowded with his costumes; but he talks with you easily in the common tongue of pop tunes and editorials. Trusting you he sleeps, boots off, into Kansas, slumbers through the scene of one of his triumphs, a roadside park where he spent a day replacing, by himself, a piston. A piston is a thing you remember to have occurred in high school physics in a four-stage diagram, and, from bitter experience with repairmen, to involve rings. O Western Ulysses, man of stratagems! Awaking, he offers a cigarette, and suddenly, in his red-and-white package colored like a plug to lure fishermen and large-mouthed bass, you see, like the travelers from Emmaus, what resurrection of the West he represents: the Marlboro Man.

> Christmas Season
> Here's the Reason
>
> Buy your tree
> Locally!
>
> Canadian trees
> Cut before freeze
>
> Without a doubt
> They dry out.
>
> St. John Tree Farm
> St. John Kan.
>
> Cuts them fresh,
> They're the best!
>
> See you in
> St. John!

Counting the miles measured by handlettered verses you talk wheat, speculating how long before Gerald reaches each yellow field. At lunch in St. John's Grill and Texaco Station you talk wheat, wheat, praising by implication his work, his independence, his pluck.

"I wouldn't want to do this all my life, though," he says. He pays for two meals, tycooning on a credit card.

"But what else?" He has harvested from Mexico to Canada, from March to December. "What else is there?"

He drives through the oil wells near Great Bend, where donkey engines masked by billboards (Grainbelt Beer, Kill Rootworms Fast!) do the work of a thousand John Henrys.

"Something important," he says. "Like . . . your job."

Your office returns in manila folders, gray fluorescent tubes, sweat smell imbedded in suits because the voice of authority breaks down deodorant.

"Something a hundred other guys can't do."

By a law of life the youngest child seeks new ways to excel: the others are farmers so he's an operator, yes, but excellence is always far off. Boss of two rigs, two trucks, he despairs at the earthquake rumble of outfits from Saskatchewan and Alberta and Colorado moving ten, twelve, sixteen combines and a platoon of men: he can't bear it, he wants, you can tell by his driving, to be first on the road.

"I been thinking about the Army," he says.

There are special deals in the Army where your way is paid through college—he wishes now he'd gone—and some guys make the military a career. Why not? Liberal and peaceable by nature, you hate shouters, and with what weapon should the pacifist attack the military? Moving north through Kansas where five-ranked windbreaks (cedar, olive, cottonwood, olive, cedar) guard the chartreuse wheatfields from the snow, you see how softness needs a shell. All those Pentecostals and Brethren shared their freedom and loved one another nestled within America's tightest system, a place for everyone and everyone in his place, while in the free and open North the grim-lipped Calvinist must place himself. Those neat green dairy farms, islands of rural bliss, are, like the home of every contentment, totalitarian Edens, strapped down and squared away like their tight-capped silos; this Prussian land makes milk for babies, mothers being the first, best militarists. Brian has a mind of his own, this self-made Marlboro Man has the dignity of human freedom too; and so you say nothing.

Once out of Kansas he sleeps, boots off, in the back, trusting you to take him where the mother readies his uniform and kit. No side trips east or west, Chicago decadence or untilled height of the Rockies; the journey is predestined north. In Red Cloud, Nebraska, the Willa Cather museum and curio shop is about to close. An hour to Grand Island, ninety minutes to the head of the sandhill country. You amuse yourself with your allegory, the final proof of which is the allegory itself—for it is at this period of life, when the sun slides slowly north and the journey approaches its end, that we cease testing what has been and planning what must be done, and keep ourselves awake imagining that the whole of it has some meaning, anticipating, perhaps, a smile from those who wait, or homebaked pie in the kitchen bye and bye, when the machine at last stops and the roaring in our ears, the nerves' vibration, the cramp in the legs, dissolves and dwindles away. Life as a recapitulative journey, old age with the freedom of youth, senility as infancy: a pleasing thought as you note how evening echoes morning, how in a lush green field cow leaps upon cow, nature performing civilized perversions, nothing new under the sun, as biologists tell of incest and cannibalism among the lower orders and the noble red elk of Scotland abusing himself on a log. A long aching drive through grass and cattle and horses (patiently doubled, head to withers) with the sun in your eyes: you long for darkness though it means the end of the road. Just north of Spencer, where all are ready for bed, a deer rushes up from the ditch in yellow-blue light—the only deer you have ever seen where the signs warn DEER CROSSING, and you fancy it as a glimpse of beyond. Soon, crossing the Missouri in dusk, the sun glowing blue like a footlight beneath earth's rim, you'll be an hour from the last stop of all, in total dark.

And to what end? To bring a young man one step from peace to war. Yes, and to bring yourself memories: sky, cloud, grass, trees, springtime and harvest, arc of light and orbit of man. And knowledge—ah, twice seven-hundred miles, like seventy years, gives a man a great gust of the world and makes him know what it is to be alive! The Dakota border, a goal you have set. Brian takes the wheel and you sink to a passenger's quiescence, let the dark wind rush as it will. A star fades in, your eyes close. Is it really knowledge, then, when one does nothing, acts on nothing, feels nothing? Last night you pissed on the beans in the dark, playing Henry David Thoreau . . . A whiff of smoke, Brian's Marlboro. You fall from him as last night Gerald set you free. Floating on the earth's thin crust, which floats on fire like a face (Gerald's, Brian's, your own) masking certain disaster, why should a man put down his hand? Drowsy, the mind blinks: pheasant in horizontal flight, black-bibbed yellow-vested lark, fiery wheat, heavy harvesters, red dirt and white dust, sunlight's stab on glass, gravel, oil, wide Slavic forehead, Grainbelt, Champlin, Allis-Chalmers, and, aloft with the merest forward effort, a hawk and a boy on a bike, yes you would do it again, touching nothing, changing nothing, doing nothing at all, but my God what a delight, just to travel through!

Other Electricities

ANDER MONSON

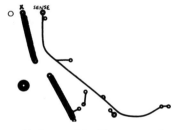

MY FATHER HAD MOVED UP in the attic with all the radios and the best connection to the main antenna. He had gotten a call sign and had begun to shape the air with his voice. You could listen to him in the night. It was good to see him controlling something. Good for him and good for us. The night was filled with him, though you had to tune in right to listen—had to find his frequency and call sign, or scan the air for the rhythms of his voice. The night was filled with him upstairs and my brother and I below. You had to have the right equipment. Amps and SWL receivers. Mobile or stationary antennas, encoders and decoders, coaxial goodness. Circuit boards traced to spec. A couple hundred feet of insulated wire, shortwave radios, the code books, FCC licensing manuals. A license to use the language.

On the radio, they speak in code. Words that are not words. Words that are words, but not the words you think they are. That displace language. Shift it back and forth like light across a room as the day changes. Charge up the air. Charge right through it. Make it opaque.

He stopped going to work. He told us he had enough money stashed to keep us up for a year. He kept provisions downstairs and would make excursions down once or twice a night for salty snacks. He was always up in the night. Radiating some signal of distress.

My relationship with him was off and on, binary, like square or sawtooth waves. Like a switch. He was all there or not at all. Days he slept and nights he didn't. When I asked, he told me there's better reception at night. More range. Something about clouds. Noninterference from the sun.

Noninterference from the kids.

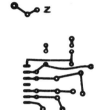

High cloud ceilings and reflection off the ionosphere (which is somehow denser at night) carry signals further. They increase your reach. I looked it up. I think he was saying something about grief, too. Some need to spread it out. Pass the news. That kid had died a week before. The latest in the string of deaths. It was like our father took it personally. It was like those kids—always someone else's—were in line for it. Like they had taken numbers and sat in the mall in queues. Getting drunk or getting dumb or getting ready.

Dear, distance must begin somewhere

You couldn't turn on the news without hearing about it. But the anchors related the news with no emotion, no surprise. Nothing to convey the importance of these deaths. You'd see their faces crease more when the DOW went down.

The Radio Amateur Is Patriotic. That's what the manual says. It is your responsibility as an amateur radio operator to pass the word in times of trouble, times of war. Times of danger or disaster. Times of tragic loss. During flood or blizzard. Pass it along. Make everyone aware. This is the Amateur's Code. You need to know it.

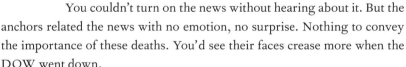
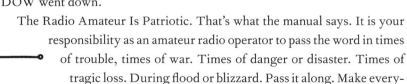

A guy held up the bank downtown in a snowstorm, took hostages, got taken out by sharpshooters through a huge pour of snow. It caused quite a local splash—all over the papers, the broadcast news. Books being composed about it. Murder in the snow. The guy kept

Dear, distance = rate x time

screaming things about being filled with voices. Conspiracies. The need for someone to listen. He found his audience.

He had a pirate radio station running somewhere in the area. You could hear him most nights on the low end of the FM, around 89.3 until the holdup, hostage-taking, and his death.

The Radio Amateur Is Well-Balanced.

I had got my own scanner and receiver and together with my brother I would listen for my father's voice on the radio in the night. We set it up outside in the shack with all the newspapers. We set it up above the words hidden in bags below the ground. Below the books that lined the floor. Below the gas line that we knew ran underneath. We hooked up the gasoline-powered generator to the radio when the batteries wore down.

The Radio Amateur Is Attentive.

We listened for my father. We always listen for my father. And we listened for who else was there. Another crackpot broadcasting in the night. There were lots of them, always someone crowing.

It is a life, the radio. Increasingly, our father's life. His father before him had the big old ones with barometers built in and vacuum tubes or huge coils. Installed on ferryboats moving across the Straits of Mackinac. Calling out in storms. Transmitting location, distance, weather, orientation. Useful news.

We knew he had a call sign. Everyone does. We searched the databases of current and expired and just-about-to-expire call signs for his name.

Nights would go like this: Have dinner. Wash the dishes. File away the food. Stoke the fire. Put your hands on the stove to see how hot it is. Don't burn yourself. Make sure the Saran-Wrap-like material over the windows is intact. Check for drafts. Watch your father go upstairs, say goodnight, get dressed, and go outside to reconnoiter.

——————————— *Dear, some forces act across any distance*

Our schedules changed to his. He wasn't available or as useful as he had been before. Got a cut or an abrasion? Knock on the door on the ceiling that holds the retractable stairs. If he's up, he'll answer. Bactine in the bathroom. Top shelf on the right in the closet. Directions on the box of Band-Aids: how to put them on; how not to touch the pad with your finger to avoid infection; how not to put bacitracin directly on the cut, but on the Band-Aid itself; how to keep the disinfectant uninfected.

If he wasn't up, we'd fend for ourselves. Which is not so bad. TV dinners for lunch. Sleep when we want. A lot of pop. Sugar cereal which we never had when Mom was around. We'd just go to the store and put it on our account. Bag it, bring it home.

He'd sit in the attic all night. He'd tell us sometimes who he'd talked to— some guy from Norway. What did you talk about, we'd ask, and he would not reply. Not really. Just shake his head and say something about transceivers or low-register noise, or bandwidth. Say something about something. We wouldn't say much in return. The Radio Amateur Is Nearly Always Loyal.

           * ———————— *Dear, distance is a section break*

One night while he was up top, we took the car. He didn't notice.

I drove it, gassed it up; we took it down to Paulding, Michigan, home of the Paulding Light. Which is not a light exactly. Nor anything exactly. It has no power source, no explanation, no obvious cause. It is not a hoax. It made *Unsolved Mysteries* one year. We watched it on tape a while after it aired, copied from someone who had recorded it from TV.

You go down this road and turn your lights out. You can only drive so far. Several miles down the path along the power lines into the distance—as far as an eye can follow—lights appear and seem to rock back and forth. My brother had never been there before. This was another electricity, I told him. Watch that thing.

The plaque said that it was the ghost of the miners who died in some accident. A likely lie. More likely some anomaly along the power lines—some collection of electrons. Some lovely gathering. Or power gnomes.

The lights move down the hill toward where you park. They come pretty close. Some of the kids who live around there told us the lights come right up to the cars and that you can see through them. Like electric disco balls spinning super fast, so fast they exert gravity or magnetism or some other force and cast off all the light that hits them. Tear the paint off a car. Tear your spare tire off the back. Tear hood ornaments right away. Even take a tie clip off a tie. A cross on a necklace off a neck. Here's the mark to prove it.

The Radio Amateur Is Truthful.

——————— *Dear, this distance is a light in Paulding*

The regulars each had stories about the light. There was a group of guys who set off with walkie-talkies and a shortwave radio to hunt the thing down. If you hunt it, though—someone said—it won't come. This kind of mystery is like a source, a gas or kerosene lamp, a gas-powered or hand-crank electric generator. It gives birth to stories, powers them.

My brother was silent the whole time. Like he always is around strangers. And at night. Like he has been since whatever happened—without language, mostly. Armless, quiet. Sometimes words burst out of him, like Tourette's. Sometimes his voice comes in whines and shrieks. Sometimes he's lucid, conversational. I held onto his side for a while in the car, right below the shoulder stump. That's where he likes to be touched and reassured. He was wondering about Dad. I could tell by his expression, by his look of emptiness, by the way he held his cheek to the car glass.

I had a list printed out of dead call signs. We examined it.

N9AEP	TRACY A MONSON
WH2AEX	ERIC H MONSON
WD8AFZ	JOHN F SIMONSON
KB2ALI	JOHN R SIMONSON
KB5ASU	DAVID M SIMONSON
NV5B	ROGER N SIMONSON
WB5BBF	MARY G EDMONSON
KJ5BP	RONALD E EDMONSON
WD8BVO	ROBERT R SIMONSON
KA0BZV	DONALD L SIMONSON JR
K1CJ	ROBERT J EDMONSON
KB7CVT	LAURA L MONSON
KB7CVU	ROBIN L MONSON
N0DAPDE	ETTE L MONSON
WB5DBF	THOMAS J EDMONSON
N2DEH	JOHN A MONSON
K9DGK	DARWIN T OSMONSON
N5DQM	PAUL S SIMONSON
N2EMV	MARVIN W SIMONSON
K7DRZ E	DON SIMMONSON

You couldn't tell much from the numbers or the names. We were solemn as if actually in a graveyard at night among the steam, stones, and plastic flowers.

I didn't know if you even had to have your real name to register a call sign. Or how you do it. Whom you register it with. The FCC? Some government commission? How much it costs. Whom to make the check out to. How long you get them for. Whether you can request a sign or do you have to take the one you're given. The Radio Amateur Is Curious About Things He Does Not Know.

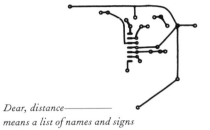

Dear, distance———
means a list of names and signs

The Radio Amateur Is Cautious, Too. The light didn't come up to us. It didn't tear the hubcaps off the car, or send us off wailing. We went home sort of awed and disappointed.

Dad was still up when we got back. You could tell by the light at the top of the house. Like the belltower in a church. Like Paul Revere. Like the strobe light up in the bridge to keep planes from ramming into it.

We had filled the gas back up to where it was. Exact. Reset the trip odometer at the right time so the miles line up right in case Dad wanted to take the car. Checked the oil like we had seen him do. I held the dipstick up to my brother's face. He smiled and it was fine. Black and thick.

On the kitchen table we found bits of further evidence. Printed out on a dot matrix printer—you could tell by the banding on the text. We didn't have a dot matrix printer, as far as I knew:

NoMWS 1999-04-02	FRED C. GEBHART, JR., TOPEKA, KS
NoNFM 1999-04-02	ELIZABETH A. LUNDSTEN, HASTINGS, MN
NoNFR 1999-04-02	PAUL A. TELEGA, DULUTH, MN
NoNFS 1999-04-02	DAVID T. GALE, SHOREWOOD, MN
NoNFV 1999-04-02	JEFFREY D. WILDE, SPRING LAKE PARK, MN

Look at that list. Like some litany of expirations. A register of those who voted for the wrong party. Landholders. A hit list. Amputation patients. Absentee parents. Those held in contempt of court. Those with past-date dues or bills that had gone unpaid for too long.

The Radio Amateur Is Knowledgeable.

Where does the power come in from? Generators, power plants, batteries. UPPCO: The Upper Peninsula Power Company. Through the lines we have been told not to touch. Through the lines we were instructed not to cut, even while wearing rubber gloves, even with large wire cutters with an insulated handle. The lines that come down in ice or heavy windstorms and twist across the road, stopping traffic in both directions. The lines that come alive. The lines that hiss and speak to my brother. The lines you can see reflected in his eyes. Lines that attract us like anything that can kill.

*

——————————— *My lead slug, my dial tone, my dumb luck, my instant distant coffee, dear*

I know about the phones. While our dad was upstairs broadcasting something to the world, and we were listening in, or trying to find his frequency for his voice, his name, his call sign across our receiver, we would give up and go out in the snow around the neighborhood with a phone rigged with alligator clips so we could listen in on others' conversations. There's something nearly sexual about this, hearing what other people are saying to their lovers, children, cousins, psychics, pastors, debtors. I would hold the phone for my brother while he listened. He'd whistle when something good was going on, or something nasty.

The Radio Amateur, However, Is Not A Voyeur, However It Might Seem.

All you have to do is find the junction box on the back of a house, or a larger junction box out by the road underneath the power lines (which we were never allowed to touch). Open it up and clip in to a tough discussion, to a life. You could make calls too, which we did sometimes. But not often because we could call from home. And who would we call? I talked to the FCC to find out who I'd have to talk to in order to get a ham radio call sign. They gave me another number. Everything is pinned to a number. Everything is handled by a tone.

Some stations just broadcast numbers. The key to some code. Something of national importance. They beam streams of digits into the night. No other programming. No anger. No malice. No bereavement. Curiosity. Politics. Love.

The Radio Amateur Is Sometimes Nosy.

We would take down messages and numbers. We would write down frequencies of tones we found on the Internet. We would go through trash out back of the Michigan Bell facility for manuals and pages of codes and notes. Diagrams. Schematics. We accumulated quite a stash of operating instructions for phone equipment. We stacked them in the shed with the rotting paper on the floor, with the words hidden below the floor in bags. We surrounded ourselves in them. They were warm when left alone, like compost. They were warm when touched or burned.

*

Yellow light from streetlights filters down through snow. Or snow filters down through streetlight light. It's hard to tell which. One is moving, one is still. My brother and I are using my pellet gun to shoot out light bulbs installed in motion detector lights on people's stairways. The Radio Amateur Is Adept With Guns.

It is good to walk through snow, to let it alight on your face as you turn up to the patterns in the sky. You can stretch out your tongue like a lizard and wait for flakes, but leaving your eyes open and allowing snow to melt on your cornea—getting bigger and bigger, you'd think, though snowflakes don't fall directly down; they shift from side to side and you can never just watch one come in; it's more like a frigid ambush when they get you—is what really marks you as being serious about sensation.

The Radio Amateur Values Sensation.

The Radio Amateur Is Friendly.

A plow comes slowly by with its lights whirling on top. We wave it down and she—an anomaly, a female driver—stops for us. The plowmen usually grin and let us in. They don't have so much to do. They make good money plowing the roads in the early morning, or whenever they are called to duty. But it is dull, I think. They are lonely mostly. They like company and conversation. Hot coffee, or too-sweet cappuccino that tastes like cocoa.

She's wearing latex gloves. She's listening to music—some old AC/DC: *Who Made Who*—on a boombox with a fading battery. It goes in and out while my armless brother holds it on his lap. She wants to know where we're from or where we're going. Which is nowhere. We are out walking. Our dad is upstairs in the house with the lights off surrounded by radio equipment. It's hard to come out with this, though. I point to my pellet gun. She nods as if she understands. My brother nods, too.

We are brothers. We are in tandem. We share secrets, cans of pop, the saliva collected in the bottoms of pop cans that makes up a small percentage of the fluid by volume as you reach the end. We share stories and last names.

You don't usually think a lot about those who plow the road. I mean, you think about the fact that the roads are plowed, and if they're not, you write letters of complaint to the city which are most likely ignored, because if the roads aren't plowed, there's usually a good reason—such as the finite (but large) budget for plowing having been plowed through already due to heavy early winter snow. You don't think about the drivers of the plows, their likes and dislikes, turn-ons and such, unless you ride along with them.

Unless you get into cars left unattended in darkness or daylight. You can find out a lot by getting into cars or abandoned machinery. People keep stuff under seats you wouldn't expect. Guns. Money. Building Plans. Pornography. Bibles and other books. *The Anarchist's Cookbook*. Cigarettes are a big one. Liquor in flasks. Half-frozen beers that explode when they open. Love notes and other things scrawled on napkins. Things that might cause grief if found.

The Longer The Radio Amateur Thinks About Things, The More Intricate They Become.

"It's not as interesting as it seems, kid," the plowman says, seeing my eyes jumping back and forth.

It has a lot of lighted dials and gauges that measure fluid levels or power. They flicker and dance when the plow jerks forward, their levels momentarily going down or up.

"I know. I've been in a few," I say.

She doesn't have much to say, which is unusual. You don't have to carry the conversation normally. You just sit alongside. Sit and listen. Listen to the on and off radio. Or the sound of the plow moving over concrete. Maybe a whump if it hits a dog or a drunk. You learn things about people.

She wears a business suit. I ask her about it. She says she's got a job interview in a couple hours and doesn't want to miss it, and what with the roads like this, she's better off taking the plow to the interview. I nod as if I understand.

She asks about my brother and I look to him. He doesn't answer, really. He hums low, trying to match the pitch of the machine. It's weird when he's really close to it because you can hear the sound beating back and forth as his pitch approaches the plow's. Then they're right in tune, and when the plowman shifts gears my brother has to play catch-up.

She gets us a mile and a half down the road before letting us out. I give her the Whatchamacallit bar I have in my pocket. The Radio Amateur, As You Know, Is Generous.

She grins and thanks me. Takes off her latex glove to grab it, shake my hand. Offers a hand to my brother, but then there's awkwardness as we pause and she retracts her hand. Her face is odd in the light that comes on when we open the door.

We get out and our breath looses itself into the air.

The plow moves down the road, burying a GMC pickup truck in a driveway.

I wonder about those latex gloves.

We make sounds with our throats, pretend we're dragons.

The Radio Amateur Is Meticulous About Appearing Hygienic.

It is later and I am telling my brother about how I only fake-wash my hands most of the time. Leave the water running long enough and divert its stream so if someone was listening, it would seem like you're doing it. Wet the soap on the top and the bottom so it looks like it's used. Always leave your hands wet in case someone checks them to see if they're washed. The Radio Amateur Is Cunning. The Radio Amateur Will Not Be Found Out.

The Radio Amateur Remembers When He Was Young, Right Before His Brother Was Born, How He'd Have To Be Driven Around In The Old Ford Fairmont Before He'd Sleep, And Even After That Car Was Long Dead And His Brother Was Alive And Without Arms, He'd Have To Rock Himself Side-to-Side To Conjure Sleep.

The Radio Amateur Remembers That Back-and-Forth. Like The Sea Or Static. That Lovely Oscillation. That Necessary Motion.

The Radio Amateur Wonders How Anything Holds Together.

We get back to the house and the lights are still off. We check some frequencies in the shed to see if Dad's still broadcasting. It's hard to figure out what they're saying out there. It's mostly mundane stuff peppered in with Bravos and Zebras and numbers tossed around like they must mean something. I think of things I'd like to tell him if only we had it set up to speak. But that equipment is much more expensive. Listening is cheap, nearly free.

There's a voice talking about the recent winter death. Probably he must be from around here. His name—he says it, unlike many—is Louie Kepler, from Lake Linden-Hubbell. It is such a tragedy. When will these kids ever learn. Was he drunk? I think he must have been. Doesn't it all come down to morals, family values? Doesn't it come down to parents ruling with an iron fist? Didn't the kid know not to go out on the ice? Didn't he see it coming?

The Radio Amateur Is Not Presumptuous.

Maybe he did see it coming, I say—though not on the air, since we don't have broadcasting equipment yet. Maybe he wanted it to come. Maybe he waited his whole life for something and it didn't come, so this was just as good to him. There are reasons to want to die. To want out of it. Maybe he felt some pressure. How do you know, I say, how do you know anything, you old ham fuck.

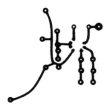

The Radio Amateur Is Empathetic.

The Radio Amateur Holds His Position If He's Sure It's Right.

The Radio Amateur Protects His Brother At All Costs.

I know nothing will bring the kid back, should he want to come back at all. I know I am not speaking to Mr. Kepler as if on the phone, nor listening to his private conversation. I doubt my words would have any more effect on him. But I think of putting a rock through his window, if only I learned where he lived.

It would be nice to be able to say it, to shove it in his face.

The Radio Amateur Knows That Power Used Is Power Lost.

The Radio Amateur Understands Needing To Know So Bad That You're Willing To Take It Home All The Way Through The Ice And See Where That Gets You.

The Radio Amateur Knows Enough To Not Reveal Or Hide Himself Away Too Long.

The Radio Amateur Is Not His Father.

The Radio Amateur Knows To Go To Bed When The Sun Comes Up.

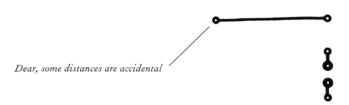

Dear, some distances are accidental

The Mausoleum

⚘

SUSAN NEVILLE

THE MAUSOLEUM. WHAT CAN I SAY? Think of a Dali painting. Dark boxes floating in clear blue space, five-sided boxes with one side opening toward you. You're rushing outward in the momentum from the thing you call your birth: you're flung, you fly, you dodge the boxes floating in the blue but somehow, still, you carom headlong into one.

And so you wait for anyone to come inside and stay with you, or better still, to pull you out where you can join the others. You lack the strength to do it for yourself because you're still accelerating, flat against the wall.

And then the sixth wall closes. And the shape of a door appears. And there's a knock. Come in, you say. Oh please come in.

Just come home, your mother says. Somehow she's got your number. You say time doesn't flow that way and besides, you've found yourself inside a box. Not that again, she says. You know, it happened to your grandmother. I was inside one myself, she says, but I escaped.

And you say you know you're not a child, but why didn't she warn you about this possibility?

She says it would have been difficult to explain.

Are you stuck inside? she asks, and you say of course, that that's the point. There's no escape, you say, looking around you at the box. You closed your eyes and leapt, you say, the endless sweep of air, and then your open eyes and all that bluescreen blue and then the rushing stars and then, at the base of your throat this joy, and then the knock and then the outstretched arms. Nothing like hers, you hasten to explain.

So you answered, she asks, and you say What else could I do? And after he came in, she says, the door closed right behind him.

And there was nothing else in the universe, you say, except his voice and skin.

And before you knew it, your mother says, there was this box surrounding you.

Exactly.

And then, you say, he disappeared.

She doesn't seem surprised. In fact, she says there's nothing she can do to help you, and so you say goodbye.

You're deeply suspicious that maybe you chose to fly into the box, that perhaps he called to you and asked you to come in. You can't be sure. Or perhaps it really was by accident and, to be quite kind, he came inside to visit. All you know with any certainty is that he comes and goes quite easily and that's something you can't do.

You've looked for the exit. You've looked for another door or a loose window. Wait for me, he said and as he vanished you said yes, because you absolutely could not do otherwise.

One day you wake up and find the box you're in has somehow changed. It's beginning to look like a motel room by the ocean. Completely dark, as usual, then suddenly an early morning gray and you can see you're lying on a bed with a cheap coverlet and on the walls of the box thick jacquard draperies, and carpet on the floor. And there's a mirror! You sit up and look. Can that be your face? You've changed. And you find that you're no longer pressed against the wall. Something, you think, has stopped, though you never felt a jolt. Or perhaps, perhaps . . . you try to remember your high school physics. Moving objects moving simultaneously move how? Something to do with spinning planets and objects such as you and you wonder if conclusions drawn from planets apply to moving boxes in which you find yourself unreasonably trapped. Your head, you believe, is now the thing that's spinning.

And then by the mirror you see, amazingly, another door. His door? You open it with trepidation, expecting a long hard fall.

Instead, you see a dim hallway! Your box has lodged inside another box which is in fact, you discover, quite honeycombed with rooms like yours, and while there are no doors leading outside the box itself (you check) there are doors to other rooms, and in each room there is, you're told by a maid with a towel-bedecked chrome cart, a human being.

And so you begin to go out into the hallway every morning and you discover there are things to eat. A banquet hall on another floor, you should be happy.

Every morning you knock on doors, but no one answers. Every afternoon you spend in the lamplit chill of your own unwindowed but becurtained box and in the evenings you wear your daytime sweater out into the humid air of a ballroom. Some days it takes hours to feel the heat and on others the contrast is so great your skin begins to sweat like you're a cup.

In the ballroom there's a window in the ceiling and they say that you can see the sky. But it's always dark, another box.

It's beautiful enough outside your box, you suppose. The green slate lobby floors are polished so they look like riverbeds with shimmering mountain water. And there are sparkling sconces and mirrored elevators, but except for in the ballroom, you're always cold. But you learn to put your foot down on that glistening riverbed and walk, and you learn to trust the hidden mechanisms that work the elevators.

Though there were many of you in the hallways in the afternoons, it seemed to be everyone's fate to be linked like this, in close proximity, and to speak in monosyllables or not at all.

While there was something resembling talk, it was empty formless sound that bubbled in the middle of eerie silence. Of course everyone had cell phones, though there seemed to be no working towers, and there were phone lines linking rooms but no one knew the numbers. If only you knew the name he went by. Down in the lobby, the receptionist who might have been of help was flossing her perfect teeth, and her glossy hair always required arranging and she could only connect the rooms if you knew the name. You try to describe the man you're looking for, but she says there are many men who answer that description.

The man who sold the water and the toiletries and stood behind the glass mahogany and chrome sold you pain relievers for your headaches and polish for your nails, but he too didn't speak.

Though the sight of other human beings was at times uplifting, for some reason you would rush back to your frigid room, into the triangle of bedside lamp, the shadows from the silly possessions you had begun to accumulate so carefully from the gift shop and which appeared smudged on the wall a grayish chalky blue. What was horrifying was the way the shadows wouldn't move, how fixed and stonelike your possessions were, like the carved stone beasts affixed to the thick limestone in the mezzanine.

The cold and dim seemed to slow you down as did the looming stone, the antique sideboards and portraits of landscapes that at one time you could perhaps actually have seen. At one time there were trees that green, the sky that shade of turquoise. There were lavender rocks in a creekbed filled with water.

One day a smell of mold came from the ventilating system, green and wet. You couldn't see the slime, but you knew the creatures were oozing into tracks throughout the ductwork.

Often, though, he would come in the afternoon, and then the time would pass more quickly. What you did inside the room couldn't be spoken of outside of it. He made that clear. He had other responsibilities. You couldn't keep him with you, no matter how much you wanted to.

Close your eyes, he says, and he has you feel a blue star burning at your knees, the inside of your thighs, your left nipple, then the right one. A star burns inside your wrists where you see the thin blue veins, inside the temples, in the fountains where the tubes flow, in the bones. Show me how you touch your breasts, he says, and there's your hand reaching up to touch them. Turn over, he says, and so you turn. Stand, he says, and there you stand. One by one he has you place the stars inside your body and he says that's where I'll touch you when I see you next and then you'll feel the burning blue, a constellation.

His fingers connect the points until there's a shape and meaning to your life inside the box, and suddenly you know you never want to leave. Your mother calls again. You tell her that you're happy.

Just wait, she says. But you don't believe her.

The phone rings late at night and you're exhilarated. It's the first time that he's called. Perhaps this marks a turn in your relationship. Your voice sounds disconnected. You hope he doesn't hear it. It's floating in the air, your voice, like balloons that aren't attached to strings. You try to will them back inside your mouth, your head, you try again to speak. He says your name, you try to connect it to your body, you try to swim inside the name as though it's yours.

Your skin feels like a fragile organ, sick of holding blood and ooze, water doming on the top of a glass until it's pierced and flows. You want to become a part of him. You want to be inside of him in that way that he's in you. You can only keep him on the line so long, and when you put the phone back in its cradle you slide the cord between your fingers, feeling for the pulse, afraid it's gone.

You wonder why he never seems to understand how much it would mean to go out in the sunlight with him, to have a simple lunch together. You're sure he knows the exit now. You'd be happy to wear any disguise he might suggest.

Yes this is him, Mother, the one I talked to you about. You'd like to tell her she was wrong, to tell your friends, We live in such-and-such a place, he likes his coffee black, he eats corn relish from a tin. You see? His beard so dense you can watch it growing indigo as he sits there with his fork, like ink it oozes out beneath his skin, you could watch that face every minute of your life. You dream of him. You walk every minute in a dream of him. In another life the two of you would have your photo taken with your children. In another life it would not have been your fate to live inside this mausoleum.

You tell him this, you tell him, and he says he understands, he does, but just for now instead to feel his cock inside, that that's enough. What you feel again is the rushing blue, the five-walled box, and it's like he's plugging in some cord and all the burning stars, you see, in the mirror across from the bed, the one he has you watch like it's a screen and you're the actors, all those stars are visible beneath your skin. He's hung you in the sky. You see a vague outline of yourself between the stars. Not everyone, he says, can leave her mark like this, and you don't know whom exactly he's referring to. You tell him that every time he leaves, the stars are less bright than the twisted wires that string them through your body.

And then one day you see him outside your room, down in the lobby. He's on his knees talking to a woman who's not you, and you catch a glow of lights underneath her skin, a subtle purplish glow but there it is. On the inside of her wrists, the elbow, underneath an anklebone, on the soft skin of her belly when she lifts her arm to smooth back a stray hair. He's on his knees in a crowd of people. The woman is sitting on a chair. She wouldn't stand up for him, she let him stoop to talk to her until that got uncomfortable for him and still she wouldn't rise, so he was on his knees. He's on his knees and you know as you draw closer and he doesn't see you, that she has free access still to any world she chooses.

She has the scent of outside air: catalpa blossoms, lemon mint. Her skin is smooth and pale, her hair is black. She's sitting on a chair, her ankles crossed, her shoes with leather straps, something about her flesh that is translucent.

If it hadn't been for that translucency, it might have taken you years to realize what was happening. She isn't as brightly lit with him as you imagine yourself to be. The blue-red light inside her veins that only he could have placed there, or rather, had her place.

Of course later, when he came to your room to sleep, he vehemently denied it.

That night you glowed with an extra ferocity and when he left the next morning you had to wait to leave the room until the lights cooled underneath your skin. No one else could shine with this intensity, you said to him. He would, you thought, be walking through his day waiting to come back in to you.

You spend the afternoon watching the television. You don't leave the room to eat. You wait for him. On every station there are girls your age on beaches dancing, and you wonder how they got there, what it is that keeps you here inside this room, how far it is from the bed where you're waiting to the place where those girls are dancing with those boys and with each other. None of them would have trusted him, would have listened when he said you would always be the only one.

How stupid can you be?

You decide to go downstairs for food and coffee. You take the polished stairs, you peer in meeting rooms, you roam. Soon you're in some cavernous space you didn't even know existed. You're afraid wherever you go that you might see her. You hate the way it feels, this hatred of her. She has, somehow, a greater power than you because you can tell she might not really want him and that he wants her way too much. The stars might even be some she's placed there by herself. But all she has to do, you think, is take his call and her own source of light will fail, like yours has.

You're willing to admit that it's a flaw in your design.

He's gone all afternoon but at night he calls and says he loves you, the contemplation of which fills your mind with some little thing outside itself. He says he loves your dark hair and olive-colored eyes, the slant of perfect eyebrow, he says he loves your breasts and tongue and curve of back, and you believe him. He calls first on the phone and whispers, wants you to wait naked on the bed. You tell him that you're shivering but you'll do it anyway. You wait under the blanket and when you hear his key turn in the door you pull the covers off as though you'd been waiting in the cold like that. What makes you lie? You smell catalpa on his skin.

You didn't make a world that works like this. You didn't ask to go inside this box. You simply focused on the emptiness, and it appeared. The mausoleum. What can I say? Think of a Dali painting.

Submarine Warfare on the Upper Mississippi

LON OTTO

THEY WOULD BE SURPRISED IF THEY KNEW we were here, they would be very surprised to know a German submarine hangs below the rippling surface of the Mississippi River, St. Paul to starboard, Minneapolis to port, they would be surprised. But here we are, a steel pike swimming almost motionless in the slow, young river, facing upstream.

How did we get here? That is what they would ask if they knew we were here. That would be their question, how did we get through the many locks, how did we slip past so many hostile eyes to come here, twelve hundred miles inland, to the "Land of Ten Thousand Lakes," to the "Land of Sky Blue Waters," how did we get here?

That is their question, it is not our question. It does not matter to us anymore, it is ancient history to us, it is "old hat." Their question is not our question. Our question is, what do we do now? Now that we have penetrated into the American State of Minnesota, an Unterseeboot of the VIIC Type, outmoded already when we sailed from Bremen, now that we are here, what do we do? That is our question, what do we do?

A prior question: why were we sent here? That is the question my First Mate asked. I had been fearing the question for a long time. What is our mission? I cannot tell him. I tell him, Willie, I cannot tell you that. You must not ask me the answer to that question.

He accepts this as if it had been an answer; he has faith in me and in the Admiralty. How can I tell him that I have not the smallest idea why we are here, why we were sent on this impossible journey, how can I tell him that, after all we have been through? That is my private question, how can I tell him? I do not know how.

The war is over for years, we know that. We are not idiots, we "know the score." The score is, Germany, o; America, 2. We know "what's up." The "jig" is up, we have known it for years.

So why have you not surrendered years ago, that is the question they would ask. The war is over for years, we don't even remember the war, what war? There has never been a war in the State of Minnesota, so what "gives"? Maybe you are part of the Sioux uprising? Maybe yours is a wild Indian submarine, ha, ha? That was our only war in Minnesota, and it was not even a war, an uprising is what it was.

We understand all this. We understand that our position, the attaining of it, the holding of it, is worse than pointless, it is ludicrous, and was so from before we, impossibly, attained it, a day we now know was fifteen days after the end of the Third Reich. We remember that day, twenty years ago, when we slid like a great savage pike between these cities, that is a day we remember, we will remember it when we have forgotten every other day. We are not stupid. We know the orders that we wait for will never come.

Today I have been talking with my First Mate, talking about the recent years, about what has come to break the monotony of this "waiting game" we hopelessly play. Not much, Herr Kapitän, he says. Willie, I say, you have it right, not much. The time we were trapped by the dredge, though, I say, that was a time, eh? That was a time, he says. We were against the American Army then, the Engineers. It was like the old days, slipping about along the bottom of the muddy river, alert always, backed further and further toward the terrible locks. It was a time, it was like the old days.

I thought then of retreating, after all these years, turning and running for the south, running for the Mexican Gulf, twelve hundred miles to the south, down the river we had forced twenty years before, forced like salmon. We will fail, Kapitän, my First Mate said. He had it right, we would have failed. We are not the men we were when we made that heroic voyage upcountry. The boat, she is not the boat she was, though we have done our best, oiling, greasing, scraping constantly, rebuilding, she is not what she was. We were magicians then, we and the boat, we could do anything, we could have sailed her up a garden hose. But not now. Willie had it right when he said that.

And so, with our propellers nearly over the dam, we made a run for it north, upstream, past the cow-like dredge, its big shovels and tangles of anchors leaving barely room for a good-sized carp. And we scraped a long and terrible sound along the web of cables and chains, the water was impossible, gravy, and we thought when we made that monstrous noise that we had "had it." But the watch must not have understood what was going on, and then nothing was, for we were past, free again in the newly scoured riverbed, which we began to learn anew.

When the worst peril was past, when we were finally past, huddled under the pilings of the railroad bridge, we felt like men, then, our blood was flowing, and Willie, he was for sending our aft torpedo downstream into the dredging barge we had so carefully evaded, and I almost said yes, yes, though we could have done that more easily when we were facing it upstream. But I said nothing. The dredge finished its work in a few more days, and was towed away.

So we are still here. We have been here a long, long time; we have not been innocent guests. We are a steel lamprey between these two northern cities, locked in the ice during the terrible winters, rusting helplessly in the summer, we are a great parasite, we have no choice. We have made raid after raid to stay here, where we do not want to be, to stay alive, though we are not alive, to keep the boat living a little longer, which is rusting to death. We have stolen food and fuel, and killed those who prevented us. We make no excuse. We are at war, we are not trying to be loved. We are not children in a fairy tale, who the birds, maybe, feed. We take what we need, like the leech, and we will not be forgiven, no matter what, who have drifted in their midst like a horrible dream.

And Willie whispers to me in the darkness, Why? Kapitän, why do we go on with this? And I tell him, Willie, don't ask, Liebchen, hush. A coal barge is passing slowly overhead. Our eyes in the darkness follow the sound of the pushing tug across our curving back. Let me sink it, he pleads, let me finish it. Not yet, my Willie, not yet, Kleine. We hug the steep curve of the sand-bank, sheltering under the warning of the buoy, as we have learned to do.

We do not know why they have not found us yet, for we have made mistakes in spite of all our deep cunning. So that is another question, why have they not found us? Fishermen have seen us, old black men fishing from the quay, and lovers along the cliff-protected shore. But maybe lovers and fishermen keep what they know to themselves, being already whole. The deserters, one by one over the years, I have expected each of them to talk, needing to win favor. Each time one fails to return from a raid into one of these cities, then I think it is over at last, they will come for us now, blast us out of this bloody stream. But no. Perhaps they disappear, truly, once they determine to leave us, having lived so long like creatures in the underworld. Or maybe the strangeness of our existence is not something the mind can hold, and they forget like newborn babies forget their other life.

But we will reach the end. Not quite yet, Willie, Lieber, not quite yet. But soon; we will not have to wait for the rust to swallow us. For I saw him tonight, Willie. Lifting the hatch under cover of the bridge for a look around before light failed, Willie, I saw him watching us, writing it down in a book. Who? Saw who? Someone who writes it down, Willie, sitting on the edge of the pretty sandstone cliffs, prettily catching the last light of the day, watching us and writing it down. Willie, Willie, don't cry, Liebchen, it is what we knew would happen, what we have been terribly waiting for, all these years, Willie, there, soon we go home, there, there, Liebchen, soon now, soon.

Wednesday Night Reflections, Edited Thursday

ERIN PRINGLE

YOU TELL ME THAT IN TEN YEARS you will live in London. Greeting the man who sings arias while selling oranges at the London market.

Vision twirls like a fan blade. Due to light-mindedness, I give you my wineglass before climbing to the floor at your feet.

When we talk, you touch my thigh. You have done this from the first time we met. I have poems to prove this.

That summer in the room without windows, I wore a short skirt and forgot to cross my legs, you told me later, and although I was embarrassed, I enjoyed the secret.

My paintings hang on the walls, surrounding us. You like that they all resemble me. I like to think it's my martyred eyes.

Two chords strung down my cheeks. Jesus, how I cry after you leave.

After you get into your car, do you sit there and sigh or just reverse out of the parking lot?

You think Wilco is the sound of Chicago, and I agree, even though I no longer live there.

You've even taken my streets, my homeless man in front of Blockbuster I took coffee to after I closed the store for the night.

You were taking me home, but you turned the other way at the traffic light and for a second, I hoped you'd forgotten the destination, that you were taking me away from this sulfur city. But before I could make love to you in the forest, we were in the library's asphalt parking lot, dropping off your daughter's books. She ignores the text and makes up her own stories to fit the pictures.

As we contemplated our own sweat, you rested your head in the curve of my spine, and I said, "he rests his head in the wheel of shadow" and you said, "you are dangerous."

Your cheek hot against me, but I'm making up the heat because temperature rarely survives memory. I know that there were Tuesdays of winter coats and scarves and Tuesdays in flip-flops.

Each time I am with you.

It is difficult, impossible really, to watch us from a different perspective. To say, the girl with the martyred eyes is in love with the man who checks the weather in Tucson.

Is it wrong to make you my muse? My Tuesday lover?

I recall our conversations without silences. But there must have been. Your foot spanning my hipbones as I watched you talk.

You are the only one who kisses me and walks away slumped. It's painful to watch. Even though it's not because of the kiss. Soft mouths without language express exactly what we were avoiding.

You sang, "Jesus, don't cry . . . ," because you knew I did.

The shadow of your anklebone. The fine black hairs on your toes.

I put you to bed that night, helped you crawl onto the mattress. Folded your jeans. But maybe they were slacks because there was a belt that you forgot on my chair in the morning.

The nightmares of missing an article of clothing in public.
The nightmares of a happier self.

No matter how much I diagram what we will say or how the shadows will cast our profiles as we talk, it's forgotten in the sound of your knock. You are the only one who forces me into present tense.

This time I thought I would kiss you immediately. Instead, I hugged and it felt false.

You say that you'll miss coming here. It doesn't make this any easier. My bruised shrine of women, their haunted eyes.

She tells him everything she's thought since they last saw each other. She collects her thoughts like dynamite and hires a guard with a pistol to keep any form of ignition away.

Kiss me before I ask.

Our intensity, the stride of our steps, even our names—it is hard to believe they are all the same. I no longer correct people who want to spell my name like yours.

It's in the sound.

We no longer laugh at the irony of homophone goodbyes.

It's taking longer to recover from your visits. Like my grandmother who must rest after the great-grandchildren visit and color on her floor and tell her knock-knock jokes and eat handfuls of M&M's out of the green candy dish with the heavy lid. I told you how she puts stickers beneath her figurines so that when she dies they go to the right grandchild, and I said you could have it to use in one of your stories.

How can you not understand why? How can you expect me to find a language to explain?

I'm going to kiss you.

In New Orleans, a wild-haired man played rows of glasses with a fork.

Your hand baring my back.

Of course it's your eyes, the beauty mark aslant from your bottom lip.

That night I broke a wineglass and later spilled another. I forgot and lay horizontal, my hair soaking up the merlot—or was it cabernet that time?—and I knew I wouldn't wash it, that I'd keep it a secret and thrill over the dry ends the next day, my wine-dyed hair as if you leaned my head over a sink and poured it over my head.

I left you there, sleeping.

You leave things at my apartment—CDs, books, your must-dusky scent that I imagine must be Arizona lingering—to ensure your return. I am your pawnshop, refusing to sell to another buyer. This can go on forever like when I was little, and it would take an hour to get home, even though I lived five minutes away from my best friend. I'd walk her home then she'd walk me home and this repeated until one of our mothers said enough.

The heat of your palm.

If you want a plot, don't ask me.

Without images, I am nothing. Not even a story. It's impossible to have one when I only see you on Tuesdays. We are in the middle of it. And if I gave you a plot, it would be what I imagined.

We don't look any different to each other than we did five years ago. As if we were expecting sudden change, something to prove that it had been too long to pick back up. But we're the weekly Soap Opera with the same characters living the same day.

If we'd met now. If we'd met tomorrow . . .

No silence.

You sing on the El. It's hard to believe, but I must because I don't lie.

Translate me if you must know why.

Your other lives spiral around the sanctuary of bruised women. It's distressing to think of you with a life outside my apartment or backyard.

"Jesus, don't cry. You can come by any time that you want. I'll be around."

Do you remember when someone stole your bicycle seat, and I gave you a ride? Or when you thought I wouldn't be able to open your CD player to see what the CD was, and I did, and it was Modest Mouse. Of course, Modest Mouse.

Why does his posture weep after kissing her?

A parable:
The lovers are meeting for the first time in twenty years. They've agreed on a diner with cracked red booths on the corner of North and Clark. He's on the #36, thinking of her. She's always early and so he knows she's already in the smoking section, pretending to ponder the menu but really pretending

she's someone else and observing the woman's chewed fingernails. He gets off the bus. He's lighting a cigarette as he crosses the street. He sees her and is suddenly slammed by a car. Skull shattering with windshield and interior mirrors. She doesn't see any of this behind the menu. Although the sirens dredge the depths of her, she ignores the feeling, adds it up to anticipation. She thinks he stood her up. She chain-smokes the hurt.

Every Tuesday. Every Tuesday. Oh.

When you're in Chicago, I convince myself I don't love you, that I just enjoy conversation. I critique us like a bad short story. And then you're knocking and no longer can I believe my illusions. Terrible.

I am telling the truth, but I'll call this fiction because who would believe that lovers like us still exist? We are as fossilized as Lancelot and Guinevere. It's our bond, the way reality often supersedes fiction, and we're the only ones left to make fiction real, to give it a believable plot.

Boy meets girl. Boy touches her arm when he talks. He's the first person to do this. She's stopped doing it herself because it makes people edgy. It's a gesture she learned from her mother.

Stop leaving your music here.

The woman across the lawn dyes her hair red. She thinks she's forgotten her natural color, but as soon as it reappears, she cannot.

Puddles like bruises.
All the Tuesdays become one.
I left you sleeping and returned to cry in the bottom sheet's indentation. Searched the pillowcases for your scent. While I was gone, you returned for your belt.

The other men were sad attempts to hate you. We both try. You beg me to hate you, so that you can take your belongings home this time. The only good thing about Hubert Selby's short stories is that they brought you back.

This may sound submissive, begging. A woman not strong enough not to care if her lover returns. This is just how it is. The games people play.

The length of our separation is equal to the number of wine glasses it takes to dizziness.

This all must seem idealized. It's not. I'll add to it: You're a Cancer, I'm a Virgo. We have a 54% chance at our relationship based on numerology. My horoscope for Monday you came over said it would be my best day in a very long time. It was.

I lied about sleeping with another lover and another and another because I like their writing, their different lives, their hoping I don't realize they'll leave me the next morning. I undress them again and again because they are not you. I'm safe because I don't care; none can enter my mind through backdoors I've locked. Any of them.

You say my expression is harsh, unapproachable. It's abstract enough to warn potential trespassers of danger.

All your women are bruised.
You are dangerous.
Why?
Jesus, don't cry.

I shouldn't be upset that you sleep with other women because we're not together. We do not say I love you, which might make this worse because of the silence where love should be—but there are no silences, right? Not in memory. We are a pawnshop. Actually, you never return what I lend. And I don't have the currency you accept.

The plot began with a short skirt and you across the room shuffling papers. Your hand on my thigh since then.

There are these panicked moments.

I thought my black hair dramatic, and although everyone else compli-
mented me, once the black was gone, I believed only you. This is problem-
atic, perhaps. Another safety on my toy gun.

It's easier to deny when only a centimeter of natural brown comes
through.

While you were in the bathroom, the bartender asked if you wanted
another glass of water. I said yes, the first time I've taken your voice or
made you decide. I wanted to hug the bartender with the joy of it, dance him
around the room.

With you, my language is flawed, susceptible. A turtle walking across
the interstate.

Promise you will pose for me. To see if I bruise even you. I, with paint.
You, with your mouth and the years I didn't know you in Arizona.

Because I watched you talk to her. I heard you comment on her beauty
when she was gone. It should've been me you were talking about. Me!

This clenching.

I only ask because you won't.

Only you refuse me the right to be another character, and therefore throw
me headlong into myself, expecting me to acclimate instantly.

In Chicago, I stood on the sidewalk across the street from American Girl,
watching you above as you served tea to little girls, dolls, and mothers. We
never met while I was there because of your schedule. Again. No matter. No
matter, right?

If we entered wholly into our daily lives, it wouldn't work. To make this a
comedy, I'd paint us in a kitchen with a vase of daisies on the table. As I cook
breakfast, you hug me from behind, your shower-wet hair dripping down

my neck. But it's tragedy. I want this and since you don't, I laugh. Pretend it's impossible.

Move with me. I'll buy the U-Haul. Move with me and be there when I wake up. I'll be quiet and creep around getting ready to go write at the diner. At the diner, I'll think of how you get out of bed and shuffle to the bathroom, tripping over my shoes. How you wait until you're dressed to look in the mirror, or maybe you don't. But you can't, and you won't meet me at any diner. You'll read my stories, but what's that mean? There is your daughter, there is London in ten years. But she could live with us in the summers. She could fly down once a month. I checked. The airport's not too far. Three cigarettes away.

Who else has loved the shadow of your anklebone?

The neighbors would hate us for not giving into pleasantries as we un-locked our front door. We'd be the writers next door.

He checks the weather in Tucson.

I fear you're waiting for me to realize something, like a poem too aloof to be analyzed completely. I'm floundering here.

The horoscope said we won't end our relationship even if it's floundering. You say, "Astrology is such a woman's creation." See me, I'm hanging up the stars right now. I'm hanging them just like your bathrobe and mine on the same hook. Knots of tissue balled in the pockets.

The Great War

JOSH RUSSELL

OPEN THE BOOK AND A SMALLER BOOK pops up. Its red cover is stamped with a gilt title too small to read—could it be French? The smaller book is on a thin-legged desk that stands on a Turkish rug before a tall, narrow window hung with curtains. Outside there is a maple tree with an octagonal trunk. All this popped up when the small red book popped up but it is the book you noticed. The curtains are yellow. They lift as if touched by a summer breeze; the leaves of the maple shiver and show their pale undersides. A cloud the dull silver of an old nickel has risen and unfolded while you marveled at the curtains and the tree. A knife of lightning stabs the maple; lines of rain slant from the belly of the cloud and come across the sash to soak the book. Its pages become wavy and thick with moisture and the book opens like a fan. Sammy's brother left the window open and Sammy's book is ruined.

Turn the page and the book and the window and the thunderhead fold away and a forest of charred stumps rises from pocked mud. A boardwalk snakes between the stumps. Its planks are gray crosshatched with a wide grain and marked by outsized nailheads. You hear the boom of cannon and the crack of rifles. There is the smell of gunpowder and burning rubbish. Three doughboys in flat helmets walk along the boardwalk singing a nursery rhyme. Sammy is the last in this short line. The soldiers' arms and legs are nearly round, but if you look closely you can see where they fold when they have to lie flat.

Turn the page and two aeroplanes rise toward each other, rattle their guns, pass so close each pilot can hear the other's curses—English from the Sopwith's cockpit, regal Prussian from the Folker's—and dive toward the lush paper grass of the mountain meadow. Below the dogfight Sammy and the two other doughboys—David from Kansas and Richard from Boston—sit on the grass. They tear a long loaf of bread into thirds, pass a canteen of wine, wipe their mouths with the backs of their hands. Above the picnic the red triplane and the moth-brown biplane rise and dive, rise and dive. A patch of wildflowers pops up and Sammy picks a bouquet and offers it to Richard. Richard pretends to be a girl and David pretends to be Richard's jealous beau. A squadron of yellow butterflies jerkily crosses the meadow while the doughboys wrestle and laugh. Sammy pins David and Richard kisses the victor. Above them a shock of orange and red fire unfolds to engulf the Sopwith's tail.

Turn the page and the landscape leaps up at you, broken trees and a bombed-out barn. The jagged wound of the trench crosses both pages. A voice from beyond the knotted wire of the no-man's land calls *Wine for tobacco? Wine for tobacco?* No moon jumps into the sky. Sammy watches over David's shoulder while David zips the pages of a dog-eared flipbook, animating the coupling of a naked man and woman. From the German trench again comes the offer to trade wine for tobacco and again the doughboys ignore it. The knee-deep water is scabbed with ice and it trembles when a shell screams over the trench and lands off its mark. David drops his flipbook into the water and curses. Richard, who had been too prudish to look, laughs. Both of their mouths are very dark, giving away the truth that they are hollow inside. A flare lights above the trench like a bulb hung on a cord. Sammy looks down and sees a torn photograph of someone's sweetheart floating on the dirty water. The gas alarm sounds and Sammy and David don their masks. Richard hunts in his rucksack and cannot find his. David pulls off his mask and puts it over Richard's face, unbuttons his pants and urinates onto his handkerchief, covers his mouth and nose with the urine-soaked rag, and screws shut his eyes.

Turn the page and the war flattens under the weight of a victory parade. Red, white, and blue bunting hangs from lampposts. Children ride their fathers' shoulders. A brass band plays and an organ grinder turns his crank and his monkey dances a stiff jig. Soldiers march in formation, legs parting and closing like scissors. Sammy is in the middle of them, a head taller than the rest so you can easily find him. A gang of wiseacres breaks rank and unfolds a banner that reads *No Beer, No War Stories*. A girl in a calico dress darts into the street and kisses one of the soldiers on his cheek. Close the book, keeping your finger between the pages to mark your place, and when you open it again you will see that she chooses a different soldier. Open and close it again and again until she kisses Sammy.

Turn the page and a house snaps up at the head of a flagstone walk, its windows bright with light. Do you recognize the maple? Each room is illuminated just long enough for one detail to be seen—Brother's baseball mitt, Father's pipe, Mother's sewing machine, Sammy's ruined book.

Turn the page and a table pops from the floor. You can smell baked apples. Mother and Father and Brother and Sammy pop up too, napkins in their laps. Father carves the ham, a brown cone marked with black grid. You hear laughter, the music of forks and knives on the good china. A banner on the wall reads *Welcome Home!* Mother covers her face with her napkin and weeps for joy, a silent tear slides down Father's cheek and hangs on the tip of his folded nose, and Sammy chews with his mouth open.

Turn the page and the small book pops up once again, the gold words on its red cover still too small to read. The desk, the window, and the maple rise as well. Sammy stands at the desk, dressed in striped pajamas, and looks out the window. The pages below wink with fireflies. A cloud moves across the flat circle of the moon, dimming the room and Sammy's face for a moment. The curtains rise and then are pulled out the window where they wave stiffly. Over and over Sammy tries to close the waterlogged book. Each time it pops open again. His chest fills and empties with a creaking sigh. He shakes his head and wets his lips with his paper tongue. Bats hunt bugs above the pages of the lawn. The book he holds becomes the book you hold, open to the pages of the victory parade, and Sammy watches the girl in the calico dress dart into the street and kiss him on his cheek.

July Snow

❧

SCOTT RUSSELL SANDERS

WITH A COPY OF *Yoga Made Simple* open before him and a greasy tarp unfurled beneath him, Gordon Milk squatted on the floor of his garage, trying to mimic the stance of the wiry young man pictured in the book. Neither wiry nor young—past fifty, in fact, and built like a stump—Gordon could not begin to wrench his body into those pretzel shapes.

In a rare stroke of unanimity, his four children had given him the yoga manual on his birthday a week earlier. "Let's face it, Dad, you're thickening like split-pea soup," one daughter observed. "You're stiffening like an old boot," a son added.

Gordon had to admit it was true. In recent years his body had come to feel more and more like a sandbag. It did not help that nowadays, what with budget cuts and a hiring freeze, the city of Red Hawk, Indiana, had him driving trucks instead of fixing them—garbage trucks, gravel trucks, delivery vans, snowplows. Sit down eight hours a day on a jouncing seat, with a cooler of food open beside you, and your butt will spread like warm butter, guaranteed. The widest men Gordon had ever seen were those who drove forklifts at the tire plant where he got his first job, and those who ran derricks at the quarry where his father used to dig limestone.

Since the birthday, Gordon had been rising at dawn each morning to spend a furtive half hour grunting and twisting on the garage floor. He kept reminding himself that he was doing this for the sake of his family, who pestered him to keep his old ticker ticking. Yet he did not want anybody watching him while he struggled to copy the poses of the wiry young man. "*The postures of yoga represent the ideal shapes that are hidden inside you,*" the book assured him. The shapes must have been hidden pretty deep, Gordon figured, because he had not come anywhere near them so far.

Even today, the Fourth of July, when he could have slept late (his only job was to follow the noontime parade through the streets of Red Hawk in a garbage truck), Gordon had rolled from bed at daybreak, careful not to wake his wife, mother, parents-in-law, or children, all of whom slept under his mortgaged roof. As he moved through the house, the only sound he made, aside from the scuffing of callused feet on the linoleum, was a gurgly humming, more like the sound of water running than a man singing, a habit he had picked up from his father.

Although the garage was already turning into an oven on this July morning, he didn't open the door, for fear that an early dog-walker or the neighbors across the street would spy on him. And thus Gordon was caught wearing his tiger-striped Cincinnati Bengals boxer shorts, lathered with sweat and groaning in one of the more painful yoga positions, when his children came bursting into the garage to announce that during the night a storm had buried the city under two feet of snow.

Before Gordon could untwist his corkscrewed body, the children flung open the door and, sure enough, a white drift slumped onto the concrete floor. While the younger two danced along the fringe, squealing in their pajamas, and the two older kids probed the snow with bare toes, Gordon pawed through the laundry basket until he found a grimy pair of coveralls to put on. Wouldn't you know it, on his morning off he would have to drive the plow. Well, at least the storm should cool things off.

"Holy cow, it's warm!" shouted Danny, the littlest. He wriggled his fingers in the drift and threw handfuls into the air. With degrees of skepticism proportional to their ages, the other children did the same, each in turn crying with amazement and delight, even Jeanne, the college sophomore, who prided herself on having put away childish things. Soon all four of them waded into the driveway.

Gordon shuffled over and poked a hand into the wall of snow. It was not so much warm as a kind of no-temperature, dry and wispy like soap flakes or confetti or the tiny Styrofoam beads used for packing boxes. Warm or cold, why did it have to snow on his morning off? The pickup and station wagon, parked on the drive so as to leave room in the garage for his yoga, were two gleaming humps. A thick frosting covered everything—the houses across the way, bushes and trees, mailboxes, telephone poles, fire hydrants. The street, untraveled so far on this holiday morning, curved away as white and smooth as a bathtub. Not a breeze moved. Not a bird sang. Not a motor revved. The world might have seemed fixed and final, if Gordon's kids hadn't been sliding down the hood of the truck on the seats of their pajamas, shouting like pirates.

None of them offered to help shovel, nor did Gordon have the heart to ask them, they were so stoked up with joy. He fetched the coal scoop from its nail in the garage and started clearing a path to the front door. At least it was light, this July snow. Lucky thing, since Gordon had a tricky back. When he threw a shovelful over his shoulder, the white flakes giddied and floated like the downy seeds of dandelions. Still, no matter how light, no matter how warm, two feet of snow was two feet of snow. Long before he reached the front door, he was sweating like a mule, his heart was thumping, and his back was twitching.

"Yoga will help you unkink your spine," Jeanne had told him on his birthday as he unwrapped the book. Far from loosening him, the exercises had made him feel like a stiff knot, the kind that tightens as you work on it. Leaning for a moment on the coal scoop to let his ticker slow down, Gordon wondered if there really was a lean and limber young man hidden somewhere inside him.

Just then an upstairs window thunked open and a voice called down, "Gordon, there's been a blizzard!" and a second voice cried, "You foolish man, you'll catch your death of cold!" and a third voice hollered, "Come indoors this minute and get some clothes on!" In this way, Gordon learned that all three grandparents were up. He went back to digging.

Presently the kitchen window opened and Mabel, his wife, shouted, "The supervisor's on the phone and says to report for snowplow duty right away. But I say you eat breakfast first."

Outnumbered as usual, Gordon allowed Mabel to stuff him with oatmeal and banana and wheat germ and skimmed milk, then, to humor the grandparents, he bundled up in winter clothes, from boots to knitted cap. As he trudged past the car and pickup, where his own children had been joined by a passel of neighborhood kids—all whooping and sliding, the youngest ones clad only in diapers or underpants because of the heat—Gordon realized that driving to work was out of the question. So he waved goodbye to his family and waded through the snow toward the city equipment yard, lunch box clunking against his leg.

As soon as he was beyond sight of the house, he took off the hat, gloves, scarf, coat, and flannel shirt, carrying them all in his arms. Still he sweated, and the flakes stuck to him like feathers. When he finally reached the lot where the snowplows were parked, it was a hard job to open the gate, for so far nobody else had made it in to work. No sooner had he climbed into his truck and started the engine than voices began to crackle at him from the CB radio.

"All available plows report immediately to the mayor's house . . . to police headquarters . . . to station WXTZ . . . to Our Lady of the Highways Hospital . . . to the Perpetual American Bank . . . to Red Hawk Bowling Lanes . . ."

Gordon tried hard to answer all these voices, zigzagging across the city in his parrot-green truck with the scooped blade in front and the blinking yellow light on top. But whenever he plowed in one direction, he was called in three other directions. He drove as fast as he dared. The snow flew away before him, airy as the goose down from pillows. In the rearview mirror he could see it settling again in his wake. He imagined himself piloting an icebreaker, parting the North Seas—or perhaps, in view of the heat, the South Seas. Twice he drove by his own house, honking at the yard full of kids, and on the second pass he found the snow as deep as ever.

Soon other green trucks were on the roads, driven by his buddies from the maintenance crew. Gordon waved as they passed, but they might as well have been plowing water, for all the good they were doing.

Unable to clear the streets, he began picking up riders, ferrying them to the places they needed to reach. Thus he carried four mailmen to the post office, three civil defense wardens to fire stations, two soldiers to the bus depot (from which, he reckoned, no buses would be leaving), a doctor to a woman in labor, a girl to a volleyball tournament, a grandfather to a birthday party, a painter to her studio, a banjo player to his banjo. The passengers could see that Gordon was busy handling the truck, so they contented themselves with brief remarks on the order of "Crazy weather, hey?" or "If you ask me, it's a sign."

With help from the passengers, Gordon's lunch box, which Mabel had packed to the brim, was empty before mid-morning. By that hour, it was so hot in the truck that Gordon had to leave the windows open, no matter how the riders complained. The snow blew in and settled on the dash, the seat, his clothes, like an albino version of the fluff that gathers under beds: widow's wool, his mother called it; whore's hair, his father called it.

The more plows joined him on the streets, the more the air filled with fluff, as though Red Hawk were being shaken inside one of those wintry glass paperweights. Snow blurred the truck's windshield faster than the wipers could scrape it clean. The white haze that separated Gordon from the world became a blank screen on which he saw, not only the young man tied in yoga postures, but also jugglers, acrobats, violinists fingering their instruments, protesters clambering over fences at missile bases, fasters reduced to skin and bones, trampoline artists, tennis pros delivering perfect forehand volleys, lovers joining in ways never before attempted. Forget it, Gordon told himself. You're not cut out for such poses.

There was nothing to do but keep driving.

Toward noon, when the marchers were lining up for the July Fourth parade, more snow began to fall, great lacy flakes that swerved on their way down, as though from the plucking of a sky full of chickens. Past the leaping cheerleaders in their short skirts, past the veterans in faded uniforms, the high school bands, the politicians with gleaming teeth, the clowns, policemen, six-legged dragons, past farmers on tractors, queens in sun dresses and kings in shirts paler than the snow, Gordon drove his plow. Hunched over the wheel, peering into the white swirl, he envisioned a map of the city: the courthouse square, the rows of houses and stores, the snaky blue river, the green patchwork of parks, his truck a dim yellow light pulsing through the web of streets, and himself inside the cab, an even dimmer light but still burning.

The Red Bow

✤

GEORGE SAUNDERS

NEXT NIGHT, WALKING OUT where it happened, I found her little red bow.

I brought it in, threw it down on the table, said: My God my God.

Take a good look at it and also I'm looking at it, said Uncle Matt. And we won't ever forget it, am I right?

First thing of course was to find the dogs. Which turns out, they were holed up back of the—the place where the little kids go, with the plastic balls in cages, they have birthday parties and so forth—holed up in this sort of nest of tree debris dragged there by the Village.

Well we lit up the debris and then shot the three of them as they ran out.

But that Mrs. Pearson, who'd seen the whole—well she said there'd been four, four dogs, and next night we found that the fourth had gotten into Mullins Run and bit the Elliotts' Sadie and that white Muskerdoo that belonged to Evan and Millie Bates next door.

Jim Elliott said he would put Sadie down himself and borrowed my gun to do it, and did it, then looked me in the eye and said he was sorry for our loss, and Evan Bates said he couldn't do it, and would I? But then finally he at least led Muskerdoo out into that sort of field they call The Concourse, where they do the barbecues and whatnot, giving it a sorrowful little kick (a gentle kick, there was nothing mean in Evan) whenever it snapped at him, saying Musker Jesus!—and then he said, *Okay, now,* when he was ready for me to do it, and I did it, and afterwards he said he was sorry for our loss.

Around midnight we found the fourth one gnawing at itself back of Bourne's place, and Bourne came out and held the flashlight as we put it down, and helped us load it into the wheelbarrow alongside Sadie and Muskerdoo, our plan being—Dr. Vincent had said this was best—to burn those we found, so no other animal would—you know, via feeding on the corpses—in any event, Dr. Vincent said it was best to burn them.

When we had the fourth in the wheelbarrow my Jason said: Mr. Bourne, what about Cookie?

Well no I don't believe so, said Bourne.

He was an old guy and had that old-guy tenderness for the dog, it being pretty much all he had left in the world, such as for example he always called it *friend-of-mine,* as in: How about a walk, friend-of-mine?

But she is mostly an outside dog? I said.

She is almost completely an outside dog, he said. But still, I don't believe so.

And Uncle Matt said: Well, Lawrence, I for one am out here tonight trying to be certain. I think you can understand that.

I can, Bourne said, I most certainly can.

And Bourne brought out Cookie and we had a look.

At first she seemed fine, but then we noticed she was doing this funny thing where a shudder would run through her and her eyes would all of a sudden go wet, and Uncle Matt said: Lawrence, is that something Cookie would normally do?

Well, ah . . . , said Mr. Bourne.

And another shudder ran through Cookie.

Oh Jesus Christ, said Mr. Bourne, and went inside.

Uncle Matt told Seth and Jason to trot out whistling into the field and Cookie would follow, which she did, and Uncle Matt ran after, with his gun, and though he was, you know, not exactly a runner, still he kept up pretty good just via sheer effort, like he wanted to make sure this thing got done right.

Which I was grateful to have him there, because I was too tired in my mind and my body to know what was right anymore, and sat down on the porch, and pretty soon heard this little pop.

Then Uncle Matt trotted back from the field and stuck his head inside and said: Lawrence do you know, did Cookie have contact with other dogs, was there another dog or dogs she might have played with, nipped, that sort of thing?

Oh get out, get away, said Bourne.

Lawrence my God, said Uncle Matt. Do you think I like this? Think of what we've been through. Do you think this is fun for me, for us?

There was a long silence and then Bourne said well all he could think of was that terrier at the Rectory, him and Cookie sometimes played when Cookie got off her lead.

When we got to the Rectory, Father Terry said he was sorry for our loss, and brought Merton out, and we watched a long time and Merton never shuddered and his eyes remained dry, you know, normal.

Looks fine, I said.

Is fine, said Father Terry. Watch this: Merton, genuflect.

And Merton did this dog stretchy thing where he sort of like bowed.

Could be fine, said Uncle Matt. But also could be he's sick but just at an early stage.

We'll have to be watchful, said Father Terry.

Yes, although, said Uncle Matt. Not knowing how it spreads and all, could it be we are in a better-safe-than-sorry type of situation? I don't know, I truly don't know. Ed, what do you think?

And I didn't know what I thought. In my mind I was all the time just going over it and over it, the before, the after, like her stepping up on that footstool to put that red bow in, saying these like lady phrases to herself, such as, Well Who Will Be There, Will There Be Cakes?

I hope you are not suggesting putting down a perfectly healthy dog, said Father Terry.

And Uncle Matt produced from his shirt pocket a red bow and said: Father, do you have any idea what this is and where we found it?

But it was not the real bow, not Emily's bow, which I kept all the time in my pocket, it was a pinker shade of red and was a little bigger than the real bow, and I recognized it as having come from our Karen's little box on her dresser.

No I do not know what that is, said Father Terry. A hair bow?

I for one am never going to forget that night, said Uncle Matt. What we all felt. I for one am going to work to make sure that no one ever again has to endure what we had to endure that night.

I have no disagreement with that at all, said Father Terry.

It is true you don't know what this is, Uncle Matt said, and put the bow back in his pocket. You really really have no experience whatsoever of what this is.

Ed, Father Terry said to me. Killing a perfectly healthy dog has nothing to do with—

Possibly healthy but possibly not, said Uncle Matt. Was Cookie bitten? Cookie was not. Was Cookie infected? Yes she was. How was Cookie infected? We do not know. And there is your dog, who interacted with Cookie in exactly the same way that Cookie interacted with the known infected animal, namely through being in close physical proximity.

It was funny about Uncle Matt, I mean funny as in great, admirable, this sudden stepping up to the plate, because previously—I mean, yes, he of course loved the kids, but had never been particularly—I mean he rarely even spoke to them, least of all to Emily, her being the youngest. Mostly he just went very quietly around the house, especially since January when he'd lost his job, avoiding the kids really, a little ashamed almost, as if knowing that, when they grew up, they would never be the out-of-work slinking-around uncle, but instead would be the owners of the house where the out-of-work slinking uncle etc., etc.

But losing her had, I suppose, made him realize for the first time how much he loved her, and this sudden strength—focus, certainty, whatever—was a comfort, because tell the truth I was not doing well at all—I had always loved autumn and now it was full autumn and you could smell woodsmoke and fallen apples but all of the world, to me, was just, you know, flat.

It is like your kid is this vessel that contains everything good. They look up at you so loving, trusting you to take care of them, and then one night—what gets me, what I can't get over, is that while she was being—while what happened was happening, I was—I had sort of snuck away downstairs to check my e-mail, see, so that while—while what happened was happening, out there in the schoolyard, a few hundred yards away, I was sitting there typing—typing!—which, okay, there is no sin in that, there was no way I could have known, and yet—do you see what I mean? Had I simply risen from my computer and walked upstairs and gone outside and for some reason, any reason, crossed the schoolyard, then believe me, there is not a dog in the world, no matter how crazy—

And my wife felt the same way and had not come out of our bedroom since the tragedy.

So Father you are saying no? said Uncle Matt. You are refusing?

I pray for you people every day, Father said. What you are going through, no one ever should have to go through.

Don't like that man, Uncle Matt said as we left the Rectory. Never have and never will.

And I knew that. They had gone to high school together and there had been something about a girl, some last-minute prom-date type of situation that had not gone in Uncle Matt's favor, and I think some shoving on a ball-field, some name-calling, but all of this was years ago, during like say the Kennedy administration.

He will not observe that dog properly, said Uncle Matt. Believe me. And if he does notice something, he won't do what is necessary. Why? Because it's his dog. *His* dog. Everything that's his? It's special, above the law.

I don't know, I said. Truly I don't.

He doesn't get it, said Uncle Matt. He wasn't there that night, he didn't see you carrying her inside.

Which, tell the truth, Uncle Matt hadn't seen me carrying her inside either, having gone out to rent a video—but still, yes, I got his drift about Father Terry, who had always had a streak of ego, with that silver hair with the ripples in it, and also he had a weight set in the Rectory basement and worked out twice a day and had, actually, a very impressive physique, which he showed off, I felt—we all felt—by ordering his priest shirts perhaps a little too tight.

Next morning during breakfast Uncle Matt was very quiet and finally said, well, he might be just a fat little unemployed guy who hadn't had the education some had, but love was love, honoring somebody's memory was honoring somebody's memory, and since he had no big expectations for his day, would I let him borrow the truck, so he could park it in the Burger

King lot and keep an eye on what was going on over at the Rectory, sort of in memory of Emily?

And the thing was, we didn't really use that truck anymore and so—it was a very uncertain time, you know, and I thought, Well, what if it turns out Merton really is sick, and somehow gets away and attacks someone else's— so I said yes, he could use the truck.

He sat all Tuesday morning and Tuesday afternoon, I mean not leaving the truck once, which for him—he was not normally a real dedicated guy, if you know what I mean. And then Tuesday night he came charging in and threw a tape in the VCR and said watch, watch this.

And there on the TV was Merton, leaning against the Rectory fence, shuddering, arching his back, shuddering again.

So we took our guns and went over.

Look I know I know, said Father Terry. But I'm handling it here, in my own way. He's had enough trouble in his life, poor thing.

Say what? said Uncle Matt. Trouble in his life? You are saying to this man, this father, who has recently lost—the dog has had *trouble in his life*?

Well, however, I should say—I mean, that was true. We all knew about Merton, who had been brought to Father Terry from this bad area, one of his ears sliced nearly off, plus it had, as I understood it, this anxiety condition, where it would sometimes faint because dinner was being served, I mean, it would literally pass out due to its own anticipation, which, you know, that couldn't have been easy.

Ed, said Father Terry. I am not saying Merton's trouble is, I am not comparing Merton's trouble to your—

Christ let's hope not, said Uncle Matt.

All's I'm saying is I'm losing something too, said Father Terry.

Ho boy, said Uncle Matt. Ho boy ho boy.

Ed, my fence is high, said Father Terry. He's not going anywhere, I've also got him on a chain in there. I want him to—I want it to happen here, just him and me. Otherwise it's too sad.

You don't know from sad, said Uncle Matt.

Sadness is sadness, said Father Terry.

Blah blah blah, said Uncle Matt. I'll be watching.

Well later that week this dog Tweeter Deux brought down a deer in the woods between the TwelvePlex and the Episcopal church, and that Tweeter

Deux was not a big dog, just, you know, crazed, and how the DeFrancinis knew she had brought down a deer was, she showed up in the living room with a chewed-off foreleg.

And that night—well the DeFrancinis' cat began racing around the house, and its eyes took on this yellow color, and at one point while running it sort of locked up and skidded into the baseboard and gave itself a concussion.

Which is when we realized the problem was bigger than we had initially thought.

The thing was, we did not know and could not know how many animals had already been infected—the original four dogs had been at large for several days before we found them, and any animal they might have infected had been at large for nearly two weeks now, and we did not even know the precise method of infection—was it bites, spit, blood, was something leaping from coat to coat? We knew it could happen to dogs, it appeared it could happen to cats—what I'm saying is, it was just a very confusing and frightening time.

So Uncle Matt got on the iMac and made up these fliers, calling a Village Meeting, and at the top was a photo he'd taken of the red bow (not the real bow but Karen's pinkish red bow, which he'd color-enhanced on the iMac to make it redder and also he had superimposed Emily's communion photo) and along the bottom it said FIGHT THE OUTRAGE, and underneath in smaller letters it said something along the lines of, you know, Why do we live in this world but to love what is ours, and when one of us has cruelly lost what we loved, it is the time to band together to stand up to that which threatens that which we love, so that no one else ever has to experience this outrage again. Now that we have known and witnessed this terrific pain, let us resolve together to fight against any and all circumstances which might cause or contribute to this or a similar outrage now or at any time in the future—and we had Seth and Jason run these around town, and on Friday night ended up with nearly four hundred people in the high school gym.

Coming in, each person got a rolled-up FIGHT THE OUTRAGE poster of the color-enhanced bow, and also on these Uncle Matt had put in—I objected to this at first, until I saw how people responded—well he had put in these tiny teethmarks, they were not meant to look real, they were just, you know, as he said, symbolic reminders, and down in one corner was Emily's communion photo and in the opposite corner a photo of her as a baby, and Uncle Matt had hung a larger version of that poster (large as a closet) up over the speaker's podium.

And I was sort of astonished by Uncle Matt, I mean, he was showing so much—I'd never seen him so motivated. This was a guy whose idea of a big day was checking the mail and getting up a few times to waggle the TV antenna—and here he was, in a suit, his face all red and sort of proud and shiny

Well Uncle Matt got up and thanked everyone for coming, and Mrs. De-Francini, owner of Tweeter Deux, held up that chewed-up foreleg, and Dr. Vincent showed slides of cross-sections of the brain of one of the original four dogs, and then at the end I talked, only I got choked up and couldn't say much except thanks to everybody, their support had meant the world to us, and I tried to say about how much we had all loved her, but couldn't go on.

Uncle Matt and Dr. Vincent had, on the iMac, on their own (not wanting to bother me) drawn up what they called a Three-Point Emergency Plan, which the three points were: (1) All Village animals must immediately undergo an Evaluation, to determine was the animal Infected, (2) All Infected or Suspected Infected animals must be destroyed at once, and (3) All Infected or Suspected Infected animals, once destroyed, must be burned at once to minimize the possibility of Second-Hand Infection.

Then someone asked could they please clarify the meaning of "suspected"?

Suspected, you know, said Uncle Matt. That means we suspect and have good reason to suspect that an animal is, or may be, Infected.

The exact methodology is currently under development, said Dr. Vincent.

How can we, how can you, ensure that this assessment will be fair and reasonable though? the guy asked.

Well that is a good question, said Uncle Matt. The key to that is, we will have the assessment done by fair-minded persons who will do the Evaluation in an objective way that seems reasonable to all.

Trust us, said Dr. Vincent. We know it is so very important.

Then Uncle Matt held up the bow—actually a new bow, very big, about the size of a lady's hat, really, I don't know where he found that—and said: All of this may seem confusing but it is not confusing if we remember that it is all about *This*, simply *This*, about honoring *This*, preventing *This*.

Then it was time for the vote, and it was something like 393 for and none against, with a handful of people abstaining (which I found sort of hurtful), but then following the vote everyone rose to their feet and, regarding me and Uncle Matt with—well they were smiling these warm smiles, some even fighting back tears—it was just a very nice, very kind moment, and I will never forget it, and will be grateful for it until the day I die.

After the meeting Uncle Matt and Trooper Kelly and a few others went and did what had to be done in terms of Merton, over poor Father Terry's objections—I mean, he was upset about it, of course, so upset it took five men to hold him back, him being so fit and all—and then they brought Merton, Merton's body, back to our place and burned it, out at the tree line where we had burned the others, and someone asked should we give Father Terry the ashes, and Uncle Matt said why take the chance, we have not ruled out the possibility of airborne transmission, and putting on the little white masks supplied by Dr. Vincent, we raked Merton's ashes into the swamp.

That night my wife came out of our bedroom for the first time since the tragedy, and we told her everything that had been happening.

And I watched her closely, to see what she thought, to see what I should think, her having always been my rock.

Kill every dog, every cat, she said very slowly. Kill every mouse, every bird. Kill every fish. Anyone objects, kill them too.

Then she went back to bed.

Well that was—I felt so bad for her, she was simply not herself—I mean, this was a woman who, finding a spider, used to make me take it outside in a cup. Although, as far as killing all dogs and cats—I mean, there was a certain—I mean, if you did that, say, killed every dog and cat, regardless of were they Infected or not, you could thereby guarantee, to 100 percent, that no other father in town would ever again have to carry in his—God there is so much I don't remember about that night but one thing I do remember is, as I brought her in, one of her little clogs thunked off onto the linoleum, and still holding her I bent down to—and she wasn't there anymore, she wasn't, you know, there, inside her body. I had passed her thousands of times on the steps, in the kitchen, had heard her little voice from everywhere in the house and why, why had I not, every single time, rushed up to her and told her everything that I—but of course you can't do that, it would malform a child, and yet—

What I'm saying is, with no dogs and no cats, the chance that another father would have to carry his animal-murdered child into their home, where the child's mother sat, doing the bills, happy or something like happy for the last time in her life, happy until the instant she looked up and saw—what I guess I'm saying is, with no dogs and no cats, the chance of that happening to someone else (or to us again) goes down to that very beautiful number of Zero.

Which is why we eventually did have to enact our policy of sacrificing all dogs and cats who had been in the vicinity of the Village at the time of the incident.

But as far as killing the mice, the birds, the fish, no, we had no evidence to support that, not at that time anyway, and had not yet added the Reasonable Suspicion Clause to the Plan, and as far as the people, well my wife wasn't herself, that's all there was to it, although soon what we found was—I mean, there was something prescient about what she'd said, because in time we did in fact have to enact some very specific rules regarding the physical process of extracting the dogs and/or cats from a home where the owner was being unreasonable—or the fish, birds, whatever—and also had to assign specific penalties should these people, for example, assault one of the Animal Removal Officers, as a few of them did, and finally also had to issue some guidelines on how to handle individuals who, for whatever reason, felt it useful to undercut our efforts by, you know, obsessively and publicly criticizing the Five- and Six-Point Plans, just very unhappy people.

But all of that was still months away.

I often think back to the end of that first Village Meeting, to that standing-ovation moment. Uncle Matt had also printed up T-shirts, and after the vote everyone pulled the T-shirt with Emily's smiling face on it over his or her own shirt, and Uncle Matt said that he wanted to say thank you from the bottom of his heart, and not just on behalf of his family, this family of his that had been sadly and irreversibly malformed by this unimaginable and profound tragedy, but also, and perhaps more so, on behalf of all the families we had just saved, via our vote, from similar future profound unimaginable tragedies.

And as I looked out over the crowd, at all those T-shirts—I don't know, I found it deeply moving, that all of those good people would feel so fondly toward her, many of whom had not even known her, and it seemed to me that somehow they had come to understand how good she had been, how precious, and were trying, with their applause, to honor her.

Medieval Land

STEVE TOMASULA

"...IN A TIME ..."

Anselm thought, Troubadours sang . . .

"... *long, long ago* . . ."

. . . others, too, until songs trapped in wax hardened into vinyl discs ever evolving—revolving—spinning in place—faster, faster—history anew?—better that than wobbly plates atop a juggler's sticks—men-with-telescopes-discovering-planets redux, griffins walking the earth again; End Times and Holy Wars. *De novo* peasants, and tyrants too—once more the earth is 5,000 years old, as it says in the Bible—and he wondered if that was how . . .

"... *though not so very far away* . . ."

. . . how, in the 21st century, he had ended up a gong farmer.

"Medieval Land!" the recorded announcer roared, and the gates were flung open, knights galloping out into the arena on their steeds, their squires jogging behind. And Anselm walked out behind them, shovel in hand.

Theological Questions

How many angels/strings/meanings/computations/black holes/singularities/galaxies can dance on the head of a pin?

Has anyone ever seen an ionic bond?

If a body is reconstituted at the end of time, what happens to the bodies of Christians who have been eaten by cannibals? What happens to the cannibals? Especially cannibals who, after having dined on Christian flesh, have themselves been baptized into Christianity? And then eaten by other cannibals. Who were in turn baptized. And then, in turn, eaten? Ad nauseam . . .

If a humanized mouse bears the genes of a tobacco plant that carries the genes of a jellyfish, that bears the genes of a rat, that has been born by a rabbit that carries the genes of stink weed is it a?—Oh, never mind.

MEDIEVAL LAND. You can see it from the highway: an enormous metal building set on a plain like those sheds that homeowners buy from Sears to store riding lawn mowers, also from Sears, only a thousand times bigger, maybe a million. A great gray box if the roofline hadn't been notched to give it the silhouette of a storybook castle. Yea, without its battle pennants, its Las Vegas-style marquee—MEDIEVAL LAND! MEDIEVAL LAND! MEDIEVAL LAND!—you might think it's just another of those gigantic box-buildings rising from a heartland paved with corn—a land so flat and plentiful that even farmers could afford it until tax rates were rigged to attract agri-factories or astrodome-sized distributors of tires, or televisions, or furniture, for the 100 serf-wage employees they might take in.

In a sense you'd be right. It was sort of a FedEx of goods, Anselm oft' considered as he pulled into the employee lot. Only instead of flying goods in to a central sorting center before they are flown out to individual addresses, here in this redistribution center, individuals—or better, whole families—were brought in and the goods returned to their addresses in the form of food in their bellies, real plastic crowns on their heads, real plastic swords in their hands, and memories . . . Real memories! Anselm, limping in sackcloth, one of them.

E thru G (from ERIC the RED's BLOG)

. . . **EXECUTIONER:** an anonymous government employee whose identity was secreted by the hood he wore; his responsibilities included torturing detainees, chopping through necks as though they were logs, parboiling heads and displaying them on pikes. Often haunted by spooks, many executioners committed suicide.

FAERIE: a mixed and varied species, from beings of light to walking scarecrows. While Faeries' dispositions range from altruistic to murderous, all are capricious and simply can't care about the consequences of their actions.

FEUDALISM: an arrangement linking power and wealth to pedigree. Feudal society eventually centered in castle life for many of the same reasons that those with means join today's gated communities.

Subjects Are to Remain in Character at All Times

All employees, as they exit the locker room into the public areas, were supposed to bow to the faux crest on the wall: a shield emblazoned with the family tree that showed links between the founder of Medieval Land and one hundred and twenty other aristocratic families, descendants all of noble stock, as well as their wholly-owned subsidiaries. Cloud Faces in each of the four corners blowing hard. *Here Be Dragons.* And The Great White House— Camelot—whose banner and arms maintained peace across all maps. A God-given right to rule. Or so it would seem.

Indeed, back on the day that the castle's marquee announced NOW HIR-ING, Anselm had found himself in a line of would-be subjects so long that it wrapped around the outer walls. Praying with the multitude for an audience within, he had fallen in with another supplicant who, like Anselm, only had to sell what God had given him. Only this peasant—Jude—had already optioned off his futures to the National Guard: "If I'm called, they'll teach me a skill—heavy equipment operator." A clean-cut boy from one of the farms that used to dot the land before there was a Medieval Land Inc., Jude could have easily ridden as a knight in the show—if he didn't look like a hick who'd grown up feeding Midwestern chickens.

In single file they approached their present judgment: a Casting Director/Personnel Manager who stood at an elevated podium between two doors. As the supplicants filed forward, their judge would assay each body, wherein was written that person's God-given station—"Royalty," "Court" or "Peasant"—sending those with photogenic smiles, healthy skin, the bodies of ex-cheerleaders and jocks to the right, while those with computer-nerd acne, or philosopher's physique, a hunch or lumps, librarian's tan, those who grew up suffering a lack of skin-care products, whose teeth had never been set in their ideal places, who grew up in want of five-dollar co-pay or no-pay health insurance, whose non-existent training in posture, walking with grace, those whose frame bore their mother's or fathers' occupation (back of a hotel maid) or place of origin or destination (lungs of the asbestos abater), or gimp, like his, were sent to the left.

GONG FARMER: (from gong, a going, passage, drain) a cleaner of privies. Any Cleaner of Shyt. The toilet seat of a castle sat atop a gong, that is, a chute that ran through its stone wall and emptied into the moat below. One of the gong farmer's duties was to kill invaders trying to gain entry through the gong. Even in times of peace, though, the gong plugged up often since Medievals used straw for toilet paper. When it did, the gong farmer would beat his drum to announce 'the hour of no shyting,' climb up into the gong and clean out corpses or other clogs. The gong farmer had such low status that nearly everyone else in the castle considered it a great prank to sneak up above him, as he went about this duty, and let loose a torrent of filth upon his head . . .

MEN'S RESTROOM No. 3. The company liked Anselm to carry out this part of his job while their "guests" were in the house, seeing him dressed in his sackcloth costume, picking up paper towels that the royal pigs left on the floor, making sure there was enough toilet paper in the stalls. He was mopping piss stains under the urinals when two princes ran in, plastic crowns on their heads, $200 Michael Jordan's on their feet, the both of them splashing right on the floor he'd just mopped. He washed his hands, something the kyds didn't do, pushing by him as he signed the log taped to the door: LAST CLEANED BY:_____. Then he went to take up his post in the arena for the show, humming to himself, *Well I haven't fought a dragon in a fortnight* . . .

Jude fought them all nightly, and twicely on Saturday night. The last portion of the show involved a display of riding skill, a contest between Christian knights and Mohammedan caliphs. Each in turn, the knights, then caliphs, bore down with sword, then scimitar, as they aimed for colored rings. Like most histories, this one was fixed, and the Christians always win.

But not ungraciously. For at this point, the stagehands used to release the dragon: a contraption with two operators inside that snorts dry-ice smoke. Jaws snapping, red-eyes flashing, animatronic tail swishing, Jude used to be in the head, operating its fiery breath, directing its steps.

But a lot has changed since the dragon first emerged from its den. Jude was gone, and since it had been the end of the summer, the company didn't want to replace him. In fact, they'd gotten rid of the whole ending to a show where the dragon's appearance used to signal all knights and caliphs to dismount. First the Christian knights would make an attack, and were repelled by the beast; then it was the turn of the Moors, who had an equal lack of success. It was only when they joined forces that they were able to defeat their common foe. With the beast dead at their feet, they used to link arms—Christian, Moor, Christian, Moor, Christian, Moor—and sing as inspirational rock music swells, "*We are the world* . . ."

But as they say, a lot has changed since then.

Church & Science in the Age of Irony

Catholic bishops denounce researchers for trying to coax stem cells into transubstantiating into heart muscle, or other new flesh, demanding that they "stop chasing after miracles."

The State in the Age of Religious War

And lo, while yet governor of Texas, the Lord came to him in a vision, or so he has claimed, and said, "I want you to run for president." Me Lord? The governor might have asked; though he did not ask, for all his life he had been among the elect and so was less surprised that God Himself, not an angel nor any other emissary, would deliver the message than he was by the scorn heaped upon him by atheists, secular humanists, and other witches who scoffed at the idea that God would choose him as His instrument, righteous finger on the button of Armageddon, ruler of the mightiest military on earth, he whose greatest ambition was to be baseball commissioner, who needed gift-grades to get to "C" (at a college where "C" spelled dunce), who was surprised (this in his first term as president) to learn that there were blacks in Brazil (this from someone who grew up not in a shack in Appalachia, nor a dark hole, but in the highest circles of power), who went missing from the military the time he himself could have fought instead of sending others. Still, with the certainty granted only to those touched by God, he continued to speak in tongues—"We need to make the pie higher"—and the faithful continued to vote, for surely, the Lord had made fishers of men from fishermen, thieves, and worse reformed drunks than him (but no harlots like Mary Magdalene), and besides, gay marriage must be defeated at all costs, and they recognized in the "funny math" that twisted the election's results, the Hand of God.

To what end, was not yet clear. But clouds were gathering in the East, ominous clouds it seemed since the governor now president oft' declared, "God is at work in world affairs." And he didn't need no advisors to remind him of Zechariah 12:1: Jerusalem will become an international problem; and Revelations 16:12: Troops will cross the Euphrates; and Revelations 11:9: The world will be able to simultaneously witness events; and Joel 3:2; and Micah 4:1; and Matthew; and Luke and four score other such passages wherein is foretold the natural disasters, rampant immorality, the rise of a world economic order—NAFTA, Starbucks, Wal-Mart—and other wondrous signs that signal the Rapture: earthquakes in divers places, famines and troubles, as well as the difference between glorious Jerusalem and wicked Baghdad, the new Babylon; and the return of the Messiah once the Jews had been returned to the land promised by God to Abraham.

Reading these signs he declared, "I believe there is a reason that history has matched this nation with this time," for truly, we have entered The End Times, the final battle between Good and Evil, which 40 million American voters believe will usher in The Second Coming, so he'd better get right with Israel, the lobby said, for a showdown there could be a "dress rehearsal of Armageddon," and God speaks clearly in opening His Seven Seals, and woe unto those who oppose His Chosen People.

As if to punctuate their words, a beast rose up and smote the United States, and unable to capture the beast for his people, the Great Leader's eyes turned to Saddam, this newly-risen Saladin; for if a rematch was in God's master plan, as it was in *True Grit; Rambo 2; Warhead; The Dirty Dozen; The President's Man: A Line in the Sand; Hell in Normandy; Fort Apache; Walker, Texas Ranger: The Final Showdown, Parts 1 & 2; Walker, Texas Ranger: A Matter of Principle; Walker, Texas Ranger: Way of the Warrior; Fighting Back; The Proud and the Damned; Eagle in a Cage; The Green Berets; Master and Commander; Moment of Truth; Blood in the Sun; Delta Force 2: The Colombian Connection; Delta Force 3: Operation Stranglehold; Hero and the Terror; Missing in Action; The Delta Force; Invasion U.S.A.; Code of Silence; Missing in Action 2; Bravo Two Zero; First Blood; Lone Wolf McQuade; Forced Vengeance; Lord of the Rings; Braddock: Missing in Action III; Silent Rage; An Eye for an Eye; A Force of One; Operation Dumbo Drop; Walker Texas Ranger 3: Deadly Re-union; Gung Ho!; Battlestar Galactica; Rambo 3; Command and Conquer, Red Alert* (for PS2); *The Sum of All Fears,* Tom Clancy's *Ghost Recon: Advanced Warfighter* and every other epic he had ever seen, and if Saddam was Saladin, the great Muslim warrior-king who repelled Richard the Lionhearted during the third crusade, that made him?——

Quoth he on the matter: "God told me to strike at al Qaida and I struck them, and then He instructed me to strike at Saddam, which I did."

And in response, Muslim clerics urged their followers to blow themselves up in "Jihad"—holy war—against America, calling this Crusade one more in a series of barbarous military operations against the Muslim world by Christian kings, who launched wave after wave of coalition armies to steal Jerusalem over the course of several hundred years.

And yea, the Great Leader warned television viewers that this effort to bring the rule of God to the four corners of the earth [Editor's note: most believe the earth is round], "this American crusade, this war agin' Evil, is gonna take a while." [*sic*]

Prayer for the Holy Innocents on the Eve of Being Caught in the Crossfire . . .

Can God create a rock so heavy He can't lift it?
Number of subatomic particles it takes to set off a nuclear war: 1.
Can people?

Eliciting Confessions in the 21st Century

The United States redefines "torture" as only those actions specifically intended to cause "organ failure or death," unless excused under the president's executive powers for some circumstances. While such circumstances are left up to the president (or his designees), methods of non-torture allowed under routine circumstances include, but are not limited to: The Ducking Stool; The Witch's Cradle; The Boot; The Collar; Burial (temporary); Electric Shocks; Testicle Clips; The Heretic's Fork; Pressing; Knotting; The Oven; The Pear; The Shin Vise; Stockades; Ordeal by Freezing Shower & Air Conditioning; Water Boarding; Ordeal by Phonebook (place on subject's head and hit with hammer—leaves no bruises); terrorizing nude detainees with dogs or by forcing them to play Russian Roulette; hooding your tired, your poor, yearning to be free, then wiring them up in a Statue of Liberty pose, telling them that if they fall off their pedestal the floor will electrocute them; stacking your naked, huddled masses into pyramids; forcing them to perform oral sex, and etc.

More Science

New studies of a fossil called *Scipionyx samniticus* reveal that dinosaurs must have breathed in much the same way as crocodiles. The fact that the biblical record contains no mention of dinosaurs has often perplexed scientists, but this new finding explains why Moses wouldn't have reported them: if they existed, they probably were just another type of crocodile to the people of his day, e.g. "the great crocodile crouching in the river" (Ezekiel 29:3).

More Religion

Big hairdos and 1-800-BELIEVE numbers . . . *You don't need to wonder why the Lord has set a plague of AIDS upon us: "And ugly and painful sores broke out upon those who had mocked Him." Revelations 16:2 . . . Abortionists, homos, the National Organization of Witches and other devils don't want you to know that it's all explained in Scripture so they can go about their business of killing babies, fornicating, and poking God in the eye!—the One who will not be mocked!* A collage of world chaos appears on screen: mushroom clouds, hurricane-bent palm trees, mind-numbing death tolls, plagues, mudslides, wild fires, rampant superstition, drought, floods, earthquakes and starving children; the tyrant of the day whipping up turbaned hordes . . .

The Soviets used to figure prominently among the atheists in these collages: bushy eyebrows and scowling faces looking down approvingly upon parades of missiles sporting Hammer-&-Sickles . . . "A bear will rise up from the East": a common pull-quote at the time was still on-screen, having survived, apparently, the Soviet fall, though Putin's face now graced the collage. A handsome man in a business suit, he could easily be one of ours, though Anselm didn't think that was the point.

Medieval doctors wore duck masks, somehow knowing that when God, with His sense of humor, ended the World, it wouldn't go with a bang, or whimper, but quack . . .

"Operating the dragon was a lot like operating a garden tiller," Jude had said.

The Children's Crusade

One spring day in 1212, a child of French farmers began to preach Crusade, claiming that Christ had appeared to him while tending sheep, and bade him to retake the Holy Land from the Muslims. Others had tried before, of course. Four times, armies led by kings had tried and failed, their efforts dissolving into spectacles of greed and barbarism since many crusaders only used religious patriotism as a pretext to plunder the Holy Land for their own enrichment. But their example was the very reason his crusade would succeed, the boy professed, since his crusade—a crusade comprised solely of children—would use no other weapon than faith and as he and his fellow children prayed down the walls of Jerusalem, their innocence would protect them. At the urging of his father, he began to march to the east—*an army of one*. Other children joined in, increasingly encouraged by their parents as their number grew—*be all you can be*—for so clearly did the innocence of the children shine out from them that they truly did seem touched by God.

Prayer for the Holy Innocents on the Eve of a Dangerous Journey

By the time they reached Rome, the army had grown to 30,000 French children—not one over twelve-years old—and another 20,000 boys and girls from Germany. The pope (named Innocent) didn't believe real innocence had a chance. So rather than dissuade them, he gave the children a blessing, and let them pass, believing that while they could not succeed, they

would shame the crowns of Europe into forming a coalition of the willing to
join in on the attack.

Pfc. Steven Acosta, 19, Company C, 67th Armored Regiment.
Hammond, Indiana, Died from friendly fire in Baquba, Iraq.

"I joined because I wanted to learn how to operate a bulldozer. I thought
that if my unit got activated it would be to clean up after a hurricane or
earthquake."

Did Jesus ever laugh?

Pfc. Paul J. Bueche, 19, Illinois Army National Guard, Aurora, Illinois.
Died when the tire he was changing on a UH-60 Black Hawk helicopter
exploded in Balad, Iraq.

Of the 20,000 children from Germany who joined The Children's Crusade, none returned and of their fate nothing is known. Of the 30,000 children from France, many fell to disease, drought, exposure, kidnappings, and
other hardships of the journey. When the rest reached the Mediterranean,
the sea did not part for them as they believed it would and they languished
at various ports, waiting for their miracle until—Reprieve!—it came: two
Christian merchants with ships to take them to the Holy Land!

Pfc. Amy A. Duerksen, 19, 4th Infantry Division. Johnston, Iowa.
Died of a non-combat related injury in Baghdad, Iraq.

Lance Cpl. Kenneth J. Butler, 19. Columbus, Ohio. Killed by a
homemade bomb near Amariya, Iraq.

Two of the seven ships that the merchants hired were lost in a storm,
though, and all of the children aboard drowned. The remaining ships were
handed over to Muslim slavers from Africa, at a destination prearranged by
the merchants. Those not sold in Algiers were later sold in the slave-markets
of Baghdad where the price for white, Frankish slaves was higher. Though
most converted to Islam, more than a few were tortured and martyred for not
accepting their new faith. Only a handful managed to make their way home
and relate the fate of the rest, whereupon the father of the original shepherd
boy, the father who had encouraged his son and other children to take up the
crusade, was beaten to death by a mob of angry parents.

Lance Cpl. Dominic C. Brown, 19, Truck Company, Eau Clair, Wisconsin. Died due to a non-combat related incident in Anbar province, Iraq. Lance Cpl. Andrew Julian Aviles, 18, Headquarters & Service Company. Lansing, Michigan. Killed by an Iraqi artillery round. Pfc. Roberto C. Baez, 19, Northfield, Minnesota. Killed by a roadside bomb. Lance Cpl. Nicholas H. Anderson, 19, Hayward, Wisconsin. Died in a vehicle incident. Pfc. Stephen P. Baldwyn, 19, Lincoln, Nebrasaka. Died of wounds. Andrew D. Bedard, 19, Missoula, Montana. Killed by a home- made bomb. Gunnar D. Becker, 19, Forestburg, South Dakoka. Died. Jeffrey F. Braun, 19, Whinfield, Kansas. Died. Daniel Scott R. Bubb, 19. Killed. James J. Arellano, 19; Anthony E. Butterfield, 19; Shayne M. Cabino, 19; Peter D. Wagler, 18; Tina M. Priest, 19; Jody W. Mis- sildine, 19; Jeremy W. Ehle, 19; Stephen P. Snowberger III, 18; Leon B. Deraps, 19; Christopher M. Eckhardt, 19; Brent B. Zoucha, 19; Ryan J. Clark, 19; Kyle R. Miller, 19; Devon J. Gibbons, 19; David N. Crombie, 19 . . .

The 12,000-Ton Blood Gutter

"You studied history," Jude had said. "In all your readings, doesn't war seem like something that just happens? Like a hurricane? Or accident? Whenever a king or whatever starts a war, the ordinary Joe always just goes, right? I mean, just because a chicken farmer does his duty doesn't make him a killer, does it?"

A man of so few words, that was the longest speech he'd ever made. Or at least the most impassioned, revealing how much going weighed. They'd been watching *X Games* on TV when a commercial came on showing a kid in the yard of a farmhouse, flying a kite, then a little older, flying a toy airplane, then older still flying a radio-controlled model plane, then jump cut to him just a little older now, features of a fine young man at the remote-controls of a surveillance-kill-drone as heroic rock music swells—the culmination of a childhood—*We've been waiting for you. The US Army!*

Before Anselm could fashion an answer comforting yet true, Jude brusquely handed him a card. "Here's my address. In case anyone at Medi- eval Land wants to write to me." FPO: *USS IOWA*. A ship named after a state paved with corn.

And on that day and all the rest, Anselm tried to imagine it as a gleaming city afloat upon a sea of green, a pastoral image, though looking it up online, he thought he understood how Jude's dragon could come to live within, carried from the Middle West to the Middle East not by the winds of chance nor the white sails of some merchant's ship, but aboard a gray device with its eight Babcock & Wilcox three drum 565psi Boilers; its two 18 foot 3 inch (5.563m) four-blade Screws; its 12.1 inches, inclined 19° (307mm) armor plating; its nine 66 foot-long, 239,000 pound, 16-inch (406-mm) / 50-caliber guns and their 2,700 pound Armor-Piercing shells; its 1,900 lb (862 kg) HC (High-Capacity), large bursting, bombardment shells (with their signature 50-foot craters, and defoliated forests); its "Katie" or kilo-ton nuclear shells; its twelve 5-inch/38 caliber DP Guns (Mark 12) (127mm); its array of 16 launch tubes, 8 Armored Box Launchers and 20mm/76 CIWS Anti-Aircraft/Missile Missiles; its 32 BGM-109 Tomahawk Cruise Missiles; 16 RGM-84 Harpoon Anti-Ship Missiles; its SPS-49 long range radar system; its SPY-1D Phased Array Radar (simultaneously tracks 128 targets); its two VTOL craft, Apache helicopters, eighty assault tanks and other armored vehicles; its eight RQ-2 Pioneer unmanned, remote-control vehicles (RPVs) and other (history-making) robots (first time ever to have enemy forces, an Iraqi army unit during Iraq War I, surrender to a robot—the dawn of a new age); its eight Westinghouse electric generators (SSTGs) and air conditioners for the comfort of 60 officers, 70 chief petty officer, 720 enlisted sailors; its 10 aircraft crew-members, 80 assault marines in power armor, and 120 marines in body armor . . . And him.

Prayer for the Holy Innocents on the Eve of Nuclear Fire

Prayer for the Holy Innocents on the Eve of a NEW and IMPROVED Ice Age!

Prayer for the Holy Innocents on the Eve of Religious War

Prayer for the Holy Innocents on the Eve of Post Humanity

Prayer for the Holy Innocents on the Eve of Extinction

O Lord, Here we are again (and by HERE I mean in Your crosshairs), rumors of doom gathering like the night with us feeling not a little like the doorman given the task to hold it back. Indeed, our Prophets tell us that You, in your infinite wisdom, periodically extinguish 95% of the life on earth. They know this from reading the strata of earth, Your book, a geological record wherein is recorded some 20 global mass extinctions which arrived with the regularity of German trains and includes the Ordovician-Silurian extinction (fickle hand on the global thermostat?), then the Late Devonian extinction (a mistaken delivery of fire?), then the Permian extinction (fire again), then the Triassic extinction (floods worse than Noah's), then the Cretaceous extinction which did in the dinosaurs when, according to Your fine print—a layer of Iridium at that strata—an enormous meteor slammed into the earth, the dust kicked up by the blast plunging us into a night so pure that it seemed to draw the final curtain for every mammal. The regularity of your timetable makes many fear that earth, Your book, is in the path of Your pen, an elliptical asteroid belt that brings the two into contact every 26 million years, and means that the period You'll put to Your current sentence—ours—is due.

Still, even if we have fallen so low as the preachers say, we beseech you to look upon those too young to have yet tried, the innocents . . .

Grant us, O Lord, a spectacular miss.

We watch the sky.

Natural Citizens

DEB OLIN UNFERTH

Resorts

AT THE END THEY TALKED about resorts—not as in sunshine and sea, but as in the phrase "last resort," and they tried them all: therapy, compromise, time apart, time together, and when there weren't any more of them and there was nothing else to do, Alex picked up his stuff, left at last, took a job in the city. He moved into the neighborhood, one of the neighborhoods where the other broken people besides himself (broken in two ways) lived—some of them also without skills, like him (Alex saw this now: he lacked skills), but most not. Most of them were immigrants and very skilled and had come to this country to live in this neighborhood and drive a taxi or clear plates, despite their skills, and there were a lot like that from all over the world, from India, Korea, and from places he'd never heard of, all here as their own resort, last or second to, and there was a park across the street where they all

walked in circles—in saris, in robes, in T-shirts, with elote carts or pets—
and he among them, another one, back in the city, alone.

Landlord

You should be comfortable here. There aren't a lot of natural citizens, he
said.

Which Alex took to mean that Alex was not a natural citizen, or not as
natural as the landlord.

In fact, Alex was pretty natural. His parents had come from someplace
else but he himself had been born in this country as naturally as anybody and
in fact he knew no languages other than the one.

Was he going to spend time making a fuss about this? No.

Citizens in the Basement

Okay, there were a couple of them, natural citizens. Two in the basement,
only they didn't seem very natural. When Alex moved in, the landlord
pointed at the basement door and said, Leo and his girlfriend live down
there. It isn't a real apartment.

Now what does that mean? Alex didn't ask, just carried his box up the
stair, but some of it began to make itself clear. Leo and the girlfriend had
no electricity, for one. So how did they listen to the TV so goddamn loud
every night for hours when Alex had to be up early for work? So loud that
he couldn't quite believe it? So loud that he moved his bed to the other end
of the apartment by the kitchen and could still hear it loudly? Leo and the
girlfriend ran an extension cord out into the hallway and plugged it into the
hallway lamp, which had an outlet on it.

One night it was so loud Alex didn't think it possible to turn a TV up that
loud. It shouldn't be possible. TVs shouldn't contain that possibility within
them. He went downstairs and knocked on their door but they couldn't hear
him of course because the TV was too goddamn loud. He went back upstairs
and banged on the floor with a mop handle but they couldn't hear him of
course because the TV was too goddamn loud. It was like stars bursting in
his head. So he went downstairs and hit the door with a flat palm, yelled,
Turn down the goddamn TV. He could hardly hear his own voice, lost in
the din.

He stared at the extension cord. Unplugged it. The building sank into
silence.

What happened to the TV? someone on the other side of the door said.

He dropped the extension cord, ran back up to his apartment.

Therapy

They had tried therapy. That had been one resort they had tried but to him it had been like talking to a telemarketer or some other person with a script or some other list of words read off a clipboard flatly or with cheer: caroler, flight attendant, salesman.

Doorbell

So the electricity and the fact that they didn't have any but did. And then the doorbell, which they had but didn't use. Their doorbell worked. Alex knew because he tried it himself one afternoon and it brought Leo to the door, yawning. So it worked but their visitors stood outside and yelled, yelled for Leo. Leo. Hey Leo. Yelled for him in the middle of the night, at one in the morning there was someone outside yelling for Leo. Alex opened the window.

Do you think it's decent, yelling like that this time of night? he said.

I'm looking for Leo, the man said. He looked afraid.

That was another thing. They looked afraid, all these citizens, natural or not, and Alex wondered if they were afraid of him or of something he should be afraid of too and the thought that he didn't know which or what did make him afraid.

Well, use the doorbell, he said.

The citizen under the window looked like he'd never heard of the word.

You know, the *door*bell. It's around the front of the building and it works.

The man stepped off into the bushes. But he was back again the next night, this time stage-whispering, Hey Leo. Leo.

Alex stuck his head out the window. You think he can hear you with that goddamn TV on so loud?

More or Less

He certainly felt less than a citizen these days. His wife was a citizen on both sides and in more than one way, what with the long line of rosy cheeks and smiling faces behind her, and forward too, into the future, he could see them, the pale-pink blush of her descendents. Unlike his own forebears and shortcomings.

Relation

There were other people in the building, natural and not natural—though mostly they seemed not. The landlord said the woman across the hall was related to the landlord's wife and would he, Alex, be kind enough to drive this relation to the grocery once a week when he himself went?

He hated driving the relation to the grocery. There was clearly something wrong with the relation and he felt like the landlord's wife was shoveling her semi-retarded relative off on him and he wasn't happy about it. He'd help the relation to the car and then drive to the grocery and she would sit beside him and read each sign as they passed, slowly, in a loud monotone. No left turn. Don't walk. No parking here to corner.

One night the relation across the hall came across the hall and knocked on the door. Alex was tired. He toed around the apartment, hoped she couldn't hear. The relation went back across the hall but returned a few minutes later and knocked again.

She knocked the same number of knocks.

She went back across the hall but returned a few minutes later and knocked again. The same number of knocks, the same pattern.

She left and came back. Then left and came back.

She kept it up for hours. It was like the relation wasn't human. It was like she was a wind-up toy, or a piece of factory machinery, or an airplane tray table moving from one upright and locked position to another, and as the night wore on, Leo turned up his TV and the knocks were nearly drowned out beneath the explosions from below—nearly but not. He could still hear the relation, like a woodpecker tapping away in a storm, and at some point Leo and his girlfriend started fighting and their shouts were so loud, they trumped everything, her accusations, his defense rising into the sky. Inside the apartment Alex moved the mattress up and down trying to find one half-peaceful spot, but could not.

He Wasn't Calling to Find Out If She Was Seeing Anyone

He was calling because they hadn't spoken in a long while now and the last time they had spoken, she had said she might come into the city for the weekend and might see him for coffee or a meal but then she had called back and left a message saying she had forgotten she had made another engagement for the weekend, something about a motorcycle or group of motorcycles, and he had called back and said, Okay, some other time. And then he had called a second time to ask since when, by the way, had she been riding around on motorcycles, which maybe she hadn't heard were *very dangerous* and by the way *with whom?* But that was what she planned to do so she didn't come and they didn't talk very long and that was the last time they had spoken and now he was calling again.

Well, she was glad he called. There was something she wanted to discuss with him.

And what was that.

She wanted him to know, she thought he should know, that she's seeing somebody now. She didn't want to make any assumptions about why he'd been calling and writing her letters and asking if he could come for a visit but she thought she should tell him.

She wanted him to know that.

Yes, that, and that maybe they should go ahead with the divorce.

One letter. He wrote her one letter and about asking if he could come for the visit, might he remind her that he does know other people in the area, having lived there for *four years,* and anyway that wasn't why he was calling?

All right. Why was he calling?

Maybe two letters. And two phone calls and besides, he's happy that she's seeing somebody. He hopes she's happy, at least as happy as he is. And he hopes they'll be happy together, the two of them, on their *motorcycles,* which she better damn well wear a helmet.

Well, she was happy anyway that he called and wrote those letters. And anyway their relationship could change now. They could be friends.

Wouldn't that be fucking nice.

Yes, well.

Advice for Citizens

Avoid contact with eyes. Careful contents may be hot. Attach no bikes. Use seat bottom cushion for floatation. Don't forget your lotto.

Citizen's Arrest

He called the police. One night the fighting was so bad, Alex was actually afraid, not for himself, and not for the girlfriend, but for Leo. The girlfriend sounded like she was beating him up down there. Her voice was deep like a man's and held the fury and inspiration of authority. Leo's voice beneath sounded like a discouraged child's. A squad car turned up. Alex watched out the window through the spinning circle of lights. They took the girlfriend out in handcuffs.

The next day she was back.

Outage

Late that summer was the great blackout. The heat rose so high the electrical systems collapsed and the entire city was plunged into darkness. It went on like that for days. It was an emergency. The electric company restored power into the neighborhoods one by one. His own neighborhood, the poorest (everyone broke in one or two ways), was listed last, must have been, because they suffered through day after day, no air-conditioning, no radios, no clocks, the cell-phones died, only the occasional flashlight gleamed a line across the dark. It was too hot in the apartments, too many citizens, not enough windows, so they brought sheets outside and slept in the park, spread out in the grass with water coolers, pillows, pets. A din, an outrage, rose over the street. Citizens started fighting. Somebody smashed a car's windows. There were gunshots. The police drove in with the ambulance. Kids threw bottles at the police, then ran down to the river. There were more shots. The neighborhood was barricaded, surrounded and cordoned off, no one allowed in or out. Alex was in. His job was out. He sweated out a whole day and night until the electric came up and the barricades came down and everything went back to normal.

Bad Behavior

One night Alex called the police and nobody came. He called again, called three or four times, waited for them to come with the phone in his hand.

Why aren't you here yet? he said to them. They're killing each other down there.

He called the landlord as well. They're crazy, he said. They're tearing the basement apart. You've got to do something.

What can I do? said the landlord, which Alex thought was like taking their side.

Don't call so late, said the landlord, which Alex thought was like saying he, Alex, wasn't being polite, which wasn't very polite considering just whose building the thing was and therefore whose fault it was that Alex was up at this hour.

One of us has to get some sleep, said the landlord, which Alex thought was so unreasonable he didn't know what. It was like he'd stumbled into a broken mirror world, one that resembled his own in the shards.

The police arrived at last. They took the girlfriend away and she was back in an hour, downstairs again, shrieking. Alex called again. She's back, can you hear her screaming? Why don't you make sure she stays away?

Fitness for Citizens

What Alex needed was some exercise. That was one way to clear the head. Some up and down, drip-sweat, park path underfoot. No reason to get all the way to thirty and give up. He had run three miles a day in college. He put on his running shoes and was standing at one end of the park. Doing some stretches, some knee-lifts. Who but Leo and the girlfriend should walk over and stop.

What are you doing? said the girlfriend. Aerobics?

Running, he said.

She was the same height as him. She had blue rimless eyes. She wore an outfit of zippers. She said, I'd like to be in your head for five minutes.

My what? My head?

It must be bliss.

Oh, you think so? Alex said.

Leo had on an outfit of snaps.

Excuse me, Alex said, and jogged off. He jogged around the corner, unlocked his car, got in. He sat.

He called the landlord. You have to get those two out, he said. They're selling drugs down there. The police are here every night. You've got to do something.

Let me ask you this, Alex said. Who pays more rent, me or them? Who pays rent at all?

All right, said the landlord. I'll make them leave.

Departure

A pickup truck arrived on a Saturday. He watched out the window. Leo and the girlfriend loaded up in the rain. A mattress, a few chairs, some bags of clothes. They tugged a piece of plastic over it all. The landlord stood on the street with his hands on his hips. They drove off. Alex sat in the window all afternoon. He said to himself, Now, that's it. He resolved to do better now, to be better. He made a list of things he could do to be better. He divided them into categories: personal, professional, and other. He divided the categories into further divisions. He wrote a list of goals and assignments, long-term, short. This could be a beginning for him, or at least not the end of him.

Self-help

He stuck a Post-it to the mirror: *See that? It's only going to get worse.*

Letters

That night he dreamed of letters from her waiting in his mailbox. He dreamed of opening the letters, the pages falling out, his wife's small handwriting, letters of apology, explanation, reconciliation. He woke.

Not Even Real Apartment

First he thought he was still dreaming. Then, that he was hearing voices in his head, had lost his sanity once and for all. Then, that they were ghosts. Then, that they had doubles who had stayed down there when the originals left. Finally he faced the truth: they were back.

He called the landlord. They're back, he said.

How can that be? I took the keys. We watched them drive away.

Apparently they drove back. They're down there fighting. I think she's going to kill him this time for sure.

Alex waited. He waited for hours while they screamed below. He called the landlord again. You better get over here, he said. They'll be gone before you arrive!

I certainly hope so, said the landlord. I don't want to come over there with them fighting like that. They're a tough two. Convicted felons.

How smart is it to rent to convicted felons? Alex said. In a not-even-real apartment? Is it even legal, that apartment?

All right, all right, said the landlord.

Departure (reprise)

Four squad cars pulled up. The landlord hid in his car across the street and Alex watched from the window.

Come on out, someone called through a bullhorn—no doorbells this time.

Leo and the girlfriend didn't come out. Alex buzzed the police through the first door because the landlord wouldn't get out of the car and unlock it even when they waved for him to. Then they broke down the second door because Leo wouldn't open it and the landlord wouldn't get out of his car with the key. Then Alex heard them yelling, everybody in there yelling. It could not have been easy to locate those two in the dark with no lights.

Leo and the girlfriend came out. They got into the squad cars. The police stood around for an hour. A couple of men carried belongings out of the basement and into the daylight, the belongings they hadn't left with the last time. They piled it on the grass. They came out with a skinny dog, which Alex hadn't known had been down there. They came out with a terrarium, which had something moving around in it but he couldn't see what. They put the dog into one of the squad cars. Then a van drove up that said Roy's Keys on the side and one man fixed the door and another changed the locks. Then everybody drove away, the squad cars, the landlord, the locksmith, the carpenter, and Alex was alone.

One More Thing Happened. No, Two.

One, his wife never came back. There were years of that, of her not coming back and the discussions of the particulars—the cars, their value to start, their value to finish, their savings and how to split it—then of her becoming someone else's wife, becoming someone else's mother, once, then again, while Alex had his own inconveniences.

Two

Alex never saw Leo again. The landlord, real or not, moved some boys down into that apartment, unnatural teenagers. They spray-painted the door with the words "KEPP OUT!!!" and had wild parties down there every night and did not fight but shouted with joy and he was too weary to do anything about it. By day they stood out on the street, talking on their cell phones or just standing.

What are you looking at? Alex demanded of one.

America, he said.

Secession, XX

KELLIE WELLS

ON THE THIRTEENTH DAY following fertilization, "we" found "ourselves" with three X's and a Y to work with, so it didn't take brain surgeons, or even budding geneticists, for the excessive zygote we were to figure out how best to assemble ourselves. We were the thwarted hermaphrodite splitting defiantly down the middle, reconciled to sharing intestines, a bit of pelvis, perhaps a spleen, but not everything. We knew enough each to claim an X, and then I

The biological impossibility of our zygosity proved no deterrent to my sister.

XXOO, she signed our postcards from summer camp (where we were the envy of all three-legged racers). This valediction was not meant to signify affectionate gestures, vouchers for kisses and hugs that could be cashed in upon our return (she occasionally drew half arrows shooting northeast out of the O's said, "Girl," and yanked the other X out of the communal stewpot. He (to be) looked on and blinked, so in burgeoning disgust I finally punted the crippled X, amputee, that hobbling, one-legged Y, over to It, deciding his him-ness. I could see that He né It, future brow in a phantom crimp, would have pondered ontological mind-benders all day had I not taken decisive action. Where would we be now had I been as equivocal as we seemed fated to be? Perhaps swapping sex like shoes—today the yob, testicles descending, Florsheims polished and reflecting redundant chins as we bent to tie them; tomorrow a filly, donning a frock, legs crossed tightly as the clasp of a coin purse, retracting the truncheon, passing it under the table like a secret, internal relay, Mary Janes kicking the curious dog as he wags by sniff-sniffing. You can imagine what fatiguing work it would be to cobble together an identity out of such fleshy ambivalence. So I drew a line in the genetic sand and it has divided us (zippered together though we are like conjoined sleeping bags) ever since.

Some nights I stroke his face as he sleeps, feel a tingle in my own. I will him not to stir and he doesn't. He heeds the messages I send him through the beats of our hearts, palpitations we've learned to compose and decipher like Morse code—thum-thump thumpity-thump: Don't Move. And I know he does the same to me, caresses me in sleep as intimately as congenital disease. A residue of sensation sometimes pinks my throat as I wake in the morning.

to make this unmistakably clear). It was she on the left and I on the right. To her, I was absence from the start. The space harnessed, circumscribed by Her.

She told me once she'd dreamt boys were small as beetles, and she caught them and put them in killing jars, prodding them with a pencil when they got too lippy, feeding them blades of grass through the holes in the lid when they pleaded for rations.

We performed theater in the summer, on a stage of rickety orange crates covered in burlap. She wrote soliloquies for me that invariably ended: HIM: (*spoken plaintively*) Y, y me?

She made my circulation quicken, her desperation for *sovereign contours.*

Her cool fingers against my cheek made me well up uncomfortably with tender feeling, and I'd begin to gulp air. It was as though I'd been knocked on my back and was struggling to recover lost breath. I did not think of her in these moments. It was my mouth I imagined kissing.

Naturally, we do everything together. Even if we weren't soldered along the torso, I don't think he would ever have left my side (though he dreamed of little else). When we were children, our parents always told us they were doubly blessed, as they grinned at us tragically. *And so are you,* they'd insist, having as we did the peculiar honor of sharing skin and bone, internal organs bridging that gulf of Otherness that renders the rest of humanity small and cheerless, discrete, forsaken (honor schmonor, anima and animus warring under one tent, launching missiles in a relentless covert land grab, thought I petulantly in those moments when I yearned for autonomy. "Beat it!" I'd sometimes bleat aloud instead of think, and my brother just clasped his hands and endured, the saucer-eyed supplicant). "That's what we all really hanker for," my mother once whispered to me, and she did frequently look upon us with eyes moist at the corners and narrowed with envy.

Most days, we took our blessing seriously. At my brother's urging, we practiced saintly behavior, gave nickels to the humpbacked, dirt-scabbed, addicted, and street-diseased people along the Paseo, people who slept in rusting, wobbly-wheeled shopping carts and donned a full wardrobe even in August, people with palm-sized army knives, packages of crumbled crackers, slim, green New Testaments, Tiparillos, and quarters cadged from blood-bank volunteers in their pockets. These people other people took circuitous routes to

I never ache to leave her, though I do occasionally dream of receiving postcards sent from places with brightly plumed tropical birds or slick-haired dictators on the stamps. XX, she signs them simply so I know it's her.

I could sometimes feel her willfully hogging our organs, like a fitful sleeper tugging the blanket to her side of the bed. I felt her trying to digest me, me, little more than tough protein to her. She always stopped with only the faintest morsel of me remaining, and, somehow, against both our wills, I rallied, persisted. I think she feared how she might be transformed if I became more fuel than aimless appendage. I imagined myself impertinent blood washing through her veins, moving her arms and mouth and feet in discord with the neurotransmission of her wishes. I was never as harmless as she convinced herself I was. It wasn't subversion. I was reserved long before I understood it to be an asset, fundamentally laconic.

I had originally been one of two boys. We were Romulus and Remus floating down the Tiber of the fallopian tube in search of the appropriate site for the avoid pressed themselves against walls as we passed. We parted crowds, crowds of those who usually made others hasten their step. We were a freak's freak.

One day, on a visit to our maternal grandparents in Michigan, walking along the shore of Asylum Lake, my brother (a subject implicit in whom is myself—there is no grammar sufficient to express the bifurcated id, et al, that rends us, joins us) became fascinated by the Jesus bugs, those splay-legged insects that skate across water, sleek as geometry and weightlessly optimized to take advantage of surface tension. He was certain we were somehow equipped to do the same, on our archless feet, large for our size, flat as platypuses, so we stepped off the dock and onto the water, and for a second we hovered there, the water heavy as ballast that kept us, grown sheer with divinity, from floating up into the sun, kept the thinning wax of being from melting off our bones. But I couldn't sustain the insubstantiality and I dropped into the drink, pulling my brother with me.

My brother has all the Jesus on his side. It was always me who ran after the kids who hurled chestnuts and hedge apples at us (in place of clever invectives, the snot-nosed galoots) as I schlepped my pacifist brother beside me like a lame appendage, so forgiving, civil, so disobedient to the genes flanking him scrappily to his right.

Sometimes we lie in the hammock, sunk deep in its belly, an inverse pregnancy. I move my mouth to his, kiss him, and it becomes confusing, whose lips are whose, whose chapped, whose

founding of an empire. My sister turned out to be the she-wolf waiting at the other end. When we came tumbling into her encampment, she pressed against her amnion and saw our chorion give, hold the shape of her hand. She gnawed an opening in her sac and then began working on ours, until she parted the curtains of membrane and stepped inside. As we would soon be bulging at the placental seams, she snipped the line at my brother's umbilicus and hooked me up to the potent generator of herself. Her hunger was not easily sated, though, and there were times when I saw her eyeing the cord, which coiled near my crown; I knew she was imagining it noosed round my neck and was willing the womb's trap door to drop so she'd be rid of me for good and could suck the choicest drops of marrow from that rope of life.

I strove to be pure, transparent as water, but I was vaguely aware that the very struggle to remain innocent made me regretfully wise. If there is anything I wanted never to be it is knowing. At our baptism, after the reverend sprinkled water on our foreheads with the dainty covertness of a person on a sodium-restricted diet salting an egg, I awoke to find the organist pressing athletically against my chest and water dribbling down my chin. I turned to see my sister glaring at me. I recalled looking up sticky, whose molar is aching at that moment, but then I taste the bitter balm of godthefather on his lips, and I remember which mouth is mine and pull it back. When we take communion on Christmas and Easter, my brother (our soul's emissary) laps the grape juice, tries discreetly to dislodge the host from his tooth with his tongue, and, try as I may, I can never stifle the belch that rises up within me from that hub of sutured selves, that centrifugal nucleus that seems to blow us out and blow us out from the inside and haunts us both with a feeling of excess. I can see the vapor of Jesus slip out of my mouth like soap bubbles, pop pop . . . pop, see Him float toward the pastor's clasped hands. The pastor gazes past us with an aspect of forbearance that seems pasted to his face with thin glue, a look that appears as though it will curl forward at any moment like improperly hung wallpaper and will reveal the hole in the wall, the bottomless despair beneath faith that makes his soul gape. An undressable wound—that's how I've always thought of faith.

The rich repast of body and blood are best taken with food or milk lest you risk an ulceration of the spirit.

When we turned thirteen, my brother became suddenly modest. Though he showed a predilection for this at an early age, fig-leafing himself with his hands, averting his eyes from the exposed charm of his other half, he quickly recognized the impracticality of such behavior and distracted himself by looking through our body like a Viewmaster to gaze upon the silvery

through gentle waves without ambition toward the water's surface.

Honestly, it wasn't the body—even our body—that anguished me so much as the fluids it produced. They were so unpredictable and abundant, new eruptions daily. I longed to be arid as desert, desiccated. At night, in an attempt to subdue all geysers burbling within, I imagined thirstless pack animals and sand-blown sultans bent against hot soul, unhampered by a bodily hedging of bets; he was buoyed by how it swam free of genitalia, floated inside us cleanly and purely with never the need to unzipper its trousers. Finally acquiescing to physical imperatives, he slumped on the toilet and occupied himself with chaste and hygienic thoughts, while I, happy to reclaim scatology from the stifling ether in which eschatology hung (it was lost on neither of us that the subtraction of the bodily from the heavenly left only a flip-flopped and befuddled "he"), always marveled at the insider information I collected at such moments.

I have always loved my body, loved running my hands across hill and dale, loved the discovery of soft puckerings of flesh hidden in uncharted fissures. At night, as my brother withdrew, my hands roamed the merged continents of our body, noting the shifting topography of Pangaea's hemispheres, parched steppe to fertile grasslands. Though my brother's half seemed to respond pleasurably, seemed to enjoy being mapped, in the morning he would be quieter hunched over his oatmeal, seem more pale, nearly translucent, the white of a cooked turnip.

At school, junior high, the administration was stumped as to which compulsory class to place us in: home ec or shop. The answer seemed to be found in our dexterity, whether sewing machine or band saw posed less of a threat to our fingers, to our overlapped physiognomy. (I knew well the picture classmates' minds conjured as their thoughts moved from the spinning jagged teeth of the saw to my brother and

siroccos. My sister, on the other hand, was perfectly at ease frolicking in any effluvium.

My body is the very shape of betrayal. It rises and stiffens and purrs against all my considered remonstrations, wicked. My sister, my puppeteer. I have always been thin, thinner than my sister, hoarder of flesh, and so any new cleft or ripple is immediately visible, and my sister fingers the putty of me at night, tries to conjure her own likeness out of my spare clay.

me, though our grain went arm to arm, not head to toe, so they'd never be able to sever us neatly. *Better stick to spice racks,* I radioed back to them with my glare.) Actually, we were quite graceful, having had to thoughtfully choreograph every move. Harmony of gesture was a matter of bald well-being; injury lurked in every step, every impulsive swipe of the hand. If we were all joined at the hip, there'd be no war.

Standing in the principal's office, surrounded by administrators, secretaries, PTA officers, the school nurse, my brother became angry and pushed me. This was the first sign of antipathy toward me my brother had ever shown, and it thrilled me. Before this show of aggression, I think we both feared he was only an appended afterthought of yin to my anchoring yang, a perfunctory gentility that merely lent a rough-hewn dignity to my intemperance. When my brother took the slingshot and pebble from my pocket and aimed it at me, our hearts clapped loudly inside us, and I understood—in this similarity of impulse—we were mete of discrete spirits, hinged, hyphenated, but fully forged.

You can imagine how the heart sank when he shot his own foot.

He was good to the root! In this moment I began to understand my own insufficiency, my lopsided wickedness, and I growled, causing Mr. Pelofsky, the principal, to drop his monogrammed fountain pen. Before, I had always quite enjoyed being a discipline problem, enjoyed hearing my brother yelp as the paddle met my backside; I held my ankles and grinned defiantly as

The economy of my disposition was partly owing to the understanding that when I did speak, it was with my sister's voice, the propulsion of her breath. She was curator of the lungs, you see. This became clear to me in junior high when we stood before the principal, waiting for him to administrate some decision with regard to our curriculum, which was gender specific and involved machinery that made them fear litigation should we injure ourselves, which seemed to those dreamless bureaucrats likely. Watching my sister sneer at the principal's shrivelled fig-faced secretary (what she was thinking as she looked at her), I suddenly realized that anything I might interject in the matter would be so thoroughly in relation to the wishes of my sister as to be moot where my own interests were concerned, and it further occurred to me that, when you got right down to it, I had no interests; if I ever had, they had long ago been so skillfully colonized as to have virtually disappeared from both mind and memory.

This realization left me momentarily fractious, until I understood, in all the erosion of self—the horror and relief such recognition brings—that, like a the disciplinarian scratched his chin and pondered the shiftiness of justice, the social contract, considered, vaguely, sacrifice, the greater good, imagined how we—that is, my brother and I— might one day complicate not only corporal but capital punishment, saw one of us hanging from a noose, the other flailing about and gasping, begging for clemency not for himself but humankind, and pleading for acknowledgment of our interdependency, the executioner himself beginning to feel the prickle and burn of taut hemp against his throat, vertebrae cracking beneath the hood.

It was decided that too many liability quandaries were posed by our working with any sort of machinery and so Mrs. Ridgeway would instruct us in deportment during seventh period. Deported is just what we, aliens accidentally washed ashore the cloying nation of the other, each secretly longed to be.

A throng of memories always throbbed inside my brother and me as isolated moments trying to assemble themselves into a parliament that could agree upon a shared history, but, frequently bellicose, or at the very least churlish, competing versions of significant events often tried to muscle one another out, filibustering until the others slumped beneath their powdered wigs and gave in, wearied into submission. I could see as far back as synkaryon, which my brother and I still remain, a fusing never meant to be/never meant to be sundered. *Sin carrion*, I sometimes thought, the decaying roadside remains of our parents' original sin, the sin of boomerang, no matter where I aimed my loathing, it somehow always bent its trajectory and dropped at my own feet. Were they my feet? I could no longer distinguish.

ill-fated genes recklessly colliding. And *sin carry-on*, fateful luggage that went with us everywhere.

The blood my body let, internal leech of menses sucking the poison of fertility out, was the final betrayal, and my brother refused to eat or sing at choir (though his voice, unlike my own, had yet to drop, and so remained dulcet during hymns) or sleep much after that. He was affronted by this exclusion, the fumbling mess it created, the desecration of clean sheets, despite the fact that it was he who had traced his fingers along an imaginary perforation at night, wishing we might be severed like stamps, like soon-to-be distinct continents giving grudgingly, eagerly, in to the whims of plate tectonics. I felt the tug in the other direction when he dreamt of lying languorously on his side, leaning with disaffected panache against a wall, when he dreamt of swimming sidestroke, imagined walking with a blank peripheral prairie spreading out to either side. He squeezed his eyes closed and forced his thoughts to stack themselves vertically, pretended lateral dominion, tried to imagine what it would be like to be utterly alone. I had been stung by the vigor of his jerking when he was in the throes of such traitorous fantasies, but I yanked him back toward my side and held his nose until his mouth popped open like a split fruit and his eyes quit their seismographic twitching beneath the lids. He always looked regretful in the morning, knowing even the shadowy terrain of his unconscious mind was hardly too formidable a frontier for a pioneer such

It's true that I wasn't at all prepared for menstruation, despite that "You're Becoming a Woman" lecture at school I was made to sit in on. The sheer gooeyness of it was certainly objectionable, not to mention the backache and lightheadedness I'd not anticipated, but what was most distressing was really the questions it raised for me regarding transubstantiation. Uncannily, the onset of the bleeding coincided with Easter communion. The heresy of this! It was clear my sister bled to prove a point. Ingesting His resurrected flesh and blood had more abiding significance for her, the grape juice transformed, flowing undeniably from her loins. My sister claimed, with more one-upped smugness than conviction, that women bled to remind us of the wounds suffered for the piggishness of mankind. I concealed my revulsion lest she oink at me.

as myself. What he desired most was secrecy, the thing he could never have stapled to a spy like me.

In eleventh grade, it came as a genuine revelation to us both (our premiere epiphany—which was itself a revelation—the first uncovering of something concealed from the both of us) that my brother and I both fancied the same classmate, Arno Unruh. Arno was lean and gawky, with birdlike limbs, wore drooping corduroy pants and neatly pressed oxford shirts rolled up at the sleeves. His hair, sandy blond, seemed to aspire to straightness but lost its resolve and kinked on the ends. He had a friendly manner well-suited to his freckled, fair skin, and he was inclined equally toward chemistry and Unitarianism. His lips were eternally chapped, but behind them he had very straight teeth and the faintest lisp. I found him thoroughly fetching and drew pictures in my notebook of the Möbius strip of our intestines linked in infinity. I asked Arno if he'd be my lab partner, which made my brother sulk, though he tried to look cheerful as he steadied the alembic for the alchemy of Rhonda Obenchain, school sorceress, his partner. Rhonda wore black clothing that occasionally shimmered and kohled circles around her eyes; an amulet fashioned of amber (which she claimed her great grandmother had smuggled from Poland, clutched tightly in her vagina as she dodged the penetrating stares of border dragoons), dangled around her neck, and the beat of my brother's heart grew faint in her presence. Though she referred to us as

Arno Unruh—those winsome good looks and ready sermons about selflessness and moral rectitude, how he'd segue easily into a discussion of unstable isotopes—he was an unwitting heartbreaker, "Bible-thumping lothario," to use Rhonda Obenchain's epithet for him. She could not fathom the attraction. I looked into Arno's watery eyes and I could see him puzzling over the logistics of my sister and me coordinating our selflessness. My sister's XX-ray eyes burned through my jersey, through to my gnarled heart murmuring its ruined hunger.

Neither she nor I could be sure of the originating locus of our desire, but the skin below my navel pulsed and smoldered when I stole glances of Arno turning on the Bunsen burner, recording data in his college-ruled notebook. This, just when I thought I'd all but shed this shambly and unpredictable skin, bequeathing all its urges to my sister. I knew any hint of my being smitten would seem mutinous to her, so I balled up my fist and held it fast to my abdomen, willed my stomach to ache.

Frick and Frack or Chang and Eng, these were endearments coming from Rhonda, and I espied appetite in her smudged eyes when she batted them at my brother. I pictured her years hence at a midtown ashram performing self-trepanation, drilling a hole in her skull that she imagined would lead her to the altar at which God himself worshipped, the heart of the heart of divinity.

Arno made corny, clean jokes as we performed our experiments, and I imagined him in the basement of his church at a youth group social performing the same shtick, hair disheveled, lopsided grin, girls in long skirts and flat shoes with dog-eared copies of the *Living Bible* clutched to their chests smiling yearningly at him with each predictable punch line. I longed to corrupt him.

One day Rhonda, who it was clear found Arno insufferable, said, "How do you make a dead baby float?"

"That's disgusting," said Arno. Rhonda looked to my brother for counterpoint. I could have told her he would not look up from the scarred, black table.

"Two scoops of ice cream, root beer, and a dead baby," she said, grinning, her braces glinting tauntingly. I could see she had practiced being spellbinding. At that moment, my brother straightened in his seat and glanced up at Arno, and I saw a meaningful look pass between them. There was a brief pause, then Arno shook his head, and my brother looked again at the table, slumped. Rhonda arched her eyebrows at me. I couldn't decode all of this swiftly enough to come to any satisfy-

I could feel Rhonda Obenchain gazing at me sometimes across the table. When I finally dared to look up, I'd catch her licking her red, candied lips. She'd cock her head suggestively, reminding me of a famished wolverine that has stumbled upon a wayward lamb grazing obliviously, far from the flock. Watching *Wild Kingdom* every Sunday night, I died a thousand deaths as those pronghorn deer, snowshoe rabbits, kangaroo rats misstepped and were snapped in the jaws or talons of cunning predators. I learned at a young age the futility of cheering on the defenseless, and I understood now that one false hop and I'd be helpless and wriggling in Rhonda's bangled clutches.

ing conclusion and spent the rest of the class period trying not to think about it, staring at the periodic chart on the wall. I cursed 39, yttrium, Y, named for a town in Sweden, Ytterby, a cold place with Y's to spare, a melting point of 1,523 °C. I pictured my brother in a bubbling cauldron. He began to kick his feet.

Several experiments later, I confronted my brother about the knowing glances he kept shamelessly lobbing at Arno, and he said, in a tone that indicated he was smiling smugly, though he wasn't, Benedict Cheshire Cat Arnold, double-agent quisling, "I am offspring of your rib. What did you expect?"

I had the lion's share of our internal apparatus, it was true, which was why we were eternally wedded, our intimacy inoperable, though *he'd* always had custody of the soul, docile lamb, bleating softly until the bequest of the earth was officially his, and this had seemed to me a reasonable division of labor. I'd sin, he'd feel penitent, each to her own vocation.

Later, when I noticed Arno's hand on my brother's knee under the lunch table, I felt suddenly and irreversibly annulled. My brother sat there innocently, unflinching, and I wondered when it was he had seceded, when he'd left me, expatriated, to form desires of his own. Perhaps, I wondered, my body throbbing with inviolate contours, it had been his appetites all along that had nudged us this way and that. Perhaps I had always been more spirit gusting beneath the shared dermis.

When we were born it was unclear how much of the body my brother would

When my sister sniffed the pheromones wafting in the air between Arno and me, I was filled with shame and regret but also, I confess, with a certain buried satisfaction that my body, heap of rusting scrap, creaky and reticent, might be stirred to impulses not entirely honorable.

ever be able to claim, and he was termed
"parasitic." Though he has always been
subtle, he confounded all prognostica-
tions, even my own, by forging an undeniable shape for himself, and talk of
excision, as if he were little more than
an ingrown toenail, ceased.

It occurred to me now that he'd been
helmsman all along. It was I who had
been indulged, spared. *He* suffered *me.*

It is the winter we have always
feared, bitter and wet. We are no fans
of intemperate weather, my brother and
I. There is never enough warmth to go
around when temperatures dip below
forty degrees. The blood races from
limb to organ, trying to keep up with
the demand.

Outside, turkey buzzards perch in
the leafless trees, looking like strange,
black fruit, oversized ornaments. They
blink their eyes at me, small heads
nestled in the fluffed pillows of their
backs. I threw a hambone out between
the trees, but the buzzards, whom I've
never known to be dissuaded from such
effortless spoils by any sort of inclement conditions, were apparently too cold
to stir, and it strikes me, as I watch the
wind ruffle their black feathers, that
they are right not to move. Eating is an
obsolete gesture, their lethargy seems to
say, survival something we've evolved
beyond. Eating only keeps you going
for another day, holds you at arm's
length from God, exactly where I've
always wanted to be, but my resolve is
thinning.

Rutherford B. Hayes, nineteenth
president of the United States, was referred to in the press and by resentful
partisans as Ruther*fraud* because he'd

won a narrow and contested electoral majority but had lost the popular vote, and this is suddenly how I feel: fraudulent, in command only by way of biological fiat. I managed to corral more cells than my brother, more fleet than he even in gestation, but now I feel a revolution percolating inside me, the fundamental goo of self quarrelling with itself, a cellular uprising, and I understand that no matter what bone anyone throws me, I will lay my head on my brother's shoulder and think, "It is too cold to stir." I imagine cartoon vultures falling dead from the trees, tongues hanging out of the sides of their beaks, XX for eyes, other vultures, eyes wide and clear—the black, empty OO of a rifle muzzle—crowded round, comically picking at the remains.

One morning as we were getting ready for school, my sister touched my creamed chin and said to me that there is no such thing as the ordinary. "The more you look at a common thing," she said, "the more refined your understanding of it becomes and, somehow, the less familiar it seems—in knowing something intimately, you defamiliarize it, grant it its due complexity.

"But the converse is also true," she said dreamily, eyes blank as portals, seeming to teeter on the brink of understanding something essential. I bristled at the philosophical cant of her head. "The more you look at an uncommon thing," she said, looking at me, then at herself, in the mirror, "the more you see how common it is. You reduce it in such a way as to make it nearly universal."

Flummoxed by this sudden combination of depth of thought and attentiveness to my ablutions, I tried to defuse the solemnity of this moment, as well as that of the grimly garbed phalanx of future moments I saw marching toward us: "Philosophers must be querulous by nature," I feebly quipped. "Must be a sleepless lot."

She laid her head on my shoulder. Oh, no, no: levity and capitulation! I knew the jig was up.

My sister has stopped eating. Like an irradiated tumor, she is shrinking. That's how she once would have thought of me, but that's not how I think of her. I think of her as ballast. She has kept us from lifting off, fleeing the planet, which we'd have done long ago had I once had my druthers. As the ballast lessens, I have to curl my toes in the carpeting, cling to banisters, so as not to rise and hover. I have no intention of increasing our notoriety.

She will not let me feed her, and she sags at my side, like a raincoat draped over my arm. As I watch her skin grow slack, see bones emerge, feel the border between us lose its elasticity, I sense that it is, after all, in the body that one knows whatever one can claim to know about God; redemption occurs, courageously, at this site of pain and decay. Where would the challenge be otherwise? Would we be so stirred, for millennia, would we still be talking about it, if it were only the *spirit* of Christ whose wispy wrists and billowing feet had been staked to the cross? It's the thought of torn tendon and cracking bone that makes us swoon.

I find this optimistic and try to prop my sister up with the news. After the resurrection, Jesus couldn't eat cabbage without expelling gas, I say. He wasn't recognizable at first, even to disciples, appeared haggard, if beatific, and a dark shimmer followed him everywhere, the body stuttering. His footprints always left behind a sticky, sweet residue, like honey, a postscript of the protoplasm of survival. And when he walked on water, he sank down to his ankles, nearly lost heart. It's no walk in the park being incorruptible, I tell her. Resurrection takes a toll. The body changes, I say, touching her cheek, but it's still necessary, if only to register the shifty spirit! She grins at me weakly, beyond revelation.

The wan changeling, my sister, erodes from girl to appendage to tumor, hurtling in the direction of idea. "XX, XX, XX!" I whisper fiercely in her ear, the code meant to gather and stitch her cells together, shape her back into girl–child.

But, even in deliquescence, it is her will that presides. I feel my heart shrinking with her, puckering, growing green, a forgotten potato. Another tack: I plant a plaintive kiss on her waxen lips. *Y,* I breathe into her, *Y you?* I think this will rouse her, and she does lift her head. Outside, birds drop from branches like black bombs, swoop toward a gristly salvation. I imagine the wafer of my sister's body placed on my tongue, imagine the salty flavor of shared organ, shared illness, disputed border, divided desire. My own body tick-ticks, the pinging of a heated engine tired of idling, awakened, animates the loosening spirit spread thin between us.

Metaphysics in the Midwest

CURTIS WHITE

1. The Insulted Brain

"YOU ARE GOD, MAN. Are you aware of that? You are God."

"I'm not God. I'm just the Commissioner."

"Commissioner Stevie is God. I'm a true believer."

"Okay, okay. Then God's telling you to keep it down or my mom will wake up."

The Commissioner was nervous. He'd been caught at this game once before and the next time would be serious. But a large part of the game was psychological, and it was important to keep the Commissioner's attention scattered. So, if I woke his mom, I was too loud; if I didn't, not loud enough. It was on that wafer, that crescent, that I played.

"Right. We be cool," I said, too loud. "You know what I'm gonna do tonight, man? You're not going to believe it. You are not going fucking to believe what I have in mind. I'm gonna bench Clemente and put that big sucker with the thirty-six ounces of salami, Wally Post, man, in right field."

Stevie jumped up. "No fair." Shocked. He was so shocked he didn't even notice his dingle poke out of his flannel PJs. I loved those pajamas. Geronimo, Davy Crockett, Custer, Tonto, the Ranger, man, they were all there.

He wants to tell me what's not fair "No way, Professor. Wally Post is on the Reds. You have to wait until a trading session, then you can trade Clemente for Post." Then he laughed at me. "If you're that dumb. Like when you pinch hit for Smokey Burgess and had to have skinny Elroy Face do the catching next inning 'cause you forgot that old Smokey was your only catcher."

He rolled around laughing with his hand over his mouth like he was keeping in marbles. "Twelve passed balls in one inning. A league record."

"I'm not dumb. You forget, I *knew* Wally Post. If he connected, it was gone. He's got two in him tonight, I can feel it. Four-baggers. His bat hung down to his knees, not like that guppy you got in front of you there."

That shut him up. He shoved it back into the flannel pocket that Cochise defended, rifle leveled, riding his palomino.

"That's why I went into the Reds organization when I played AAA. I said, when the Post-man retires, it's gonna be me and Robinson and Vada Pinson. I did it all in those days. Run, throw, hit. But then came the leg injuries. I stole so many bases I wore the flesh on my shins right down to the bone. The sky diving this summer opened those old wounds up."

"Are you a sky diver?" the Commissioner asked. "Not any more. Too old for that. But I'll take you up if you'd like to learn.

"Would I!"

"Say, what time is it? I've got office hours tonight."

He pulled this rattling Big Ben out from under his pillow. "Almost midnight."

"Gee-zus! I've got to git. I'm meeting with students."

Commissioner Stevie scoffed. Where do our children learn to "scoff" in these late days?

"You liar. You're just going to go meet women and leave me to play the whole damn game by myself."

"Stevie, I know how you feel." I did know how he felt. I remembered the uncertainties of boy-being. "You're worried about women. You wonder what you have to do with them. Well, put your fears in the Light. Let the god that is within you help. Ask for something particular. Tell the Whiteness that you'd like to feel comfortable with the idea of women."

"Don't give me that. You're just gonna get drunk."

The Commissioner looked lonely and disappointed. The red-blonde hair on his brow, the freckles, the girl's eyes. He was the very picture of your daughter pouting. But I was already out the window and standing in his mother's geraniums.

"Commissioner, let me leave you with an idea. Something to think about while I'm gone. Imagine a fly in a bottle who wants to know what the bottle looks like."

The pout liquefied. The look of the twelve-year-old Kepler, he who speculates on the gauzy firmament, took its place.

"You mean from the outside?"

"Yeah."

So I didn't feel too bad. He had a knot worthy of Dante to fiddle with and Maury Wills leading off in the top of the first. He was alright.

"You are God." That's all I have to teach in my course, "Spiritual Growth: Getting All the Way to Infusion." Yes, infusion. Like making tea. Because you've got God inside you and he is needed elsewhere. Forget about what to believe. Believe anything you want. Just let the Smiling One out

I was sitting in Benito's Downtown Tap, having the Italian beef sandwich and a beer, wondering if Laura or Melissa would need help tonight. Benito himself was seeing to the bar responsibilities, which were none too great on Tuesdays. It made for nice quiet office hours.

"Benito, a thought form has a lot of repercussions."

"What?"

"What do you make of the Bears signing Flutie?"

Benito brightened, incandescent, like someone had slapped his face. "Now that was the smartest fucking move they've ever made. That Flutie's a winner. And if McMahon is gonna be hurt all the time you can't blame . . ."

"You're right," I interrupted. "Now if they could just sign the Bronc, Nagurski, to complement Payton, they'd have an offense."

"What?"

At that moment, Laura walked in. I was surprised that it was Laura. She seemed a bit out of place in the class. Hadn't yet found her bearings. Part of the problem was that she seemed to want my class to function like other classes. I thought it would be weeks before she dared to take advantage of my office hours. But what are you going to do with today's students? All a teacher can do is make himself available.

"Laura! Fantastic! Benito, a double rum and coke, please. What would you like, Laura?"

"Nothing, thanks." She set her backpack down on the bar top. She looked young for a returning student, almost like a student-student. So there was something strange in this for me too.

"Come on, Laura. Some white wine?"

"No thanks."

"You know, part of the point of a class like ours is to learn to take a fresh perspective on things."

"You mean things like office hours?"

"Exactly."

"Okay, then how about just a coke."

She was cute with that midwestern plump cuteness. As if Illinois thought girls were like frankfurters. But I'm sure she never had an evil thought, so I liked her. I was glad she'd taken the class.

She took a sip of her coke, pulling it innocently up through the straw.

Then she said something. "Isn't it kind of weird to be having office hours this late at night in a bar? To tell you the truth, I didn't think I could stay awake this long."

"It's not weird for me."

"Oh."

"And after next week's class we won't be meeting at Schroeder Hall either. Courses offered in conjunction with the Metaphysical Frontiers Foundation are customarily held at the homes of those in the study group. It creates an important intimacy among members."

"I didn't realize that, either. I don't know how comfortable I am with that."

There was something about the way Laura moved her lips when she talked that charmed me. They made soft, wet, plopping sounds that had nothing to do with the words she spoke, that were entirely her lips' own language.

"You'll need to get beyond your fears if this course is to be of any use to you."

She shrugged her shoulders with a nice resemblance to what you see people doing.

"I'll give it a try."

Then Melissa walked in. She was a more typical student for my course. Whereas Laura expected a meeting of the Young Hegelians, Melissa came in looking for what I really had to offer: metaphor, self-realization, spiritual growth, good vibrations. However, it is important for me to admit, the one thing I've learned about teaching is that I never know who my best students are. That understanding comes about slowly, over a long period of time, and usually only after I have once again surrendered more of myself, more waxy gouges from my own thigh.

Melissa was thirty-six that semester, but she still had a young woman's figure. She dressed casually but with some gold jewelry and spangles which pleased me. She was married, had a two-year-old son, and worked in the personnel office of a local K-Mart, a position to which she'd been recently promoted from cashier. Melissa took classes like mine to keep her mind lively. Her husband, Lester, thought it was generous to allow her a few nights to herself. He stayed home with the baby. This was all only months before Melissa joined Alcoholics Anonymous.

"Melissa! Fantastic! Benito, a double rum and coke. Melissa, what can I get for you?"

"Are we going to have a drink?" She laughed loudly. "I think I'm gonna like this class. Just a beer."

"How about a shooter with that beer?"

"A shooter?"

"Yea. A little thimble of the old boyo to give the beer some kick."

"I better not."

"Okay. But timidity is failure in this class. We need to learn to release. To give up our attachments and our fears. What we think we have to lose is usually nothing at all. What we need is the freedom to get 'completely drunk,' in a manner of speaking."

"Yeah, I guess so."

Melissa really wasn't very pretty. Motherhood, marriage, avarice had been working on her face like busy worms. But there was that special little sneaky look in her eyes, that said "I want to live," which seemed to her to have something to do with sex. She was one of those women who thinks sex is a conspiracy, an underground. Her sly grin says, "If you'll bring it up, we can talk about cock and pussy all night, and no one will be the wiser."

But it was Laura who spoke first that night. "What is your background, Professor Feeling?"

"Please, call me Bill."

"Bill."

"You mean, why do I get to teach this course instead of Benito here?"

"Yes, I suppose." She giggled and took another nervous sip of her coke, which was already only a runny stain at the base of a stack of ice cubes.

"Ultimately, I get to teach the course because I'm the name on the Kankakee College Continuing Education payroll."

This amused but didn't satisfy her. Melissa, too, looked serious, fun over, as if she thought some of the mysteries might be getting started. "I mean, they must have had a reason for hiring you."

"You want to know about my credentials."

"Yes."

"I have none. You can teach the class, Laura. I'll give you all of my money."

Of course, eventually I explained that the Metaphysical Frontiers Foundation was related to the Spiritual Frontiers Fellowship which has seventy-three regional organizations in thirty-five states. Through the rituals of meditation, prayer, and group study, members focus on a God who dwells within the souls of men. I began my studies in Evanston in 1977. I came to Kankakee only recently in order to establish a metaphysics study group of my own. I felt the need to help those who might otherwise flounder.

I was still describing my interest in psychic and spiritual experience, in Meher Baba and Madame Blavatsky, when Benito announced last call for drinks.

"Say Benito, you should take my class. Next week we do 'Communication with the Dead'."

"What's that?" he asked, a little angrily.

"Another of my little Pepsis, please. And a shooter for my prize pupil."

"Are we really going to communicate with the dead?" asked Laura, rousing herself for the last time.

"Sure. I mean, we'll try. We'll see if my communicator can put us in touch."

"God. This is too much." She lifted her sea-blue pack up on her shoulder with nearly Buddhist control. She looked gorgeous. I could imagine her as a celestial detail in a Tibetan thangka. She seemed gifted to me, at that moment, in spite of her boredom and her skepticism. Her virtue shone through like the infant Dalai Lama's.

"Is there no one close to you who has gone on to the other side?"

"Yes," she acknowledged, hesitantly. "My father died of a heart attack when I was in high school."

"And wouldn't you like to talk to him again, if you could?"

"Sure."

"We'll try, sweetheart, such things can be done."

A little twist of pain caught her face. Melissa, who'd been listening to all this, said, "Wow. This class is going to be heavy." She threw back her shot, a squeeze of pain of another kind on her face.

As we left, I took Melissa by the elbow. "Do you have a car?"

"A little Honda Civic," she replied.

"Can you give me a ride home?"

"Sure."

"Better yet, would you like to visit the Commissioner?"

"The Commissioner?"

"The Commissioner is God," I said, penetrating the puddle of her blue eyes.

Next thing, I had both hands on the butt of Melissa's blue jeans, pushing her through Stevie's bedroom window. She landed on his bed, all over the Commissioner, in fact, waking and scaring him.

"Oh God, Professor, what are you doing here? What time is it? I'm gonna get in so much trouble."

"Dr. Feeling, there's someone in here. A little boy."

"That's the Commissioner." I turned on his Zorro night light. "How'd the game come out?"

"Dodgers two–zip behind Koufax."

"Shit. What did Post do?"

"I told you, Wally Post could not play."

"You see that mastery, Melissa? That's why he's the Commissioner."

"This is so weird. It's three o'clock in the morning and I'm sitting with my college professor on a bed with a ten-year-old boy."

"What were you expecting?"

"I don't know. I thought 'going to see the Commissioner' was like 'going to the submarine races.'"

"Sorry. Say, get me the box score, Stevie, I want to see who got the big hits."

The Commissioner got out of bed, his pajamas dragging around his girlish hips. "Here, but keep it down or my mom is gonna kill me."

"No sweat. By the way, Commissioner, this is Melissa. She's one of the women you were so worried about. I thought you'd like to meet her."

"Glad to meet you."

"Glad to meet you, Stevie."

We gathered our knees together on the Commissioner's bed, Indian style, like we were kids sitting around a campfire. Or we could have been disciples practicing zazen. Then I said, "You see, she's not so frightening, is she?" Boy, he got embarrassed at that. "Melissa, give the Commissioner a hug."

"Are you kidding?"

"No, that's okay, really. I like her."

"He's got insecurities about girls and I want to help him. Give him a goddamn hug."

"Be quiet, Professor!"

"I don't know . . ."

"He's just a goddamn little kid, so give him a fucking hug."

Animal paralysis seemed to set in with those two.

"Alright, I'll show you how." I took Stevie's arms, stiff as a little Frankenstein's, and reached for Melissa.

Then there was a huge knocking at the door. Big rattling of the handle.

"Steven! Steven Bruce! What's going on in there? Open this door."

"Nothing, Mom. (Get out of here, you guys.) I'm sleeping."

"It doesn't sound like you're sleeping. Who's in there?"

"No one. It's just me being Vin Scully for my baseball game."

"Let me see you. Open this door."

We were out the window. "Bye Commissioner." Melissa wanted to run (what a nice scene: a middle-aged housewife sprinting from a ten-year-old's bed), but I pulled her up against the house, behind a bush, hoping there would be more. Sure enough, Mrs. Commissioner stuck her head out the window. "Why is this open? It's freezing in here." She had the light on and I liked what I saw, Mom in her glowing nightie. In theosophy, constellations are named after such visions.

2. The Ego as Defined by Its Absence

Although Laura was reluctant to commit herself to the unorthodox education offered by Metaphysics, she had relevant needs and a familiar desperation.

Not only had her father died a few years before, but she'd recently gone through a searing divorce. It was one of those affairs in which the woman commits herself headlong but naively, with no self-knowledge—no knowledge period—and then is amazed to see the husband drunk, violent, roaring the family chopper around the duplex at two o'clock in the morning, doing doughnuts on the neighbor's lawn and leaving it up to the wife to explain to furious Mr. and Mrs. Nextdoor. But as wrong as this first life decision is, these spontaneous creatures seem to have an uncanny nose for remedies, although those remedies are chastened and far from immediate: they get jobs, their own little apartments, they enroll in college. In short, they furnish the void.

This was precisely Laura's situation. She discovered my adult education class in Metaphysics in the same way every other resident of Kankakee had—through a brochure addressed to "Boxholder." Also offered by the "K.J.C. Adult Ed. Prog." were courses on belly dancing, Christmas crafts and psychology. She took Metaphysics because it fit her schedule and appeared more rigorous and academic than the others. Her impression of the class after actually attending a session was that it was perhaps even less rigorous than Christmas crafts, but she came quickly to hope that—beyond my eccentric pedagogy—this might be a course about exactly what she was most troubled by: the absence of meaningfulness in her life. What I wanted to say to her from the very first was yes, yes, yes, that's right.

"Thousands of people die miserable every day for lack of the study I suggest to you." That's what I said to them in week five, ten, twelve, whatever it was, in Laura's little apartment. "To avoid desolation—what after all our death culture has most to offer—and discover real knowledge, you must move from a merely customary awareness of material existence to a plane of true intuition at which love and knowledge may be actualized."

Laura and Melissa never did figure how to respond to such proclamations. They stared like a couple of stunned carp, with no notion of what sort of response they might appropriately risk. At least, on that night, Melissa was willing to say something.

"I have a lot of trouble knowing what to say about this stuff. I guess I feel inadequate. You and the books we read are too much smarter than I am. I'm sure it has to do with my self-image problem."

"Melissa, consider the virus. What is it? A genetic code wrapped in a protein shield. And what does it want? It wants every other living cell to devote itself to reproducing the virus's own vainglorious, naughty-sneaky genetic message. It's like a combination lock with Ghengis Khan's will to power. So, the virus has no self-image problem. But is what we're after here the willingness to assert oneself as infinitely desirable? It's entirely the wrong question. The real problem is to get beyond issues of personal worth, and on to the issue of making the God-unit, fragmented as it now is, whole again."

"I think I see what you mean," said Laura, almost unaware that she was saying anything. More like she was talking to herself.

"You're talking about a kind of 'availability.'"

"Yes."

"A kind of availability and a denial of even minimal engagements with trivial preoccupations."

A star was born. Melissa, on the other side, looked crestfallen, confused and marooned. I didn't want Laura's breakthrough to be Melissa's falling away, so I stood and abruptly dismissed class. That is, suggested that Melissa and I should be going.

"I've got to meet the Commissioner yet this evening."

"The Commissioner?" asked Laura. "Who's that?"

"It's a funny thing to explain, actually. When I first moved to town about two years ago, I read an ad in the classifieds by a young boy who was looking for someone to form a statistical baseball league with. I responded, we became friends and now on several nights each week we get together to play the '62 Giants against the '69 Mets. Or the '63 Dodgers against the '75 Reds. There's something so beautiful about the way the game insists: time is nothing, identity is undecidable, only the Event matters, and it is universal and perfect regardless of how it comes out."

"Oh. That is strange, but kind of nice I guess. That you have a friendship with a little boy."

"He's basically without a proper father."

"Well then it's very nice. But his mother sure lets him stay up late. It's almost eleven now."

"Yes, doesn't she?"

"Does that mean that there won't be time for a beer this evening?" Melissa squeaked desperately, her aura throbbing with fear of abandonment.

"There's always time for a little beer," I counseled. "Then can you drop me off at the Commissioner's?"

"Love to."

Much later that evening, in the top of the fifth, I squatted on the Commissioner's bed giggling and staring at the wall. Elston Howard had just hit one into the gap and Kubek, Mantle, and Maris had skipped giddily to the plate making it a 7-1 ballgame. The Commissioner was pissed off.

"You're not even paying attention. It's not fun for me to win if you don't care if you lose."

He was right. I was too amused to concentrate that night.

He continued. "And why did you pick the '64 Cubbies against the '62 Yankees? And pinch hit for Ernie Banks with men on in the fourth? It's stupid."

"I had a hunch."

"Don Zimmer for the great Ernie Banks is not a hunch."

The kid was right and ordinarily I'd have been kicking myself. But I was thinking about the conversation Melissa and Laura would be having the next day. Melissa was surely going to tell all, and who would be more impressed than Laura?

"Laura, I've got to tell you what happened last night."

"Last night? What?" Laura a little afraid, a little depressed.

"You know I went out with Professor Feeling for a beer after class and then I drove him over to the Commissioner's. Boy, is that arrangement weird, but that's another story. Anyway, I stopped the car a few houses down from where I should have. I admit, I started it."

"Started what?" Panic.

"I gave him that kiss-me look."

"Oh God."

"So we kissed for a few minutes and then he told me to take off all my clothes. Well, you know his manner, I couldn't say no. It was so exciting. He wouldn't even let me leave my socks on. Right in the middle of the street, practically. And then . . ."

"And then?"

"Maybe I shouldn't tell the rest. It might not be fair to Willie."

"Willie? God damn you, don't stop, finish the story." Something real in that urgency.

"It sounds almost too strange to say, now that I think about it. Maybe I should be ashamed."

"What?"

"He introduced me to a friend of his, 'Shy Bob.' Laura, he carries a vibrator with him in that old leather briefcase. He said Bob's friends just call him Buzz."

3. The Wisdom Event

"So you guys are lovers now?"

"Well," completely pleased with herself, "You might say."

That's how we concluded that incredible conversation. I was depressed, and I was upset about being depressed. I seemed to care about something in this. I had to admit that, once again, I had given myself over to what Professor Feeling called the "torment of hope." And now I was obliged to see that I not only hoped for wisdom or at least some kind of self-knowledge through our study, but I hoped for something from Feeling himself. I was jealous. I felt a failure. And what the hell kind of horrible person was Melissa anyway? She had a husband and a little boy! And doing it in the street like a slut with that porn shop sex toy. I was disgusted.

I had to talk to Professor Feeling. So, I called him and asked if I could come over to get his comments on the journal I'd been keeping.

"Come in, Laura."

He hadn't gotten up to greet me. When I opened his door, he was sitting in the lotus position on a kitchen chair—apparently the only piece of furniture in the apartment—with a tumbler of water at his side. Through our talk he never opened his eyes and only occasionally drank from his glass.

"Welcome. Have a seat." He motioned to a squat meditation cushion on the floor before him.

"I'm sorry to interrupt you, Professor." I was. I was now completely confused about my motives. Really, all I wanted to say was "How could you?" But how could he what? Have a sex life? Prefer Melissa? Own a vibrator? Live without me?

"No problem. I'm just in middle intensity meditation. If you don't mind if I keep my eyes closed, we can talk."

"That's fine."

"Then why don't you just read to me from your journal."

I started reading one of the exercises he had assigned us, about visualizing the body of a giant: "His arteries are soft and elastic and at first I feel a little confined, but when I allow myself to flow, stream with the little blood balloons, I realize that even here in the most constricted place in the giant's body I am in infinite space, free to rise, expand, like smoke infusing the universe." My tongue clucked along, and I soon lost all contact with what I was reading. The words spilled like gibberish. I might have imagined that, the Professor and I were sharing a mystic moment, that our thoughts were one, except that when I looked up to see the glow of similar recognition in the Professor's eyes, I saw instead that he was now in very deep meditation indeed. He was asleep. So much for psychic oneness. It was then that I saw, propped behind him up against a wall, his worn leather briefcase. I had to look. I crept to the briefcase and, one item at a time, removed:

an issue of *The Bill James Baseball Abstract*

an empty half-pint of Jose Cuervo

a small stuffed toy parrot

thirteen Bic pens, marked "Property of Kankakee Junior College"

a dozen pages of confused notes

a wine glass

a bottle of Advil

a frisbee

Space, Time, Knowledge by Tartang Tulku

and a nightlight with a picture of Zorro on it

But no Shy Bob vibrator.

"Good night, Laura."

I turned to see Professor Feeling fall from his seat and land on his face. For the first time I noticed the smell of alcohol. The now empty tumbler was still pungent with gin.

I found a blanket, covered him there on the floor, and left.

Two nights later I called Professor Feeling again. I had decided that he was clearly no guru, but he was nonetheless unlike any other man in the midwest. That much was easy to say. It was true that he had a drinking problem that I didn't understand, but a stable relationship with someone who really cared for him would surely help. And he had something to give me, strange though that something often was. I would tell him how I felt.

But he didn't answer his phone. I was afraid he was with Melissa, so I called her. Lester answered.

"She's not home now. Who is this, please?"

"This is a friend of hers. Laura Harper."

"You're in the evening class with her, aren't you? With that psycho?"

"Yes, I am. What do you mean psycho?"

"I mean lunatic. Would you like to know where I'm going right now? With our little boy in my arms? I'm going down to City Hall to bail her out of jail. She and that son of a bitch have been arrested."

"Oh no."

"Breaking and entering, sexual misconduct with a minor, drunk and disorderly. That fucker has ruined my life."

"I'm sorry. I'm so sorry"

"Listen, I've got to go."

"But just a minute. Is Professor Feeling in jail too?"

"I was told he'd been taken to the psycho hold at the hospital."

"So he's at Mt. Mercy."

"I think so."

"Thank you. And I hope things turn out okay."

It was the next morning before I was allowed to speak with him. But first I talked with Dr. Simon Able, chief of staff in psychiatry.

"Would you like to know what happened, Miss Harper?"

"Yes, please."

He was serious about this and not even friendly with me. As if somehow my desire to talk to the poor guy implicated me.

"The police report indicates that at around ten PM last evening the police received a phone call from a Mrs. Eileen Warden with a burglary-in-progress complaint. The police arrived in moments and were directed by Mrs. Warden to her son's room. The door was locked and the police forced entry. What they found was this: your so-called professor was drunk and unconscious on the boy's floor. Your friend Melissa was found similarly intoxicated, in partial undress, sitting on the bed with the boy. She could provide no reasonable excuse for her presence or her state, so she was arrested under suspicion of a number of things including child molesting."

"She wouldn't do that," I protested, "she has a little boy of her own."

"I can't speak for her, but I can tell you, as a result of my own examination, that Feeling is a disturbed and potentially dangerous man."

"You don't know him. He's just different."

"Miss Harper," more than a little contempt in the way he said that, "This guy has suffered major insult to a number of important organs due to his alcoholism. Not least among these organs is his brain. His liver has a lethal resemblance to a puff fish, and that's not to be ignored, but his brain, his brain . . ."

The appropriate comparison was testing him.

"Pudding. Tapioca pudding. Just lumpy enough to allow the circuitry to bump into transmission now and then, but generally much impaired."

"Listen. I'd just like to speak to him."

"Of course you may."

The Professor was wide awake and quite calm in bed. "Laura! Fantastic!"

"Hello, Professor Feeling."

"What can I offer you? Grapefruit sections? Oatmeal? Java? I don't have any brandy for the coffee, I'm sorry to say."

"That's alright. I don't want anything."

"So what brings you here?"

"I've come to see you, obviously. It's not like you could come to see me. Some terrible things happened to you last night."

"Like what?"

"You were arrested and so was Melissa."

"Oh, she'll be okay. And I'll be out of here shortly. I just need to talk to a few people."

"I don't think you understand. You're under arrest for burglary and child molesting."

"Oh that!" He laughed. "Of course, the Commissioner let us in. And what interest would I or Melissa have in Stevie sexually? That part's really funny."

"I was told that Melissa was undressed."

"All they saw was her blouse was undone. Big deal. Stevie's old enough he needs to know and accept as unremarkable that women are different. It's nothing his mother would ever tell him. And I didn't want him to grow up frightened and obsessed by those differences. As it is, we were probably too late. He said it looked like the face of a sad monkey."

"What are you talking about?"

"I'm saying I love the Commissioner and I've done him no harm."

"Dr. Able says he'll need several years with a good child psychologist."

Just a moment of doubt and dread, perhaps. "No. That's false. He already understands more than any of them. When they're done, they'll admit that."

"Professor, child molesting is serious business. You are likely to go to jail."

"I spent a month in a Cong cage in Nam up to my neck in putrid swamp water. They pissed on my head for fun."

"I don't believe that."

"And besides the Commissioner has already begun work on a benefit concert for me. This is just like the Dead bust in New Orleans. A frame-up. Rock stars are going to be there—Peter Townsend, man, and Sting, and Paul McCartney—and baseball greats, too, like Mays and Roger Maris. Whitey Ford if he can get away from some commitments. These people are in my corner, Laura."

"None of this can be true."

"Can you see McCartney and Stan Musial singing 'Fool on the Hill' for me?"

To that I said nothing.

"You look sad, Laura."

"I am sad."

"Why?"

"I feel disappointed."

"You know, the most beautiful thing that ever happened for Stevie and me in our baseball game was one night through a peculiar and rare combination of rolls the game was rained out in the third inning. Were we ever excited. Imagine, a rain-out! We climbed out the window together and sat on the curb in front of his house and Stevie had his first warm beer and the moon was there and cars rolled by ecstatic. I told you, Laura, the Event is universal and perfect no matter how it turns out."

I didn't feel like doing anything with the rest of the day, so I went home and turned on the TV. I watched the episode of *I Love Lucy* where she gets caught in Richard Widmark's den hiding beneath a grizzly bear skin. At the moment where Ricky and Widmark stand above her—she sunk in the stink of that hide, peeping up from under its jaw like something just eaten; Widmark focusing an elephant gun on her head—I got up, pulled down my

jeans, spread myself before the dressing mirror and scrutinized the organization of bits locked there. It didn't look anything like the face of a monkey.
More madness. Unless he meant the kind of red-lipped, know-nothing monkey moms make out of socks. You could think of it that way. Of course, once
I'd thought of it that way, I couldn't think of it any other. It had the nasty
insistence of a radio jingle you can't get out of your head. Like, "Eat Eskimo
Pie. Eat Eskimo Pie."

Luna Moth

MICHAEL WILKERSON

MR. PETERS SHOWED US TWO specimens from his boyhood. They were louse-riddled, encased in glass-covered Riker mounts that had allowed the incandescent light of his study to fade the wings to grey. Rick turned away from the long-dead creatures, and I followed him to the bicycles. He had caught Luna moths before, one night when I had stayed home ill. Mr. Peters walked outside with us. The moon had come up, and its light he saw the moth first, flapping its great wings slowly against the dark spruce tree in the center of his huge yard.

"There's a Luna now," he said, violating the awe of the moment with his flat tone, his indifferent shrug, his turning away toward the indoors. The nets were on the other side of the porch from us; instead of getting mine, I watched the Luna relay the moon's white light through its faintly green wings, its long curved tails carving a brilliant orbit path around the spruce. My brother returned with a net, but this moth was not to be caught; it vanished while I stared at the tree. We rode the half-mile home, avoiding the dark places that were chuckholes in the chip-and-seal road. All the way we searched the pavement for dead moths that might have been hit by cars, but found none.

We spent part of the Christmas of 1968 with an aunt and uncle in Franklin, Indiana; Borman, Lovell and Anders sent us their carefully orchestrated *Genesis* against the stark backdrop of the televised moon. Aunt Bonnie, then 85, said repeatedly, "It's a hoax, they're not really there, why, they'll never go to the moon." The simulated moon that Walter Cronkite showed was back-lit incorrectly, my Uncle Jack claimed. "It looks so small, like you could catch it," Rick said. In the morning we got up early to search the woods for cocoons. Unlike those of the other moths in its family, the Luna's cocoon separates from the trees on which it is spun, and mixes with the dead leaves on the ground.

There was a new kind of light in Indiana in the early 1960s. We moved west 40 miles, from Columbus to Bloomington. I cried all the way. Mother described the workings of the brilliant blue-white mercury vapor light. We counted the bulbs we saw at business and farms along Highway 46. "You have to rent it from the power company," she said. "Four dollars a month, forty-eight dollars a year. A lot of money." My faint tears and as-yet-undiscovered myopia made the lights seem magical and shimmering; I wanted one.

In Bloomington we lived in a graduate student apartment building; Dad sought a doctorate in education. I looked out from the balcony at the mercury lights in the parking lot. The night John Kennedy died, we went for an aimless drive in the rain. We had just acquired a fading Oldsmobile with sculptured fins. In spring my brother and I collected leaves for school. The teacher did not allow shoes in her classroom. Mother knitted us slippers of grey-white yarn. In them, we shuffled quietly around the classroom, mounting and preserving our accumulated leaves.

Rick and I were also fossil hunters in Bloomington; the bedroom was filled with jars of crinoid stems we had taken from the neighborhood ditches that cut through the grass and bared the blood-red clay. We learned in class that Bloomington was the world capital of crinoid stems. We considered our collection of grey-white sea plants an investment, hard and unbreakable like promises. Crinoids were most easily found at night, when the mercury lights accented them against the clay.

Illinois was our next home; we joined 4–H to fill the summer and hunted insects in the fields around the housing developments. Dad worked at the university in a floodlit limestone administration building that looked like a castle at night. We were day hunters then, chasing Giant, Tiger and Zebra butterflies through the alfalfa blooms. Fishing, I caught a snapping turtle in Teachers College Pond; it came to the surface heaving and covered with dark green weeds that displayed shining beads of water to the sun.

We left Illinois after only a year, transferring to Terre Haute as if in flight. We bought a two-story brick home that had once been a stop on the Underground Railroad. From the basement, a tunnel led to Honey Creek near the Peters' home. We found farm artifacts near the bank: square cobbler's nails, blades, decaying knives and saws. The rural mercury lights drew moths and beetles in far greater numbers than the old yellow-tinged incandescents. We read that blue was the best color for attracting insects, and that white was second. Mother, though, would buy only the yellow incandescents; we complained about their uselessness. The future was mercury. In less than six months, we knew the location of every mercury light in southern Vigo County. We bought large mesh nets from the Farm Bureau and made friends with the children of homeowners who had paid the extra rent to the power company.

The best place to hunt was the Hacienda Motel—inside were aging waitresses with pale, cracked makeup on their white features, a bar with a pool table, and moon-faced twenty-year-olds gathered to rage against the draft and to dodge the state alcohol police. The moths spread their huge wings on juniper bushes that grew beneath the motel's blue neon sign. Biting dobsonflies made the hunt dangerous. Metallic green attack beetles impeded our progress. Large cars turned in and out of the driveway, stopping at the cabins at odd times. We caught the myth-named Saturniid family one-by-one: Cecropia, Promethia, Io, Polyphemus—all of them oversized, slow, delicate, and winged in prominent hues of yellow, brown and purple. The last still eluding our nets was the green Luna.

One night I stayed home with the flu, watching the wavering light of the new Magnavox TV—our family's first color set. I chased my mother's cat with a flashlight beam while Rick went to the Hacienda. The next morning, the breakfast table was covered with the faint green dust of Luna wings. I was thirteen years old. That night, Rick went to a friend's house, telling me I was too young to accompany him. That same month he demanded that we forever stop calling him Ricky. Mother bought me a pastel green shirt from the semiannual sale downtown. "This is you," she said.

On the day that Bobby Kennedy was to be shot I brought home a perfect Zebra Swallowtail—a butterfly with dogged, fascinating habits, found only in small hollows and roadsides in certain areas of the Midwest. It was a whitish-green specimen with long, razor-straight tails, more fragile than those of the Luna; its wings were striped with jagged slashes of black. Dad's graduate assistant stayed with us that night, while our parents went out and the California election returns came in. In the morning the red pilot light on my radio glared; there were sirens in the background of a man's tired voice. Dad's graduate assistant was a Catholic and told us he was unable to talk about the shooting. "There was a large green moth on the porch last night," he said. "Right before I went to bed, just as the primary ended. It kept banging against the screen, trying to get in the house, but I shooed it away." I went to the porch and stared at the screen, seeking any evidence I could find. I watched the incandescent floodlight; for numerous minutes, I stood on the empty porch and tried to imagine the scene Dad's graduate assistant had viewed.

Moths usually have one to three hatching seasons per summer. These seasons, called broods, are like volatile windows during which the adults are plentiful. They disappear in days. Despite their long tongues, called probosci, most adult moths, including the Saturniids, do not feed. The Luna's broods are in late spring and early to mid-August. Mating is the sole purpose of the adults. The August brood has a more pronounced blood-red stripe on the forewings; in the early brood, the stripe is a fresh hue of purple. Walter Cronkite once told us of the few times when the Apollo rockets could be launched. "If we don't make this three-day window, we'll have to wait for another time when the moon is an accessible target," he said. I watched the landing of Apollo 11 on the big Magnavox. I took a picture of the set when Neil Armstrong stepped on the lunar surface, but it came out glowing, grey, indistinguishable.

Having conquered all the Saturniids, Rick turned his attention to other orders—primarily Coleoptera, the beetles. "Spotted dung beetle," he'd say, slamming a jar on top of a crawling, round, black object. "Caterpillar hunter. Carrion beetle." One day he brought home from the woods a greenish-white apple borer with long, curved antennae that wavered for about twenty minutes after the insect should have died from the carbon tetrachloride in the jar. "I wonder if it's sending out a message with those antennae," Mother said. "Maybe it's crying." "Bugs don't feel pain," I said.

My great-grandmother was 98 when she died in 1975. "You boys stop killing those poor bugs," she had said four years earlier. "How do you know they don't hurt?" Not bugs, I thought. Surely not bugs. Half senile and stooped with cancer, she was taken to a nursing home. We picked round and sour gooseberries on her property. At her funeral my great aunt—her eldest daughter—said, "She was so out of it those last few months, she didn't feel anything."

All the turkeys in Turkey Run State Park had been killed long ago, and now the land was a hilly, wooded refuge for campers and hikers. We drove up the gently curving pavement of Highway 63 to hunt there. Mercury lights dominated the parking lot. We started eagerly, spending the daylight hours filling cigar boxes with wings that were scattered on the grass medians. Mother and Dad walked in the woods. At dinner we had white chicken meat and green beans under yellow candlelight. Dad spilled red wine on his chicken. After dinner, Mother and Dad retrieved an army blanket from the car and went to the outdoor theatre to watch a state-sponsored melodrama. I hated melodrama—the villains too villainous, the heroes too heroic, the faces too pasty and made-up. Like my brother, I preferred to stand in the parking lot with net in hand, feeling its rough wooden handle, tracing the wind-changed curves of the green mesh netting, waiting for the Luna to flounce its elegant, mercury-lit shadows on the pavement. "God, I hope we get a Luna," I said. Rick asked, "Have you seen how my Lunas are fading? I need one, too."

The first big moth to fly in was a Polyphemus: common, huge and almost entirely dusk-brown. It came from the West like a weather pattern and flapped near the lightpole. We blocked out the bulb by lining the handles of our nets in front of our squinting eyes. The moth circled the white-blue aura twice, then flew to the north. We pivoted, tracking it, and saw a sudden rush of blackness followed by the four wings' slow drift to the pavement. "Bats," Rick said. "They take the body but don't eat the wings." We interred the Polyphemus in the cigar box and waited. I saw it first—a beetle, enormous and one-horned, rutting across the stripes of the parking stalls beneath the light. "A Unicorn!" Rick said, awed at something I had found for the first time since the Zebra. The Unicorn was about two inches long and almost an inch wide; its bristly legs scratched my fingers. I dropped it into the killing jar, and its huge body almost took up the entire surface of the jar's false cardboard bottom, through which the carbon tetrachloride fumed. The beetle was spotted—dark brown on a field of green that I knew would fade to black in a few months. As I watched it die, Rick caught a Luna moth.

"God damn you!" I was almost in tears. "You promised the first one to me."

"There wasn't time. It would have flown away, or the bats would have gotten it. Anyway, you got a Unicorn. Everyone has a Luna; almost no one has a Unicorn."

I didn't answer; I was completely unable to look at him. I went to another side of the parking lot. The hunting there did not seem as good. I was sure that all the most coveted moths were stopping first at Rick's brighter and better-located light. He caught two more Lunas in the next hour. Then the melodrama ended, and Mother and Dad shooed us into the car for the trip home. I watched the little moths and beetles fly into the headlights of our new white Chrysler, for which we'd traded the Oldsmobile. The headlights distorted the tiny half-inch millers and made them seem gigantic, larger than Lunas. Drained, I slept until we hit the Holiday Inn and Honey Creek Square, whose neon and mercury lights gave the carless parking lot the quality of a desolate moonscape. At home, I tried to trade the Unicorn beetle to Rick, but he refused, saying I would just demand it back later.

We spent the summer of 1970 in Nebraska, still hunting. I fell further behind Rick in my overall collection. I was thinking more and catching less. The excessive sun made the alfalfa fields pale. At night, we didn't know where many good mercury lights were in that strange, new territory; driving to an over-illuminated power plant, we crossed a set of railroad tracks that reflected the rays from a row of harsh orange-pink bulbs. No insects approached these lights, and we wondered what they were. For me, Turkey Run had rendered the hunt of the Luna joyless, but I finally succeeded that summer in Lincoln. My first Luna was a perfect specimen, all four quadrants an exact and brilliantly haunting shade of green, bright as a young apple, but delicately translucent. Pale dust wafted off the furry white body into my hands as I gently touched the long-sought insect. I put it in a special box for our trip home to Indiana in August, when I displayed it at the Vigo County Fair.

All the buildings at the fairgrounds were of prefab aluminum; the exhibit hall had been painted green, which was the dominant color of 4–H. "I pledge my head to clearer thinking," I said. "My heart to greater loyalty, my hands to larger service, and my health to better living, for my club, my community, and my country." People continued to make positive remarks about my two-year-old Unicorn. I stayed at the fairgrounds until the last possible hour of every day, talking with other 4–H'ers about Apollo 13's crisis and the upcoming Junior Leader elections. "Don't you guys ever talk about girls?" said a friend, who then, in the near-total darkness of the new moon, gave an exhaustive account of his premeditated exploits of young women. Uninterested, Rick and I took our nets to the Speedway, where the Midget races had drawn spectators in great numbers. We looked for beetles but found only dropped dollar bills under the incandescent lights near the Midway.

I finally put my net away in 1971, when we moved again to Bloomington. There were other things to collect in that place—money, albums, parts in plays, tools for my new car. Rick had enrolled at Purdue as an Entomology major but transferred to Broadcasting after one semester. One night, the radio station posted his lottery number; Mother sat picking at the finish of the kitchen table and crying. Along Jordan Avenue, trees stayed awake 24 hours a day under the harsh influence of proliferating sodium-vapor lights. A friend's father bought a moon-grey car from Mr. Peters in Terre Haute.

There were too many mercury lights to count; the moths had no way of knowing where to congregate.

I spent a summer counseling at a conservation camp, where I taught entomology. I had a net but no killing jar, and I slept in a green canvas tent. One night during a new moon, some campers and I set an insect trap of beer and sugar water beneath a parking-lot mercury light. We checked it about 11:30, after a campfire during which I'd performed a medley of outdated protest songs. In the trap, swimming and trying not to drown, were two Luna moths. Their blood-red wing stripes seemed less prominent than I had remembered. The male waved feathery antennae at me. "He's talking to you," one of the campers said. "That's a romantic notion," I replied. "He's receiving sex impulses from the female." There was no more talk. To the south, I pointed out the orange sky of illuminated Indianapolis, where 750,000 people slept. I fought and defeated an urge to keep the Luna moths. I had given my collection and my brother's to the state nature center; I was not interested in preserving the past. I freed the struggling moths and led the way through the jungle-like trail, back to the camp. A woman counselor, who had sung harmony to some of my protest songs, took my hand in the darkness and asked me what the flying object was. I said I didn't know, that I had missed it. Maybe I had tried to avoid seeing it. I think Rick would have pursued it, but I held my fellow counselor's hand and led the group back to their tents; like everyone else, I had already been to the moon.

Baby · Pornography

❧

DIANE WILLIAMS

Baby

NOBODY WAS GETTING UP CLOSE to me, whispering, "Do you get a lot of sex?" Nobody was making my mouth fall open by running his finger up and down my spine, or anything like that, or talking dirty about dirty pictures and did I have those or anything like those, so I could tell him what I keep— what I have been keeping for so long in my bureau drawer underneath my cable-knit pink crew—so I could tell him what I count on happening to me every time I take it out from under there. Because it was a baby party for one thing, so we had cone paper hats and blowers, so we had James Beard's mother's cake with turquoise icing, and it was all done up inside with scarlet and pea-green squiggles, and the baby got toys.

Nobody was saying, "Everybody has slept with my wife, because everybody has slept with everybody, so why don't we sleep together?" so I could say at last, "Yes, please. Thank you for thinking of me." I would be polite.

Just as it was nothing out of the ordinary when the five-year-old slugged the eleven-year-old on the back and they kept on playing, looking as if they could kill for a couple of seconds. We didn't know why. And then the baby cried in a bloodthirsty way.

My husband sat stony-faced throughout. I don't think he moved from his chair once. What the fuck was wrong with him? He left the party early, without me; he said to get a little—I don't know how he was spelling it—I'll spell it *peace.*

I spoke to a mustached man right after my husband left. He was the first man all night I had tried to speak to. I know he loves sports. I said to him, "I think sports are wonderful. There are triumphs. It is so exciting. But first, you have to know what is going on."

Then my boy was whining, "Mom, I want to go home." He was sounding unbearably tired.

The baby's aunt said she'd take us. She didn't mind. She had to back up her car on the icy drive. She said, "I don't know how we'll get out of here," when we got into the car, "the windows are all fogged up." She said, "I don't think I can do it." She opened the window and poked her head out. She said, "I don't think so."

When she closed the window, we went backward terrifically fast. I don't know how she knew when to spin us around into the street. It was like being in one of those movies I have seen the previews for. It was like watching one of those faces on those people who try to give you the willies. It was like that, watching her—while she tried to get us out.

Pornography

I just had a terrible experience—I'm sorry. I was yelling at my boy, "Don't you ever!" I saw this crash. I saw this little old man. The door of the car opened and I saw this little old man tottering out. Somebody said, "I saw him!" The same somebody said, "He's already hit two cars."

There was this kid. He wasn't a kid. He was about nineteen. He was screaming and screaming on a bicycle.

Then I saw him, the kid, on the stretcher.

That little old man did more for me than any sex has ever done for me. I got these shudders.

The same thing with another kid—this one tiny, the same thing, on a stretcher, absolutely quiet in a playground, and I was far enough away so that I did not know what had happened. I never found out. Same thing, shudders that I tried to make last, because I thought it would be wonderful if they would last for at least the four blocks it took me to get home and they were lasting and then I saw two more boys on their bicycles looking to get hit, not with any menace like they wanted to *do* anything to me, because I wasn't even over the white crossing line, not yet, and the only reason I saw either one of them was because I was ready to turn and I was looking at the script unlit yellow neon *ı* on the cleaner's marquee which was kitty-corner to me, when just off that *ı* I saw the red and the orange and my driver's leg struck up and down hard on the brake without my thinking, even though I think I was ready to go full out at that time, because where was I going, anyway? Back home to my boy?

My car was rocking, the nose of it, against the T-shirts of those boys, first the red one, and then the orange one, and they, each of them, they looked me in the eye.

Back home, my boy, he's only five, he's going to show me, making himself into a bicycle streak down our drive, heading, he says, for my mother's house, heading for that dangerous curve where so many horrible accidents have happened or have almost happened. What I did was yell at him DON'T YOU DO THAT! but he was already off, and then this goddamn little thing, this animal, this tiny chipmunk thing races with all its stripes right up at me, but not all the way *to* me, and then the thing, it whips around and runs away, like right now with my boy—I can't—there is no other way to put it—I *can't come.*

Credits

For Photos

For Previous Publication

"All You Can Eat," by Robin Hemley, first appeared in *New Letters* and then in his story collection *All You Can Eat* and in the anthology *A Literary Feast*.

"Happy Film," by Laird Hunt, first appeared in *Conjunctions*.

"Anton's Album," by Janet Kauffman, first appeared in *The Quarterly* and then in the short story collection *Obscene Gestures for Women*.

"A History of Indiana," by Jesse Lee Kercheval, first appeared in the book *The Dogeater*. © Jesse Lee Kercheval. Reprinted by permission of the author.

"Still Life with Insects," by Brian Kiteley, was published by various publishers in 1989, 1990, and 1993. © Brian Kiteley. Reprinted by permission of the author.

"Mobile Axis: A Triptych," by Clarence Major. © 1990 by Clarence Major. Reprinted by permission of the author.

"The Digitally Enhanced Image of Cary Grant Appears in a Cornfield in Indiana," by Michael Martone, first appeared in *Paper Placemats*, edited by Paul Maliszewski.

"Talking to my Old Science Teacher about Drawing in which I Killed Him," by Brian McMullen, a real interview with a real person (illustrated by real drawings), first appeared in *Cabinet*.

"A Harvest," by Glenn Meeter, first appeared in *Epoch* and then in *Innovative Fiction*, edited by Jerome Klinkowitz and John Somer, and *Experimentelle Amerikanische Prosa*, edited by Brigitte Scheer-Schatzler.

"Other Electricities," by Ander Monson, first appeared in *Fugue* and then in his book *Other Electricities*.

"The Mausoleum," by Susan Neville, first appeared in *Gargoyle Magazine*.

"Submarine Warfare on the Upper Mississippi," by Lon Otto, first appeared in his book *A Nest of Hooks*.

"Wednesday Night Reflections, Edited Thursday," by Erin Pringle, first appeared in *Quarter After Eight*.

"The Great War," by Josh Russell, first appeared in *Colorado Review*.

"July Snow," by Scott Russell Sanders, first appeared in *Hopewell Review*.

"The Red Bow," by George Saunders, first appeared in *Esquire* and then in his collection *In Persuasion Nation*.

"Medieval Land," by Steve Tomasula, is excerpted from the author's novella *Medieval Times*. Excerpts have also appeared in *American Letters & Commentary*, *Western Humanities Review*, and *Ninth Letter*.

"Natural Citizens," by Deb Olin Unferth, first appeared in *The New York Tyrant*.

"Seccession, XX," by Kellie Wells, first appeared in *The Kenyon Review* and then in her collection of stories *Compression Scars*.

"Metaphysics of the Midwest," by Curtis White, first appeared in his book *Metaphysics in the Midwest*.

"Luna Moth," by Michael Wilkerson, first appeared in the *Iowa Review*.

"Baby/Pornography," by Diane Williams, first appeared in the following:
"Baby" first appeared in *The Quarterly*, "Pornography" in *Conjunctions*, and both appeared in her collection *Excitability: Selected Stories*.

Contributors

Max Apple: 700 Broadway, Grand Rapids, Michigan—Hebrew International.

Joel Brouwer: If you travel to the northern tip of the Leelanau peninsula, turn your back on the Grand Traverse Lighthouse and wade out into Lake Michigan's shallow, ice-clear waters. Stepping carefully across the stony bottom, you will find a place about thirty feet out which death has never discovered. I've instructed my family to dump my ashes and a pint of blueberries there.

Robert Day: I live these days in the fictional town of Bly, Kansas (four streets, the mayor is a dead dog—but a very fine dog she was), where the non-fiction Committee to Save the World meets. Mornings, mainly. We have only three rules: There shall be no rules. There shall be no votes. And everyone in the world is a member. Once, a few years ago, I asked one of the charter members if there had ever been a Mercedes in Bly. There was silence. Then he said: Yes, Bobby. 1987. But she was lost. Don't bother to look for us on the map.

Rikki Ducornet: Noticed, could not help but notice; noticed to my dismay again and again, how potatoes were smugly offered, as if a benefit to us all, in infinite yet drear progressions, as though the imagination were crippled by an obscure dogmatism. This was Minnesota. The potatoes came with white bread and were followed by white cake. One paled. And yet the waitress was always pink. Her cheeks and lips, her gums and elbows: pink. Mongrelized, one slept fitfully.

Stuart Dybek: I'm in Japan, I meet with Murakami later today. I'm visiting also with my wonderful translator who was featured in a Japanese magazine earlier this year and pictured in his old Tokyo 'hood, the caption on that photo read: the South Side of Tokyo. He took me there, because that place is why he translates me and it had the power scene you seek, an industrial river in a mist of factory smoke spanned by railroad bridges, iron and smoke and what passes for and as water.

Mark Ehling: One summer, as a child, I was wandering through the back-channel of the St. Anthony Falls hydro plant in Minneapolis, Minnesota—a series of little inlets and forest trails—and as I approached the spillway, I almost immediately fell into a trance. The falling water mesmerized me—I was lulled by the rushing sound. And I sat there in a kind of stupor when something huge and dark shot from the spillway and was launched over my head.

At first I thought, *That's a big log*. But it was actually—and I only had a second to see before it crashed back into the tailrace—a fish. A gigantic carp. When it hung for that one second in air, I could see its eyes.

The strangeness of this scene—the Zen trance, the sudden appearance and airborne-ness of the fish, its grotesque size—has stayed with me.

St. Anthony Falls is a beautiful place (I'm hardly the first to say so; it was revered by the Dakota and the Ojibwa, and then white settlers made it ground-zero for the birth of a city), but I love it just as much for what's missing: the dead tributaries, the sunken islands, abandoned bridge pilings, all things that are hidden, then revealed, then hidden again.

Louise Erdrich: The intersection of I-29 and I-94 lies about 45 minutes north of my parents' home in North Dakota, and is a place of perverse and nefarious power. It is vast, swooping concrete interchange—a weird tangle of signage. There is never much traffic and so the effect of all that road is disorienting. I worked tying steel rebar on the I-29 overpass which lies too far from Wahpeton to be of any economic benefit to our town. I'm honestly sorry that I helped I-29 into existence, although I must say I am very attached to I-94, which takes me almost directly from my house in Minneapolis to Wahpeton. Almost directly, that is, except for a stretch of Highway 210 that is perhaps the flattest and most exquisite landscape I know. This stretch of land is also a power crossroads, but there is no central locus. You can see the horizon to each direction from almost any point on this road, so in a way you are yourself a traveling crossroads of insignificance.

Robin Hemley: Woolworth's, Athens, Ohio, Court Street, circa April 12, 3:32 PM, 1968. I'm sitting at the counter with my best friend, Gary Keller, eating banana splits. We've come here after fishing quarters with bobby pins from the change slot of the pinball machines at Campus Sundry. Gary has the touch, a jewel thief's deft ability to evade the high-security apparatus, the cameras and death rays employed by Bob, owner of Campus Sundry. The banana splits are by way of celebration. I will leave a generous tip for Sally, the Woolworth's counter waitress, treat her to a Diet plate if she likes. "You know where I would hide if the Mafia was chasing me," I ask Gary. He nods, whip cream on his chin. "Woolworth's bathroom," I say. "No one would ever think to look for me there." He nods. Agreed. I rub my hand on the counter, wondering how they get those flecks to sparkle in Formica.

Lily Hoang: Michigan/31/933 (because every street in South Bend has multiple names) & Jefferson: where good coffee makes creative writing.

Laird Hunt: My Midwest place of great power? Rural Route 3, Box 97, Frankfort, IN, 46041, where my Great-Grandfather, a reluctant farmer, used to pull stone axe and arrow heads from the fields, one of which years later I set on the desk in my attic bedroom, in the house said Great-Grandfather had built, and wrote my first fictions. The axe head is still there. The writing is long gone.

Sandy Huss: The site of midwestern telluric power most vivid to me right now is a spot in Harman Cemetery, Putnam County, Ohio, where a gravestone (If love could have saved you, you would have lived forever) is surrounded by a plaster cherub, a US flag, and an Obama/Biden poster. In the background, a rolling field of corn stubble. Thanks to the Piermans, an Ohio farming family of long standing, for the alluring photo.

Lily James: Bowling Green, Ohio, is flat. It's a town that looks like a map of a town. However, there is one hill that sticks up on its own, like a foot under the blankets. In the winter, people sled on it, and in the summer, they make out there. I've heard that people from Northwest Ohio are only waiting to be people from somewhere else. Could this one lonely hill, for locals, be a jumping-off place to distant urban centers, or a life without virginity?

Janet Kauffman: The Black Swamp of northern Ohio and southern Michigan still seethes. It's gone underground, under flatland fields from Lake Erie to Fort Wayne—corn on corn on corn. But the Swamp Thing is waiting. Buried alive a hundred years ago, its waters ditched and drained, streams piped underground, its tangle of bladdernut, pawpaw, nannyberry chopped and burned—that's nothing. Pipes break, people come and go, seeds grow in ashes, water finds its level. A hundred years, a drop in the bucket.

Jesse Lee Kercheval: To me the most midwestern place I have ever been is the middle of a frozen lake.

Madison, Wisconsin, where I live now, is on a narrow isthmus between two large lakes whose names sound confusingly similar to newcomers, Lake Mendota and Lake Monona. My house is on Monona. My office at the University of Wisconsin is on Mendota. When I first moved to Wisconsin from Florida, someone told me Mendota froze so hard in the winter that in the old days they used to park cars on it during basketball games. I thought they were kidding. How did the fish breathe under all that ice? But after a winter or two, I started to look forward to the concrete white of the frozen lakes in winter.

The ice creates open space in a town that, in the summer, feels crowded on its narrow bridge of land. In the winter, people walk their dogs on the ice, sweep circles of snow off the ice to skate. On Mendota, there are ice boating regattas. The brave even sailboard on the ice—and really fly. People ice fish; the hardcore fishermen drag huts out onto the lake for the duration while the more casual just perch, bundled up, on overturned drywall buckets. Once, from my 6th floor office, I watched a man ride his bicycle the two miles across a frozen Lake Mendota to the student union, park his bike, and stroll inside.

Still, it took me a couple of winters before I could bring myself to trust the ice. I walked to the public park behind my house and down to the swimming beach, put one boot onto the rough frozen waves at Lake Monona's edge. Then I stepped onto the ice. Nothing cracked underfoot or even groaned. I did not plunge through the ice into bone-chilling water. Instead the sky stood blue and still above me, the lake dazzling white in front of me. I wrapped my muffler around my lower face, put my gloved hands deep in my pockets, and marched out to the sparkling diamond middle. Then I turned around and looked back. On shore, I could see the changing house, the lifeguard stand a foot deep in snow. I could see all the big Victorians at the edge of Monona that were so clearly lakefront houses even if their docks were now piled in their front yards, their boats in storage. By god, I was standing in the middle of a lake on my own two feet. And it struck me as a miracle. Like Jesus, I had walked upon the water.

Brian Kiteley: When I was in college in southern Minnesota, my friends and I would occasionally drive a few miles away to Dundas. Beer prices were cheap there because the town had more relaxed liquor licensing rules than Northfield, next door. We arrived one day to find a C&NW freight train stopped on the railroad tracks that ran through the center of this very small town, just before the level crossing at Hester Street. The engineer and two other C&NW employees climbed down from the locomotive and walked to the same bar we were going to. This image has stayed with me of a half-mile-long freight train idling in a small midwestern town so the crew could enjoy a beer. Trains on the Great Plains must have done this regularly, and the crews must have known which counties were dry, and, more importantly, which were not.

Clarence Major: I grew up in Chicago and for me its Art Institute was a place of magical power during the whole time. I spent as much time as I could there. I go back there as often as I can to reconnect with that magic.

Michael Martone: For me, it is the state road that follows the old Wabash mainline that follows the ruins of the old Wabash and Erie Canal that follows the Wabash River that follows the leavings of the last end moraine of the last ice age's last glacier, running south-southwest from Logansport to Lafayette, Indiana. Indiana, of course.

Brian McMullen: I once made a girl cry by smashing her windshield with my back at the intersection of Hill Road and Centennial Road in Holland, Ohio. Her speeding westbound Oldsmobile broadsided my southbound bike and 15-year-old self at 2:25 PM on Friday, April 1, 1994. When I got done caroming off the windshield, flying through the air, and cracking the Styrofoam of my little-worn helmet in half by landing on my head, I jumped up—pain-free, injury-free—and saw the crying driver running toward me, her checker-flanneled arms open wide. The accident was my fault—99 percent through with a three-hour spring-break bike ride, I'd

missed the last major STOP sign before my house—but the girl wasn't angry. She just wanted to make sure I was okay. We hugged and exchanged
phone numbers before the police and the EMTs arrived to ask us, "Where
is the victim?" When I told the cop that I was the one who had been hit, he
didn't believe me. He thought it was an April Fools' joke.

Glenn Meeter: St. Margaret's Hospital in Hammond, Indiana, across the
line from my parents' home in Lansing, Illinois, where I was born in 1934
and left uncircumcised because of the 94-degree heat that day, in that time
before air-conditioning, and where my brother and sister were born in 1937
and 1942. And where in 1957 my daughter Barbara was born, incidentally
saving me from the draft at age 23. A fine old Catholic hospital with crucifixes and sculptures of saints (one spearing a dragon, one pin-cushioned
with arrows) and a picture of Jesus wearing his glowing heart on his tunic,
and nuns and priests in black-and-white regalia, all weird to us Protestants
but numinously powerful. Where Marlene, my wife, while waiting to nurse
our baby, heard from the bed on the other side of her room's thin divider
a Polish immigrant confessing her sins ("and I mumble mumble with my
husband four times, and mumble with my mother twice"), never hearing
the sins but only the frequency. And heard her object strenuously to cir-
cumcision for her son, fearing he would be taken for a Jew, we gathered, in
some future pogrom.

And where one of the nuns, accompanying our small family in the elevator as we left St. Margaret's, said cheerily, "See you next year!" and my
Protestant mother-in-law from South Dakota, who had herself borne five
children and would number grandchildren in the twenties, said "O, I hope
not!"—but where we were again, nevertheless, almost exactly one year
later, with our second daughter, Nancy, whose bandaged feet had endured
innumerable pinpricks over seven days to test the bilirubin count in her
blood, which if it reached the level of 21 would trigger a complete blood-
replacement transfusion; and where the doctor told me brusquely "deaf
baby, blind baby, dead baby" when I asked what might happen without
such a transfusion, and where we prayed as never before or since, Marlene
for seven days in the hospital and me driving to work each day and home
again to help our two mothers in sequence take care of one-year-old Barbara, saying prayers in the car on the road, and then to the hospital at night
saying prayers with Marlene, while priests walked the corridors to hear

confessions in other rooms, until the count crested at 20 and then at last came down, down, down, and after seven days we brought Nancy home rejoicing with her feet swaddled in bandages.

And then I sold my first short story to *The Atlantic* (August 1958, you can look it up), and the three hundred dollars went to pay, in full, for the doctor (with all his brusqueness), the nurses and nuns and blood-count technician, the birthing and the daily testing and lab work and monitoring and board and room and medicines and bandages and constant care for mother and daughter over seven days and seven nights, as they say in the Bible, 24/7 as we say nowadays, at St. Margaret's Hospital in Hammond, Indiana.

Which was good, because we had no insurance.

Ander Monson: Ames, Iowa, just west of the city. Y Avenue south of Lincoln Way, where it crosses over US-30, nighttime, summer, faint smell of at least two kinds of manure, overpass. There is very little traffic. You are alone. A woman whom you do not know yet that you love has just left and, not satisfied with being alone, you are lonely. Soon enough you will be leaving too. This is a rare spot of interface with nature, before you will have enough of it and give it up. This is not nature, proper—it is a cultivated nature, squares of farmland, corn and soy and more, repeating into the distance. There is a radio tower in the distance blinking out its Morse into the night. You can drive in any direction, and oftentimes you will think about it, just getting on any road and driving with the pizzas you are meant to deliver off into the night and not stopping until eventually you have to stop. It is two and a half miles to the base of the tower. Your car is off and you are above the highway. Each car is an event happening for miles, meaning minutes, and you are above them, witness to their approach and their disappearing into the horizon. Everything is flatness, and in the winter it will be whiteness. All around you are a half a million fireflies. There is some magic in the world beyond our easy grasp of it.

Susan Neville: Always and again New Harmony, Indiana: final resting place of Paul Tillich's ashes, a suicide garden, pear trees pruned to resemble cathedral windows, a roofless church, a yellow tavern, an angel's footprints in stone, a museum of hair and postcards, and the epicenter of all midwestern earthquakes, both past and potential.

Lon Otto: I live in St. Paul, Minnesota, a few blocks from the patch of deer-haunted, inner city wasteland where the old Selby Avenue streetcar tunnel plunges into the Mississippi River bluffs below the cathedral. The tunnel entrance is blockaded with concrete. The tunnel feels its way westward in the dark.

Erin Pringle: The road that runs past the house where I grew up in Illinois. It was RR# when I was a child and then renamed into a numerical street for the ease of 911 operators. Whenever I need to imagine what a mile is, I imagine driving or running from the stop sign at the bottom of the hill to the yield sign out near the stone quarry. My mom walked up and down that road when she was pregnant with me, I learned how to ride my bike on that road, and my first cat was killed on that road on my fifth birthday. It's a powerful road that leads to and from everything I know.

Josh Russell: Ruth & Arthur "Red" Martin, RR1, Tonica, Illinois 61370. When the snowplow appeared on the distant edge of the white winter landscape after we'd been snowed in on my grandparents' farm one Christmas, my mother and father and my aunts and uncles cheered, and my grandmother and my grandfather, sitting at the huge kitchen table, drinking coffee, shared a relieved glance behind their backs. I was, what, eight? Ten?

We visited from Normal, fifty miles south, only on weekends and holidays; rarely did I see Grandpa Red at work in the seventy-nine acres of corn and soybeans surrounding the acre on which their house stood.

One night, when I was maybe twelve years old, I walked out of the circle of yellow light beneath the back door's bug bulb and kept walking until the hand I held in front of my face disappeared. Raised beneath streetlights, I'd never before experienced darkness so complete.

I went with my grandfather to meet a neighbor at the old railbed to negotiate who would farm a strip of land that my grandfather owned on the neighbor's side. I was sixteen or seventeen and it was 1984 or 1985: imagine my haircut. The neighbor tried to chat, but my grandfather stared over his shoulder so fixedly that the man peeked to see if someone was sneaking up on him. At some point Red and the neighbor came to an agreement, though in my memory my grandfather doesn't speak a single word.

Grandma Ruth found it impossible to live there alone, exposed by landscape and widowhood. One day while she was gone to town, someone broke in, flipped the pillows on her bed looking for guns she did not have, and opened the ornamental box holding Grandpa Red's ashes, mistaking it, perhaps, for the jewelry box my grandmother did not have. When she moved, she sent me a set of toy Ford tractors that someone had given my grandfather.

Scott Russell Sanders: Just south of my home in Bloomington, Indiana, near the village of Oolitic, beside a graveyard, there's an enormous rectangular hole in the ground, out of which the limestone for the Empire State Building was quarried. That stone began as ground-up bits of shells from creatures that swam in tropical waters when the land that would become Indiana lay under a shallow sea near the equator, some three hundred million years ago. When I am feeling exasperated by my upstart species—including myself—I visit the Empire State quarry, scrape aside the bullet casings and rifle shells left there on the lip by gun-happy Hoosiers, step over the spray-painted declarations of teenage love, seat myself on the brink, and gaze down along the terraced walls to the sea-green water, which gives back reflections of the sky, a realm even older than stone. Why that view into deep time should comfort me, I cannot say; but it does.

George Saunders: Not far from my house, in Oak Forest, Illinois, south of Chicago, there was a vast undeveloped tract we called just The Field: wild strawberries, weird little fetid creeks, inexplicable sewer manholes in the middle of a thicket, the occasional muddy man's parka just cast over a bush, et cetera. We played all of the usual games there, plus a few we invented, like the one where we jumped our sleds over a semi-frozen creek and the rule was you had to run home when you fell in, to avoid frostbite; or one called Manhunt, which we played with BB guns, where it was prohibited to shoot in the groin, unless you felt you really wanted to. This was a place of power because we were allowed to go in there and stay as long as we wanted and do whatever we liked: like a scale model of the imagination. It's now a very nice public park, all mowed and tidy.

Steve Tomasula: A brief lexicon of words useful in Northwest Indiana/South Chicago: Blood Sausage. Carcinogenic. Steam Pipe.

Deb Olin Unferth: Lawrence, Kansas, where I now reside, is, by any method of measurement, the exact center of the United States.

Kellie Wells: I, Kellie Wells (née Ingeborg Traumschlaf), was born on an inclement night in 1872, in the village of Röcken bei Lützen. My father, a struggling cobbler, made and repaired only left shoes and always longed for a life on the German stage. A loquacious sleeper, Theodor Traumschlaf could be heard throughout the town delivering nightly somniloquys as he slept; my mother, Elisabetta Traumschlaf, twittered in her sleep like a zebra finch, and thus the Theatre of Dreaming was born. She died at the age of twenty-seven, giving birth to my older sister, Ludmilla (who would later sleep professionally). I was discovered selling winter dreams of questionable provenance on the streets of Vladivostok, discovered by Herr Dr. Sigmund Freud himself, the very sight of whom produced in me aphonia. I later confided to the doctor I'd spent each night of my adolescence dreaming of him, dreamt he lay naked, save for a decorative beard, in a field of timothy, which he informed me meant I would soon lose my teeth, and I did. I died standing up, toothless and singing, in 1984, in Kingdom Come, Kansas, the capital of misspent sleep.

Curtis White: My place of power in the Midwest is all too earnest: the great room at the state lodge at Starved Rock State Park near Ottawa, Ill. The enormous limestone slabs in the building, the enormous wooden beams in the ceiling, the Paul Bunyan-like furniture, all created by hand by workers in the WPA. I like the mythic idea of a Midwest that was once a place where people made big beautiful things rather than what we see now: a race of "malignant dwarfs" (as Nietzsche put it) turning the land into a vast toxic factory floor, now complete with wind generators.

Michael Wilkerson: I teach a form of sorcery formally known as "Arts Management" at American University in Washington, D.C. My non-normal flyover area is Bloomington, Indiana, where I lived until the Great Mitch Daniels Emigrations of 2007–2008. I fondly remember the intersection of Maple Grove Road and Maple Grove Road, between Ellettsville and Bloomington. Only a local—nay, a resident of the neighborhood—could tell one Maple Grove from the other, and if one had to ask, one didn't belong, and never could. Maple Grove and Maple Grove occupies a leafy, hilly spot from which one can see every stereotypical midwestern icon—winding roads, trees, a creek, rundown old farmhouses, a cheesy new development with vinyl siding, and power lines keeping even our most remote brethren plugged into the growing abnormalcy of the twenty-first century. One can travel north, south, east, or west, but one will always and forever be on Maple Grove Road, no matter what the destination.

Diane Williams: Lake Michigan. I go to the lake because I believe the lake is better than I am and I want to be in good company. Its beauty, its success, its remote aspect, its inability to speak, hints at intelligence and virtue more pure than my mine, better. . . . Occasionally the lake looks at me coldly which gives me the creeps.

Michael Martone

is Professor of English at the University of
Alabama–Tuscaloosa. He is the author of
seven works of fiction, including *The Blue
Guide to Indiana* and *Michael Martone;* three
collections of nonfiction, *The Flatness and
Other Landscapes*, *Racing in Place*, and
*Unconventions: Attempting the Art of Craft
and the Craft of Art; Double-wide*,
collected early fiction published by
Indiana University Press; and
editor of six volumes.